CALL ME CROCKETT

I0598111

CALL ME CROCKETT

David Lewis
With Lisa Dugas

Leonard Press

Copyright ©2006 by David Lewis. All rights reserved. Printed in the United States of America. No part of this book may be used or reproduced in any manner whatsoever without written permission except in the case of brief quotations embodied in critical articles and reviews.

Leonard Press
Bolivar, MO 65613-0752

For other titles, prices, and order information:
www.leonardpress.com

ISBN 0-9769114-9-3
[ISBN 978-0-9769114-9-4]
Library of Congress Control Number: 2006930122

Cover Art: Anastasios Kazapedies

My gratitude to the usual suspects who have given so selflessly of their
time and effort to get this project up and running.
Special thanks go out to
Software Savior and dive buddy,
Wade Berlin.

The Guinness is in the mail.

For the many happy hours that he has given me over the years, this
book is fondly dedicated to the master storyteller,

Robert B. Parker

ONE

Rachael Get Your Gun

DOCTOR RUBY LACOST ADJUSTED HER GLASSES and looked at the young woman sitting across from her.

"You're going to what?" she said.

The young woman's face was as immobile as porcelain.

"I'm going to buy a gun," she said.

"Ah, Rachael, I'm not sure that's your best possible course of action at this time."

"Spoken like a true psychologist," Rachael said, the hint of a smile teasing her glossed lips.

"You're dealing with memories you've kept repressed for well over half your life. Now is not the time to get involved with a firearm!"

"I've made up my mind."

Ruby noted Rachael's rigid posture.

"It's your father, isn't it?"

Rachael looked at her blankly.

"Every time you're dealing with something about your father," Ruby continued, "you go on emotional hold. You become neutral and separate from it all. You tuck in behind your newsreader identity. It's how you choose to protect yourself from him."

"That's why I want a gun," Rachael said. "To protect myself from my father."

"You haven't even seen the man in years. Why now?"

"He knows that if I'm going to a psychologist, some things could turn up that would be dangerous to him."

"How long has it been since you've seen your father?"

"Fifteen years or so. Ever since I went to live with Aunt Ivy."

"Does she have any connection to him?"

"She despises the man."

"If you haven't had any communication with him in that long, what makes you think he knows where you are or what you're doing?"

Rachael plucked absently at the hem of her skirt. Her shoulders sagged and she lifted tear-filled eyes to look at Ruby.

"He knows," she said. "He makes it his business to know. I'm a loose end. Daddy hates loose ends."

"And you've decided to get a gun."

Rachael nodded.

"Do you know anything about guns? Have you ever even shot a gun?"

"There are a couple of places that give lessons."

Ruby fiddled with her pen as she stalled for time.

"Okay," she said. "I know somebody who might be able to help. Will you give me a day or two?"

After Rachael left, Ruby reached for the phone. Crockett answered on the third ring.

"Gotta gun?" Ruby said.

"What?"

"A gun. You know, bang-bang, innocent bystanders lying in the street, blood in the gutter, that kinda stuff."

Crockett lowered his voice into a stage whisper. "Ruby, if someone is forcing you to make this call, clear your throat."

"I have a client."

"One of your own? I told you that 900 number would work!"

Ruby grinned. "If you can drag yourself out of that quagmire of isolation and self-pity you laughingly refer to as your life," she said, "meet me for lunch."

"Gee, I don't know. My calendar's pretty full."

"Bullshit."

"Is this, like, a date?"

"Business," Ruby said. "I'll buy."

"Must be serious."

"Possibly. The Classic Cup, on the Plaza, one-thirty."

She hung up quickly, knowing that the Classic Cup did not compliment Crockett's self image, half expecting him to call back and bitch. He didn't.

Crockett remained on the couch for a while, feeling like he'd come in during the middle of the movie, a not unusual sensation when he dealt with Ruby. He realized that making him play catch-up was one of her ploys to keep him off balance, but today was different. Today was obviously not just fun and games. She wanted his cooperation. The fact that she needed his assistance for some reason didn't mean that he had any sort of advantage. Ruby didn't give advantages. Whatever was on her devious mind would be more than met the casual eye. Still, it was nice to be needed, even if he had no idea why. Sighing, he rose, compensated for the kink in his back, grimaced at the pain in his hip, and limped into his bathroom. He brushed his teeth in the shower, slipped into some faded jeans and a nearly clean flannel shirt, and prepared to venture out into the world.

Kansas City's Country Club Plaza is one of the more celebrated up-scale shopping districts in the country. Luxury cars adorn its curbs, jowly businessmen its bars, young lions its pubs, junior leaguers its shops, and pretension its restaurants. Ordinarily Crockett avoided the area at all costs. Ordinarily Ruby didn't ask him if he had a gun.

Parking was a predictable hassle. He left Thumper on Ward Park-way and walked to the Classic Cup, wishing he'd brought his cane. Ruby was waiting just inside the door when he arrived. As usual, her slow grin brought butterflies to his nether regions, and he gave her a peck on the cheek as they were approached by a waitperson that looked a great deal like Uma Thurman. Uma raised his eyebrows and looked at Crockett. Crockett raised his and looked back. They held their mutual pose for a couple of beats and Ruby snorted.

"Two," she said. "A sidewalk table please. He smokes."

Uma permitted one eyebrow to fall and curled his lip. "This way," he oozed, and led them outside.

Crockett looked at Ruby as they walked to the table. She hadn't changed much over the years. Still the thick mane of nearly black hair, still the oversized mouth and eyes, still the flawless olive complexion. At five-ten and about one-forty he found her wonderfully substantial. In heels they stood nearly at eye level, with him on the short end. Ruby never went out in public without heels.

Ruby smiled as she sat.

"You didn't have to get dressed up just for me," she said.

"Clothes do not make the man, Ms. LaCost."

"No, but they evidently do make mistakes."

"My underwear's silk," Crockett said. "Chinese. Raw."

"I wouldn't know."

"There's still time."

Ruby blew him a tiny kiss.

"It is possible that I may require your assistance," she said.

Crockett bumped his eyebrows.

"I have a client who believes she needs to learn how to use a gun to protect herself. I have attempted to dissuade her from that course of action."

Crockett peered at her over the top of his menu. "Of course you have," he said. Their waitress arrived.

Ruby ordered something with the oxymoronical title of Southwestern Pizza. Crockett had a turkey sandwich, hold the sprouts, hold the avocado, hold the cilantro, hold the orange-mustard sauce, add some mayo, tomato, and lettuce. The young woman looked at him askance.

He lit a Sherman and Ruby smiled.

"My client needs to be handled with kid gloves. I am concerned that she will purchase a firearm and cause herself injury, or patronize a less than scrupulous instructor, or find herself immersed in a situation with which she, as emotionally fragile as she is, will be unable to cope."

"No shit?"

Ruby broke out in laughter, a rich contralto that was irresistible.

"Do you really talk like that to those poor unsuspecting victims of yours?" Crockett said.

Ruby rested her chin in her hand and twinkled.

"None of this stuff works on you, does it?"

"Probably not."

"Crockett, no matter what I say, this woman is going to get involved with firearms. I want you to teach her how to handle a gun safely. I trust you. I believe she will, too."

Crockett knew Ruby's seemingly open declaration of purpose and need was not the whole story. She had other motives. Ruby always had other motives.

"I'm not qualified," he said.

"You used to be a cop. You are a truly sensitive and honorable man. This woman is very vulnerable. You would never take advantage of that."

"I wouldn't?"

"I'll discuss it with her. If she goes for it, I'll set up a meeting for the two of you. Feel free to charge her something unreasonable for this service. She can afford it."

"You're being both civil and complimentary," Crockett said. "I'm a little scared."

"Of course you are."

"Aroused, too."

"Of course you are."

"Ruby, you know I don't like guns."

"Yes, but you need my approval so badly that you will most certainly do as I ask."

He gave up. "Alright. I've got a session tomorrow morning. Tell her to call me after ten. I should be home by then. She can buy me dinner or something. I want to spend some time with her in a semi-social situation before I hand her a loaded gun. Nothing can screw up a brand new relationship like getting shot in the foot."

Ruby grinned.

"No shit?"

TWO
Born to Rust

PUTTING A SINCERE SMILE IN HIS VOICE, Crockett said, "Bob Bailey Homes, Olathe, Shawnee, and Overland Park."

"That's it," squeaked his headphones. He took them off and walked out of the booth to where Rob sat amid his recorders, processors, computers, and speakers. The little girl from the advertising agency, who thought she was a copywriter, a producer, and terribly sexy, beamed at him.

"Really great job, Mr. Crockett, really. It's always really great to work with a professional."

"It is, isn't it? That Rob's a helluva guy."

She giggled in what she assumed was a fetching manner and crossed her legs. "We've got some other stuff coming up in a couple of weeks," she said. "We're gonna need kind of a hillbilly country voice, and a real nervous wimpy guy."

"That would be me," Crockett said.

"Really great. We'll be in touch. You'll invoice us for today?"

"Count on it," he said, easing out the door.

"That'll be really great," she said. "Really."

Crockett left the truck in his drive, quietly opened the gate to the backyard, and was almost to the door when he heard the snarls and barking. Two giant schnauzers came bristling and roaring around the corner of the house.

"Sit!"

They slid to a halt on their butts about three feet from him, grinning and wagging their stubby tails. It was all part of the routine. Their owner, a mousy woman named Charlene, rented the second floor of his house, a big old stone monstrosity that Crockett bought for a song nearly 20 years before, when he first came to Kansas City. Over the years he replaced the plumbing, the wiring, the windows and the doors. He insulated and sealed, painted and peeled and, because of

11

all that and the fact that the Valentine district had worked very hard to become respectable, the place was now worth nearly ten times what he paid for it. Because he didn't need over four thousand square feet, Charlene had the second floor, he kept the ground floor and basement, and the third floor remained untouched. Charlene's rent covered Crockett's utilities and taxes and her large toothy dogs covered his ass. The Valentine district wasn't that respectable.

When Crockett opened his back door the hounds charged inside. Treat time. Charlene had named the canines Wolfgang and Hildegard. He called them Stupid and Shithead. Shithead was the one with the blue collar. They waited for him by the refrigerator. In the middle of the kitchen floor, carefully avoided by the dogs, ever hopeful of hanging a claw in a curious muzzle, sat over thirty pounds of one-eared, buff-colored, feline attitude. Nudge.

Crockett grabbed two turkey hot dogs and a small chunk of broiled chicken out of the fridge. The dogs inhaled the franks and whined at Nudge as he daintily consumed his treat, one tiny morsel at a time, often stopping to peer at the hounds as they circled him and begged, hoping one of them would come within reach. They both had. Once. Nudge didn't take any shit.

An hour later Crockett was sitting on the couch with Nudge purring on his lap, contemplating the possibility of lunch. The phone rang.

"Hello."

"Mister Crockett?"

"Yes."

"Mr. Crockett, my name is Rachael Moore. Ruby LaCost suggested that I contact you. She said you are a man worthy of trust."

"The fruit baskets are finally paying off."

"I beg your pardon?"

"Nothing, Miss Moore, just a feeble attempt at humor."

"I see. Ruby suggested I buy you dinner."

"Or lunch. Or a new truck. Your choice."

"Lunch will be fine. Today?"

"Where and when?"

"Let's say the Classic Cup on the Plaza, in thirty minutes?"

"My favorite."

"How will I know you, Mr. Crockett?"

"I'll have a white gardenia in my cleavage."

"Excuse me?"

"I'll be the worst dressed man there."

"Very well. In thirty minutes then. Thank you, Mr. Crockett."

She disconnected. Crockett called Ruby.

A client had cancelled and Ruby was contemplating what to do with the extra hour, when the phone rang.

"This could very easily be an obscene phone call," Crockett said.

12

"Sorry. I have to wash my hair."

"Tell me about Rachael."

"I can't tell you much."

"Don't violate your ethics."

"She is a very closed person, frightened and fearful. Abused as a child, definitely suspicious of men. She needs the opportunity to relax a bit and open up to a non-threatening male."

"A what?"

"A non-threatening male."

"C'mon, LaCost. What are you getting me into? I'm not a therapist. I don't want anything to do with guns. And, since I have you, why the hell do I need another crazy woman in my life?"

Enjoying Crockett's obligatory complaining, knowing it was part of his process for dealing with the world, and glad to participate in his emotional ritual, Ruby replied, "I have every confidence you shall fare well".

"I can't win here, can I?"

"But you will win, Honey. You'll get to go out in public, see new things, make new friends, and learn to work and play well with others. Just think, if we can get you socialized, the next time we go for a walk in the park, I can take your leash off and let you run loose. Wouldn't that be fun?"

"I don't like the park," Crockett said. "The geese scare me."

"As I said before, she'll pay you."

"Sounds good to me!" Crockett said. "Can't talk, Ruby. Gotta go. Got a heavy date with a real babe for lunch. I found her phone number off the men's room wall at Denny's. She sounds really nice. What's a Chinese wax job?"

Ruby chuckled. "Have fun," she said.

"You too. Pat yourself on the bottom for me."

"In progress, Crockett. 'Bye."

In therapy, Crockett and Ruby had seen each other at least twice a month for over three years. He had been more open and willing than she'd expected him to be. Crockett had felt responsible for a failed marriage and the death of his partner on the police department. He seemed to enjoy the fact that Ruby wouldn't knuckle under to him, that he couldn't push her around or intimidate her.

Ruby adored Crockett. And now, once again, she was dragging him out of his cave. She smiled. It was true. Therapy is never finished. It is just abandoned.

For Crockett, the only redeeming aspect of venturing onto the Plaza was taking his truck. The natives found Thumper distasteful. Actually, almost everybody found Thumper distasteful. Constructed in the years before Chevrolet found a way to really rustproof their vehicles,

Thumper began his life as a diesel work truck. After many years in that incarnation, he was obtained by a hot-rodder who painted him an unfortunate shade of blue, removed the original motor, and installed a 454 with about four hundred twenty-five horsepower. Crockett had had the truck for eight years. Thumper's body was falling apart, his four-wheel drive ride was rough, his exhaust loud, his tires huge, his seat ripped, and not once had Crockett given him a bath. The truck bore the only bumper sticker Crockett had ever put on a vehicle, "Born to Rust." Thumper was tall, ugly, noisy, had neither a radio nor air-conditioning, and the doors wouldn't lock. Crockett didn't get out much.

Driving through the erratic traffic on the Country Club Plaza was one of the tiny joys in Crockett's life. One look at the truck, and then at him, and the lesser vehicles parted in much the way the Red Sea did for Charlton Heston. It was easy to see that neither Thumper or Crockett had anything to lose. Finding a rare parking space, he eased the truck in behind a BMW around the corner from the Classic Cup. Several pedestrians issued furtive glances. When Crockett slammed the door, a small piece of rusty rocker panel fell into the street.

As he approached the restaurant, so did Rachael Moore. Crockett recognized her immediately. She was the relatively new news anchor for channel 36 or 32 or some popular independent station. Her picture graced several billboards and a few city bus flanks. Five-six, early thirties, great cheekbones, ash blond hair, socially acceptable thin figure, good skin, impeccable make-up, expensive shoes, fixed smile, green eyes, and the solid warmth of bathroom tile. They arrived at the door together.

"Miss Moore," he said. "Forgive me, I misplaced my gardenia."

"Ah," she said, "you would be Mr. Crockett."

"Only because I don't have a choice."

"Ruby cautioned me about your sense of humor."

Crockett opened the door. "Ruby who?" he said. They came face to face with Uma.

He and Crockett looked at each other. Uma raised his eyebrows. Declining the opening gambit, Crockett left his in a fixed position.

"Two please," he said, "outside if possible. She smokes." Uma turned to Crockett's companion and brightened considerably.

"Miss Moore, how nice to see you! It's so good of you to drop by today. This way, please." Turning expertly on one heel, he swept them to a sunlit table, seated Rachael and, with a flourish, presented her menu. He dropped Crockett's on the tablecloth.

"Your waitress will be with you in a moment. If you need anything at all, Miss Moore, just call," Uma gushed.

She smiled at him. "Thank you, Ricky." He darted away.

"His name's Ricky?" Crockett said.

"Yes, it is."

14

"I woulda gone with Uma."

A tiny smile flickered on her penciled lips as she scanned the menu. "No, it's Ricky, Mr. Crockett."

"Let's loosen up a little. If you don't mind, I'll call you Rachael and you can call me Crockett."

"What's your first name?"

"David."

"David? David Crockett? *Davey Crockett?*"

"See? I knew it would come to this. It always does."

Rachael smiled. "Well, Crockett, it's better than Uma."

"So," he said, "who do you want to kill?"

Crockett watched an amazing range of emotions flicker over her face in the next second. Rachael quickly composed herself and settled on insulted. She glared at him and whispered.

"Maybe this is a mistake," she said.

"Probably."

"Look, I've already phoned a place called The Bull's-Eye. They said they have a two hour session to teach people how to shoot."

Their waitress arrived. Rachael ordered some sort of ethnic Czechoslovakian greenery, and herbal tea. Crockett chose what appeared to be a tuna salad sandwich and lemonade.

"Here's the deal," he said. "I am not a mental health professional, but I have an autographed picture of Doctor Phil on the wall above my bed. I will not teach you how to defend yourself with a handgun. That implies you are waiting to be victimized and I don't like the entire victim mindset. It is my intention, if you decide to do this, to teach you how to respond to lethal threat with overwhelming counterattack. You will learn how, when the situation offers no other alternative, to kill another human being."

Crockett cleared his throat and leaned over the table toward Rachael.

"This is some very serious shit, Sweetheart. It is not two hours with ten other students blazing away at cute little targets. It is not fun and games in a group of gigglers. It is a course of action that will result in you knowing how and when to take someone's life! If you are not prepared to take another life to protect your own, you don't need a gun or shooting lessons. You need a bodyguard or something else to hide behind."

Rachael looked at him for a moment.

"Are you trying to scare me?"

"Is it working?"

"I've thought about this a lot. I really think I could kill someone to save my own life."

Crockett smiled. "Nothing to it," he said. "Child's play."

Rachael's eyes narrowed. "Well, how 'bout you, then, tough guy. You ever killed anyone?"

"Yes."

"Really? You have?"

"But not this week."

Rachael drew a deep breath and studied her hands for a moment. When she again looked up, it seemed to Crockett her eyes were darker.

"Okay," she said. "You got me."

"It's mutual, Kiddo".

Crockett's tuna salad had grapes in it. The lemonade was pink, with a black straw.

When he arrived home, a phone message was waiting from Ruby.

"Have a good lunch? Why don't you come by tonight, if you can remember where I live. Bring dinner. I have a cute little Australian merlot we can try. It has an excellent nose, great legs, and finishes well. Me too. See ya around seven."

Crockett filled a pot with water, dropped in three diced potatoes and put a fourth in the oven. In a sauce pan he installed a half pint of heavy whipping cream, a small can of chicken broth, half a stick of butter, dried dill, cracked pepper, some lemon juice, and a half-pound wedge of brie with that nasty white stuff cut off. When the potatoes were about done, he poured off the starchy liquid, replaced it with fresh water and allowed them to cool. The baked potato, minus the skin, went in the pan where it disintegrated into the sauce. He poured the water off the potatoes, added a handful of diced green onions, a cup of sour cream, and the contents of the saucepan, then set the whole thing on slow simmer and headed downstairs to throw in a load of laundry. By five, Crockett's famous potato soup was cooling in the fridge and he was in a hot tub, trying to get his hip and leg to settle down.

He picked up some sourdough rolls on the way to Ruby's place, an apartment over by the Nelson Art Museum. In her ongoing attempt to defraud the federal government, Ruby actually had two apartments. One was a small one-bedroom where she received clients and claimed, for tax purposes, she lived. The other was across the hall, a two-story, three-bedroom extravaganza where she lived and claimed, for tax purposes, she received clients. The guard at the gate looked at Crockett and his truck with thinly disguised disgust. His nametag read "Larry".

"Deliveries go through the back drive," he said.

"I'm sure they do Larry," Crockett said. "I, however, am not a delivery. I am a visitor."

"To who?"

"Whom."

"What?"

"To whom am I a visitor."

Larry squinted at him. "Who you here to see, Mister?"

"I am here to join in the company of Ms. Ruby LaCost, apartment 203 or 204, depending on whether I give or receive therapy."

Larry consulted his clipboard. "Don't got no guests listed here."

"Perhaps if you were to call her, this matter would be easily resolved."

Larry had had about all the conversation he wanted. Crockett could feel him yearning for a gun to go with his snappy uniform.

"Miss LaCost?" he intoned into his official phone, "there's a guy says he's here to see ya." His eyes drifted to Crockett as he listened. "What's yer name?"

Crockett smiled. "Just tell her it's Raoul the pool boy," he said.

THREE
Single Malt and Cigars

WHEN LARRY PHONED and confirmed Crockett's arrival, Ruby was surprised to find that she was a little nervous. She had never called on an ex-patient to assist a current patient before, and was still struggling with a list of unintended consequences that could crop up from such an arrangement. Still, she had great faith in Crockett's innate ability to read people and behave accordingly. Plus, she knew he was anything but a predator. Sure, he exhibited testosterone-powered behavior with her from time to time, but that was part of their play. Both of them were free to behave outrageously if they chose to, trusting the other one not call their bluff. Liberating to be sure. Frustrating from time to time for Crockett, no doubt, but great fun for Ruby.

When she realized part of her nervousness came from the anticipation of continuing her relationship with Crockett in relatively intimate surroundings, she was actually embarrassed. She checked her face in the entryway mirror and decided a bit more lipstick was called for. It would have to wait. Crockett was knocking.

She answered the door wearing a man-tailored black silk blouse over white calf-length tights. Her feet were bare, her hair loose, her grin wide. She looked Crockett up and down as he stood in the doorway.

"Raoul, you've come."

"Carmelita, I could no longer stay away."

"Damn, Crockett! A jacket? You wore a jacket?"

"The best Sport Coats 'R' Us had to offer."

"Those lapels are hand stitched."

"I didn't want the wine to be embarrassed."

"And slacks!"

"I even brushed my teeth," Crockett said. "Didn't want to offend Larry."

"Well get your bad self on up in here!" Ruby said, stepping back from the door.

18

He regarded her feet.

"The least you could have done was put on shoes. I haven't been here in nearly a year."

"You haven't been here in nearly two years," Ruby said. "Put the sack in the kitchen." She headed off up the stairs.

Crockett wandered through the massive living area, through the overly large dining area, into the huge, stainless steel encrusted kitchen area. He had just finished putting the pot on her six-burner stove to warm, when she walked in, now wearing earrings and darker lipstick. Jesus. The sight of her always brought a flutter. She assaulted him with a long, full-bodied hug that he enjoyed immensely.

"What's in the pot?"

"Potato soup."

Ruby arched a perfect eyebrow.

"Potato soup?" she said.

Crockett enjoyed the contact of her palms on his shoulders and his forearms on her ribs.

"You haven't been here for dinner in almost two years and you bring me potato soup?"

Crockett caressed her chin with a forefinger and allowed his voice to drop an octave. "Once its succulent creaminess passes those pouting lips and warmly caresses that ever so sharp tongue of yours," he said, "you will never again want another, but will yearn only for mine."

Ruby smiled and slipped out of his arms to collect dinnerware. "Open the wine, Hotshot," she said.

Thirty minutes later she pushed her empty bowl away with a tiny belch.

"Ambrosia, Crockett, goddammed ambrosia. I never tasted anything like it. Bet it goes straight to my thighs."

"An appealing thought, but not true. Crockett's famous potato-brie sludge never gets past the heart. That's why I hardly ever make it."

"To the terrace, Raoul, and breathe. I'll be right there."

Crockett walked out through the sliding glass doors and flopped on her patio couch. Night was coming on and the air was beginning to cool. He looked at the Kansas City lights reflected off low cloud cover and rolled Ruby over in his mind. As always, she remained an enigma. During the infrequent occasions when they spent time together, he was never sure if it was therapy or social. The only thing he *was* sure about, was that it would never escalate into anything romantic.

A minute later Ruby came out, handed Crockett a short scotch, and reclined on the remainder of the couch. Unable to resist teasing him, she draped her calves across his lap. As usual, Crockett did his best to remain casual.

"Twenty-five year old, single malt," she said, then reached into the pocket of her shirt and removed two cigars. She clipped the ends off both, lit one for him, the other for herself. Smoke wafting slowly from her lips, she grinned.

"Macanudo Maduros and good scotch, Son. This is surely better than either of us deserve."

Lightly rubbing her calves, Crockett said, "What's going on, Ruby?"

"Could be seduction," she said.

"As I recall, you don't sleep with men."

"I don't fuck men."

"So, is this therapy?" he said.

"Crockett, every minute I spend with your tired old ass is therapy for me."

Crockett leered, drawing his finger lightly along the bottom of her foot. "Think how therapeutic I could be if I really tried," he said.

Ruby shivered, stood up, leaned over, and kissed him lightly on the lips.

"I'll be back with more scotch and a quilt," she said. "Don't move."

When she'd settled in again, Ruby asked, "What about Rachael?"

"That is a very troubled woman," Crockett said.

"You have no idea how troubled. I suspect that I don't either."

"She's pretty cute," he said. "Nice bod. So I've decided to gain her confidence, have my manly way with her, and cast her cruelly aside. It's a guy thing. Like football."

Ruby flipped a cigar ash in his general direction. "When do you see her again?"

"I've got an early recording session at Airbourn Studios in the morning, then I'm meeting her for breakfast at the IHOP by I-35, then we're going to the Bull's-Eye and blaze away."

"How do you feel about that?"

"See? Now there you go," Crockett said. "I didn't go to all the trouble of building my potato masterpiece just to let you pick my brain. Why can't we just get along?"

"Fess up. How do you feel about that?"

"Well, Doctor LaCost," Crockett whined, wringing his hands, "I feel that my feelings are feeling that they feel a feeling that feels full of feelings. Can you feel how full that feels?"

"C'mon, Asshole."

Crockett thought for a moment.

"All right," he said. "Rachael has a lot of snakes crawling just below the surface, but I think she'll be okay. I'm a little worried about how I should deal with her."

"You'll deal with her fine," Ruby said. "It's instinctive with you. Don't concern yourself. You're not here because I'm worried about Rachael. You're here because we have been too long apart and this was a perfect excuse to spend time with you. Christ, Crockett, the Classic Cup was the first time I'd seen you in forever. You spend more time with Uma than you do with me."

"Yeah, but I like Uma."

"Fickle bitch that you are."

"And I've got a better chance of scoring with Uma than I do with you."

"When's the last time you fired a gun?" Ruby asked.

"What?"

"You heard me."

"I don't know."

"Bullshit. You know. You know exactly. C'mon, Crockett."

"The night I got shot, I guess."

"The night Paul Case was killed."

"Yeah. The night I got shot," Crockett said, feeling an all too familiar flutter in his chest.

Relentless, Ruby kept after him.

"That would be the night Paul died, right?"

Cold emptiness surged behind Crockett's heart and the taste of metal leaked into his mouth.

"Yes," he said. "The night my partner and friend, Paul Case, was shot to death, Doctor LaCost. March third, nineteen eighty-four. The night that Margie became a widow, the night that Clifford and Janet didn't have a daddy anymore, the night a useless piece of shit named Clevant Pelmore took it upon himself to shoot me and kill my partner. The night that I popped a cap on that same useless piece of shit and sent his dog-ass into the cold hard ground. That shot, Doctor LaCost, is the last time I fired a gun!"

Shoulders sagging, Crockett lurched to his feet. Ruby reached for him, but he brushed her hand away and stalked off through the apartment. The sound of the slamming door was flat and final.

Fog had formed at ground level and Crockett surged through it on the way to his truck, the pale vapor swirling behind him. He got in and put the key in the ignition before the cold behind his heart overtook him. Fingernails digging into his palms, he rested his forehead on the unyielding steering wheel and let the tears come.

21

FOUR

Ilene at the IHOP

THE NEXT MORNING while Crockett was grinding the last of his stash of Blue Kona beans, Airbourn Audio called to re-schedule his recording session. The scripts would not be in until after the weekend. Great. He could use the extra time to visit the Bull's-Eye shooting range before meeting Rachael for their ten o'clock breakfast. He loaded the grind into the magic machine and watched the double load of espresso begin to trickle into the carafe, then readied some half and half for latte. The instant Crockett opened the valve to steam the cream, Nudge was doing Olympic floor exercise on the counter.

"What the hell do you want, you old fool?"

Nudge myrrphed at him and bumped Crocket's forearm with his head. It felt a lot like getting hit with a cantaloupe.

"Meeaaoowfff," Nudge continued, flopping on his side to poke at Crockett's wrist with a paw nearly the size of a coaster. Sometime during his misspent youth, Nudge lost his right front fang. It forever colored his speech with impediment.

"Dammit, Nudge, quit!" Crockett said, as the cat continued his assault.

"Ruffth, ruffth, ruffth," Nudge urged, trying to pull Crocket's arm and the container of foam to him. He was not de-clawed. Quickly dragging a saucer out of the cabinet to minimize blood loss, Crockett spooned a bit of the foam onto it. Safe! After he poured the frothy cream in his coffee he dribbled what was left onto Nudge's saucer. The cat was so busy lapping he didn't even notice. Ungrateful wretch. Waiting outside the back door, Stupid and Shithead grinned in the sunshine. Lighting a Sherman and carrying his coffee to the table, Crockett called them names through the screen.

The Bull's-Eye had just opened when Crockett arrived. Inside, three men stood behind the counter, intently discussing the eminent confiscation of all handguns in the entire United States by blue-helmeted

United Nations' troops. They ignored him. The room was long, narrow, tall and dark. Glass cases contained a wide variety of handguns. Crockett began to browse.

He was familiar with most of the revolvers, but less than half of the autoloaders. Technology had passed him by. Eventually, an employee approached. Very short hair, black horn-rimmed glasses, huge gadget-encrusted wristwatch, short-sleeved sport shirt stretched tight across a round stomach, about thirty-five. He wore a nicely re-done Colt model 1911 in a high-rise belt holster and eyed Crockett suspiciously

"'Nam?" he said.

"What?"

"Noticed your limp. You're the right age. 'Nam?"

"Felon. Used to be a cop."

"What'd he git you with?"

"Poodle shooter."

"A nine, huh."

"Browning High Power."

"Nice gun."

Crockett shrugged.

"Depends on where you're standing," he said.

The guy snickered and stuck his hand over the counter.

"Name's Chuck."

"Call me Crockett," Crockett said.

His credentials had been established.

For the next half-hour he took the tour. The cement floor didn't do his hip and leg much good, so when Crockett de-trucked at the IHOP to meet Rachael, he carried his cane.

Rachael was sitting in the rear of the restaurant when he entered the dining area. She smiled as he made his way to her table.

"Good morning, Crockett."

She was wearing an expensive dark blue sweat suit and matching ball cap with a ponytail pulled through above the backstrap, black hightop running shoes, aviator style prescription glasses, and no makeup. Her cheeks were slightly flushed and she appeared to be about eighteen. Feeling old, Crockett looked down at her.

"That's a good look for you," he said. "Teen-aged determined shootist in training. The guys at the range will love it."

He sat down.

"I went by The Bull's Eye earlier. Gun shop in front, shooting range in back. Lane shooting in two rooms on the ground floor, open shooting in two rooms in the basement.

"I notice you use a cane," Rachael said. "You didn't have it at the restaurant."

"No, I didn't. I was on my feet in the Bull's-Eye for quite a while this morning, preparing for your possible arrival. They have cement floors."

"It's a very unusual cane."

"Rosewood," Crockett said. "The wirework on the shaft is brass, the duck's head handle is solid pewter. A guy at the Renaissance Festival made it for me. It has magical powers."

"Injury?"

"You're gonna fit right in with the guys at the Bull's Eye, girlfriend. Ol' Chuck asked me about my limp not an hour ago."

Rachael smiled down at the table for a moment, then looked at him.

"Why do you have the limp?"

"I got shot once."

"I'm nosey by nature. Wanna talk about it?"

Crockett shook his head.

"Not today," he said.

"Want me to shut up?"

"Not today."

Rachael paused to refresh her tea from a small metal pitcher.

"What do you mean, my *possible* arrival at the range?"

"When I was there, I had yet to decide if I was prepared to stand beside you while you waved a loaded gun around."

"So, I'm on trial?"

"Not any more. You're good to go."

"You've decided already?"

Crockett nodded.

"Just on the strength of our short conversation?"

"That, and the fact that just the thought of seeing you in that outfit while wielding a deadly weapon makes me want to have your children."

Rachael stifled a smile.

"Sorry," she said. "I'm sterile. War wound."

Crockett grinned.

"Where's *your* cane?" he said.

"I left it at home. Didn't want your pity."

The waitress arrived. Rachael selected some type of fruit plate that wouldn't sustain a canary and Crockett ordered a waffle with two over easy and a side of bacon. His companion raised an eyebrow in obvious disapproval.

"Good news," Crockett said. "My anorexia is in remission."

She giggled.

"Will I have to show identification at the range?"

"You bet. These places want to know exactly who they're dealing with."

"My driver's license is in my real name."

"Pandora Fozdick?"

"Ilene Rachael Morrison."

24

"That'll work."

"Good. I really don't want these people to recognize me."

"Which brings us to this," Crockett said. "I am as sworn to secrecy as Ruby is. While not a legal mandate, it is an ethical mandate."

"Thank you. Ruby said that you'd make that kind of statement."

"I've never really liked Ruby."

"She said you'd say something like that, too."

"Then I also need to say this. Whatever happens stays between us. Without your permission, I won't even discuss it with Ruby."

"Wow. You're serious about this."

"Ruby didn't put us together by accident. She is a sneaky, manipulative, nasty bitch with devious motives that only she knows."

Rachael regarded him for a moment.

"What kind of devious motives?" she asked.

Crockett shrugged and did not answer.

"I'm in," she said. "I wouldn't miss it."

"I'm going to charge you an outrageous amount of money, teach you how to slay your fellow man, and stick you with the breakfast check."

"My hero."

"That's what I was going for."

FIVE

The Bull's Eye

"WHERE IS THIS PLACE?" Rachael asked. They were standing in the post-breakfast sunshine outside the IHOP.

"About six blocks or so. We'll take Thumper."

"Thumper?"

"A more right-wing image," Crockett said.

He walked to the truck and opened the passenger side door. It creaked and groaned. Rachael scrambled inside.

"Nice upholstery," she said.

"I had it covered with a blanket for a while, but the water that comes through the floor boards rotted it away."

He got in and slammed the door twice to get it to stay shut. The motor rumbled into life, vibrating the cab.

Rachael nodded.

"Three-quarter ton, big block, six inch lift, thirty-five inch tires, six miles to the gallon in town if you're lucky, about ten on the highway," she said.

Crockett grinned.

"Where is the stiff, frightened, prissy young woman of yesteryear?"

"Crockett, I decided to trust you. I intend to try to make our very serious business fun if I can. I don't have much fun. I expect you to assist. Let's go shoot."

Crockett loved surprises.

They stood in the Bull's-Eye's parking lot for a while so Crockett could smoke a cigarette. He scuffed a foot in the gravel.

"Okay, Scooter-pie, here's what's goin' on," he said. "You and I are going to become members of the Bull's-Eye shooting range today. This will cost you about twenty-five bucks apiece. We are then going to rent a revolver and an auto-loading pistol for you to shoot. That will cost about ten bucks. We will also buy fifty rounds of ammunition for each gun, four man-sized silhouette targets, and rent earphones. That'll be around twenty-five bucks, and the lane rental fee is six dollars, but that's good for all day. My fee is a hundred dollars per session. Sessions can run from thirty minutes to three hours, it depends on you. My fee stays the same. You up for that?"

Rachael nodded.

"Here are the two rules. Rule number one. When a weapon is involved, the democratic process is over. What I say goes. You will do nothing that I do not instruct you to do. You will do everything that I do instruct you to do. Are we absolutely clear on that?"

"Yessir."

"Good. Rule number two. See rule number one. Are we absolutely clear on *that*?"

"We are."

"Excellent."

Crockett dropped the butt into the gravel and headed for the building. Rachael walked beside him.

There were shooters inside and the big exhaust fans were on, creating negative air pressure in the structure. It took most of what Crockett had to pull the front door open. They were standing in the darkened showroom, letting their eyes adjust, when Chuck spotted them. He glanced at Crockett's cane.

"You're back," he said. His eyes quickly settled on Rachael and he sucked his stomach in a bit.

"Chuck," Crockett said, "this is my friend Ilene. She wants to become a world-class shooter in three easy lessons. Set us up, will ya?"

"Nice to meetcha, Ilene. We're always glad to have women shoot."

Rachael laid a seventy-five watt smile on the poor bastard. "Hi, Chuck," she gushed. She sidled up to Crockett and wrapped an arm around his, shooting him a sappy grin. "Mister Crockett's gonna teach me how to shoot. I like him a lot."

Chuck attempted to swallow the tennis ball that had magically appeared in his throat.

"I'll get the paperwork together and we'll get you two signed up."

"I want Mister Crockett to show me some of the guns." Nearly climbing his arm, Rachael began to pull Crockett toward the cases.

"Sure," Chuck said.

Crockett looked down at her. "Jesus Christ, Ilene," he said.

"Rachael Moore would never act like that, would she?" Rachael said.

"No, she wouldn't."

Rachael grinned, exposing just the tip of her tongue and lightly traced the bottom of her lower lip with an index finger.

"You'd never tell on me, would you, Mister Crockett?"

"Miss Morrison, you're secret is safe with me."

She clutched his arm even tighter.

"Then let's look at some of these guns," she said. "But not the big ugly black ones. I want to look at the cute little silver ones. Then I want to see my new friend Chuck again, then I want to go shoot some bullets and see what it's like!"

She turned to face him, and the spacey, excited grin fell away.

"I'm scared, Crockett."

"That makes two of us."

SIX
Something for the Lady

RACHAEL DID OKAY. By the time the basic instruction on what end the bullet comes out of, and why it's not good to drop the thing was over, she was trembling. After thirty rounds from the .38 caliber revolver, she had settled down. After thirty rounds from the .45 caliber auto-loader, she was getting the shots within eighteen inches of where she wanted them to go. At about twenty feet, Rachael was putting nearly every shot into the black of a man size target.

When Crockett told her it was time to quit for the day, she seemed relieved. They hung around for a while and looked at guns, then headed for the truck. Halfway across the parking lot they were approached by a redheaded older man carrying a shooter's bag.

"'Scuse me, folks," he said. "Somethin' for the lady?"

"Yes," said the lady.

"Got a nice little piece with me. Nine millimeter, single-stack Smith, in stainless steel. My son travels a lot. Got it for his wife. I tried to tell him she was too big a wimp to get near it, but he wouldn't believe me. Bought it right here. Ain't never been shot."

Rachael moved next to him as he fumbled in the bag.

"It's one a them double action only automatics. No hammer spur, no thumb safety. Holds eight rounds, lightweight, won't rust." He pulled a dark blue Smith & Wesson box from the bag and opened it up.

"Safe as a revolver, nice fit for a woman's hand. Take the gun inside with ya. They'll look up the serial number and tell ya that John Anderbur just bought the thing from 'em a couple of weeks ago."

Rachael checked to make sure the pistol was not loaded, dropped into a Weaver stance, and pointed the gun around the parking lot. She glanced at Crockett. He nodded.

"That won't be necessary, Mr. Anderbur. How much?"

"Three hundred and fifty dollars, M'am. No tax. I'll write ya out a bill of sale, and I need to see some I.D."

"Done."

Back at the IHOP, Rachael put the gun in her trunk and they went inside for coffee. Crockett had water.

"Don't you drink coffee?"

"Not restaurant. I'm a coffee snob."

"How'd I do?"

"Real well. You didn't fall apart. You did everything I asked you to."

"Am I any good?"

"You suck."

Rachael laughed.

"Be nice to me," she said. "I'm armed."

"I've seen you shoot."

"Okay, I suck. What now?"

"Take your gun home. Do not load it. Practice the stance and aim at stuff. Once the stance feels fairly natural, tie a pair of running shoes together by the laces and hang 'em over the gun. Swing the shoes and try to hold your sight pattern on target. It'll help you hold more steady on the range."

"Shoes swinging from the gun?"

"And aim at a lot of things. Your stereo, your cat, your toaster, a door knob, whatever. That builds muscle memory. The shoes will help build muscle strength. Carry the Smith with you around the house. Get used to it. The feel, the weight, the texture, the purpose. Use both hands. You need to get to know the weapon. It's a nice little piece."

"What kind of gun do you have?"

Crockett shook his head.

"I haven't even held a gun since you were in about third grade," he said.

"What will you shoot?"

"I won't. I don't have to shoot to teach you how."

"Where did you learn?"

"What are you, some kind of reporter?"

"How long have you known Ruby?"

"Long time."

"How'd you meet?"

"What's your bra size?"

Rachael flushed. "Sorry, Crockett. 34B."

"Nothing to be sorry about. 34B is fine."

"Tit for tat. Ask me a question."

"I just did," Crockett said.

"How long have you been in Kansas City?"

"Nearly twenty years. How 'bout you?"

"About a year. Why did you stop being a cop?"

"Got shot. Where'd you live before here?"

"Omaha. Where'd you get shot?"

"Low back," Crockett said. "Where before Omaha?"

"Rockford, Illinois. Ever Married?"

"Once. You?"

"No. Why'd you get divorced?"

"She didn't like me. Why are you afraid of men?"

Rachael looked at Crockett. Christ, he'd gone too far.

"I'm sorry," he said.

"I'm not afraid of *you*."

"I consider that a compliment."

"I accept your apology, Crockett. I didn't answer your last question."

"That's okay."

"I will answer it, just not today. Sometime over alcohol."

"You got it," he said.

"Why are you afraid of guns?"

"Sometime over alcohol."

"You got it," Rachael said.

SEVEN
Ruby Regroups

RUBY LACOST LOOKED at the clock. Nearly six. She was restless, she was hungry, and her four o'clock session had worn her out.

LeAnn had been coming to Ruby once a week for about six months. She was thirty, she was large, she was loud, she was gay, and she preferred to be called Lee. Living off an inheritance, LeAnn did not have the satisfaction of accomplishment that comes from work. Extremely demanding, her relationships were fleeting. She despised men almost as much as she despised herself, and looked only to others as the source of her problems.

Their sessions were short on therapy and long on bitching. She did none of the exercises Ruby asked her to do. She would not keep a journal. She called three or four times a week, and she was in a nearly constant state of righteous indignation. Ruby couldn't seem to get the woman's attention. Something had to give, or she was going to send LeAnn to another therapist. Ruby refused to carry clients that made no effort to participate in the process. Sitting in her treatment room, she felt the front door slam when LeAnn entered.

"C'mon back, Lee," Ruby said, and steeled herself for the onslaught.

The woman entered the room like a water buffalo, shoved the door shut, and flopped into Ruby's overstuffed leather recliner.

"Sonofabitch!" she snarled.

Ruby swallowed a smile. Fuck it.

"Upset?" she said.

"You know what that snot-nosed little gate guard said to me? I parked my truck on the street, told him my name and shit so I could get in, and that little motherfucker looked at me and said, 'Thank you, Sir!' Cocksucker."

"That seems to have irritated you somewhat."

"Whatthefuck do you think? Little fucking shithead!"

Ruby sighed.

"All right, Lee. You asked for it. How tall are you?"

"I'm five-ten. Whatthefuck has that—"

"How much do you weigh? Don't lie."

LeAnn glared at her. Ruby slipped into cobra mode and held the woman's gaze. It didn't take long.

"Almost two-eighty, okay? Jesus!"

"Now let's examine your wardrobe. You're wearing combat boots, blue jeans with a four-inch cuff, a studded leather belt, a trucker's wallet on a chain, a long-sleeved white shirt over a black t-thirt, steel-rimmed glasses, and your hair is cut in a flat top. The guard, who is only about half your size, sees you getting out of a pickup truck and lumbering across the street in his direction. From his standpoint, calling you m'am would have been an insult. Look at yourself! You're about as feminine as a jockstrap! He made a natural mistake."

"I can dress any way I—"

"Yes, you can. You have every right to take the whole lesbian-in-drag thing as far as you like, as long as you're prepared to accept the consequences. If you insist on dressing, looking, and acting like some male refugee from a biker bar, you have no right to be pissed off if somebody believes you."

"What the fuck would you know about it!"

"Know anybody in Cleveland, Lee?"

"No."

"Nobody in Cleveland knows you either. Nobody in Cleveland gives a damn that somebody called you sir. As a matter of fact, nobody in Cleveland gives a shit if you live or die."

LeAnn stared at the floor.

"What are you tryin' to do?"

"You are only the center of *your* universe, Lee, not the center of *the* universe. You expect people to allow you to deal with them on your terms, but you will not extend them the same courtesy. You have to make a very simple choice. Do you want to feel right, or do you want to be happy?"

Tears filled LeAnn's eyes. She leaned back in the chair and began to weep.

Ruby rose from behind her desk and picked up a box of Kleenex.

"That's a start," she said. "Let me know what you decide. We're done for the day. No charge."

She dropped the tissues in LeAnn's lap and walked out the door.

By seven o'clock Ruby was ravenous and needed to put the day away. She phoned Crockett.

"So, Raoul, whacha doin'?"

"Currently I am engaged in the delightful labor of shoveling Nudge poop."

"I'm proud of you, Crockett. You've finally found your true station in life. Get over here."

"Road runs both ways."

"Park my Lexus in that neighborhood?"

"Stupid and Shithead are in the yard," Crockett said. "They'll watch your ride."

"Pizza?"

"Sure."

"Thirty minutes."

"I'll count each and every one," Crockett said.

"You can't count to thirty," Ruby said. "Say goodbye, Gracie."

She hung up.

Crockett, excited by the prospect of a visit from Ruby, hustled up scooping out the litter, lit a stick of incense, jumped in and out of the shower and put plates and glasses on the coffee table, complete with two candles and four paper towels. He was wiping down the john when he heard the dogs barking. Up the front walk came Ruby, swaying on the broken concrete in four-inch heels, clutching a bottle of Chianti and palming a large pizza box. He opened the door.

She passed him the pizza.

"Food," she said. "Booze," she continued, handing him the wine. "Me," she went on, slipping her arms around his neck as he tried to balance the box and bottle, giving Crockett a luscious, if unreturnable, hug.

"All three completely suitable for consumption," he said.

Ruby leaned back and fixed him with a slow smile.

"Don't you just say the sweetest things to little old me?"

"We keep seeing each other this often and I'm gonna exhaust all my good lines."

"Crockett, you don't have any good lines, but I'll take my chances."

"Any chance you'll take your arms from about my neck so I can put this stuff down?"

She released him, and Crockett lurched to the table. Ruby began yelling.

"Nudgie? Nudgie? Where's my big ol' Nudge man?"

Nudge, a cat who never came to anybody, a feline that had not seen Ruby LaCost in over a year, streaked into the living room and slid into her shins with an audible thump. She grunted with effort as she picked the cat up and rolled him onto his back like a baby. Ruby was in full make-up and jewelry, wearing a six hundred dollar teal silk pantsuit, and she was completely safe. Nudge would not only never extend a claw, he would not even shed. They gazed longingly at each other as she swayed back and forth. He reached up and patted her face with his paw.

Ruby crooned. "How's my wittle Nudgie-wudgie," she said. "Has my wittle baby been a good kitty-boy?" Nudge slow blinked at her and cooed.

Crockett flopped to his backside on the couch and opened the wine so it could breathe, then began to un-box the pizza. Ruby sat beside him, still holding the cat. Nudge, realizing how out of character he was, rubbed his forehead on her chin and began to gently squirm. She released him and he slipped to the floor.

"If I manhandled Nudge like that," Crockett said, "I'd bleed for a week." Ruby looked at him and grinned.

"I'd say manhandled is the operative term here," she said. "It's been my position for many years that pussy responds much better to a woman's touch."

Crockett smiled and lit the candles.

"You romantic fool," Ruby said. "Candles for me?"

"In case you want to roast marshmallows."

Ruby traced small circles on the back of his neck.

"Crockett, your ponytail is damp," she said. "A damp ponytail indicates a recent encounter with water of some type. Let us pause and examine this situation." She shifted her position on the couch and looked at him with big eyes. "A late supper of tactile food and semi-sweet wine, candlelight casting sensuous shadows about the slightly seedy room, you freshly scrubbed from head to toe. Oh, my goodness! Be still my beating heart."

Crockett laughed. "Damn, Ruby, you are wrapped tight tonight."

"Guess I'm just going to have to take it out, so to speak, on you. Give me wine." He did.

She drained the entire glass, took a saucer-size bite of the pizza, leaned back, kicked off her shoes, put her feet on the edge of the table, and began to chew. Crockett left his feet on the floor and did the same. They were halfway through the pizza before conversation was resumed.

"Wine, Raoul, and be quick about it."

Crockett poured her another glass. She drank it all in two gulps and handed it back. He refilled it. She drank half of that in one long swallow, then placed the remainder on the table.

Ruby stretched her neck and groaned. "God! I feel as if I may be able to go on now. How'd it go with Rachael?"

"Pretty well.

"Relax Galahad, the fair maid and I have spoken. She said you indicated that I might have some sort of secret agenda concerning the two of you."

"Feeble ramblings of an unstable mind."

"Yours or hers?"

"I thought that if I communicated with her, she would be more inclined to communicate with me."

35

"She said the same thing." Ruby's marvelous smile slowly overtook her face.

"Damn!" Crockett muttered.

"Somebody's gotta do something, Crockett. You hole up in this joint like a goddam hermit. You only step outside this dump to work, go to the store, or spend a little time with me. And you don't spend much time with me."

She killed her wine and held the glass out for a refill, then grabbed another piece of pizza. All of the food and most of the wine had disappeared before anyone spoke again.

Crockett refilled her glass and emptied the bottle, about two ounces, into his. He'd had a glass and a half. Ruby took a sip, placed the balance on the table, swiveled on her butt, leaned back across his lap, and smiled up at him.

"Go ahead, Sweetie" she said. "Relate, relate."

Crockett told her all he could remember about their trip to the Bullet Hole.

"The Ilene identity act is interesting," Ruby said.

"I thought she was pretty resourceful."

"She plays roles, Crockett. She's a newsreader! The good ones are some of the best actors on the planet. Not only are they thespians, they are thespians of the utmost subtlety. That's the bad news."

"Terrific. What's the good news?"

"She likes you. She longs to be honest. You just naturally bring that out in people, even me." She placed a hand on his cheek. "It is well to spend time with you again, Crockett. I have missed you."

Crockett patted her on the head. "That's just the booze talking," he said.

"Probably. Help me up."

"Are you okay to drive?"

"The horse knows the way to carry the sleigh."

Crockett pushed her to a sitting position and she slipped into her heels. If Ruby could walk in those, she could drive a bus during rush hour. They stood. With Crockett's sock feet and her four-inch stilts, she was nearly two inches taller than he.

"Walk me to the car."

They stopped beside the fender. She entwined her arms around his neck and kissed the end of his nose.

She held on for a long moment, then leaned away to look at him.

"If things were different," Ruby whispered.

"I understand," Crockett said. "I too, am a lesbian. Sadly, I'm trapped in a man's body."

"Slut," Ruby said, and turned away.

EIGHT
Second Opinion

THE NEXT THREE SATURDAYS Rachael and Crockett met at the range, chatted for a bit, spent an hour or two with her blazing away, then went their separate ways. Rachael made good progress. Her stance solidified well, she handled the little Smith with respectful confidence and she shifted to double tap shooting nicely. Things were fine. Things were not right.

Standing twenty-five yards away from a round target attempting to group all your shots in the X-ring is an emotionless endeavor of precision and control. Good shooters fire between heartbeats with lungs half full, striving to perform in the exact same way every time. Target shooting is as free of variables as possible.

Combat shooting is different. Dropping into a stance and putting two rounds into the center of a man-size silhouette in less than one second, on cue, from a distance of twenty feet or so requires passion. It requires aggression. Rachael didn't have it.

She was willing enough. She practiced stance and sighting at home. She worked on her speed. She shot until her hand was sore and her eyes red and puffy. She did everything Crockett asked of her, but remained distant from the process. She wanted to learn to shoot, but she didn't *like* to shoot. She took no pleasure in her improvement, found no joy in learning a new skill. An experience that should have brought her satisfaction, didn't. Instead she seemed to be withdrawing a bit, becoming more mechanical, more distant from the exercise, more distant from him. Crockett didn't like it. He called Ruby.

"Doctor LaCost."

"You're home."

"Firm grasp on the obvious, Crockett."

"It's Friday night. Why aren't you out tripping the light fantastic, or whatever it is that you people do on Friday night."

"I could describe some of our secret lesbian rituals, but I'd be afraid for your heart, Old Man."

"I'd be afraid too, but not necessarily for my heart," Crockett said. "It hasn't been in my possession since the first time I saw you."

"You silver-tongued devil."

Crockett laughed. "I haven't seen you in three weeks. We need to talk."

Instant switch. "What's up?"

He told her about Rachael.

"Don't help her climb any farther. If push comes to shove, see what she does after you kick her lovely little ass."

"It is, isn't it?"

"Why, Crockett! I didn't think you'd noticed."

"*You* noticed."

"I am a health care professional! A trained vessel of knowledge and compassion."

"So let's say I find a way to kick her ass—"

"Lovely little ass."

"… lovely little ass. What's going to happen?"

"How the hell do I know? Educated guess would be that she will either recover her enthusiasm, or stop. Either way, it'll be better for you."

"What's really going on here, LaCost?"

Ruby laughed. "Life, Crockett," she said. "Something in which you participate as selectively as possible and as seldom as you can. Just life. The hassle of being human. Hang in there. It'll do you good."

Crockett knew he'd get no more out of her.

"Back to Rachael," Ruby went on. "Right now you are more invested in her training than she is. That ain't good, Sweetie."

"I've got an idea I've been playing with."

"Trust yourself. You feel yourself to be flawed, so you are tolerant of flaws in others."

"That right?"

"It's one of the reasons you put up with my teasing. You believe I see you as flawed, and you view my sexual preference as a flaw. Someday you will come to see flaws for what they really are. Differences."

"You're a helluva woman, Ruby."

"Except for one tiny flaw, I'm perfect," she said. "It's a little mole right down beside my, well, sometime when I just can't stand it anymore, *Davey*, I'll show it to you. You'll like it a lot."

"Thanks for all the good words, Ruby."

"Crockett, do me a favor tonight, will you?"

"Sure."

"Don't think about Rachael's ass."

She was laughing when Crockett hung up on her.

NINE
Breakdown

ON THE WAY TO THE BULL'S-EYE the next morning Crockett stopped by Ace Hardware and picked up two 24-inch lengths of 1x2 pine board and two spring-loaded clamps. He arrived in the parking lot just as Rachael was getting out of her Land Cruiser. She waved and waited for him, then looked puzzled as he walked toward her, sack in hand.

"Morning, Crockett. What's in the bag?"

"Bad guys."

Rachael's eyes became slightly wary, but she smiled.

Inside they picked up a hundred rounds of nine-millimeter target loads, four targets, and headed out to their assigned lane. For the first hour, things were pretty much customary. Rachael would place the loaded pistol on the carpeted board before her, the target twenty feet or so distant. Crockett would tap her on the shoulder. At that signal, she would pick up the weapon, hit her stance, find the front sight, and discharge the gun twice as rapidly as she could pull the trigger, attempting to place two rounds back to back with only one sighting.

Rachael, despite her wandering commitment, had made significant progress. Her double taps were most always within eight or ten inches of each other, her total time from cue to fire less three seconds, her two-shot groups nearly always within the center trunk of the target. The problem was not ability, but attitude. She was passive.

After about an hour of practice, Crockett laid out a fresh target, a man-size silhouette in black on white. Across the bottom of the paper sheet, one on the underside and one on top, he placed the two 1x2 boards and secured them to the heavy paper with the two clamps. He hung the target from the overhead rack and cranked it out to about thirty feet distant.

Rachael walked to the line and looked at the target.

"Why the wood?"

"To hold the target straight. Load eight and safe your weapon downrange please."

She smacked in a fresh magazine, laid the gun on the shelf with the muzzle pointed toward the target.

"Chamber a round."

She snapped back and released the slide. The pistol was ready to fire. Crockett stepped to her left and slightly behind her and put a hand on the crank to move the target.

"You will begin firing, double tap, when I signal, until the magazine is empty. Take your stance!"

She raised the weapon, rotated her body thirty degrees, and took her sight, right arm straight, left arm bent with the elbow braced, right hand held by the left hand, right arm pushing, left arm pulling. The Weaver stance. He paused and let her wait a few seconds to add to her uncertainty, then touched her on the shoulder and began to crank the target as rapidly as he could, directly at her.

She didn't fire. She held position for a beat or two, then moaned and began to collapse. Crockett grabbed the pistol from her hand before she could drop it, and Rachael screamed as she sank to the floor.

"No, Daddy, please! Please!! I'll be good!"

She hugged her knees to her chest and keened, a high wailing sound of despair and fear. Crockett knelt beside her. Rachael looked up at him and her empty eyes slipped in and out of focus a few times before she began to sob. Crockett kneeled and held her until the sobs slowed to hiccups and the hiccups finally stopped. He stood her up and Rachael clung to his waist. Slipping her Smith & Wesson into his hip pocket, he led her outside into the sunshine.

They leaned against the fender of her Toyota as she went from sniffing to crying to sniffing to crying several times. At length she released him, leaned over with her hands braced on her knees, and vomited onto the gravel. Chuck opened the rear door of the building, walked outside, and handed Crockett a cold can of Pepsi and a damp hand towel. When Rachael finally stood up, he wiped her face and handed her the cold drink.

Gradually Rachael's breathing slowed.

"I'm so embarrassed."

"Me too," Crockett said. "I don't know how I can ever be seen in there again. Chuck and I are wearing the same shirt."

She turned her head away and smiled.

"This is my fault," Crockett said. "I have that effect on women. They throw up around me all the time."

Rachael drew in a shaky breath. "I'm doing better now," she said. "Where's my gun?"

"In my pocket."

"Thanks. If you'd get the rest of my stuff for me, I think I'll just go home."

"Not a chance."

"What?"

"Not a chance. You've gotta get through this. I don't care what it takes. I want you past this bullshit!"

"But—"

"You and I are going to walk back in there and you are going to do this thing. This time you will do as you are told. You will shoot a series of four double taps. You will hit the goddammed target. You will do what you have been trained to do. Any questions?"

Her eyes traveled up to his face. She cleared her throat. "No," she said.

"Suck it up. I'll follow you. Lead on."

Damned if she didn't.

Rachael walked right through the showroom and back out onto the range with Crockett on her heels. He stepped out onto the lane and laid her pistol on the shelf in front of her. She checked the load.

"Ready on the firing line?"

"Ready!"

"You will begin firing, double tap, on my signal. Take your stance."

She did. He gave it a beat or two, then touched her on the shoulder and began to crank the target toward her. She didn't move. Crockett roared.

"*Kill the motherfucker!!*"

Rachael released a wail of anguish and eight rounds, in four sets of two, in less than three seconds. The target was only about ten feet from her when she finished. She continued to hold the stance for a moment, then began to shake and lowered the gun to the shelf. Crockett looked at the target. Every round was in the heart and lungs. Every one.

"Not bad for a girl," he said. "We'll quit for the day."

Rachael stood stock still for at least ten seconds, staring at the silhouette. Then she turned slowly and looked at Crockett.

"Okay," she said, and hit him like a cat on a phone pole. Arms around his neck, legs around his waist, laughing and crying in his ear through the headset.

"I did it, Crockett! We did it, Crockett! *You* did it, Crockett!!

"*You* did it, Sweetheart. *You did it!*"

They stood, Rachael weightless in his arms, shouting through each other's ear cups, enjoying the moment, when Crockett became aware that ten or twelve other shooters were watching them, all grinning and applauding in appreciation. Rachael climbed down off him, but would not release his hand. They were self-consciously smiling at the spectators and each other when Crockett noticed tears running down his cheeks.

"Damn," he muttered.

TEN
Rubber Duckie

CROCKETT GOT HOME about one-thirty, feeling pretty good about the events of the day. He threw a ball around the backyard for Stupid and Shithead a while, gave them each a treat, opened a can of tuna for Nudge, fixed himself a ham sandwich and a small salad and filled the tub. His bathtub was as old as the house, an oversized, cast iron, claw-footed monster that held about sixty gallons and accommodated his six-foot, two hundred twenty pound frame with ease. He gathered up an old Robert B. Parker Spenser epic, grabbed a couple of Shermans and an ash tray, collected the phone, found a small bag of cashews, poured an insulated glass of iced tea, added a few drops of pepper-mint, birch, blue tansy, spruce, and clove oils to the running water and eased himself, complete with aching hip and numb leg, into the brew. Bliss! He settled back, lit a cigarette, and picked up the book, prepared for two hours of uninterrupted joy.

The goddamned phone went off.

"You sound pissed, Raoul."

"Just annoyed."

"Busy?"

"Relaxing."

"You sound like you're in a cave."

"I'm in the tub."

Ruby's voice dropped to a throaty purr. "Oooh!" she said. "What are you wearing?"

"A leopard-skin loincloth, swim fins, a really darling smile, and my Captain Video decoder ring."

"Maybe I should rush over and see if your rubber duckie can still float."

"Did you want something in particular?" Crockett said, "or just somehow know I'd be languishing in a tepid pool, eagerly awaiting your dulcet tones."

"How am I doin' so far?"

42

"Gimme a minute while I check with the duck."

"Should I hum while I wait?"

"I assume you are calling to glean some information about the session with Rachael?"

"Changing the subject, Crockett?"

"Yep. But it in no way alters the fact that I sculpt your navel in my oatmeal every morning."

"As well you should. So what about the gunslinger? Did you kick her ass?"

"Lovely little ass."

"Lovely little ass?"

"Pretty much."

Crockett told her about the lesson, but did not mention his tears.

"Well, when I said 'kick her lovely little ass', I did not expect you to become a drill sergeant. It would appear, however, that my faith in you was not misplaced. Once again, I excel."

"Yada, yada, yada."

"I find the climbing of your person and the clinging thereto, interesting," Ruby said.

"Christ, LaCost. Let it lay."

"I'm serious, Crockett. Rachael is not prone to that level of self-expression. She, unless she is acting, simply does not behave in such a demonstrative fashion. She not only clung to you when she failed, she physically celebrated all over you when she succeeded. Fear and joy, Crockett. She shared those with you. I would venture to say, at this point in her life, you are the only man on the planet with whom she could have been that emotionally honest."

Ruby paused.

"Crockett, don't lie. Did you cry?"

They were silent for a moment while Crockett worked on the lump in his throat and opened the hot water tap a bit with his toe.

"Okay," he said. "Now what?"

"She will either be very withdrawn around you, perhaps even forsake your company entirely for a time, or she will seek you out for increased social interaction."

"Increased social interaction. What the hell does that mean?"

"Your company is good for her."

"Oh, boy."

"Relax. You are not responsible for her actions, only your own. You are not her therapist. Be her friend. Do what friends do."

"I'm not sure what friends do."

"Of course you're not. This ain't rocket surgery, Crockett, it's called a relationship. Can you say relationship?"

"Aaarrrgggghh."

"Very good. You know, it would not be the end of the goddamned world if somebody other than me got to know you a little bit!"

"Hey, Ruby!"

"What?"

"You are a manipulative, devious, controlling, scheming, calculating bitch."

"That's my boy. Say goodbye to the duck for me." She hung up.

Crockett shut off the hot water, slid down to earlobe level in the tub, retrieved the book, munched a cashew or two and settled back into the business at hand. He was drifting away with Spenser when the damn phone rang again.

"Hi, it's Rachael."

"How are ya?"

"I never would have done what I did today if it wasn't for you and I just wanna show my appreciation for everything you've done and get to know you a little bit better and goouttoeatand …"

"Rachael."

"Yes?"

"Just say you'd like to buy me dinner."

"Crockett, I'd like to buy you dinner."

"When?"

"Tonight."

"That would be good."

"How 'bout Ruth's Chris Steakhouse?"

"That also would be good."

"Great!" Rachael said. "Pick me up around eight."

She hung up.

Crockett looked at the phone for a moment, digesting what had just happened.

Christ. LaCost was something else.

ELEVEN
Off the Range

CROCKETT SPENT ANOTHER HOUR soaking in the tub trying to read, but not even Hawk could hold his attention. Ruby, as usual, had screwed with his head too much. He analyzed the situation until he caught himself analyzing the situation, then spent the rest of the time trying to analyze why he was analyzing the situation. Jesus!

The horrible truth was simple. He was excited. Crockett drained the tub, showered, shaved, trimmed his 'stash, brushed his teeth and caught himself whistling. Twice. He smoked three Shermans in less than thirty minutes and brushed his teeth again. Pawing through a closet, he pulled out the only jacket he possessed, a light brown, classic, hand-stitched gabardine, in continental cut. With it he grabbed a new pair of dark brown jeans, a dark brown corduroy shirt and one of the two pairs of shoes he owned. Dark brown.

Tucking his shirttail in for a change, Crockett reflected on the fact that he could easily be the official poster child for the National Association of Liposuckers. At seven-thirty he installed himself in Thumper and set off. On the way to Rachael's he swung by the little florist shop on Westport Road and dropped three-fifty on a single pale-yellow rose. It felt like he was going to the goddammed prom. He could have sworn he heard Ruby laughing.

Rachael lived in one of the high-rise condos bordering the Country Club Plaza, an official cliff dweller. Crockett parked Thumper on the street and walked to the front door. Beside it was a panel with numbers and buttons. He pushed hers. The speaker above it crackled.

"Yes?"

"Just a young swain, come to call," he said.

"I'll buzz you into the lobby. Down in a minute."

In the fishbowl loitering area, Crockett took a seat. He stood up. He paced, he leaned, he looked out the windows, he peered out the door, he watched traffic, he peeked at pedestrians. He heard the elevator door open. He turned around. Rachael walked toward him and smiled.

She was wearing a short, collarless, gray silk jacket over a blue camisole and a knee-length charcoal gray skirt, slit a bit over the front of her left thigh. Her hose had a slight gray sheen, her two-inch pumps and her small handbag were black suede. She wore no jewelry except a black velvet choker set with a blue topaz on delicate silver. Her blond hair was down and flipped under, providing an oval frame for her face. Crockett had gotten used to her nearly teen-age, sweat-suited appearance at the range. He was not prepared for the woman who walked out of the elevator. His face showed it.

"Hello, Crockett," she said, and he could see uncertainty in her eyes.

"Rachael. You look wonderful."

"You think so?"

His mouth was suddenly dry. "Jesus, yes," he said.

"I wasn't sure. You looked a little stunned."

"That's only because I was. You're lovely." He handed her the rose.

"That's nice, Crockett."

"Well, it was either that or a deep fried corn-dog."

Rachael smiled. "Good choice," she said, and rose on tiptoe to kiss him on the cheek. "Thank you."

Crockett stood there like a rube and grinned back. When the silence got fairly loud, Rachael jumped in.

"Our reservation is in twenty minutes. It's about four blocks away. Can you hoof it?"

Crockett brandished his cane.

"Got all the help I need," he said.

On the sidewalk they became shy and walked about a foot apart, saying very little. Rachael sniffed the rose from time to time and smiled. Crockett didn't quite whistle.

TWELVE

Ruth's

THE HOSTESS GREETED THEM. "Ms. Moore, Mr. Crockett, it is our pleasure to have you join us for the evening. Henry will seat you in the bar as you requested, Ms. Moore."

Henry appeared out of nowhere and led them to a horseshoe booth that could have easily seated six.

After Henry departed, Crockett turned to Rachael. "High class joint."

Rachael carefully avoided looking into his eyes.

"I'm nervous," she said.

"I can understand that. Being this close to me without a gun in your hand has got to be a little unsettling." The waitress arrived.

"Ms. Moore, Mr. Crockett ... welcome to Ruth's. My name is Carol. May I get you something to drink?"

Crockett looked at Rachael. "Two Beefeater martinis, Carol. Three olives each. Thanks."

The waitress left.

They sat in silence for a moment. "Me, too," Crockett said.

"Me, too?"

"Yeah. Nervous."

"I can't imagine that," Rachael said. "Why don't we just get acquainted. You know what I do. What do you do?"

Crockett whipped out a business card and handed it to her. His card read Silverthroat. Under that it said voices.

"Silverthroat?"

"Yeah. I do accents, dialects, character voices, stuff like that. Freelance."

"I don't recall hearing you anywhere."

"Let's see ... the talking cartoon dog for Pet Town Stores, the old man whose voice you hear for the steamboat museum, the voice that screams for the Dodge dealers, the cheesy cockney accent for the Ren-

47

aissance Festival, all those strange characters in the spots for The Golden Beach tanning salons. That's me."

She laughed.

"You do *all* those voices? My goodness, I'm in the presence of real talent."

Crockett cocked an eyebrow and stared into the distance.

"Perhaps you'd be enriched if you touched the hem of my garment," he said.

The drinks and menus arrived. They sipped in silence for a moment.

"So," she said, "How did you get to K.C.?"

"I got divorced, then I got shot and my partner got killed. I spent about a year and a half in treatment and therapy, stuck in a wheelchair or on crutches, before my settlement and pension came through. My ex-wife's brother, not a bad guy, was program director at a radio station here in Kaycee and offered me a job on overnights, pushing buttons, recording the weather, stuff like that."

Crockett paused to sip his drink.

"After the settlement I got myself to a chiropractor so I could walk, went cold turkey off my codeine addiction and came to Kansas City. Three years later I realized how fucked in the head I was and went to see Ruby. The rest of my time has been spent waiting until I could turn you loose, armed and dangerous, upon the world."

Rachael munched an olive.

"Good martini," she said. "You a big eater?"

"Not excessively. I just got this way 'cause I'm lazy."

"Then may I make some suggestions?"

"Please."

"No appetizer. Go for the small K.C. strip or the large fillet. Side dishes are huge. I recommend we split an order of asparagus and an order of the garlic-gouda mashed potatoes. Crème brule for dessert." She tossed down the rest of her martini and looked at him expectantly as she chewed the last of her three olives.

Crockett knocked back his drink. "Sounds good," he said. "The fillet for me, I think. Eight ounce."

Rachael twirled her rose and touched a petal gently to her chin.

"How old are you?" she said.

"I'm fifty-one."

"I'm thirty-three. You have a problem with that?"

"I feel like I should have a problem with it."

"I just wanted to let you know that I don't," Rachael said.

Crockett smiled. She rested her chin on his shoulder.

"Want some wine with dinner?"

"Gotta be careful," Crockett said. "There is sometimes an awful lot of truth in the bottom of a wine bottle."

"That's why you drink the whole thing. I'm going to have wine. You may join me if you like."

When the waitress arrived, Rachael ordered for both of them. The wine was some rich, dark, mysterious liquid that the server poured after handing Crockett the cork to sniff. Rachael extended her glass.

"To friends and layers," she said.

"Onions, one and all," Crockett said. They drank.

"Sweet Jesus!" Crockett blurted. "If you rubbed that stuff on your elbow, you'd taste it in your mouth! That's the damnedest wine I ever had. It explodes in your head! Rachael, this is wonderful!"

"I'm glad you like it. There's more where that came from. Don't be shy, drink up. I'll be right back. Excuse me."

While she was gone, Crockett went through the wine list. He was double-checking the nearly four hundred dollar price tag when Rachael arrived. He felt his ears get hot as he blushed.

"Three-hundred eighty-five dollars a bottle," she said. "It's a pretty good wine."

"Rachael—"

"Shut up and listen. I have a lot of money. I get paid well at the television station and my salary there doesn't even begin to cover the taxes on my real income, and I pay very little tax. My mother died when I was three years old and left me an annuity administered by my aunt, worth in excess of two million dollars, thirty years ago. She also provided a separate income for my care that is now mine. She also left me a significant portfolio. I am not telling you this to impress you, or buy your affection. I am telling you this because I could feel you worrying about how much money I was spending on you. It's been a while since somebody worried about me like that. I appreciate it, Crockett. Thank you."

For the second time, she kissed him on the cheek. This one lingered just a bit.

"In that case," he said, "when we leave, could we get a six-pack of this to go?"

Rachael laughed. "I'll send you a case," she said.

"Naw. I'll drink it with you, but I won't drink it without you. However, if you'd like me to drink it with you in Cancun for the next six months, I'll clear my calendar."

She lifted her glass. "To Cancun," she said.

They took nearly three hours over dinner and desert and were both a little tipsy on the walk back to Rachael's building. She held onto Crockett's arm and swayed with him, as they prattled mindlessly. It had been a long time for Crockett and he enjoyed the sidewalk intimacy. Just as they entered Rachael's lobby, it began to rain. They broke contact and were suddenly shy. Crockett felt like stobbing his toe in the carpet and tugging on his forelock, if he'd had a forelock. They faced each other by the elevator.

"Crockett, tonight was really nice."

"Yeah. I had a great—"

"Me too. You want to come up?"

"Oh yeah, but I'm not going to," Crockett said. "By the time I get home though, I'm gonna be pretty pissed that I didn't."

"Good. I find that very encouraging. See ya Saturday?"

"Or before."

"Before?"

"If you like."

"I like, Crockett," Rachael said.

"I'll call you."

"Kiss me, you fool."

He did.

When Crockett got home Nudge was waiting with the third degree, accusing him of all sorts of infidelities. Way too charged up to go to bed, he slipped into some sweats, turned on the TV, made a mug of green tea and almost called Rachael a dozen times. He felt like a lunatic, hip-deep in infatuation, a sappy grin on his foolish face. Unable to settle down and bored by re-runs, he finally gave up and turned in. The message machine on the bedroom phone was blinking. A touch of the button and Rachel's voice filled the room.

"Hiya, Crockett. Getting' ready for bed and kept thinkin' about you. Just had to call. I wanted my voice to be the last one you heard tonight. God, I'm so embarrassed! I feel like I'm fifteen! Goodnight."

She didn't get her wish. Message number two was from Ruby. It was simple and to the point.

"Heh, heh, heh, heh ... heh, heh, heh. Sleep tight, Raoul. Heh, heh, heh."

Damn.

THIRTEEN
Girl Talk

WHEN RUBY'S ALARM WENT OFF on Sunday morning, she hit the snooze button and lay in bed a few moments, missing smoking. Even though she had not had a cigarette in over fifteen years, she longed for the luxury of procrastinating in bed during the first smoke of the day.

Sunday. No clients, no seminars, no obligations, no company. Not that company would have been a problem. She'd met Victoria for drinks the night before, but Victoria was just not working out. Ruby had no false hopes. Any relationship was a crapshoot and everybody carried excess baggage but, as time went on, she found herself less equipped to be understanding and more likely to be impatient. And with Vic, as it was with many women, the drama of being lesbian seemed to be more important than the intimacy of being human.

Not that Ruby didn't like Victoria, she did. But spending time with her was simply too much work. And Vic was becoming dependant. Their relationship had turned more to therapy and less to sharing, more to seeking advice and less to enjoying company. The plain truth was, for a hundred and twenty-five dollars an hour, Ruby could put up with a lot of self-serving bullshit. For free, it was just a hassle.

At about nine she'd given Victoria a peck goodnight, come home, bagged up the few things of Vic's that were in the apartment, and put everything in the hall closet to deliver later. She'd eaten some cold chicken, poured a glass of wine, picked up her latest from Mary Wings, and gone to bed. The book didn't hold her interest and, two more glasses of wine later, she'd called Crockett's machine and left a semi-lewd message, shut off the light, and waited for sleep.

When the alarm went off the second time, Ruby groaned and swung her feet to the floor. Nude, she padded into the bathroom and peered at herself in the mirror. Oh, God. Gray roots everywhere. Time to get her hair done again. Probably time to whiten her teeth again, too. She turned sideways and sucked in her tummy. Ruby was not thin. She did not desire to be thin, but Rubenesque was out of the question. An extra session per week on the bowflex should take care of that problem. Holding it together got more difficult every year and she knew it was a battle she'd eventually lose, but, so far, she was doing okay. No lifts, no tucks, no silicone, no liposuction.

Ruby took care of herself and had pride in her appearance. The necessity of looking good could easily be passed off to the nature of her job and the relationship with her clients, and those were valid reasons, but she suffered few illusions. Ruby liked to look good. She enjoyed the attention, she appreciated the leverage, and she loved the impact.

Deciding against a shower, she pulled her hair back with clips, put on her glasses, slipped into her old velour robe and ratty sheepskin slippers, and felt her Achilles tendons complain as she walked downstairs flatfooted after a week of wearing heels. She made coffee, slathered a toasted bagel with cream cheese, sprinkled dried dill on top, then remembered the little extra poundage and dropped the bagel in the trash.

After her second cup of coffee, Ruby went across the hall to her office and checked her messages. Three patients in what they assumed were various types of crisis. She declined to phone any of them back, knowing nothing was happening they couldn't, and shouldn't, handle by themselves. As she stood to leave, another call came in. Rachael. She picked up.

"Ruby! I was hoping to catch you."

"Is this therapy or conversation, Rachael?"

"Conversation."

"Nuts. My Sunday rates are triple time."

"Let me make it up to you. Breakfast is on me. First Watch in Westport in thirty minutes?"

"How 'bout here? I'm up for company, but I'm not up for crowds."

"Great! We deliver. See you soon."

Ruby hustled upstairs, hit the shower, ran a brush through her hair, slapped on some makeup and lipstick, put in her contacts, slipped on a deep maroon cotton and silk blend coverall, some black ballet slippers, and made it back downstairs in time to answer the security phone to allow Rachael into the visitors parking area.

"You look bushy-tailed this morning," Ruby said as Rachael brushed past her carrying a bag full of Styrofoam containers.

Rachel grinned and put the package on the counter.

"We have hash brown potatoes, we have shrimp omelets, we have fresh melon and fruit, and we have a pint container of sausage gravy," she said. "And I am bushy-tailed."

"Nice evening?"

"Wonderful evening."

Ruby smiled. "Pass the gravy and potatoes. I don't think I can hear this on an empty stomach."

Ruby poured fresh coffees as Rachael pushed the remains of her omelet away.

"And you spent the night alone?"

"Sadly, yes," Rachael said. "I wanted Crockett to come up, but he declined."

Ruby smiled. "And you didn't feel comfortable pulling him into the elevator by his hair?"

"That might have been too assertive for a first date," Rachael said. "Actually, I think it was really sweet that he didn't come up. That's the way he was all night, sweet. Kind and understanding and sweet. A lesser man, well ..."

"Does that surprise you?"

"A little. I mean, I'm not used to it. Last night was the only time we've been together without our focus being on shooting. He's much nicer when I'm not armed."

"Funny," Ruby said. "You'd think it'd be the other way around."

Rachael smiled. "When we're shooting he's much more intense. Almost military or something, like a drill sergeant. When I freaked out on the range yesterday and threw up in the parking lot, he really got in my face, Ruby. Yelled at me. Didn't give me a choice. Made me go back inside. Made me shoot."

"How do you feel about that?"

"I didn't like it much at the time, but I'm glad he did. The guy I was with last night was a lot different."

"So now what? Wait for him to call?"

Rachael shook her head. "I'm thinking about feeding him wine and cheese in the park this afternoon."

Ruby leaned back in her stool and grinned.

"You go, girl," she said.

After Rachael left, Ruby's curiosity got the better of her. She phoned Crockett.

"Good morning!"

"I have known you for nearly twenty years and I have never heard you answer the phone like that."

"Hi, Ruby."

"Could it be that you were expecting a call from a lovely lass other than myself?"

"Anything is possible."

Ruby smiled. "Really? Is anything possible?"

"Sure feels like it today."

"Things went well on your little outing with Rachael?"

"Don't you know?"

"I'm manipulative, Crockett, not psychic."

"Things went fine, I think. I got your sleazy message around midnight."

"You came home?"

"I did."

"Exactly the kind of judgment I thought you'd display. God, I'm good."

"It was a great night, Ruby."

"Spare me the details. It's just good to hear you sound so happy."

"LaCost, I don't have the faintest idea what I'm doing."

"Good. There is no protocol. Just relax and take care of yourself. Keep this in the moment. Acceptance, not expectation."

"I have a question," Crockett said. "It didn't occur to me until this morning. When Rachael fell out at the range yesterday, one of the things she screamed was 'Daddy'."

"Daddy?"

"'No, Daddy,' or "I'll be good, Daddy.' Something like that. Am I some kind of father figure?"

"You are a non-threatening male, you provide a place of safety, you are her teacher, and now, it would seem, you have become a romantic interest. All of those things play into a woman's perfect picture of a father, but that does not mean she sees you as a father figure. She is patterning you slightly, however."

"What's that mean?"

"We talked before about how she is an actor. Many actors have a poor sense of self. That is one of the reasons they adapt to playing other people so well. Combine that with the relationship you and she have developed, and patterning is to be expected. She has adopted some of your speech, she has begun viewing the world with a more cynical eye, even her sense of humor has shifted a little."

"Ruby, I don't mean to—"

"Of course you don't," Ruby said. "Don't worry about it. Consider it a compliment. She wasn't referring to you when she shouted anyway. At that point, she was probably only about six years old and screaming at her father. That's who she killed when you brought her back inside, you know."

"Jesus."

"Sometimes that type of thing is called modeling. Don't concern yourself. It's part of the process."

"Okay, Ruby. Thanks."

"If you can tear yourself away sometime, we'll drink Scotch, smoke cigars, and swap lies."

"I'd love it," Crockett said. "Just name the day."

"You really came home to your cold and lonely bed?"

"That's right."

Ruby chuckled.

54

"Performance anxiety, Crockett?"

Before he could reply, she hung up.

Crockett was staring at a glass of V-8 as it warmed on the counter, turning the conversation with Ruby over in his mind, when his phone went off again.

"Hi, Crockett."

"Rachael!"

"I know you said you'd call and I don't want to seem pushy, but it's a really beautiful day and where do you live?"

"On 38th, in the Valentine district, just off the trafficway."

"I'm heading your direction. Grab a hat and some sunglasses. I have wine, I have cheese, I have bread, I have a blanket, I have pillows. You and I are going to Loose Park where we will lie on that blanket, dine on merlot and triple cream brie, and look for animals in the clouds."

"I haven't showered or shaved yet."

"Sorry, no time."

"At least let me brush my teeth."

"Just lay the phone down, I'll wait."

Crockett left the phone on the counter and hurried into the bathroom. He brushed like a madman, wiped on some deodorant, tied his hair back, threw on a shirt and shoes and hustled back to the phone.

"Took you long enough," Rachael said. "Now hang up the phone and step out onto the porch."

Rachael was in his driveway, perched on the fender of her Land Cruiser, wearing a t-shirt, cutoffs, flip-flops, and a big grin.

"If you don't want to be found, Crockett, you shouldn't park Thumper in the driveway."

"It's all part of my plan."

"I can't wait to hear the rest of it."

After lunch, Ruby was contorted on the couch, giving herself a pedicure, when her cell phone sounded. She glanced at the display. Victoria.

With a sigh, she put the phone down and returned to her toes.

FOURTEEN
Fishooks in the Park

LOOSE PARK COVERS SEVERAL SQUARE BLOCKS in a semi-upscale area of Kansas City. It is mostly a large rolling lawn that occasionally sprouts a copse of trees, some scattered evergreens, a running and bicycle track, the occasional large oak or elm, and a man-made lake rimmed in cement, artfully bridged, sporting a fountain in the center. It is a place where suntans are developed, Tai-Chi is practiced, dogs are allowed to run free, kites are flown, Frisbees are tossed and two-year-olds chase waterfowl.

They parked on the west side, walked through the only heavily planted belt of trees, and chose a spot on a slight slope near a stand of three lovely spruces. Mother nature at her most controlled and choreographed. Crockett lugged the blanket, pillows and such in a canvas bag. Rachael carried a wicker picnic basket and a bottle of high intensity sunscreen. He couldn't stop grinning.

The wine was magnificent.

They talked and necked, ate and drank, hugged and smooched, laughed and giggled, and just generally behaved like some 1962 Technicolor wide-screen version of Splendor In The Park. It was so cheesy, it was perfect. A black Lab, escaped from his owner, even joined in for a while, begging bites of brie and bread. In the middle of a gigantic cliché, they lay on their backs, holding hands and looking at the clouds.

"Where ya from?"

"I was born in Urbana, Illinois," Rachael said.

"Champaign-Urbana?"

"Do you know it?"

"I spent the first thirty years of my life there. I was a cop in Champaign for eight years," Crockett said. "You're from Urbana?"

"Not exactly. I'm from Hyatt County."

"Farm country. Corn, soybeans, like that."

"I got my degree in broadcast journalism at the University Of Illinois, worked as a gopher and low level producer at WCIA in Champaign—"

"I grew up with WCIA."

"Went from there to a station in Rockford, then to Omaha, then here." She assumed a look of dignified importance. "And now I am a talking head in a low level major market. Just another bubble-headed bleached blond."

"Tell me this. With all the money you have, why work at all?"

"I don't want time on my hands, Rachael said. "It's important for me to stay busy. Maybe Chicago is next, and maybe not. I'm starting to like Kansas City a lot."

"Another question and then I'll shut up," Crockett said. "What frightens you enough that I'm teaching you how to kill people?"

She sighed.

"I think I'm starting to burn. Rub some sunscreen on my legs, willya? It'll give you a good excuse to fondle my lower limbs." As he sat up and grabbed the bottle, Crockett felt her withdraw a bit, then slowly return while he applied the lotion.

She was getting a little pink. Rubbing on the sunscreen, he noticed very tiny, faint scars on her thighs. Looking her over, he saw several on her arms too. They were not obvious, only close inspection made them visible, but they were there, many of them.

"What happened to you?" Crockett said.

She raised up on an elbow. "What?"

"All these little bitty scars. What happened?"

"Fish hooks," Rachael said.

Crockett watched her eyes lose focus. She held rock-still for a few seconds, then blinked rapidly three or four times. Her eyes refocused on him and Rachael smiled. "What?" she said.

"Flip over. You're well basted on this side."

"My pleasure," she said, and did, the fish hooks neatly filed away.

FIFTEEN

Getaway

THINGS PROGRESSED WITH RACHAEL. She and Crockett talked on the phone daily. Wednesday he took her to lunch at Otto's for blue cheese burgers, curly fries and the absolute best chocolate malts in the metroplex. She was appropriately astounded by his culinary insight and volunteered to pay for both their precautionary bypass surgeries, proof the way to a woman's heart is with a greaseburger. Saturday at the range, Rachael's attitude was markedly different. She was enthusiastic, celebrated when she did well and was much more aggressive on the line. Outside in the parking lot, Crockett told her how proud he was.

"Do I get a reward?" she said.

"Name it."

"Go home. I'll be right behind you."

When they arrived in Crockett's driveway, Rachael leaned out her car's window.

"Put your truck in the garage, go inside and pack a change of clothes, your toiletries and razor, and get back out here."

"What's going on?"

"My reward, Crockett. You."

An hour and a half later they were on River Road in St. Joseph Missouri, ordering a late lunch at a nice little log cabin restaurant, sitting on the shaded terrace overlooking the Missouri River.

"This is beautiful," Crockett said.

Rachael squinted out across the water. "It's one of my favorite places," she said. "Bald eagles fly around here. I found it last fall when we came up to do a fluff piece on some guy retracing the Lewis and Clark route."

They talked, they ate, and as they were leaving, the manager handed Rachael a key.

"Everything is as you asked, Ms. Moore. Your bags are waiting. Have a wonderful time."

When they stepped outside, Rachael began to walk down the gravel road that paralleled the river. She smiled over her shoulder.

"Follow the leader, Crockett."

The leader led him a hundred yards or so to a two-story log cabin about sixty feet up the slope from the river. Rachael unlocked the door and held it open. Crockett went inside. It was lovely.

Deeply carpeted and constructed of hand-hewn logs, the room was about thirty feet square. An L-shaped kitchen occupied one corner. The living area contained two suede leather couches and matching chairs, a stacked-stone fireplace, and sliding glass doors that opened onto a covered patio. The patio, complete with several chairs, a gas grill and an immense hot tub, was fenced on both sides for privacy and open to the river. Beside the glass door was a spiral staircase leading to the second level. Rachael was already on the way up.

The top floor was hardwood, covered here and there with oriental rugs. It contained a bathroom with a huge shower, a bidet, and a Jacuzzi tub of even larger capacity than the cast-iron antique Crockett had at home. The bed was king size and covered with what appeared to be a buffalo-hide spread. Another stacked-stone fireplace occupied a corner, sliding glass doors led onto a deck with chairs and a deeply padded double chaise lounge. Their bags were beside the bed.

Rachael grinned. "Whatcha think?"

"It's perfect. It's just perfect."

"The fridge is stocked," she said. "We have bacon, we have eggs, we have veggies, we have salad, we have potatoes, we have aged fillet, we have fresh red snapper. The bar is full. We have scotch, we have vodka, we have mescal, we have wine, we have champagne. We do not have a phone, we do not have a television. We have the place through noon Monday and we have each other."

"I don't know what to say."

"Crockett, I love it that you're shy. I love it that you're concerned about the difference in our ages. Go shave, brush your teeth and all that stuff, then get in the shower. You are a very nice man and you have been the perfect gentleman. Now it's time to move on. Go get wet."

It was the first time Crockett ever drank wine in a shower.

It was nearly dusk when Crockett turned the steaks on the grill. He heard the sliding glass door open and Rachael's arms came around him from behind. Her forehead was pressed into the nape of his neck. Goose bumps crawled up the back of his arms. Her warm breath tickled.

"Crockett?"

"Hmmm?"

"I don't think I could ever be afraid if you were with me."

He turned around and smiled at her.

59

"I have never been happier that I am right this moment," he said.

Rachael batted her eyelashes. "Really?" she said.

The steaks burned.

As usual Crockett's leg got him up earlier than he would have liked. He eased out of bed, hit the bathroom, then limped down the stairs and out to the hot tub. He was sitting in the swirling water, eyes closed, Sherman in hand, feeling the life crawl back into his hip, when Rachael's voice blossomed in his ear.

"You didn't fix breakfast?"

"Don't bother me," Crockett said. "I'm trying to resurrect the dead."

"That's my job," she said.

"I'm talking about my leg, you wanton slut."

Rachael dropped her robe and slipped into the swirling water.

"Maybe if I rub it," she said.

"Rachael?"

"Yes, Dear?"

"That's not my leg."

"God, Crockett, can't you think about anybody but yourself?"

Crockett scrambled eggs for breakfast while Rachael cut up a melon and mixed orange juice and champagne. They rented a small pontoon boat and plowed up and down the river for a while, calling each other Lewis and Clark. They walked to the restaurant for lunch. They held hands, giggled at stupid stuff, made outrageous sexual innuendo, patted each other's bottoms in public, played in bed, made fun of one another, got mildly drunk in the hot tub at three in the morning, fed each other strawberries with their eyes closed and fell a little bit in love.

As they pulled out of the parking lot to drive back to Kaycee, Rachael smiled.

"Crockett," she said, "that was the most fun I ever had with my clothes off."

"Ha!"

"I mean it," she said.

"Don't bullshit a bullshitter," Crockett said. "I'm old, I'm fat, I'm going bald, and I got a bum leg. I remember what life was like when I was your age. I can try, but I can't compete with that."

Rachael slammed on the brakes and slid to a halt on the shoulder. Crockett braced against the dashboard to keep from kissing the windshield. When they stopped she whirled on him, tears collecting in the bottoms of her eyes.

"Is that what you think this is, some kind of stupid contest?"

"Rachael—"

60

"Shut up! Some kind of performance oriented, dirty weekend, cock hunt?"

"Rachael—"

"I said shut up! Now you listen to me, you poor, tired, fat, old, balding, insecure shithead! I went up to that cabin with you, not some suited-up, slick-haired refugee from a Plaza coffee bar. I didn't go up there with you to get laid. I went up there with you to get loved! And I got loved. I got loved by a caring, gentle, funny, wonderful man, and I wouldn't trade ten minutes with *that* man for a week with some twenty-eight year old, designer beer swilling, self-important, junior investment advisor. Are we clear?"

"Ah—"

"Just what part of shut up do you fail to understand? Do you think I dragged you up there just to see if some old guy could get it up? Jesus Christ, Crockett! Do you know what Ruby said about you? Answer me!"

"No."

"Ruby said that you were the best man she had ever known. I happen to agree with her. Don't you dare run yourself down to me, David Allen Crockett. I won't have it!"

"I'm sorry."

"Don't talk to me," she said, backhanding tears from her face. "Just sit there and be quiet until I settle down, you shit."

They pulled in Crockett's driveway before she spoke again.

"I'm sorry I blew up like that. I took what you said too seriously."

"I'm not sure you did. Can I ask you a question?"

"Sure."

"Was that really the most fun you ever had with your clothes off?"

Rachael smiled. "Yes, it was," she said.

"It was the best weekend of my life, Rachael. Without a doubt."

"Crockett, I don't know what it's like to be in love. I have nothing to compare it to, but I suspect it feels a lot like this."

He touched her cheek with the tip of his index finger.

"Take my word for it," Crockett said. "It feels exactly like this."

SIXTEEN
Revenge of the Nudge

NUDGE PUNISHED CROCKETT for abandoning him, yammering, then walking away whenever Crockett reached to pet him. Crockett followed him around the house for a while, then gave up. He returned a phone call to an agency, spent an hour in the tub in vain effort to ease his misused back and hip, washed and dried a load of whites, ate some mac n' cheese and applesauce for a late lunch, and realized how really tired he was.

About three, he took to the couch for a nap. He crawled out of the black hole near six, his neck cricked, his eyes itchy, his tongue furry, his nose stopped up, and Nudge firmly draped around his head. He felt like hell, but he still couldn't get rid of his sappy smile.

Crockett washed his face, brushed his teeth, rubbed some Tiger Balm into his neck, dumped some saline into both eyes, lit a Sherman, microwaved some stale coffee, took a sip, and burned his tongue. The ice cube in his mouth had almost melted when the phone rang.

"Heh, heh, heh, heh, heh …"

"Gimme a break, Ruby. I just burned my tongue."

"I could kiss it, and make it all better."

"LaCost, I love you."

"That's no distinction. You love everybody right now."

"Yeah, but I loved you before."

"You sound stopped up."

"I'm allergic to cats. I took a nap and Nudge slept with me, wrapped around my head."

"Me next. I'll be right over."

Crockett laughed. "Come ahead on," he said. "You'll be perfectly safe."

"Speaking of safe, how are … things?"

"Wonderful."

"At the risk of changing the course of what could become a ribald conversation, I cannot think of anyone more deserving of some joy than you, Old Son, except, of course, me."

"Find yourself a good woman, Ruby."

"The search continues," she said. "Unfortunately, the gay community is so fraught with gamesmanship, a simple hello is frequently more taxing than a Monopoly marathon."

"You are not a gamesperson."

"No," Ruby said. "I am not."

"Nor do you suffer fools gladly."

"No. The soap opera mentality of the average confused queer is difficult for me to digest. It was much easier before being lesbian became fashionable. Enough about me and the trials of being trapped between hairy bull-daggers and swooning tin lezzies."

"I can't thank you enough, Ruby."

"Crockett, it is not my habit to make matches for either current or past clients. It was obvious to me that Rachael was going to get a gun and go shoot the goddamned thing. I knew you'd do the right thing, even if you didn't know what it was. This tryst is certainly none of my doing. So, is her ass as lovely as I believe it to be?"

"You will never know."

Ruby sighed. "Alas. How's it feel to not be thirty again?"

"It is an immense relief," Crockett said. "Acceptance is much easier to live with than expectation."

"Hot damn, Crockett! You have just grasped one of the cosmic truths of the universe. One, I might add, that only a tiny fraction of people ever come to comprehend. You are now officially wise beyond your years."

"Have you talked to Rachael?" Crockett said.

"We spoke via landline briefly this very afternoon. She is spun. She is in the moment. She is happy. You done good."

"I'm not her therapist."

"But you have facilitated that process. In just the past week or so, she has become much more open, self-confident and settled."

"Tell me about the fish hooks, Ruby."

"What?"

"You heard me."

"Aw, Crockett, I can't. How'd you find out about them?"

He told her about the incident in the park.

"Interesting. How'd you feel about her shut-down?"

"It scared me a little, but I just let it slide."

"Once again, you did the right thing."

"And you can't tell me about the fishhooks?"

"It would violate confidence," Ruby said. "I will tell you this, however. She didn't tell you about them because she did not want to, but because she was constrained not to."

"Constrained?"

"That's all I can say about it."

"Terriffic. Okay. I understand your ethical situation. I don't like it, but I understand it."

"Crockett, if you know this woman another fifty years, you may never learn one more thing about her past that you are already are aware of. By the same token, you may learn it all in only a few months. What you are giving her is infinitely more important that what she has received in the past. Scratching at scabs may not be the way for the wounds to heal. Apply salve and be patient."

"I yield to your expertise."

"Ah, Crockett, to hear 'I yield' cross your tempting lips, in spite of that ratty mustache, is almost more than I can bear. How's your back and hip?"

"Sore."

"Perhaps a rubdown is advisable. I could come over. You could rub me with oil, then I could rub you with me. How's that sound?"

"Like prostate problems."

"Then, like Nudge, I could sleep wrapped around your face."

"Nudge was wrapped around my head."

"My error."

"Besides, I told you I was allergic."

"To cats, Crockett. Evidently not to pussy."

"Jesus Christ, Ruby, hang up!"

"Purrrrr," she said.

SEVENTEEN
The Kitchen

CROCKETT WAS PUTTING ON his old flannel robe when Rachael's voice floated back to the bedroom.

"Your refrigerator sucks!"

He padded into the dark kitchen.

"How kind of you to say so," he said.

She was wearing white socks with the tops rolled around her ankles and one of his threadbare white shirts as she bent over and peered into the disheveled maw of Crockett's old Amana. The light from the fridge shone through the thin broadcloth in a fetching manner and he was enjoying the tableau when Rachael spoke again.

"Just look at this!"

"Okay," Crockett said, resting his butt against the edge of the kitchen table to more appreciate the view. "Could you move a couple of inches to your right? The light's a little better."

Rachael shook her bottom, closed the door, backed up until she was leaning full length against him and turned her face up to be kissed. As Crockett attempted to respond, she took a bite of carrot and began to chew noisily, smacking her lips.

"Well, that pretty much destroys the mood," he said.

Looking over her shoulder, carrot juice on her chin, Rachael gazed into Crockett's eyes.

"Thas noght my refribaraduh!" she said.

"That's a great refrigerator," Crockett said.

"Bullshit. Lemme get you a new one."

"It's fine."

She turned around and pointed half a carrot in his face. "Crockett, don't go all macho and male on me."

He cringed. "What are you going to do with that carrot?"

"It has no door storage, the shelves are rusting, the freezer is choked with ice, and it doesn't keep milk cold enough!"

"I'm emotionally involved with that fridge. It was here when I bought the house."

"I gotta have cold milk, Crockett. I just gotta!"

"Okay."

"Really?"

"Just not a side by side."

She put her arms around his neck and batted her eyes. "Oh, Crockett! You've made me the happiest woman on the face of the earth!"

"Yeah, yeah, yeah."

"We'll measure in the morning. Now, about that stove."

"The stove?"

"It's worse than the fridge!"

"Oh, man!"

"And you really need a dishwasher."

"What?"

"Of course, we'd have to refit with a new base cabinet for the sink."

Crockett slumped into a chair.

Rachael turned on the overhead light and began to look about.

"A garbage compactor here, an eye-level oven over there with a built-in microwave. We really should replace these old sinks, they're not nearly deep enough. These counter tops have to go, we'll need all new cabinetry, this floor is awful, and the ceiling? Yuk! How 'bout it?" She waived the carrot stub. "A new kitchen, top to bottom!"

"All that so you can have cold milk?"

Rachael took a thoughtful bite of her carrot.

"Just knowing this kitchen exists could have a negative effect on my libido. Who can say?"

"Are you threatening to withhold sex for freezer space?" Crockett said.

"Could happen."

"I certainly wouldn't want to be responsible for something like that."

"Of course you wouldn't."

"All right. If it will help you, I'll do it!"

Rachael tossed the last chunk of carrot into the sink.

"The sacrifices you make," she said.

EIGHTEEN
Italian with the Italian

CROCKETT LURCHED OUT OF THE BATHROOM at around ten-thirty the next morning. Rachael was fully dressed in one of his flannel shirts, sharing her coffee with Nudge at the kitchen table and talking on the phone. She smiled at him. Crockett scowled.

"No, Arthur," she said, "no external renovation, doors, windows, or anything like that. Just interior. No, we won't have time for custom built, just top of the line prefabs ... right ... sure ... oh, granite. All new, the old ones are awful! Stainless is terrific ... you're right. Really? That's wonderful! You have the address ... marvelous! I'll be right here. It will be good to see you, too. 'Bye."

"What's going on," Crockett said.

"Arthur," Rachael said.

"Who's Arthur?"

"Arthur is the man who is going to install your new kitchen. He's very good."

"And very expensive."

"Don't do this Crockett. Don't bring up money. This is something I want to do. Just let me have fun."

"Okay, okay. Bring on Arthur."

"Good. He'll be here around noon. You have to go away."

"Do I have anything to say about this?"

"Not much. Do you prefer dark, rich wood, or light, bright wood?"

"Light and bright, I guess."

Rachael punched in a phone number and turned on the speaker. Ruby answered her phone.

"Hi, Ruby! It's Rachael."

"Good morning, Rachael, am I on speaker?"

"Yep. This is an unofficial call. You busy?"

"Not until late this afternoon."

"I'm at Crockett's."

"I'm sorry. Is he there?"

"Sitting right across from me."

"Be afraid, Rachael. Be very afraid."

"Take him to lunch, willya? I've got some things to do around here and he'll just be in the way."

"Haz-Mat coming over?"

"Sorta. Crockett's getting a new kitchen. I talked him into it."

"You're amazing! I couldn't even talk him into changing his socks! If I may remove the Hulk from your presence I consider it my civic duty."

"So she's putting in a whole new kitchen to keep her milk cold," Crockett said, watching Ruby eat spaghetti in that offhand way that Italians eat spaghetti.

She was sitting across the booth from him in the Italian Gardens, an ancient little pasta eatery near 12th and Baltimore in downtown Kansas City. Ruby was dressed for a day off. Beige suit in a silk blend, short skirt, no blouse, red scarf, red four-inch heels with open toes and an ankle strap, gold jewelry, and perfect make-up. As usual, she was the dominant feature in the room.

"Cold milk is very important," she said.

"It must be. It's gonna cost her ten or twelve grand."

"Ha!"

"What, ha?"

"That kitchen will cost her an easy forty grand."

"Forty thousand dollars?"

"At least. Maybe more."

"*For a kitchen?*"

"Yes, but it will be a very nice kitchen."

"Holy shit, Ruby!" Crockett said. "I didn't spend that much on the whole house!"

"Forget the money. The money is not important to her."

"It's important to me!"

"Why? It's not your money."

"Well, it's …"

"Yes?"

"I never thought of it like that."

"Think of it like that," Ruby said.

"That kitchen will cost more money than I make in a year."

"Big deal. You make shit. I earn more than that in three or four months."

"But—"

"Crockett, this woman was raised in a house with nine bedrooms and thirteen baths. Her lawn was over sixty acres. This kitchen doesn't mean squat to her. You do. With all your bullshit and out of date maleness, you are so far ahead of anything as trivial as money, that it is positively laughable. She's nesting!"

68

"Nesting?"

"Nesting! She won't live with you, you wouldn't live with her, so the next best thing is some common ground. A kitchen. A stupid kitchen. A place that's part of you because it will be where you live and part of her because she will create it. Something the two of you will have together. Do you understand, together?"

"Yes, I understand together."

"It's a way for her to give you something of herself, to create a place of intimacy that has nothing to do with sex, or even gender. In some ways this is the most important thing she has ever done in her life. You have given her that opportunity, Crockett. You can't imagine what that means to her, but it would serve you well to try."

"Wow."

"Understand that this whole nesting thing does not mean a lifetime commitment, picket fences, and rose gardens. It is not an effort to entrap, but to enjoy. She enjoys you, Crockett, as do I. You are the only person with whom I sit and smoke cigars. Cigars and a couch. That's my little Crockett nest."

"Damn!"

Ruby grinned. "Now don't get all misty on me, Big Boy," she said. "We fill needs for each other. You love to fantasize about my heaving bosoms beneath your sweating chest, I love to embarrass you in conversation. They're my little Crockett moments."

"Am I that transparent?"

"No. I'm just unusually perceptive."

"That you are, Sweetheart."

"I assume then," Ruby said, "we have reached an understanding?"

"Yes."

"Good. Now, onto more important matters. How much would you enjoy watching me eat a cannoli?"

"C'mon, LaCost!"

Ruby picked up the pastry and smiled.

"Another Crockett moment," she said.

NINETEEN
Arthur Excited

WHEN CROCKETT RETURNED HOME around two, Rachael was gone, and Arthur, flapping about the kitchen with a tape measure and a cynical eye, remained. He was about forty; small and slight, and wearing very tight black slacks, short boots and a white silk shirt. All that was missing was an ascot and a riding crop. He impaled Crockett with a reproachful eye.

"Sir, this kitchen is atrocious! Fear not, Arthur is here, and all shall be well. The floor space is acceptable, nearly twenty-two by eighteen, but, my God, this puts rustic in a whole new category! This floor, that ceiling! A Neanderthal wouldn't have wasted paint on these walls. Had he, he would have been pummeled and cast from the tribe!"

"Why, thank you, Arthur."

"Oh dear. I fear I have offended you! *Pardonez-moi*. Please excuse me, it's just that Ms. Moore has given me such a marvelously tacky canvass on which to apply my art, that I have become positively boisterous! Forgive my excitement, Mr. Crockett. Sometimes I am too emotionally expansive."

Crockett swallowed a smile. "Me too, Arthur," he said. "It has taken me years to learn to control myself. You can do it."

Arthur began to stride about the kitchen as he waved his arms in a random manner.

"After speaking with the lovely Ms. Moore and finishing my preliminary measurements, I think I can give you a total of twenty-five feet of counter space, a nice cold area, a more than adequate surface cooking area, double pull-out pantries, ovenage suitable to your needs--"

"Jeeze, I hope so, Arthur. I'm pretty big on ovenage."

"And a very nice center space for snacking and the majority of your water usage."

"Sounds just right," Crockett said. Arthur beamed.

"Of course, all ten of the major appliances will be stainless—"

70

"Ten?"

"*Mais, certainement!*"

"Ten major appliances?"

"Three cooling units, the refrigerator, the wine cellar, and the sub-zero freezer."

"Ah."

"Plus the dishwasher, the garbage compactor, the stovetop, the grill, the eye-level oven, the microwave-convection oven, the flash oven and the hood over the cooking area."

"That's eleven."

"So it is. All three sinks will be stainless, too."

"Three?"

"Two in the island, one small one, also with a disposer, in the cooling area."

"Oh, yeah. I forgot about the cooling area."

"Countertops in a dusky balance of gray and blue. Polished granite of course."

"Of course."

"Slate flooring a complimentary color to the counters, but slightly darker in value, with just the faintest hint of cranberry."

"That's good, Arthur."

"We'll drop this ten-foot ceiling to seven and a half around the walls to touch the cabinet tops and vault it in the center to the full height. Two stainless ceiling fans overhead at the peak, track lighting a bit farther down."

"I like vaulted."

"Cabinetry in a pale birch, with the slightest hint of blue in a very light wash. Walls in very light gray and the palest mauve, with cranberry accents. Hidden under-cabinet lighting throughout. Very masculine, without being too butch."

"Wouldn't wanna be too butch, Arthur. It all sounds perfect."

Arthur clapped his hands. "That's just wonderful! I'll get the final measurements with our structural designer next week and the cabineteer will also drop by to do his preliminary sketches. We've decided to go totally custom, much more individualistic. Ms. Moore wants us to keep our disruption time to an absolute minimum. We'll prepare as much as possible off site, so we can just whisk it in and install it. When everything is ready to go, we'll assemble double crews, work from seven A to eleven P, Monday through Saturday, and be on site no more than two and a half weeks. We should be able to begin in about six weeks. I will oversee and coordinate every inch and detail. It will be a lovely little kitchen."

"A lovely little kitchen."

"Oh, yes. Quite charming."

"How much?"

"Well, Ms. Moore said—"

"How much, Arthur?"

"Ms. Moore—"

"I won't tell you told, Arthur, but you *will* tell."

Arthur actually managed to look down his nose and up at Crockett at the same time.

"Very well," he said. "Quite reasonable, actually. This is not a large or complicated project. Under forty-five I should think. Perhaps even under forty-three. I was sworn to secrecy, Mr. Crockett."

"Not a peep, Arthur. I was just curious."

"It will be very nice. Light, airy, the complete kitchen for the complete man."

"Such as I."

"Congratulations, Mr. Crockett," Arthur said, striding to the front door. "You may rest assured that Arthur shall take care of everything. Ta!"

Rachael called after her late newscast.

"How'd you and Arthur get along?"

"Arthur's a doll," Crockett said.

"Isn't he?"

"He said I would have a kitchen that would be masculine, but not butch."

"Crockett, your masculinity is not in doubt."

"Aw."

"Arthur gets emotional."

"He seemed excited."

"So am I," Rachael said.

"Are you?"

"Oh, yes," she breathed, her voice dropping into a stage whisper. "The thought of all that cold milk—"

"I could rush to Quick Trip and put a quart of two percent on ice."

"It makes me all warm inside."

"Make that a half gallon."

"Maybe I should come over."

"A gallon of whole milk, a quart of cottage cheese, a half pint of heavy cream, two cans of Milnot, and a carton of ricotta. I'll do it!"

"Get a couple hour's rest, Crockett. I'll be there in twenty minutes."

Christ. He'd never survive a whole new kitchen.

TWENTY
The Towel Boy

FOR THE NEXT THREE OR FOUR WEEKS Rachael and Crockett spent a great deal of time together. Her TV station picked him up and he made a nice piece of change voicing a series of liners and bumpers for them. Two or three nights a week they spent at his place or her condo, weekends they were nearly inseparable. They even managed a couple of Royals games in her company box seats, striving to find value in sports-based frustration.

With Rachael's break-through on the range, the two of them went shooting every Wednesday and Saturday, renting one of the big downstairs rooms for a couple of hours each time. She shot multiple silhouettes at varying distances, low light, flashlight, and a second-rate Hogan's Ally course used by one of the local cop shops. Crockett got Rachael a shoulder rig and a breakaway purse to carry the little Smith, and twelve more rounds of Glasers so she wouldn't shoot through walls or sacrifice knockdown power. His little student blossomed. By the time September rolled around, she was an official, Crockett designated, Shootist. A hundred rounds or so every couple of weeks would keep her sharper than most cops.

"Well, that's it, Hotshot," Crockett said, as they stood in the parking lot after a mid-week session. "You have officially graduated."

"That's all there is?"

"You're done. Crank out a few now and then for fun, and you'll stay good enough to scare Wyatt Earp."

A thoughtful expression on her face, Rachael looked at Crockett.

"So I guess we'll never see each other again, huh?" she said.

"You've had your way with me," Crockett said. "You've taken all I have to give."

"It was worth it. I shoot pretty good."

"So now I'll have each and every weekend all by myself," Crockett said. "I don't know, maybe I'll get a bird."

"Considering that cougar that lives with you," Rachael snorted, "it better be an ostrich!"

"Here I am, pouring out my heart, and you make jokes about Nudge."

"Pour your heart into this," she said. "Chicago, hotel suite, marvelous food, wonderful drink, room service, Lakeshore Drive and me. A graduation celebration. We'll leave Friday night after I get off."

"So to speak," Crockett said.

"Interested?"

"Always and forever."

"Good," Rachael said. "Gotta go clean up and get to work. I'll be in touch."

She kissed him, bailed into the Land Cruiser, and roared off in a cloud of dust.

When Crockett shut Thumper off in the drive, he heard the phone ringing. Stupid and Shithead delayed his entry through the back door and he missed the call entirely. Ruby was on the recorder.

"Crockett. Shake the blond and drag your tired old ass over here tonight. I need a man. Failing that, I called you. Shrimp and Shiraz, Macanudos and scotch. Sevenish. Warmest regards, Doctor LaCost."

Crockett pulled Thumper up to the gate and beamed at the slouching security guard.

"Larry!" he said. "Long time no see."

"You got a delivery?" asked the guard.

"No, that was last time."

"Huh?"

"I'm here to see Ms. LaCost in 204."

Larry rifled through his clipboard. "Don't see no guest on my list."

"Larry, I bet if you call Ms. LaCost, she'll tell you to admit me forthwith."

Larry was annoyed. Crockett could see it in his beady little bloodshot eyes. The guard picked up his offical security phone.

"Mrs. LaCost," Larry said. "Sorry. *Miss* LaCost, there's a guy here ta see ya." He looked at Crockett. "What's yer name?"

"Tell her it's Arturo, the towel boy."

Ruby flung her front door aside and peered suspiciously at Crockett. "Who are you, and what have you done with Raoul?" she said.

"I locked him in a Quick Trip restroom. I, Arturo, am here in his stead. He has told me many things about you."

Ruby was wearing a white pullover top with capped sleeves and a bare midriff, green and white seersucker short-shorts and very tall sandals. She looked slightly down at Crockett and stepped back from the doorway.

"Arturo, you smooth-talking devil, come in and be ready with a towel. I could get wet at any moment."

Crockett felt his ears get hot.

"Crockett, you cutie, you're blushing! That's precious."

Ruby turned and headed for the kitchen, swaying a bit too much.

"Like my outfit? I'm celebrating the end of summer."

"Ah, Ruby," Crockett said. "I hate to see you go, but I dearly love to watch you leave."

She sauntered out of the kitchen carrying a shrimp dripping sauce and fed it to him.

"Okay?"

"Excellent," Crockett said.

Ruby slowly licked a drop of sauce off her index finger and bumped her eyebrows.

"Good," she said, "who knows what further delights are to come?"

"Just being here with you is a delight."

Ruby grinned and wrapped her arms around his neck. "For me too, Pal," Ruby said. "I need a full-body, double-breasted, monkey-munch of a hug, Crockett, and you are going to give it to me."

He did his best.

They ate a pound and a half of shrimp, a wedge of Stilton and a full bottle of wine in record time, then went out on the terrace. Crockett flopped on the couch and Ruby brought him a Macanudo Maduro and a double shot of scotch. She reclined on a couple of pillows, lit her cigar, and laid her legs across his lap.

"How ya doin, Davey?"

"Shrimp was good."

"Don't dodge."

"Great, Ruby. Really great. So great, I'm kind of waiting for the other shoe to drop."

"Stay in the moment, Sweetcakes."

"I'm really trying to. I said okay to a new kitchen, for chrissakes. What the hell am I going to do with granite counter tops, and eleven stainless steel major appliances?"

"Be totally embarrassed by the rest of your house."

Crockett laughed. "You got that right."

"Having fun?"

"Oh yeah. A lot."

"You're entitled. So is she. How do you feel about her, Crockett?"

"Jesus. Ruby, every time I'm around her I feel lucky to be around her, y'know?"

"Lucky is good. Deserving would be better."

"She's the first thing on my mind in the morning and the last thing at night."

"Really?" Ruby said.

Crockett chuckled and rubbed his forehead. "What do you want from me?" he said.

"A confession."

"Shit. I love her, Ruby. I'm happier than I've ever been in my life. I can't imagine what it would be like to be without her and I'm scared to death that I'll find out. You did this, LaCost."

Ruby sat up, leaned toward Crockett, took his face in her hands, and gave him a gentle, warm kiss on the lips.

"I put the pieces in place," she said. "You and Rachael did it. Welcome back, Crockett. I now pronounce you officially readmitted into the human race."

She leaned back on the pillows, put her arms under her head and glowed at him for a while, then got a decided twinkle in her eyes.

"So," she said. "Where's my towel, Boy? I'm feeling a little damp."

TWENTY-ONE
Heelless

THURSDAY MORNING Crockett called Rachael's apartment to talk about their trip to Chicago, but she wasn't home. He left a message that he'd call back, but by the time he was done with a studio session, it was too late. He tried again after her work that night, but she hadn't arrived back at the condo. The next morning Arthur and a couple of his minions arrived and measured for two hours, then showed him a raft of pictures and samples. They didn't leave until after lunchtime. He tried Rachael, but she'd already gone to work. He killed time, fussing around the house, cleaning and straightening, considering what to pack for Lakeshore Drive.

Ruby, dressed in sweats and Reeboks, had taken the afternoon off. When the phone rang, she almost let it go to her service, but something told her to answer. It was a short call. She put the phone down, swept up her car keys, and headed out the door in one motion, trembling enough that it was difficult to get her key in the ignition. Part of her coolly observed her span of emotions on the ten-minute drive to Crockett's house. Part of her wanted to collapse and bawl. Part of her wanted to rage and spit in God's eye. All of her parked the car in front of his house and started up the walk on wooden feet.

The barking dogs gave her approach away. Crockett stepped out on the porch and smiled at her, until he noticed she wasn't wearing heels. His mouth went dry and he leaned on the railing for support.

"Ruby," he said. "What's going on?"

Tears shining in her eyes, Ruby put her arms around his neck and gathered him in, kissing him on the cheek.

"Aw, Crockett," she whispered. "Rachael's dead."

TWENTY-TWO

Time Lost

RUBY WAS SITTING at Crockett's kitchen table when she heard him finally stirring. Damn. Of all the possible things to have gone wrong in his life, this had to be the worst. More than the devastating loss of a woman he loved, this could, in many ways, become nearly the loss of his existence. For years, Crockett's defense against pain had been to withdraw. Rachael had countered that. On the strength of their relationship Crockett had reentered his life. Now, that very life that had been so full of promise, could easily collapse under the cruel weight of Rachael's death. For his sake, she could not let him give up. For her sake, she could not let him crawl away from her and back down into his comfortable darkness.

Ruby took a sip of coffee and watched Crockett through bedroom door as he lurched into a sitting position. She blinked back tears as he thrust himself to his feet, holding his back, and limped in her direction. He stopped just inside the dark doorway to peer at her.

Ruby smiled. "You came back," she said. "Good."

"What time is it?"

"Quarter of two."

"Rachael and I should be arriving in Chicago about now," Crockett said.

"No, Sweetheart. It's Sunday morning, not Saturday morning."

"What?"

"You've been gone a while."

"It's Sunday?"

Ruby noticed him pale a bit.

"Yes, it is, Love," she said.

"I lost a *day*?"

"You certainly did. Hungry?"

"No. Yes. Yes, I am."

"Food would be good thing at this point. Soft scrambled eggs and pale toast coming right up. No coffee yet. I'll fix you some weak tea."

"Weak tea?"

"You had a bout of heavy vomiting about twelve hours ago. Gotta take it easy 'til we see how you're little tummy is, Big Boy."

"You been here the whole time?"

"Where else?" Ruby said. "You know how much I like Nudge."

Crockett smiled, and tears leapt to his eyes. He dropped into a chair and began to cry. Ruby slid next to him and pulled his head onto her shoulder.

"Good job, Crockett. Let it happen, Sweetie. Just let it happen."

Ruby fed him food that he ate mechanically, then filled the tub and exiled Crockett to the bath. When dawn came, she was sitting on the floor beside the tub, her hair gone limp in the steaming room, sharing small slugs of Cutty with him, right out of the bottle. When she judged Crockett to be both physically and emotionally numb, she retrieved his ratty blue bathrobe from the bedroom, kissed him lightly on the lips, and pulled the plug in the tub. She guided him directly to the bedroom, eased him onto the bed, and covered him with the free half of the bedspread. He began to snore softly within seconds.

Ruby tucked him in, spread his wet ponytail out on the pillow, and kissed his cheek.

"You're the best of the bunch, Crockett," she whispered. "You can't give up and I won't give up. Dream sweet dreams. You deserve 'em. We all do."

It was mid-afternoon when Crockett walked out of the bedroom. Ruby was stretched out on the couch, reading.

"Scooter Pie," he said.

She swung her feet to the floor and stood. "It walks, it talks," she said. "How ya doin?"

"Some better. It's not Thursday or anything like that, is it?"

Ruby patted his chest and kissed him on the nose. "I know time flies in my company, Sweetheart," she said, "but it's still Sunday. You didn't go away again, just slept. So did I. I was gonna get you up anyway. Baked potatoes'll be ready soon, lotsa butter and sour cream."

"Okay."

"Sit at the kitchen table and relax. I'll pour you a big glass of chocolate milk and some coffee. Jamaican Blue Mountain. Should be suitable for even your snobbish palate."

"I haven't had chocolate milk since I was a kid."

"Comfort food, Crockett. I have an abundance of both. Comfort and food."

"Ruby, I really appreciate you staying with me like this, but you've got things you need to—"

"Shut up, Raoul. The only thing in my life that takes precedence over you right now is if I have to pee. Don't start a bunch of unselfish bullshit with me. You have every right to be selfish. So do I, and I am.

I'm taking it out on you. If you don't take advantage of that, you are an idiot."

Crockett rubbed the center of his chest.

"Ruby," he said, "I feel like my heart is really broken."

"It is," she said. "But that also means there's more room in there for me. Let me in."

Again, he began to cry.

At a late dinner that evening, it registered on Crockett that he had no idea how Rachael had died.

"Suicide," Ruby said. "I checked with some people I know that have contacts. She was a fairly high-profile person. The cops were thorough. I wouldn't have figured on suicide at this point in her life, but the plain truth is, you just never know. Evidently it happened late Wednesday night or early Thursday morning. No sign of forced entry, no sign of a struggle. A brief note in her handwriting that checks out. In the tub, slit wrists, no booze, no drugs, nothing. There was a cop here to see you yesterday while you were sleeping. He interviewed me, and I told him to go away and come back when you were awake."

"I don't believe it," Crockett said.

"I did, too," Ruby said. "I told him the only way I would wake you up would be with a warrant."

"No. I mean I don't believe she committed suicide."

"Oh. Of course not."

"That was not a comment of despair, Ruby. I don't believe it. I wasn't in the note."

"How do you know you weren't in her note?"

"If she'd mentioned my name, the cops would have been all over me. You would never have been able to turn one away. That means they really bought the suicide story. This investigation may have been extensive, but it damn sure wasn't thorough. Once they figured suicide, they just went through the motions. I should have been in the note, Ruby. She loved me."

"Yes, she did."

"Plus," Crockett said, "women are planners. She planned our trip for days. She would not have planned that trip and then killed herself. She would have planned the suicide."

"Maybe."

"Goddammit, she was happy! Happy people don't off themselves, Ruby! Happy people go do happy things. They take trips and they buy kitchens. They don't cut their wrists and bleed to fucking death. Oh, shit. The kitchen! Christ, I don't want that kitchen."

"Forgive me, but I spoke for you. I already called the designer. Arthur is it?"

"Yeah, Arthur."

"I told him what had happened. He was so sorry. The refund check will arrive in a few days. He'll send it to you."

"Me?"

"He insisted. It was to be your kitchen, he said. It would be your refund. He would not have it any other way. Over nineteen thousand dollars."

"Nineteen thousand dollars!"

"Rachael paid nearly half down. Don't be noble, Crockett. Take it. Put away your male bullshit and take the damn money. Arthur is right, and so am I."

"We'll see. What about a funeral?"

"Nope. No service of any kind. She was cremated locally after the autopsy and her ashes sent home to her father. Her belongings will be removed as soon as the police release the crime scene. That may have happened by now. I assume the condo will be sold."

"Nice and tidy. Nice and quick. It may be what it appears to be. It may not. It doesn't add up, Ruby. She was planning the trip, she was happy and I wasn't in the note."

"I don't think so either," she said. "I would have mentioned something, but I didn't want to influence you."

Crockett grinned at her. "Then that's the first time since I've known you that you didn't want to influence me," he said.

Ruby pounced. "Awww. Look at that," she said. "You smiled. Except for that cheesy mustache in the way, I really love it when you smile."

TWENTY-THREE
Mutual Advantage

OVER THE NEXT COUPLE OF WEEKS, Ruby superintended Crockett's deconstruction and reconstruction. From disillusionment to despair, from sanctimony to self-pity, from denial to defeat, it was a rough time. She stayed in close touch, encouraging Crockett, supporting and loving him, telling him he was better than he thought he was. She was glad to see several recording jobs come through so Crockett was thrust out into the world for brief periods.

A young detective who thought wash n' wear suits and cowboy boots went well together, stopped by and talked briefly with Crockett. A check from Arthur for nearly twenty thousand dollars arrived. Crockett took Ruby's advice and kept it. He also bought a new fridge and a gallon of milk that sat, unopened, on the top shelf.

Ruby and he talked about Rachael several times. More often than Crockett wanted to, less often than Ruby wanted him to. They hashed over the fact that he wasn't in the suicide note and the other irregularities, and could come up with no definite conclusions, except that there were no facts to support anything other than suicide. Logically, Crockett knew that Rachael was a very troubled woman, and as such, was capable of extremely irrational behavior. Pragmatically, he viewed it as a cop. Emotionally, it wouldn't stop gnawing at him and he hated it. Ruby hung in there until he was stable.

On the fourth Friday after the event, Crockett arrived home late in the day from a session at Audio Post. The phone was ringing.

The voice was male with a controlled southwestern accent. "David Allen Crockett?" it said.

"Speaking."

"Mr. Crockett, my name is Cletus Marshal. Please hold for Ms. Cabot." Violin music came on the line for a few seconds.

"Mr. Crockett?" Elderly female, excellent diction, no accent.

"That's correct."

"Mr. Crockett, please excuse this intrusion on your privacy. My name is Cabot. I am, or rather was, Ilene Rachael Morrison's aunt. Please accept my condolences on your very personal loss."

"Thank you, M'am. And mine on yours."

"You are very kind, sir. Rachael spoke well of you. She said you are a man of character. Men of character are in short supply, Mr. Crockett."

"Forgive me, Ms. Cabot, but you do not feel to me to be the kind of woman who calls for a casual chat. How may I be of service to you?"

"Rachael also said you were direct. It would seem she was correct. I would like to invite you to lunch, Mr. Crockett. With me. Here. Tomorrow."

"Where's here?"

"Northern Illinois, near Barrington Hills."

"Why?"

"Several reasons, Mr. Crockett, not the least of which is curiosity. I loved my niece, Sir. In many ways, she was the daughter I never had. It interests me to meet someone who was as important to her as you seem to have been. Plus, I would discuss some things with a man of character. Will you join me?"

"I wouldn't miss it."

"Excellent," she said. "And Ms. LaCost, could you induce her to also make the trip?"

"Perhaps. I'll do what I can."

"Very well. Let me encourage you to bring an overnight bag in the event you, and hopefully Ms. LaCost, decide to stay the weekend. It's quite lovely here."

"Anything else?"

"Ah," the old woman said. "You feel you are being manipulated. You are, but it is to our mutual advantage. At about nine in the morning a car shall call for you and Ms. LaCost, should she decide to come. I will see you at midday."

"Would you like my address?"

"That won't be necessary. I am privy to certain information about you, Sir."

"Call me Crockett. I'll see you tomorrow."

"Indeed you shall, Crockett," she said. "And I shall see you."

Ruby answered on the second ring.

"Crockett. How's your heart?"

"Hangin' in there."

"How's your head?"

"Intrigued."

"Oh?"

He told her about the phone call.

83

"Great!" she said. "A diversion is welcome at this time. I'll throw some things in a bag and come over. We'll have dinner and talk. I'll spend the night and we'll leave in the morning."

"Oh, yeah?"

"Yeah. And don't get your hopes up, Big Boy. Nudge and I will be very comfortable on the couch."

"Suppose I sneak up on you in the darkness of night?"

"Sneak ain't in your nature, Crockett."

"Suppose you sneak up on *me* in the darkness of night?"

Ruby's voice dropped into its throaty contralto gurgle. "Now there's a luscious thought," she said. "I'll mull that over while I take a long, hot bath in that immense old tub of yours. If you're lucky, maybe I'll even play with the duck."

"Aw, Ruby!"

She chuckled. "Gotcha, Sweetie. I'll take a shower, grab some things and be over in a couple of hours. That'll give you time to settle down."

"Sweet respite."

"You're doin' fine, Son," Ruby said. "You really are."

TWENTY-FOUR

Ivy

A RETIRED PILOT FRIEND once offered Crockett some advice.

"If it don't fly above thirty thousand feet and ain't got no radar, don't git in the damn thing."

He got in anyway.

A limo had stopped by the house a little after nine the next morning and driven Ruby and Crockett to the downtown airport, where a man named Virgil had loaded them onto what Crockett considered to be a twin-engine death trap, and off they soared where neither lark nor eagle flew. Ruby, disgustingly calm in Crockett's estimation, promptly shoved her nose in verbiage by Tom Clancy.

Declining the offer to ride shotgun, Crockett gripped the armrests of his rear seat and wished he were Catholic or Buddhist or a Cub Scout, or something. About twelve hours into the three-hour flight, Virgil banked the plane to the left in a maneuver that put Crockett's stomach somewhere behind his right ear.

"There's the house," Virgil said.

Ruby closed the book and looked out her window.

"Jesus," she said. "When did we cross the Atlantic?"

Crockett gaped. The place was huge. It looked as if it had been imported from England, a country manor or something like he'd visualized a country manor to be. Built in an "H", three and a half stories, copper roof, heavy gray stone, it would have used Jed Clampett's manse as an outhouse. The top uprights of the "H" were connected by a greenhouse that looked only slightly smaller than the deck of an aircraft carrier. In the near distance was a strip of asphalt running for some way between two low hills. Virgil banked the plane even more steeply and headed for it. Crockett had to look away.

Once they had de-planed and a queasy Crockett had kissed the blessed earth, a golf cart arrived bearing a white male, early-forties, with slightly thinning light brown hair, heavy crows-feet, and startlingly white teeth that he displayed in an easy grin. He was wearing dark brown slacks, a white sport shirt and a light brown windbreaker that did not conceal the Glock nine-millimeter pistol above his right kidney. Almost Crockett's height and thirty pounds lighter, he was slim in the waist and muscular through the chest and shoulders. Removing his aviator-style sunglasses, he regarded the newly arrived guests.

"Mr. Crockett," he said. "Good of ya'll to come. I'm Cletus Marshal."

His hand was dry and firm. He reminded Crockett a little of Eastwood as Harry Callahan.

"Nice to meet you, Mr. Marshal. Call me Crockett."

"Name's Clete, Crockett," he said.

Ruby, wearing black slacks, four-inch ankle-strapped heels and a dark gray man-tailored shirt tied about her waist, moved to beside Crockett. Cletus' gaze flicked over her.

"Oh, my goodness," he said. "This could only be the redoubtable Dr. LaCost. Howdy, M'am."

Ruby allowed her gaze to drift leisurely from his feet to his head, then permitted a slow smile to overtake her perfectly penciled mouth.

"Hell, Clete," she drawled. "You really think that West Texas shit is gonna work on l'il ol'me?"

His laugh was loose and easy.

"Naw, I speck not, Miz Ruby. Damn shame it won't though."

"Possibly," she said, and they shook hands.

Clete delivered Ruby and Crockett to the house and turned them over to a maid who, after passing their luggage to a houseman, led them on about a four-mile trek to the atrium and seated them in immense wicker chairs. Ruby watched the maid leave and turned her attention to Crockett.

"Good thing I didn't wear dark velvet," she said. "My ass would look like a blackened waffle."

"Strawberries and whipped cream with that?" Crockett said.

"Blueberries, Darling. They're smaller."

"Damn."

Ruby grinned. "Crockett, I love your persistence. You cannot outsleaze me and yet you continue to try. It shows a lot of courage."

"I appreciate that you notice," he said, "and I admire the way you handled, so to speak, Clete."

"Clete was easy. Unlike you, Dear Boy, he leads with his libido. You lead with your heart. That's why you'll always be my favorite man."

The maid showed back up carrying a tray table, the houseman behind her with a silver service of coffee that must have weighed fifteen pounds. Behind them came a gray-haired woman about seventy years old. Extremely erect, very thin, and perfectly poised, she wore a light beige pantsuit in heavy linen, low heels and impeccable make-up. Her jewelry was understated, her complexion flawless, her eyes quick and green. They rose. She crossed to Ruby.

"Ms. LaCost," she said, her voice still full and well modulated. "So kind of you to accept my invitation. You are truly lovely."

"Thank you, Ms. Cabot," Ruby said.

The old woman turned to Crockett. "And you, David Allen Crockett. I cannot tell you how saddened I am for the loss of your future with my niece, or how glad I am she had her time with you."

Crockett swallowed the lump in his throat and felt tears collect against his lower lashes.

"Ms. Cabot," he said.

She took his hands in hers. They were warm and had the rasp of the aged.

"Indulge me, Sir," she said, and kissed Crockett dryly on each cheek. She then released one of his hands and reached for one of Ruby's. Holding them, she smiled.

"The two of you did more for that unfortunate child than you can know. The last weeks of her life were the happiest weeks of her life. As much as there is reason for sorrow, there is also reason for celebration. Now, the two of you who have done so much, have more to do. I will quell your curiosity soon enough. First we will have coffee, then we will eat. Then I will nap. Then we shall talk some more." She looked at both of them, and her eyes twinkled.

"It is not uncommon for a homosexual man and a heterosexual woman to be dear friends. It *is* uncommon for a homosexual woman and a heterosexual man to be close. Most men wouldn't have the patience. Most women wouldn't have the tolerance. Congratulations. Rachael said the two of you loved each other. Does she require a great deal of patience, Crockett?"

He smiled. "You have no idea, Ms. Cabot."

"And you, Ruby," she continued. "Is he tolerable?"

"Only barely. At least he uses silverware."

"Very well. No more 'Ms. Cabot.' My name is Ivolee Minerva. I hesitate to consider what alternatives my misguided parents discarded. Call me Ivy. I am truly happy you came to visit. Let us have coffee. I believe it will be to your taste, Crockett. Then we will enjoy lunch. I am told Jackson has prepared some lovely pecan trout with truffles and watercress. We will chat a bit over wine. Australian wine actually. I believe Shiraz is to your taste, Ruby."

TWENTY-FIVE
The Men's Club and the Whorehouse

AFTER LUNCH Ivy went to nap and Clete took both their photographs with a digital camera, something that was done with every visitor, he said. He escorted them to the second floor and showed them to their rooms. Crockett looked about his in awe.

It was about the size of a tennis court, with a ceiling that nearly disappeared in the haze. The walls were wainscoted to head height in dark rich panels beneath dusky green wallpaper. Heavy beams interlocked overhead. Windows, flanked by dense velvet draperies, climbed to about fourteen feet, and the polished oak floor, which did not creak or sigh, was graced by Persian rugs an inch thick.

The bed, an antique four-poster, was slightly over waist high, had steps to mount it and corner spires to ten feet. An immense, polished stone fireplace with five-foot andirons graced one wall, several leather armchairs and tables were scattered about, and stern faces peered at him from gilt, or perhaps even guilt, frames. A walk-in closet stood open, Crockett's stuff arranged neatly inside. He felt like the incredible shrinking man. Everything was so big, so solid, so old.

The room was dense and ponderous, weighty and grave. Whoever had desired this intensity, who had created this thickness of surroundings, was looking for something that did not exist. Permanence. Crockett found it oddly comforting.

His bath was the size of a comfortable living room, with black and white tile floor and walls, a huge shower, oversize tub, toilet, bidet, and a urinal. A door opened off of it into a small steam room suitable for about five people. He walked back out into the bedroom just as two oak doors set into the sidewall swung open. Ruby stepped in and glanced around.

"Yuk," she said. "Where's your smoking jacket, Basil?" Spying the bed, she continued. "Jesus Christ, Crockett, be careful! Fall outa that

88

monstrosity at the wrong moment and all the King's horses and all the King's men—"

"It's a small place, but we love it," he said.

"Yeah, well, forsake the men's club and come on over to the whorehouse. It's much more suited to my sensibilities."

Ruby's place was as bright and airy as Crockett's was dark and heavy. Thick eggshell carpet covered the entire floor below pale peach walls. Off-white sheers graced expansive windows, and an off-white bed, canopied in peach satin, perched on a corner dais that covered a third of the room three steps up from floor level. Scattered about were armchairs upholstered in light gray damask. Instead of a fireplace, Ruby had a bathtub.

About eight feet square, it gave the appearance of being carved from a solid piece of gold-veined, white marble. The tub itself was about six feet on a side and thirty inches deep, festooned with whirlpool jets. A round tapering column on each corner supported a synthetic marble canopy that housed four heat lamps and a television. The hardware was gold, the surrounding floor marbled tile to match the tub, and to one side stood an electrically heated towel rack.

"Would I look good all slick and soapy in that, or what, Big Boy?"

"Ruby, you would look good hip-deep in a pile of rotting whitefish."

"Why, Mr. Crockett, you do say the sweetest things. You are going to turn my head!"

"Or your stomach."

"How's your back and hip? You seem to be limping more than usual."

"Small planes and wicker chairs don't do me a lot of good."

"You got a whirlpool in your tub?"

"No."

Ruby brightened. "You can use mine, Crockett. I won't peek."

Crockett played along. "Do you promise?" he said.

Ruby clasped her hands behind her back and nodded. "Honest!"

"Well … okay," Crockett replied, enjoying the fantasy against his better judgment.

"There's probably a guest robe in your bathroom someplace," Ruby said. "Put it on, then get back in here and soak."

"Yes, Dear," he said.

Crockett's hip was stiff and it took him some time to get undressed and into a dark green satin robe. When he returned to Ruby's room the tub was nearly full, towels were warming on the rack and two of the heat lamps were turned on. She was sitting twenty feet away on the edge of the bed, legs crossed, wearing a peach colored silk wrap and smiling.

"Took you long enough."

Crockett glared at her. "I'm old," he said, and checked the water, adding a little cold.

When he turned back around, Ruby had moved to a chair within six feet of the tub and was grinning at him. Her toenails were dark red.

"Ruby!"

"Don't mind me. Go ahead and get in the tub. I'll just sit here and close my eyes."

Trying to ignore the fact that his ears were getting warm, Crockett laid the robe on the floor and eased into the swirling water.

"God, this feels good."

"Must be hot," Ruby said. "You seem flushed already."

"No fault of yours," Crockett grumbled.

Ruby stood and walked toward her bathroom.

"Oh, okay. If you're gonna get all snippy, I'll just take a shower and do my make-up."

One stride from the doorway, she let her wrap fall.

Crockett gaped at the empty door, wondering if what had just happened had just happened. Inside her bath, Ruby leaned against the wall and whispered.

"We'll get through this, Crockett," she said. "Whatever it takes. Almost."

TWENTY-SIX
Motivation

WARM BREATH IN CROCKETT'S EAR brought him back. He opened his eyes to see Ruby's face close enough that her features blurred.

"Time to get up, Sweetie," she said. "You've been snoring for about an hour. We've got to meet Ivy in forty-five minutes for tea. How's the hip?"

He sat up in the tub. "What hip?"

Ruby grinned. She was wearing a lacy lime green teddy with dark green hose and heels.

"Jesus," Crockett said. "that'll get Clete's attention."

Ruby moved about the room without self-consciousness of any kind.

"Crockett, this would get anybody's attention," she said. "Get up, dry off, go to your room, get dressed, and come back. Now." She walked into her bathroom.

Crockett did as ordered.

When he returned to her room, Ruby had added a knee-length, dark green wraparound skirt and a medium gray long-sleeved blouse with a neckline low enough the teddy just peeked over the top. Malachite earrings and a jade bracelet completed the look, highlighted by light green eye shadow.

"LaCost, you look great."

Ruby glanced at Crockett's chinos, chambray shirt, and second pair of shoes.

"That makes one of us," she said. "We gotta get you some clothes, Son, if you're gonna run in company like this."

The maid escorted them to a parlor where their hostess was waiting. The room was nearly as traditionally plush as Crockett's.

"Ivy, your home is lovely," Ruby said.

Ivy smiled. "You are a very kind liar, My Dear," she said. "This place is a mausoleum. Only about a third of it is open. I stay here because I like the land and the solarium. My first husband's grandfather built it as a country home. He, evidently, thrived on pretension. Tea?"

The maid served and Ivy continued.

"Crockett, when you entered the room, you seemed to be leaning less upon your cane. I trust your leg is feeling better. Gunshot, was it not?"

"Yes, M'am."

"The night that your partner was killed."

"Yes."

"The night that you killed the man who killed him and shot you."

"That's right."

"Forgive me, Sir. I say these things to better acquaint myself with your mettle, not to insult or impress you. I felt the steel rise in your blood at the mention of these private matters. I suspect, Crocket, that you are a compassionate person who can be quite ruthless. A non-violent man who is capable of extreme violence. Would I be correct in my assessment, Dr. LaCost?"

"Dead on," Ruby said.

Ivy laughed. "Good," she said, "I do so love being right."

Her eyes twinkled, and Crockett could not repress a grin. Ruby chuckled. Ivy took a sip of her tea, fixed her gaze on Crockett.

"Sir, my niece did not kill herself."

"The evidence suggests otherwise," Crockett said.

"Of course it does. It is false. She was the victim of murder most foul, murder at the hands of, or at direction from, her father, the man who was once my brother-in-law. I am also convinced he is responsible for the death, thirty years ago, of my sister, Othaline Marie. Feel free to smile. Our parents did have a way with names."

"Why would he do such things?"

"Convenience and fear, Crockett. Two very powerful motivators. He killed my sister because she became inconvenient. She told me once, when Rachael was only a little over two years old, that she observed her husband torturing the child with a needle. When she confronted him, he seemed excited, even aroused, but attempted to cover his passion and showed her a splinter of wood in the child's arm, claiming to be only concerned with its removal. She felt he was lying. It was the only time we spoke of the incident, indeed nearly the last time we spoke at all. Her contact with me was curtailed severely for the next few months. She then died of a fall onto a patio from the third floor balcony of her studio. The railing gave way. A tragic accident. Her husband was despondent."

"Only it wasn't an accident."

"No. Marie was deathly afraid of heights. She would have had no difficulty with a third floor studio. She would never have used a third floor balcony. I protested the ruling at the time, but was ignored. There was no proof. Rachael was left in the company of her father and his older sister who came to live with him, share his business and care for the child."

"What was his business?"

"He was, and is, a psychiatrist. A child psychiatrist."

"Let me guess," Ruby said. "When Rachael was small, her father was very controlling. Most likely he would not let her visit you, or come in contact with almost anyone, unless he was present. He probably even schooled her at home until she was ten or so. As she neared puberty, he would have allowed her much more freedom, perhaps even losing almost all interest in her. That would have been the time when you and she would have become so close. Unless I miss my guess, you put her in a girl's school to get her out of his house."

"I believe the term dead on applies," Ivy said.

"Did she live here?"

"From age twelve to eighteen she returned here when she wasn't in school at that conservatory. When she went to college, she would return for holidays and such. She attended university twelve months of the year. She was a delightful young woman and a brilliant student. Please excuse my indulgence in pride. When I said she was like the daughter I never had, I was not overstating."

"Any contact with her father?" Crockett said.

"Almost none. I don't believe she'd even seen him since she left Champaign-Urbana."

"I'll bet he had seen her," Ruby said. "Jesus, this is perfect. Who better to control another person than an individual with training, legal access to drugs and expertise in things like hypnosis? What more convenient victim than his child, a person to whom he had constant legal access? Ivy! Do you know if Rachael had ever been to a psychologist before?"

"Not to my knowledge."

"But you can bet her father knew she was going to one the past few months."

"Oh, yes."

"He probably knows about Crockett, too."

"Most assuredly."

"So it was time to move. She might remember."

"She had become inconvenient," Ivy said.

"And she knew how to use a gun."

Ivy smiled. "Rachael had become dangerous," she said.

Both women turned to Crockett.

"Do you understand what's going on here?" Ruby said.

"The sonofabitch killed the mother for access to the child, then killed the child to protect himself."

"Perfect summation, Crockett," Ivy said, "but there's more. This man is respected in his field, he has friends, he has money, and he has a clinic where he houses six to eight patients at a time. A place where he has medical access to young children twenty-four hours a day in his own home. He and his sister have held sway over babies for a quarter of a century and now my niece, Ruby's patient, and your love, is dead, if not at his hands certainly at his will."

"We've got to do something," Crockett said.

Ivy smiled and her eyes glittered. "Indeed we do, Crockett," Ivy said. "First we will have dinner. Then we will visit with Cletus."

TWENTY-SEVEN
Instigation

CROCKETT LOOKED AROUND THE DINING ROOM and contemplated playing shuffleboard on the table. The three of them were clustered at one end under a massive chandelier in a heavy wood-ridden room trimmed in light oak with gold velvet-covered walls. Crockett was laboring through a very colorful presentation of some sort of dark fish under some sort of yellowish sauce, trimmed in what were once green beans, highlighted by little red things and slivers of some crunchy stuff, wishing for a hot turkey sandwich and mashed potatoes, when Ivy spoke.

"I am an excessively wealthy woman," she said. "Both of my husbands were sole survivors from wealth, as now, with the death of my niece, am I. As such, I have the resources to make things happen and happen they shall. Martin Morrison, Rachael's father, is an evil man. He must be made responsible for his actions. I have called the two of you here to ask your help in this matter. With your assistance, he and his equally morally bankrupt sister, shall be brought low. I have no stratagem to achieve this end, children, but I *shall* achieve it."

Crockett took the opportunity to slide his plate away and look at her.

"Ivy, believe me, I share your feelings, but I'm not sure what I can do to help. This needs to go to the police."

"You were a policeman."

"That's true, but I was just a patrolman, a grunt. I was not an investigator. I'm not qualified."

"You are a graduate of the University of Illinois Police Training Institute in both basic and advanced police procedures. You also trained in crime scene investigation, criminal psychology, interrogation, and domestic intervention."

"Well—"

"At the time you took your test to become a police officer you achieved the highest score to that date on the examination. You were

95

the youngest police officer ever hired by the Champaign City Police Department, twenty-one years and eleven days."

"Jesus."

"You passed your attempt at the sergeant's examination on your first try, but were passed over four times for promotion, primarily because of your mouth and attitude. You are a graduate of the special weapons and tactics course administered by the Federal Bureau of Investigation and you were cited three times for actions above and beyond the call of duty. Crockett, you are qualified."

"I'm not a cop."

"Another qualification. Policemen are bound by certain legal and ethical restraints. They must move inside the law. You and I both know that the average citizen has, in some ways, more power and flexibility than the police."

"Ivy, I'm old, I'm outa shape, I got a bum leg and a cane. I'm past it."

Ivy smiled. "Once upon a time," she said, "a young bull and an old bull were standing together on a grassy hill, overlooking a green and fertile valley. On the floor of that valley was a herd of lovely young cows. The youthful bull became quite excited at the prospects that lay before him and began to paw the earth and snort. He strutted, he postured, he bellowed to the heavens of his power and prowess. The old bull stood and watched. Finally, after working himself into a lather and breathing heavily, the virile youngster turned to his calm counterpart. 'Let's run down there,' he said, 'and screw one of those cows!' The mature bull regarded him placidly for a moment, then smiled. 'Take it easy, son,' he said. 'Let's *walk* down there and screw *all* those cows.'"

Ruby laughed. Ivy continued.

"Crockett, you are a man of substance and determination. You are not one to waste energy on posture and promise. If a man were to want to fight you and began to remove his jacket, you would strike him with a chair while his arms were entangled in his coat sleeves. You would not initiate the battle, but there is very little you would not do to conclude it."

Ruby grinned. "Dead on," she said.

"I will now lay before you my final argument. If this does not sway you, I am done. It is very simple. David Allen Crockett, this man, by word or deed, killed Rachael. He destroyed her future and, indirectly, yours. You will never again laugh and love with that remarkable young woman. Martin Morrison did that. Now, what are you prepared to do about him?"

"Aw, Ivy," Crockett said, "whatever the hell it takes."

Ruby nodded. "I'm in."

Ivy smiled. "Bread pudding for desert, children," she said.

96

TWENTY-EIGHT
Cletus

AFTER DINNER they took to the parlor and the houseman brought coffee, very pointedly placing a large crystal ashtray by Crockett's chair. Crockett lit a Sherman and took a sip of excellent Jamaican dark roast, just as Cletus Marshal entered the room. He was carrying a folder that he placed on a table.

"Evenin' all," he said.

"How good of you to join us, Cletus," Ivy said.

"My pleasure, M'am."

Ivy turned to Ruby and Crockett. "Cletus is my joy," she said. "I first met him when Barbara Bush came to visit some time after she left the Whitehouse. Cletus had been assigned to her by the Secret Service. I attempted at that time to steal him away from her, but was cruelly rebuffed. After the buffoon from Arkansas became Caesar for the second time, still accompanied by that bleached-blond gangster to whom he was wed, Cletus heeded my entreaty and fled the service of his country."

"She made me an offer I couldn't refuse," Clete said.

"The Secret Service lost. I gained."

"She pays much better than Uncle Sam."

"My perception of true value is more clear. Hence, his talent is now at my disposal and, because it is, it is also at yours. Cletus ..."

"Ruby, Crockett," he said. "The alliance that has been formed here is going to massively disrupt your lives. Your usual day-to-day existence is over, at least for a while. Ruby, during the last twelve months your gross income was around one hundred thirty thousand dollars."

"Approximately."

"Because you won't be able maintain your practice due to your commitment, and the fact that your life could be in danger if you did, here is payment of slightly more than that yearly income."

He handed her a check. Ruby took it, but did not look at it.

"Crockett. There is no way to compensate you for your loss. To help deal with the trauma to your life that will occur because of our alliance, you will accept this payment."

Cletus handed over a folded check. Crockett placed it in his pocket and took a drink of coffee.

"Mr. Morrison probably doesn't know what either one of you look like. But he most likely is aware of your names, addresses and such through credit card and bank records. Because of that, I have taken the liberty of getting you both a temporary residence in a town house in the Quality Hill area of Kansas City. It is rented in the name of one of Ms. Cabot's companies, with an open-ended lease. You two may use it as long as you care to. The fax confirming rental as well as the address and such are in this envelope." He passed it to Ruby.

"In the garage of that property are two leased vehicles, also in the company name. Since it will not be very smart for either of you to drive your customary transportation, these are at your disposal for as long as it takes. Because in the course of the investigation you may have to travel to other locations, it would be advisable for you, even if you drive to that location, to rent a local vehicle upon your arrival. To help with that, and to provide ya'll background and cover, I have some supplementary identification for each of you."

Clete passed Ruby another envelope. "This," he said, "contains a Nebraska driver's license, an ATM card and a gold credit card in the name of Randi DeMoss. You are from Lincoln."

"Randi, huh?" Ruby smiled. "Clete, this is perfect. I've been called Randi, off and on, for years. But I think the spelling may have been different."

He flushed and Ivy chuckled.

"Also in that envelope, *Randi*," Clete said, "is your Nebraska license to practice therapy and some business cards complete with your office address and phone number. I assure you, it *is* your office, and the phone will be answered by your assistant."

Handing Crockett an envelope, he continued.

"Crockett, here's your Illinois driver's license under the name of Daniel Beckett, with ATM and gold credit cards. You are a resident of Alton, Illinois, across the river from St. Louis. Also in your packet is your commission and badge as special investigator for the Justice Department and the same showing you to be an agent for the Illinois Bureau of Investigation."

"Damn," Crockett said.

"Should anyone enquire of either of these agencies as to your credentials, we gotcha covered."

"I'm amazed."

"One of Clete's jobs is to open or close doors, Crockett," Ivy said. "He is very good at it."

98

"I also suggest," said Clete, "that the two of you change your appearances a bit."

"Lose the 'stash and ponytail," Crockett said. "New wardrobe, dress more upscale, avoid usual haunts, drop the recording sessions, stay clear of the homestead, like that."

"Exactly. You know what you're doing. Dump the ear jewelry."

"Oh, yeah."

"I'll find somebody else to handle my clients," Ruby said, "and change my hair color, dress down a bit."

"A bit?" Crockett said.

"Anything you buy," Clete said, "put on the company cards, even gasoline. If you need it, buy it. Don't be bashful. Spend whatever you need to spend, on whatever you need to spend it on. Frugality is not at issue here. There is no budget. If you need something and you can't get it, call me. I'll get it for you. That brings us to weapons. Ruby, do you know how to use a gun?"

"God no!"

"Liberal," Crockett said.

Clete grinned. "Okay. What can I get for you, Crockett?"

"Not a thing."

"What?"

"Nothing. I don't want a gun. I have no taste for it."

Clete shook his head. "Suit yourself. Everybody's got the right to get stupid now and then. I also have a couple of cell phones for you. I'll give them to you tomorrow when I brief you on Mr. Morrison's location and such. There is also some work to do on the I.D.'s, signatures and things like that. I'll let you go now. It'll give you time to come up with any questions you may have, or additional things you might need."

"How 'bout the Mississippi National Guard?" Crockett said.

Clete grinned. "Too noisy," he said. "We'll talk in the morning, before you fly back to Kaycee."

"We're not flying back to Kansas City," Crockett said. "We'll fly to Columbia, spend a day or so, get outfitted and drive back in a car rented by Randi DeMoss, whoever the hell she is."

Clete looked at Crockett for a moment, then smiled. "More than meets the eye, Son."

"Always is," Crockett said.

TWENTY-NINE
Magic Elixir

RUBY AND CROCKETT TALKED WELL INTO THE NIGHT. Everything was moving so fast, they were both a little numb. After they looked at the checks, they became a lot numb. The total was slightly over a quarter of a million dollars. That, combined with everything Clete had thrown their way, left them running to catch up. It was about three when they hugged goodnight.

The wake-up knocks came at six-thirty. The coffee arrived in Crockett's room fifteen minutes later. Ruby, in Crockett's opinion disgustingly bright and pretty, showed up at seven, while he complained he couldn't walk without tripping over his eyebrows. At seven-thirty they were escorted to the atrium for breakfast. He grumbled a lot on the way down.

Ivy was dressed in white lounging pajamas with a long white robe. Her hair and make-up were perfect. She was sipping tea and smiling.

"Good morning, children," she said.

"Ivy," Crockett grunted, "if you don't stop being so damned bright and lovely, I'm gonna start breaking windows."

"Ignore him," Ruby said. "He usually doesn't quit throwing up until well after noon."

"Oh, it's quite all right," Ivy said. "As one of the two newest members of what we laughingly call 'Ivy's Sunday Morning Fun Club', he is about to feel much better. Here comes the reason now."

Clete entered the room bearing a tray and a grin.

"Mornin' ya'll. Libation for everyone. Welcome to the Fun Club and an early morning ration of Mother Marshal's Magic Elixir and Paint Remover."

"Sweet Jesus," Crockett said.

"Step right up, Podnuh. I am about to start your heart. Don't want ya'll face down in yer breakfast." Undaunted by a threat from Crockett's cane, he continued. "This here will git ya up an' runnin' in a San Francisco second."

100

He stirred the contents of a silver pitcher, poured a red liquid over ice into a milkshake glass, and handed it to Crockett.

"Worst off drinks first," Clete said.

"A Bloody Mary?"

"Not even close. Try it."

Crockett sipped.

"Woof!"

"Thank ya."

"What's in this?"

"V-8, beef broth, cilantro, A-1, cracked pepper, fresh horseradish, lemon zest, vodka, bitters, and a touch of tonic water. Sounds awful, don't it?"

"Terrible."

"Tastes pretty fair though."

"You got that right," Crockett said. "Ruby, testride this stuff."

She took a sip, paused, then took a drink and grinned.

"Marshal," she said, "I can't offer you much more than friendly companionship, but I'd be real happy if you'd marry me."

"Give it up, Ruby," Ivy said. "I have tendered the same offer to this young man every Sunday morning for years, to no avail. You should feel complimented, however. You two are the first guests to whom he has ever confessed his list of ingredients."

Clete flopped into a chair. "Moment of weakness," he said. "This is my first glass. I'm usually more fortified before I make my entrance. Beats the hell outa goin' to church though, don't it."

"A religious experience of the first level," Crockett said, and raised his glass.

After breakfast, Clete presented them with cell phones, showed Crockett where to sign the back of his Department of Justice commission, gave them a number to call to reach him anytime of the night or day, and went through a myriad of details. Finally Ruby could contain her curiosity no longer.

"Clete," she said, "how the hell did you manage to do all this so quickly?"

"I started this project two weeks ago," Clete said. "Your townhouse, for instance, has been rented for over a week. You've had an office in Lincoln, Nebraska since last Wednesday. Your leased vehicles have been in your garage since Friday morning."

"The two of you must have been sure we'd go for all this."

"My niece spoke well and at length with me about both of you," Ivy said. "I had every confidence the two of you would acquiesce. You are both individuals of honor. Honor demands that you assist."

"But why us? With all your resources and contacts, why us?"

"Passion, Dear, a vanishing commodity. It is more elusive than gold, more precious than diamonds. The two of you have it by the

101

cargo. My resources and contacts are at your disposal, but it is that passion that will win the day. Of that, I have no doubt."

"Passion and Mother Marshal's Magic Elixir," Crockett said.

"I cannot tell you how I have enjoyed your time here," the old woman said. "My usual visitors are rather stogy and self-important types. They bore me. You do not. At my age, relief from boredom is precious. I must now take my leave of you. When this is over, I hope you will visit me from time to time. Your company is appreciated."

Ivy rose, kissed Ruby on the cheek, then crossed to Crockett and did the same.

"Take care of each other," she said, and walked away.

Clete watched her go. He looked at Crockett.

"Dialysis," he said. "Twice a week. She's tough."

"Quite a woman," Ruby said.

"When I came to work for her," Clete said, "she fully vested my retirement on that day. If I care to, in another year I can kick back on twice as much as the Service paid me for working full time. Six years ago my daddy was diagnosed with cancer. She sent him to some big deal clinic for state of the art treatment. Saved his life, paid all the bills, even income while he was laid up. In many ways Rachael was just like her."

Clete paused and shook his head, his eyes narrowed into slits.

"We are gonna get this sonofabitch, boys and girls. We are gonna knock his dick in the dirt!"

His hands were trembling. In a few seconds he settled down, and looked at them with an embarrassed smile.

"Your bags'll be at the front door by now. C'mon, I'll wheel ya down to the strip and put ya on the plane. Go to your new place, get some furniture, relax for a few days and take it easy. Then start thinkin' how you're gonna nail this guy. Take your time, set your own pace. Nobody is in a hurry. Call me if ya need anything, or even if ya just want to talk. Middle of the day, middle of the night, don't make a shit to me. Let's do this thing."

Ruby gave him a kiss on the cheek. "You'll do, Marshal," she said.

Clete's posture softened and he chuckled.

"Yes, M'am," he said. "Any damn thing you'd like."

THIRTY

Homeward Bound

CROCKETT WOULD HAVE BEEN VERY HAPPY with a Motel Six or something of that nature, but Ruby would not hear of it. After they deplaned at the Columbia, Missouri airport and Crockett recuperated slightly from a seething bout of air-sickness, she and Randi DeMoss rented an auto, a Lincoln Towne Car to be exact, and she got directions to an upscale, executive-style motel. Leaving queasy Crockett in the car, she got them a mini-suite complete with a fireplace, a small kitchen, a bedroom, a living room with a hide-a-bed couch and a bathroom/dressing area that contained a large whirlpool tub.

"Jesus, Ruby. Why didn't you get the bridal suite?"

"I tried but it was booked. This is the Getaway Suite."

"How much?"

"Don't be such an old woman, Crockett. Who gives a shit how much? It's not your money, it's one of Ivy's companies' money. Besides, I thought you needed to relax. Feeling better?"

"I am marginally acceptable. Thanks for thinkin' of me."

"Judging by the way you were limping after you got off the plane, I thought a big car and a whirlpool would give your tired old frame a break."

"It could use it."

"Why don't you use the whirlpool and I'll go pick us up some wine. We'll get mildly drunk, take a nap, go out to dinner and turn in early. Then tomorrow we'll make some calls to take care of business, go shopping for you some duds, and relax. Next day we'll head for Kaycee and check out the new digs."

"I feel like we're wasting time."

"Of course you do. That's because Clete handed you Ivy's check for more money than you make in three years. You feel a debt to her and debts make you edgy. It's all part of your sense of honor. Let me tell you about honor, Crockett. Honor is committing to do what you have committed to do. Nobody doubts your honor."

103

Ruby lifted her small suitcase to the bed.

"That check was Ivy's way of telling you that her commitment to this unholy alliance is as deep as yours," she said. "The absolute surest way for you to screw this whole thing up is to beat yourself over the head with it. You know what the objective is. Now is the time to let things happen. Slow down. There is no time limit. There is no hurry. Nobody is looking over your shoulder. This is your baby."

"Yeah, well—"

"You know I'm right. That's my function, to keep you on the straight and narrow by reminding you that I am right. Your function is to stress out and worry. We're the perfect team. I chastise and berate, you investigate. You save the world from the bad guys, I save you from yourself."

"Sounds workable, I guess."

"D. A. Crockett. Private dick."

"Private duck," Crockett said.

"You and the private duck get in the tub and loosen up. I'll be back with some wine and assist in that process. You've got those creases between your eyebrows, Crockett. We gotta do something about those. Go play in the tub like a good boy and try not to splash water on the floor."

Earlobe deep in the warm swirling water, Crockett was almost asleep when Ruby returned. After fussing around in the kitchen for a while, she sauntered into the bath carrying a cup.

"Bailey's and coffee," she said, setting the cup on the edge of the tub.

Grabbing a bath towel, she disappeared back into the other room.

Sipping and soaking, Crockett had just about convinced himself that he truly deserved to live in such a manner, when Ruby, clad only in the towel, walked back in carrying her own cup and a lit Sherman. She placed the cigarette between his lips, sat on the side of the tub, swung her legs over, and eased her feet into the water under Crockett's left knee.

"Ahhh," she said. "If I didn't look so good in heels, I wouldn't wear the goddammed things."

"Vanity, thy name is Ruby."

"I've got good legs, Crockett."

"I can only agree."

"In heels, I have *great* legs. So, I wear heels. Now I will soak my poor, tired dogs for a while, as you soak your poor, tired leg. How ya doin?"

"In heaven, with an angel perched on the edge of my cloud."

"Exactly the effect I was going for," Ruby said, rubbing the underside of his knee with her toes.

Crockett looked at her through a cloud of cigarette smoke. "You're right, you know," he said.

"Of course I am. About what?"

"About keeping me level in this whole thing with Rachael's father. I need to go at it slowly and methodically. You will have to remind me of that from time to time."

"And a lot of other things."

"Probably."

"You are going to have the inclination to want to get this over with, to hit it too hard, to let it consume your life," Ruby said. "You cannot transform the passion you had for her into the motivation to deal with him. Determination is the desired emotion. Stack the bricks, Big Boy, and the wall appears all by itself."

"Yep," he said, and drained the last of his coffee.

Ruby removed her feet from the tub, collected Crockett's cup and the cigarette butt from between his lips and walked out. In a moment she returned and handed him a fresh drink, walked to the large frosted glass shower stall, and stepped inside. She hung her towel over the top, started the tap, and turned to face the tub. Her contralto wafted above the rush of the water.

"Hey, Crockett," she said.

"Yeah?"

"Can you see me?"

"Almost."

Ruby's chuckle cascaded off the tile walls.

"That, too, is exactly the effect I was going for," she said.

THIRTY-ONE
New Digs

RUBY AND CROCKETT DIDN'T GO OUT TO DINNER. They didn't go shopping the next day. They did drag themselves out to lunch, then schlepped back to the room like zombies. Crockett felt like he'd been run over by a rhino. Ruby said it was stress rebounding from the visit to Ivy, the decisions they'd made, and the fact that their lives had so quickly changed, but he still kept an eye out for the rhino.

Crockett phoned his tenant and mother of Stupid and Shithead, Charlene, and explained to her that he had been called away for some time. The prospect of living rent free made her very happy to care for Nudge and forward his mail to Randi DeMoss at the Quality Hill address. He also called his agent and a couple of the studios where he often worked, to offer some sort of explanation for his absence. Ruby did the same with her patients, referring them to other doctors she trusted to continue their therapy. She also phoned her psychologist to discontinue her sessions for a time.

"Okay, Crockett, now that I am adrift, it's gonna be up to you to give me the therapy I need."

"The entire National Institution for the Restitution of Destitution couldn't keep up with your twisted batch of neurosis, LaCost. Christ! You're an exhibitionist, a scarlet woman, a tease, a floozy and you prefer sex with members of your own gender! Now you've even taken on a second identity to help you facilitate some sort of nefarious plan. You are beyond salvation. Why the hell do you think I can do anything?"

"Because you love me."

"Okay."

"And because hope springs eternal."

"There's that."

"Yes, there is, Crockett. There is always that."

Tuesday morning Crockett and Ruby were still beat, but they drug their tired frames out of town at around nine and headed for Kansas City. As they passed Grain Valley on I-70, Crockett phoned the rental company, informed them he and Ruby were inbound, and requested someone meet them at the town house with the keys and anything else they might need. A little before eleven they found the address and parked on the street. An excessively bubbly and very curious young woman bounced up to them, briefly inspected the confirmation fax, and turned keys and a sheet with her office and some emergency numbers over to them. After she left, they went inside.

The two-story structure was brick and large. The kitchen was massive and very state-of-the-art, the living room about thirty feet square with the obligatory fireplace, the dining room ample and cozy. The ground floor was completed by a large bathroom and a small library/sitting room. Upstairs were the master bedroom, dressing room, and bath suite and two more bedrooms, each with its own smaller bath. The unexpected basement was half the square footage of the ground floor and consisted of storage and a three-car garage that opened onto ground level at the rear of the home. In the garage were a Chevrolet Corvette and a four-wheel drive, full size Chevy pick-up with an extended cab.

"Damn sight better than that piece of shit truck you usually drive," Ruby said.

"Me? I'm taking the Corvette. Clete said he got the truck for you."

"We'll take *my* Corvette, drop off the Lincoln and get a room at the Downtown Marriott until we can get some furniture in this place."

"Suits me, but lets take the truck. I need to feel all that massive power through the seat. It a guy-thing."

"Put your guy-thing back where it belongs and get over it. That Neanderthal on wheels won't fit in the hotel's underground parking. There's an envelope on the kitchen counter with a Chevy emblem on it. It's probably the keys and insurance and stuff. Let's rock and roll, Crockett. I wanna return the car, register at the hotel, and go furniture shopping. With luck, we can get the place furnished tomorrow. Then we get you furnished. I can't wait to go clothes shopping with you. That oughta be the treat of the century!"

"I happen to have very discriminating tastes."

"In your mouth."

"Okay, Ruby, here's the deal. We get the hotel room and you drop me off back here. I'll go clothes shopping, you go furniture shopping. We'll meet back at the hotel. I'll park here and walk over."

She looked at him, and Crockett saw it in her eyes. He was all she had.

"Naw, bad idea," he continued. "You're right. We should go shopping together."

Ruby smiled.

"Thanks, Crockett."

THIRTY-TWO

Re-birth

THERE IS AN OLD ADAGE that when a couple enters into a relationship, the woman goes into the arrangement hoping the man will change, while the man hopes the woman won't. Nearly ecstatic at the lump of Crockett clay that lay beneath her fingers, after they checked into the Marriott, Ruby took charge. She wheeled the Corvette through Kansas City traffic with such style and grace that Crockett wished he was back on the plane. Less than twenty minutes after they pulled out of the parking garage, they pulled into the House of Denmark. Ruby grinned at Crockett while he panted.

"So, Raoul, what kind of furniture ya like?"

"Furniture that doesn't move," he gulped.

"Knowing you, I figured you prefer solid, simple pieces. Leather, few frills, plain lines, boring stuff like that, right?"

"Yeah."

"Have you ever actually been furniture shopping before," she said, "or did you just get all your stuff from Goodwill?"

"What do you think?"

"First time for everything," Ruby said. "Let's go." She got out and slammed the door.

Crockett limped along behind.

Three hours later, they'd also been to Benchmark, were sitting in the hotel restaurant, and Daniel Beckett had spent over twenty-two thousand dollars. It was very liberating.

Ruby slumped in her chair. "I'm done for the day, Crockett," she said. "Spending all that money just wore me out."

"I'm surprised at some of the stuff we bought," he said. "I didn't think it would be to your refined taste."

"Most of it wasn't, but it's your furniture."

"Mine?"

108

"Sure. After this is over, all that stuff goes to your place. You just got a houseful of new furniture, Crockett."

Shortly after they arrived in the suite, room service delivered a bottle of Shiraz. Ruby, a mysterious smile on her face, poured Crockett a glass.

"Drink that," she said.

He did. She poured another.

"One more."

He complied.

"Now, take a nice hot shower. I'll get you a warm fluffy robe from the health club and when you are all squeaky clean, I am going to make you a new man."

"Should I be aroused?"

She put her arms around his neck and kissed him chastely on the lips.

"I can't wait any longer," she said. "Get in the shower, get out, and get ready for me."

When Crockett stepped out of the shower, Ruby's voice floated in from the bedroom.

"The robe is on the john. Towel off, put it on, and get in here. This is something I cannot do without you."

Crockett put on the robe and walked into the bedroom. Ruby, also wearing a robe, sat with crossed legs on the edge of the bed, grinning at him. She brandished a pair of scissors.

"They're comin' off, Crockett. That cheesy mustache, that ratty ponytail, that wispy thing in the middle of your chin. Say goodbye."

"Ruby, I've had my ponytail and 'stash for almost twenty years. The least you could do is show a little remorse."

"Remorse, my ass. You're stalling. Sit down."

He did.

Ruby pulled her fingers through his hair a few times and gathered it loosely at the back of his head.

"Christ, Crockett. We need to save this and get some glue. You're really thin on top."

"What you interpret as a bald spot is, in reality, a solar collector for a sex machine."

Ruby snorted and chopped off about a foot of his hair.

Thirty minutes later Crockett's face was smooth as the wrinkles and lines would let it be, and Ruby was fussing.

"Look at this, Crockett. Your hair is curly where I cut it," Ruby said, patting and poking.

"Fine."

"*Fine.* Don't be bitter," she said. "Now when we go clothes shopping, I won't have to be seen with some refugee from Woodstock."

"You could do worse."

"Damn straight, I could. I'll be in the john for a while. In about forty-five minutes order me a double cappuccino, a turkey club on whole wheat, a dinner salad and something not too sweet for desert. And get us another bottle of wine."

Crockett turned on the TV.

The food arrived about an hour later. After they ate, Ruby, wearing a towel the size of a washtub around her head, disappeared back into the bathroom for another thirty minutes. The next time Crockett saw her, her nearly black hair was light auburn with blond highlights and six inches shorter.

"Jesus," he said.

"Whadaya think?"

"I like it."

"Really?"

"I've never known you with anything other than long dark hair. It sure changes your appearance. It kinda turns me on, LaCost."

"Oh, yeah?"

"You look just like my fifth grade teacher, Mrs. Simons. If I bring you an apple, will you let me watch you erase the blackboard?"

"Have you ever considered therapy?"

"Therapists always remind me of my fifth grade teacher, Mrs. Simons."

Ruby dug her cheesecake out of the fridge, sat on the edge of the bed and began to eat it with her fingers.

"Sick," she said. "Sick, sick, sick."

"There's a fork on the table."

Ruby poked a cheesecake-encrusted digit in the general direction of his mouth. "I like fingers," she said. "More sensual, don't you think?"

"I would like to remind you of the eleventh commandment, Ruby."

"The eleventh commandment?"

"Yep. Words to the wise. Thou shalt not push thy luck."

She grinned and shoved another fingerful of cheesecake between her lips.

"Lemme see if I got that. I shalt not push thy duck. Right?"

Crockett laughed. "Close enough," he said.

THIRTY-THREE
Roommates

RUBY AND CROCKETT WERE AT THE NEW TOWNHOUSE by nine the next morning. The truck from Benchmark arrived about ten minutes later. Ruby, in an oversized black t-shirt, blue jeans and heels, shivered a bit in mid-morning cool. Her new hair was pulled back into a very short ponytail, she wore little make-up, no jewelry, and seemed a bit self-conscious.

"You look great, Kid," Crockett said. "Sweet, scrubbed, almost virginal."

"Me?"

"I find the new Ruby very erotic."

Ruby grinned. "Does the term unrequited mean anything to you?"

"You're a cold woman, LaCost."

"I am, actually. The back of my neck misses my hair."

"How 'bout a nice kiss to warm it up?"

Ruby smiled and dropped her chin.

"Does the term unrequited mean anything to you?" Crockett said, and returned his attention to the movers.

It took the Benchmark guys only about thirty minutes to unload and another thirty minutes or so to set up the TV, sound system and recliners in the dining room because Ruby said she would not be plagued with a television in the living room. Crockett also had a TV installed in his bedroom.

As the benchmark truck was leaving the Danish bunch arrived, and by noon they had couches, chairs, tables, beds, dressers, end tables, all the stuff a handsome young couple could want.

"We need a toaster," Ruby said.

"And an espresso machine," Crockett added.

"And dishes."

"And pots and pans."

"Crockett, I've got a lot of shopping to do. We have to set up a basic kitchen, we need groceries, we still have to both get new clothes—"

111

"And I have to get to work."

"I know you do. Let's go out and grab some lunch and go shopping for you. On the way home we'll pick up some paper plates and stuff like that. Tonight we'll order pizza, tomorrow while you work, I'll go shopping for me and us. Okay?"

"We'll take the truck. Manly transportation for manly men and their manly shopping."

"Jesus," Ruby said.

They went to Independence Center, well away from the Plaza and related areas.

At Crockett's insistence, their first stop was to get Ruby a white satin windbreaker, some white socks and a pair of penny loafers. She eyeballed herself in a full-length mirror.

"Different, Crockett. Not bad, just different."

"Different is good," he said.

"I got your difference right here. Let's find a good men's store."

"No men's store. We need a men's department. Penny's, Sears, something like that."

"What?"

"Yup. I'm Justice or IBI. Most cops can't afford upscale men's stores. They don't go top of the line. I won't either."

By late afternoon Crockett had two new suits, two new jackets, four pairs of slacks, underwear, socks, shirts and, for the first time in his life, men's hosiery. All that was topped off by three pairs of shoes, a couple of belts, four or five ties, and a dark gray trench coat with a zip-out lining. Contrary to Ruby's sense of fashion, only one of the suit jackets was double breasted. Cops carry guns. Double breasted gets in the way. Even though Crockett did not intend to carry a gun, he had to play the part. On the way out of the mall they purchased bed linens, towels, and related items, then stopped by the grocery on the way home and staggered into the living room at dusk.

"Christ, what a day," Ruby moaned.

Crockett grunted as he dropped a load of garment bags across the back of the couch.

"You got that right," he said.

"Oh, shit. Crockett, you're limping terribly. I pulled you all over that mall today without a thought for your leg. I'm really sorry. Take a short soak to loosen up and I'll give you a massage."

"Promises, promises," he said.

"I'm serious! Use the big tub in the master bath. When you're done, I'll give you a rubdown. Then we'll order pizza and I'll get you buzzed on wine. You deserve it."

Smiling, Crockett turned toward the stairs.

This whole roommate thing could have some real advantages.

THIRTY-FOUR

The Defective

THE NEXT MORNING Ruby and Crockett went to First Watch for breakfast. Good service, bad gravy, no smoking. When they finished she headed off for a bout of shopping. He went home and called the cops.

"Kansas City Police Department." Female, not too young, professional.

"Investigation division, please."

"One moment." Three minutes.

"Investigations, Parker." Male, mid-thirties, black.

"Officer Parker or Detective Parker?"

"Detective Parker. How may I help you?"

"Detective Parker, my name is Daniel Beckett. I'm with a division of the federal government. I certainly do not expect you to take only my word for that, but what I would like you to do is to put me in contact with one of your troops who investigated a recent D.B. that was ruled to be a suicide."

"Who was the dead body?"

"A white female, early thirties, named Ilene Rachael Morrison. Found in her apartment in the Country Club Plaza area about five or six weeks ago, I believe."

"Ilene Rachael ... oh! Rachael Moore."

"That's correct."

"Hang on a minute." Two minutes.

"Detective Jamison." Older male, dry scratchy voice, bored.

"Detective Jamison, my name is Daniel Beckett. I'm an investigator for a branch of the federal government. I would like to speak with you about the Rachael Moore suicide."

"Case is closed."

"I am aware of that. I want to come see you."

"Oh sure, I'll just drop everything for Uncle Sam. How soon can ya get here?"

113

"Twenty minutes."

"Well, make it snappy. I gotta lot a stuff to do."

"Glazed or cake?"

"Huh?"

"See you soon, Detective."

Crockett made it in eighteen minutes. Just inside the squad room door a pretty brunette eyeballed his cane, then pointed out a fat guy sitting at a desk in a honeycomb of cubicles with shoulder-high walls. There were four or five other detectives working in the room. Crockett walked over.

Gray haired with the florid complexion and veined nose of a boozer, the man was forty pounds overweight and maybe fifty years old. A tired, burned-out veteran who stopped being a cop a decade ago and went to seed. Close to his pension, he was trying to be a tough guy. He wasn't good at it. He probably wasn't good at anything.

"Detective Jamison?" Crockett said.

Jamison didn't offer to shake hands.

"Yeah," he said. "You the Fed?"

"I'm the Fed."

"Lemme see some ID."

Crockett passed over the case containing his Justice Department badge and commission.

"Feel free to make any calls to verify my credentials that you care to," Crockett said. "I appreciate you taking time to speak with me."

Crockett watched while Jamison went through the motions of studying his commission for a moment. The guy wouldn't have known a valid Federal ID if it bit him on the ass.

"What can I do for ya, Beckett?"

"First off, you can show me the courtesy of offering me a seat."

Jamison looked at Crockett's suit, then at his cane, then removed his feet from the chair beside his desk and snorted as he shifted position.

"Siddown," he said.

Controlling his urge to drop Jamison out of a window, Crockett took a seat.

"Kind of you," he said. "Ilene Rachael Morrison."

Jamison looked confused.

"Who?"

"Rachael Moore?"

"Oh, yeah," Jamison said. "Suicide. Damn shame. Usta watch her on the news. Great lookin' little piece. Nice tits."

Crockett smiled. "You the primary investigator?"

"Naw. I was the first one there after the blues went in. Lieutenant Pike was the investigator. He's on vacation. I stayed on after they loaded up the corpse and hung around with forensics. Gotta keep a

114

dick on the scene, chain of evidence and like that. Place was clean. Medical examiner ruled it a suicide. Case is closed."

"I need copies of the reports and photos. Crime scene, autopsy, everything."

"What for? Fuckin' case is closed."

"It has come to the attention of some people that perhaps the case was not given the attention it deserved."

Jamison leaned toward Crockett, his complexion picking up a shade of red.

"Attention it deserved?" he said. "I was there, Bucko. Nothing disturbed, nothin' outa place. Just this once upon a time good lookin' blonde cunt sittin' in bathwater and blood, wrists slashed, dead as a goddammed hammer!"

"We still think the case needs a little extra work."

Jamison's respiration rate increased.

"Bullshit! TV star couldn't take the pressure of makin' all that fuckin' money and offed herself. Poor baby. Crime scene got nothin', forensics got nothin', latents got nothin', nobody got nothin' because there wasn't nothin'. The fuckin' case is closed. We don't need no goddam Federal badge jockey showin' up to re-open nothin'. You get my drift?"

Crockett lowered his woice to just above a whisper.

"Jamison," he said, "if you sit real quietly and listen, you may actually survive this. If you continue to give me attitude, this will be one of the worst days of your shit-filled life."

Some of the color drained from Jamison's face. He had plenty to spare.

"Who the fuck do you think you're talking to?" he said.

"I know who you are, Jamison. I've known assholes like you for years. Do yourself a favor. Reach into the bottom drawer of your desk, sneak out the bottle of booze you keep there and take a big slug. It'll help you focus. I want you real fucking focused."

Crockett waited until the man had taken a drink and returned the bottle to the drawer.

"Now then," he said, "listen very closely. I want copies of everything, and I mean everything, written about this investigation. I want the investigator's reports from every specialty, the autopsy, tenant interviews, reporting civilian, blues on the scene, every scrap, every flake, every mote, every tiny piece. You will see to this, Jamison. You will see to this because if you do not, I will own your fat ass. You will be audited by the Infernal Revenue Service. The Justice Department will tail you twenty-four hours a day for as long as I want them to. Every contact you have will be logged and filed. I will bug your car, I will tap your phone, I will watch your house."

Crockett leaned until his face was just inches from the florid man and sniffed.

"You are dirty, you sonofabitch. You know it and I know it. I can smell it on you. I will catch you, Jamison, and I will have your pathetic little pension. I have the funds, I have the resources, I have the time, and I have the will. You will become my personal project for as long as it takes. You fuckin' play games with me, *Bucko*, and you will bleed from the eyes. Do you understand your rights as I have advised you of them?"

Jamison had nothing left. His skin was gray, his hands were clenched, he was sweating and slumped forward, staring at the floor.

"Yeah," he said.

"What?"

"Yessir."

Crockett smiled and raised his voice so cops in the surrounding cubicles could hear him. "Great! Everything is fine then, isn't it, Detective?"

"Yeah, sure. Fine."

"I can't tell you how much your help means to me and the Department of Justice. I know that you'll tend to this personally and have that packet ready for me at the front desk in two hours, right?"

"Yeah."

"Good," Crockett said. "I'll just drop back by and pick it up there, that way I won't have to trouble you again. I know it will be complete, but just in case, I'll make some additional inquiries as time goes on. If it should happen that something I needed from you is missing, I'll look you up personally and we'll discuss the problem. That okay with you?"

"Oh, sure. That's great."

"Well, thanks again, Detective Jamison. Always a pleasure to work with a dedicated officer. Sit still, I'll see myself out."

Crockett sat in the truck at the curb for nearly ten minutes, until he settled down enough to drive. He ate a Tums to quiet his sudden case of heartburn and headed for the townhouse, a little embarrassed that he'd let Jamison get to him.

Asshole.

THIRTY-FIVE

Pink Flannel

WHEN CROCKETT GOT HOME he changed into lightweight sweats and began to go through the material from the cop shop. Ruby showed up about four. He heard her key rattling in the front door and went to let her in. The door swung open and she stood there, packages in hand, grinning at him.

"Damn, Crockett. Good to see you. Kinda nice havin' somebody home when you get there." He accepted part of the burden and followed her into the kitchen.

"What's this stuff?"

"We got everything from an espresso machine to a can opener. Gimme a hug, then check out my new vines."

Crockett put his packages on the counter and Ruby moved into his arms.

"Vines?" he said.

"Yeah, you know, threads, drapes ... clothes!" She pulled away and posed.

Ruby was wearing a maroon canvas stockman-style jacket over a chambray shirt, off-white chinos, and ankle-cut hiking boots with speed laces and cleated soles.

"Wadaya think?" she said.

Crockett smiled. "Sort of a Junior League meets Eddie Bauer thing goin' on there," he said.

"Not bad for a sleazy exhibitionist, huh?"

"There is an alarming amount of you covered up."

"I know. So, I got a new malachite-green silk teddy and a short white silk robe, trimmed in dark green, to go over it."

"Ah."

"And a pair of green and white three-inch mules so my lovely feet won't get cold. Help me drag all the stuff in from the car, then I'll take a shower while you fix dinner, then we will dine. I'll slip into some-

117

thing more comfortable and we shall sit on the couch, drink, and not talk about that stuff you have scattered all over the table in the study."

"Okay."

Ruby reached out and took his hand. "You have had a very difficult day," she said. "I can see it in your eyes and body. It is now time for relief. I simply will not allow you to succumb to all this. We will compartmentalize. I will help."

"I count on that."

"Thank you, Crockett. That is a marvelous compliment."

It took ten minutes to pry all the stuff out of the Corvette. With her new clothes hung neatly away, the kitchen hardware stashed in appropriate places, and groceries stowed, Ruby sighed and slipped an arm around Crockett's waist.

"Now I feel like I live here," she said.

"Nesting?"

"A little. You got a problem with that?"

"Not one damn bit. Usually, I am very comfortable around you."

Ruby sidled up against him. "Usually?" she said.

"Yeah. Usually."

"God knows, Crockett, the last thing I ever want is to make you even the slightest bit uncomfortable," she said. "I'm just gonna go up to the master bath, take off all my clothes, and slip into a nice warm shower. Okay, Honey?"

"LaCost—"

"And don't you dare think about me getting all wet and soapy. I wouldn't want you to be uncomfortable."

In the kitchen, Crockett found some Jerusalem artichoke angel hair pasta and put water on to boil. Among the pans Ruby had purchased was a deep skillet. He set it over high heat and prowled through the fridge. He grabbed a nice butterfly-cut pork chop and diced it into half-inch squares, sliced up a good sized shallot, washed some fresh pea pods and opened a can of water chestnuts.

When the skillet was hot, he added olive oil and dumped in the shallots and some minced garlic that he found in the cabinet. When the garlic was lightly browned, he dropped in the pork and turned the pot of water down to a low boil. Keeping the cubes of meat moving, he shook on some dried dill and white cracked pepper. When the pork was nearly cooked through, he drizzled on honey from one of those little plastic bears and dumped in a spoonful of hot Chinese mustard.

Crockett stirred the pork until it was covered with the honey and mustard and put it in a bowl. Then he paper-toweled the gunk out of the hot skillet, added a little oil and soy sauce and dropped in the pea pods and sliced water chestnuts. He slid the pasta into the boiling water and turned the flame up, then stirred both the pot and the skillet.

When the veggies were mostly done, he pushed them to the outside of the pan, dumped the meat in the center, and heard the shower shut off.

"'Bout ready!" he yelled.

"Me, too!" came the reply.

He poured the water and pasta into a colander, stirred the meat and veggies together, shut off the pan, dropped on a lid and pulled plates out of the cabinet. He put the angel hair on the plates, spooned on the meat and vegetables, and carried them to the kitchen table. He had just laid out paper towels and silverware and was fixing ice water, when Ruby walked into the kitchen.

She was completely devoid of make-up, wearing a pink floor-length, flannel housecoat, zipped from chin to ankles, some awful pink fluffy slippers about the dimension of bass boats, and over-sized glasses with tortoise-shell frames. The housecoat had a thin edge of white lace around a Peter Pan collar and she had enough pink terry-cloth wrapped around her head to carpet Rhode Island.

"Dinner ready?" she asked.

He couldn't speak.

Ruby's eyes were wide and her face the picture of innocence.

"What?" she said.

Crockett gained a bit of control.

"Nice look," he said.

"You like?"

"Oh, yeah. It's you."

"That's kinda what I thought when I bought it today. I was thinking about you and how I wouldn't ever want to make you uncomfortable."

"What if I told you that pink flannel really turns me on?"

"I'd say you need food," Ruby said.

Half and hour later Ruby pushed her plate away and peered at Crockett through her really ugly glasses. Her eyes looked about twice their normal size explaining why she wore contacts.

"That's it, Old Son," she said. "You have permanent kitchen duty."

Crockett smiled as he got up to clear the table.

"Kitchen duty and pink flannel, too," he said. "My libido is reduced to the size of a pecan."

"I feel I am forced to re-think the whole flannel protocol," Ruby said.

"Just when I was getting used to it?"

"That very statement speaks volumes in itself, Crockett. I am compelled to admit that flannel may make you too docile. I would much prefer you to be, at least in this stage of your treatment, relaxed, but alert, as opposed to lethargic and complacent."

"Of course," Crockett said, "none of this has anything to do with the fact that you are a self-confessed sleazy exhibitionist."

"Absolutely not!"

"I see," he said.

"But not nearly enough. I put some scotch in one of the cabinets. Find and open it please. I shall return."

She sauntered seductively toward the stairs, a nearly impossible feat in big fuzzy slippers and flannel.

Crockett cleaned up the mess and put the hardware in the dishwasher, located the scotch and opened it, gathered up some glasses and placed them and the whisky on the coffee table. He grabbed an ashtray and a box of Shermans, lit the gas log, lowered the lights, hit the couch, poured himself a short one, and propped up his feet. He heard her bedroom door open and there on the landing was Ruby.

She had shaken out her hair and applied a little make up. The glasses, housecoat, and slippers were gone, replaced by her new green teddy and short white robe. The mules completed her ensemble.

"Holy shit," Crockett said.

Ruby smiled and walked slowly down the stairs in that one-foot crossing over the other way that models walk. Her clothes rustled when she sat down on the couch and Crockett heard a whisper of nylon as she crossed her legs. Ruby rotated her torso toward him, smiled, handed Crockett a cigar and kept one for herself.

"Hey, Davey," she growled, "want me to lick your Macanudo?"

"Aw, Jesus. Ruby!"

Crockett saw her eyes dance.

"Another Crockett moment," she said.

THIRTY-SIX
A Cold and Case Files

CROCKETT AND RUBY STAYED HOME for the next three days and went through the information that Detective Jamison had been kind enough to provide. Crockett developed a head cold and Ruby pummeled him with various patent nostrums, each falsely guaranteed to bring immediate relief. She offered the premise that his illness was a way to punish himself because Rachael was dead. He offered the premise that she was full of shit. Crockett examined every scrap of the considerable information except the autopsy pictures and crime scene photos of the body. That he left to Ruby. Women are tougher than men.

Crockett tried to put his emotional attachment to things away and view the case from as neutral a position as possible. There was absolutely nothing to suggest Rachael's death was anything other than a suicide. Fixing the time of death was made a bit more difficult because she had bled out in a warm tub of water, but estimates placed it at between noon and five PM on the Thursday before they were due to head for Chicago. The only definitive fingerprints at the scene were hers. There were a few smeared latents, some of which were probably his, but the place had been thoroughly cleaned before her death. Rachael was a neat person getting ready to go out of town. Nothing sinister could be assumed from the recent cleaning.

The body was found by the police after concerned prompting from her supervisor at the television station, when she had not shown up for work in two days and had not been responsive to phone calls. The building superintendent opened the door for them, but waited outside and was not admitted to the scene.

The apartment was in order, nearly pristine. Nothing appeared to be out of place, there was no sign of a struggle, no evidence of a search. Examination of her nails revealed nothing out of the ordinary, there was no bruising on the body, no defensive wounds, no drugs in her blood stream, just a deep vertical slash, four to five inches long, up

121

the inside of each forearm. There was no blood spray on the walls, no splashing on the floor. The wounds were consistent with a small kitchen knife found under water in the tub. The blade, high-carbon steel and very sharp, was confirmed to be the fatal instrument.

The carpets had been vacuumed for foreign substances to no avail, and her clothes, found rumpled on the bathroom floor, yielded nothing unusual, but that was inconclusive. The Kansas City Police Department is not equipped for a truly high-tech examination and, since the death seemed to be from so obvious a cause, nothing was sent to a federal lab. No unusual materials or possessions were found in a search of the condo except her pistol, which, although not common, was certainly not illegal.

It was impossible to determine if she had received a visitor on the day of her death. None of the other tenants questioned saw anyone unusual and the building had no doorman or security personnel. Her answering machine contained several calls from her job and the ones from Crockett. Nothing else.

He went over the whole thing several times, thinking about it from as many angles as he could. Something should be amiss, but no matter how hard Crockett looked, he could not find it. Eventually he passed it off as paranoia. He considered, he conjectured, he cogitated. He put it away, he went back, he gave up, he re-started, he studied, he read, he cursed, he wept, and finally, on the third night while Ruby was making supper, he quit.

Crockett schlepped into the kitchen as Ruby put a skillet on the stove, and slipped an arm around her sweat-suited waist.

"What's for dinner?" he said.

"Comfort food, Carnivore. Big old cheeseburgers made with ground Angus fillets, with some really awesome cheddar I found, and homemade French fries with vinegar and sea salt. You've been very good through this whole cold of yours, lotsa fruit juice and veggies, yogurt and fiber. This supper and kind words from me are your reward. It will be worth the illness."

She removed a small package from the fridge and began to shape a couple of thick ground beef patties.

"Ruby, could Rachael really have killed herself?"

"Sure."

"Could Ivy have been so wrapped up in her loss that she made her accusations based on nothing but emotion?"

"Sure."

"Could I be so concerned with remaining objective, that I'm missing something?"

"Sure."

"I'm stumped," Crockett said. "I don't think that the police missed anything. Every assumption they came to seems valid to me. If I had been assigned to investigate this case, I would have reached the exact same conclusion. Suicide makes sense. The evidence suggests nothing else. Some of the things in the autopsy report are strange, but may or may not mean a damn thing. I got no place to go with this. What do you think?"

"You stink."

"What?"

"You smell like a large man with a cold. Go take a shower, put on a robe. You've been in sweats for three days. Brush your teeth."

"It's almost time to eat."

"I will delay putting on the burgers until I hear the shower stop. Change is necessary. You are about to change your food intake. Take a shower for a change, put on a robe for a change, eat a big meal for a change. After dinner we will talk, and perhaps something will surface amid all these changes."

He headed for the shower.

Crockett toweled his hair dry, easy to do with it so short, slipped on some sweat socks and a long terry robe, and padded into the kitchen just as Ruby turned the burgers. She scooped a pile of French fries into a paper towel lined bowl and started spooning vanilla ice cream into a blender.

"Make yourself useful," she said. "Put the rest of those potato slices into the fryer."

"Homemade French fries?"

"Not just homemade, Sweetcakes. Homemade and fried in real lard, just like grandma used to make. Damn the cholesterol and full speed ahead!"

"Wow."

Ruby poured chocolate syrup on the ice cream.

"Cheeseburgers, fries and chocolate shakes," she said. "If you're good, later I'll let you ask me to the prom." She dumped a cup of Bailey's into the mix and fired up the blender.

Crockett stepped back from the popping lard. "Why mess with the prom?" he said. "After dinner, let's head straight for Inspiration Point."

"You're about to be inspired," Ruby said. "Be careful of that grease. If your robe slips open, burgers and fries could mean crispy duck." She put buns on a plate, and slipped slices of cheddar onto the patties. "There's sea salt on the counter and a bottle of malt vinegar. Put the salt on the fries and the vinegar on the table, while I pour the shakes."

Crockett scooped the rest of the fries onto the pile and salted them, then carried the fries and vinegar to the table with some paper towels to use as napkins. Ruby poured the shakes into tall glasses, added fat straws, gathered up ketchup and mustard, took all that to the table, and lit two candles.

"Before you get me to inspiration point, Big Boy, it's gonna take a corsage, a nice dinner, and a half-pint of sloe gin. What kinda girl do you think I am?"

Crockett smiled at her. "All girl," he said. "From the top of your lovely head to the tips of your succulent toes."

"What a shame my formal is at the cleaners. At least we have the nice dinner and alcoholic milk shakes. There's some fresh oregano in the crisper. It's not exactly an orchid, but it might possibly do. Let's eat and see."

"Acceptance," he said. "Not expectation."

"Very good, Ruby said. "Anticipation, however, can be awfully nice."

THIRTY-SEVEN
Fold 'em

THE DINNER WAS TERRIFIC. The best French fries Crockett had had in forty years. The beef was outstanding, the shakes were marvelous, and the Bailey's left a little buzz. He began to gather the plates and Ruby stood up.

"Damn, Crockett! Am I good, or what? You clean up the mess, fire up the logs, open us some wine, and arrange yourself seductively upon yon couch. I'm gonna go scrape off the cobwebs. When I return, I expect you to ply me with liquor in vain attempt to pat the dimples on my lovely knees." She vanished up the stairs.

Crockett did as ordered. They were out of Shiraz, but did have a chubby little Merlot that he liked. He opened it, found the rest of that great cheddar, dug out two Macanudo Maduros he'd been saving, and took the whole assemblage to the coffee table.

Smiling, he grabbed a green onion out of the fridge and sat on the couch. As he heard Ruby open her bedroom door, he slipped the robe off his right shoulder and put the onion between his teeth. When she appeared at the top of the stairs, he gave her a toothy grin and bounced his eyebrows a few times. Ruby laughed.

She was wearing dark blue, silky, man-style pajamas and black mules with impossible heels. The effect, in the reflected light from the kitchen and the glow of the fire, was startling. Except for the hair color, this was the old Ruby. He'd missed her.

"Woof, LaCost. You'd give Gandhi a case of the munchies!"

Ruby turned in a slow circle.

"Sweet-talker," she said. "You like?"

"You amaze me," Crockett said. "You are covered from ankle to throat and most women could work for two weeks and never get half as sexy as you are right now."

"It's all attitude. What goes on between the ears is so much more important than what happens below the neck. But you know that, you sly devil. In ten words, you can turn a girl's head farther than a two dollar chiropractor."

Crockett felt his ears get warm.

"Zat Right?" he said.

"You know damn good and well it is. You get embarrassed, you play the shy guy, you lay that 'Aw, shucks, Ruby' bullshit all over the place, but you can't fool me, Old Son. I have wallowed in your life for too many years. You specialize in giving me a way out. If any other woman on this planet treated you the way I do, you'd either kick her off the mountain or drag her into the cave by her hair, even if she was a dyke. But not me."

She eased down, cross-legged, next to Crockett on the couch and turned so she was facing him. Her knees touched his left side.

"You play the bumpkin and I play the harlot because we like to play," Ruby said. "We are familiar with each other in those roles, we find them a safe way to maintain emotional distance during sexual tension, and we are both frightened we could lose each other if one of us made the wrong move."

Crockett smiled at her candor.

"Exactly," he said.

"So, Crockett," Ruby said. "You wanna play hide the salami, or what?"

"Damn!"

Ruby laughed. "Tag!" she said. "You're it."

The cigars were gone, the wine almost gone, and Ruby was sitting on a pillow on the floor, leaning back between Crockett's knees, while he rubbed her shoulders.

"You said something bothered you about the autopsy report," she said. "What bothers you?"

"The examiner listed several old fractures. Fingers, three or four ribs, a wrist, even a low-level skull fracture. There were also some nearly invisible burn scars. The report states that they were probably from early childhood. He also noted the small scars I told you about. The ones I mentioned to Rachael when she said fish hooks. I'm curious about the injuries."

"Beatings and torture," Ruby said.

"What?"

She swiveled on her butt, put her hands lightly on his thighs, and looked up at him.

"Beatings and torture. Now get a grip, Crockett. I'm going to tell you what little I know. I can tell you now because Rachael is dead and because I'm sure Ivy would not object. When Rachael was a child, probably from age three or so until she was about ten, she was abused by both her father and her aunt, his sister."

"Aw, shit."

"The mistreatment, although not sexual in nature for the child, was almost certainly sexual in nature for the adults. Rachael could not freely recall very much about the events, but from what I did learn from her, I can deduce the broken fingers and such were deliberate acts perpetrated upon her by those two people. I'm sure they enjoyed hearing her scream. Burns also work very well for that."

"My God," Crockett muttered, rubbing his hands together and staring at the coffee table.

"Should I continue? You're shaking."

"Go on."

"A child with a couple of fish hooks embedded in each arm and thigh can be restrained quite easily when tethered by strings tied to those hooks. I should imagine the adults in question, as they shot her with a pellet pistol and threw darts at her, were quite entertained."

"Oh, Christ. Ruby, can that be true?"

"That and other things. You must understand, you absolutely *must* understand, that I do not know if all she told me was accurate. I do know that Rachael believed it had happened. I had no reason to doubt her."

"But, how can someone do that to a child?"

"That, and much worse is all too common, Crockett."

"Goddammit! I know it. I just don't want to know it."

"She also stated her father belonged to some sort of child abuse ring, or club. That once or twice a year, a number of people from around the country would come to his home, each bringing at least one child, for a weekend of swapping and abuse of all types."

Crockett hung his head toward the floor. Sweat stung his eyes and he felt sick to his stomach.

"No."

"Yes. Crockett, listen to me. Listen to me! You must know that Rachael did not suffer from continuous memories of these events. They were blocked from her conscious mind almost completely. Only during intense therapy did they begin to surface. She did not actively remember these things. They affected her, to be sure. She maintained a distance from everyone with whom she came in contact, until she met you."

Ruby took his hands in hers and looked at the pain in Crockett's eyes.

"You offered her some control. You wanted nothing from her. You helped her change the way she viewed herself within the context of her past and present. You were the first person, other than Ivy, she was ever really close to in her adult life. You made her life joyous, David Allen Crockett, and if you allow what I have told you of her childhood to push that marvelous fact from your mind, you are a self-indulgent fool! Do I make myself clear? Answer me, Crockett!"

"You make yourself clear."

"Okay. How you doin'?"

"I'm pissed, Ruby."

"Pissed is good. Go with pissed."

"I'm pissed that anybody would do that to a child, I'm horrified that there could be clubs, for crissake, for that kinda thing, and I am fucking furious that none of this, none of it, means that low-life sonofabitch killed her!"

"No, it doesn't."

"Not only does it not prove one goddammed thing legally, it doesn't even make me certain it wasn't a suicide. If anything, it points more to the likelihood of suicide! Not even the fact that she didn't mention me in that non-committal note she left proves anything. It was her handwriting. The expert who looked it over said he didn't even detect any significant stress in the script! We got nothin'. Not a damned thing. Christ, I'm tired."

"Why don't you go to bed," Ruby said.

Crockett smiled. "Naw. You go ahead. I couldn't sleep right now."

Ruby rose to her knees and slid between his to hug him.

"Be a cop," she said. "Get your mind around this, don't let this get around your mind. If there is nothing we can do, we will do nothing. If there is something to be done, we will do it. Time will reveal all. This is not a race. Settle back and let it come to something or nothing. Don't push it. Okay?"

"You are a good woman, LaCost."

"Damn site better than you'll ever know."

"You're probably right, but the duck has his suspicions."

"I knew I could never fool the duck," she said, and kissed him on the nose. "I'm going to bed, Crockett. I'll let you sleep in the morning."

It was after six when Crockett realized he'd been sitting on the couch all night. He brushed his teeth, got dressed, jumped in the truck, and went to a coffee shop to pick up some cinnamon rolls and a half-pound of Jamaican Blue Mountain. Then he swung by a Q.T. and bought a cheap lavender rose. By the time Crockett got all that accomplished it was after seven-thirty. He ground some beans, fired up the espresso maker, popped the rolls in the micro-cave, foamed up some half and half, dropped the rose in a tall water glass, poured the coffee and cream into two tumblers, put the whole mess on a cutting board, carefully carried it upstairs, and eased into Ruby's bedroom. She stirred as he came in, opened an eye, and smiled.

"Trying to sneak up on me, Davey?"

Crockett crossed the room to place the cutting board on her end table, and noticed Ruby's pajamas folded on a chair.

"Well now," he said.

"Well now, what?"

"Let me see," he said. "You are here in bed, and your peejays are way over there on that chair."

"So what?"

"I was just wondering what you might be wearing all snuggled up in those crisp sheets? And, if you are wearing only what I think you're wearing, you are gonna have to eat pretty much lying down, or they will close Minsky's. Here, Sweetheart, let me put this stuff down and help you sit up."

"Crockett. It wouldn't surprise me a bit to see the average man behave like this, but of you, I thought better."

Crockett put his burden on her end table.

"You have appealed to my puritan instincts," he said. "I will deliver your pajamas to you, at least the top, turn my back, at least mostly, and we shall dine when you're decent."

"That could take some time," she said. "You know, Crockett, if I were you, I'd—"

"I'll be damned," he said, staring at Ruby's pajamas where they lay folded on a chair.

"What?"

Crockett sat on the edge of the bed.

"Ruby LaCost," he said, "it wasn't a suicide!"

"It wasn't?"

"Not only no, but hell no."

"Fine. Why not?"

"You're a woman, right?"

"Can't get anything past you, can I?"

"Rachael was a woman."

"You really are a trained investigator, huh?"

"Just play along, willya?" Crockett said. "At the end of the day, what do you do with your clothes?"

"I put 'em in a hamper or hang 'em up."

"Exactly. Women do that."

"A sexist remark, but true," Ruby said.

"What if you don't hang your clothes up or put 'em in a hamper? Then what?"

"I fold them. So What?"

"At the end of her life, would Rachael have left her clothes crumpled up on the bathroom floor?"

Ruby stared at Crockett for a beat or two, and the light bulb came on.

"Rachael would have folded her clothes," she said.

"But she didn't," Crockett said.

Ruby stared at him for a moment.

"Jesus Christ, Crockett! There's your proof. He killed her!"

"It's nothing that would even begin to hold up in court, but you can bet your sweet ass he did. That's what's been bothering me this whole time. Those clothes just left lying on the bathroom floor. One way or another, the sonofabitch killed her."

THIRTY-EIGHT
Planning

CROCKETT CARRIED THE COFFEE AND ROLLS DOWN to the kitchen table and Ruby, wrapped in a robe, joined him a few minutes later.

"Now what?" she asked.

"Now we take it to this guy. We start poking around to find out more about Martin Morrison and his sister. What's her name?"

"Marian. It's in the stuff that Clete gave us. Pictures of them, couple of shots of their house, estate is more like it, a photo or two of the place from a plane, some articles he's written for various journals, things like that."

"Stuff I need to go through."

Ruby studied him for a moment. "Crockett, have you been up all night?"

"Yeah."

"Lemme get this straight. You're still half sick from that cold, you've been without sleep for over twenty-four hours, and your first thoughts of this day were to bring to me this lovely pastry, this delicious coffee, and this substandard rose?"

"Sorta."

"Sorta?"

"Actually, I had hoped to fondle you in your sleep."

Ruby grinned. "Crockett, I'm thrilled! You are a romantic fool."

"Silly me."

"Go up to my bathroom, get into my whirlpool tub full of warm water that I have already prepared, turn on the jets, and relax. I'll be there shortly with fresh coffee. We will continue this conversation and then you will go, sadly alone, to bed."

"Missed again, huh?"

Ruby smiled. "Yes, you did, Sweetheart. But not by much."

The minute he hit the warm, swirling water, Crockett started to fade away. Ruby came in with two screwdrivers made with orange and papaya juice, pulled up a stool, lit a Sherman for him, and sat down.

"This ain't coffee," he said.

"You need sleep, Son."

"When I get outa here, I'm gonna take a nap and you are going to set some things in motion."

"Oooh!" Ruby said. "I love setting things in motion." She slipped her feet into the tub. "Whacha got in mind?"

"Nothing that would interest a woman of your proclivities, I'm afraid."

Ruby rubbed her toes on his thigh. "I don't know, Crockett," she said. "Just being here while you relax in that rush of warm water, makes me come over queer."

"Ruby," he said, "you are queer."

"Alas," she said. "What am I going to set in motion?"

"You are going to visit Martin Morrison."

"I am?"

"Yes, you are. It seems that Randi DeMoss has a patient whose family is having a very difficult time with their youngster. About a five year old girl, I think."

"And I, of course, have read some of the good Doctor's writings on behavioral modification in children."

"Indeed."

"And I think that were I to visit his clinic and discuss the matter with him, look over his facilities, and learn more about his very effective protocol, it is entirely possible that I could persuade these wealthy people to turn their extremely troubled daughter over to him for a time."

"All, of course, for the benefit of the child."

"Of course. Money and the availability of some fresh meat would have nothing to do with it."

Crockett smiled. "That's the idea."

"Oh, Crockett," Ruby said, "you have no idea what being exposed to the devious side of you does for me."

"You are about to be exposed to more than that. I gotta get out of this tub, and get to bed before I sink outa sight. Fetch my robe and then go away. Shortly thereafter I will join you in the downstairs."

Ruby was sitting at the kitchen shuffling through some papers, when Crockett padded into the living room.

"Whacha doin'?" he asked.

"I'm preparing a letter to Martin Morrison from Randi DeMoss. Clete even included some letterhead stationary in this packet. I will process it on my computer, as soon as I go out and buy a computer, mail it to my office in Lincoln, they will mail it to the Morrison Clinic, and contact will be initiated."

"God, you lesbians are a sneaky race."

"It's because, deep down in our little hearts, we all want to be men."

"Give it up, Cutie. Male is something you don't come close to."

Ruby rose and headed toward him.

"As a rule, no, Crockett," she said. "But it would seem that you are the exception. Sometimes I quite enjoy being close to you."

She slipped her arms around Crockett's neck and smiled at him.

"Coming close to you is amother matter, I'm afraid. Go to bed."

As he went up the stairs, Crockett lifted the back of his robe and mooned her. Even after he closed his bedroom door, he could still hear Ruby laughing.

THIRTY-NINE

Warrior

CROCKETT DRUG HIMSELF out of bed about two that afternoon and struggled into some clean sweats. He hated sleeping during the day because he always seemed to wake up in worse shape than when he laid down. Stopped-up, bleary-eyed, and severely rumpled, he lurched out of the bedroom and staggered down the stairs. Ruby was working on a computer in the small study. She looked at him.

"Yuk! No wonder you never got married again. You look like hell, Crockett."

"Give coffee," he groaned. "Food now. Me hungry. Need eat. Make strong."

"My goodness," Ruby said, "jutting brow, weak chin, shambling gait. I thought you people were extinct."

"You woman. Me like. Make hump."

"This elemental side of you is very refreshing."

"Ugh," Crockett said. "Duck cold. Come here. Make warm."

Twenty minutes later Crockett was on his second cup of coffee, leaning on the kitchen table as Ruby slid a plate of scrambled eggs and toast in from of him. Outside the window, leaves were swirling in the blustery wind.

"Jesus," Crockett said. "Winter's not that far away. What happened to fall?"

"We missed it," Ruby said. "You especially. The loss of someone close has a way of distorting time."

Crockett didn't answer. His mouth was full.

"I called Randi's office in Lincoln, Nebraska," Ruby said. "Spoke with a lady named Rose, Randi's office manager. Tomorrow I'll send her the letter for Morrison and she'll forward it. Then we see what happens."

"Good," Crockett said. "We'll mail the letter on our way out of town."

"Where we goin'?"

"Champaign, Illinois."

"Your hometown. How come?"

"Champaign is only thirty miles or so from the Morrison Clinic. If anybody that remembers me is still at the cop shop, maybe I can get some grease on my skids to get cooperation from the Champaign County Sheriff's Department. Champaign County borders Hyatt County wherein lies Morrison's clinic. I'd like to gather as much intel as possible."

"Why not go to the Hyatt County authorities?"

"Morrison, if he is as important and moneyed as Ivy claims, probably owns a few of them. Plus, there is considerable jealousy in law enforcement from county to county. The folks in Champaign County will probably be more prone to tell me what I need to know about their neighbors. Compared to Champaign County, Hyatt is backward and poor, much more like the South, more wary of strangers, more clannish. I don't want to walk in there cold."

"I thought cops were cops."

"For the most part, you're right," Crockett said. "Especially on a person-to-person basis. Police departments are a lot like clubs or religions. They'll all band together to fight off the heathens, but each one knows that they are the best. Jealousy between cops is not, as a rule, as common as jealousy between departments. It all comes back to the group mentality. It even occurs between different shifts on the same department. Kind of a microcosm of the species."

"I suppose I shouldn't be surprised by that."

"Cops are just like everybody else, only different."

"Right," Ruby said.

"So I need a way in. My credentials are nice, but not enough. I need to talk with these people as much as an inside equal as possible. If I have to throw my Federal or State weight around, I'd rather save that for the folks in Hyatt County. Very probably Morrison will know I'm there within fifteen minutes after I arrive. That's not a bad thing. As a matter of fact it can work to our advantage to make him nervous. But I want to be sure I control when that happens."

"You are a threat."

"You got that right. Tomorrow we go to Champaign for a couple of days, and I start nibbling around the edges of this thing."

Ruby was looking at him curiously, a slight smile on her lips.

"What?" Crockett said.

"The change that has come over you as you talk about cops and robbers is relatively subtle, but extremely obvious."

"You got a problem with that, M'am?"

"It's like you've gone on alert to Def-Con three."

"C'mon, Ruby."

134

"I just got a peek at Crockett the cop. There was a flicker of flame in the furnace, Old Son. I suspect Rachael saw some of this when you were teaching her how to shoot. To have that in a friend would be very comforting. To have it in an enemy would be very daunting."

"You're serious, aren't you?"

Ruby nodded. "It's part of the warrior mentality. As old and tired as you claim to be, you are a warrior. It is your nature to fight the good fight. Before you lies what you see as a good fight, your first one in a long time. Emotionally, you are much more settled than you were twenty years ago. The warrior in you recognizes that you are perhaps more formidable at this point in your life than you have ever been. That's what Rachael saw. It provides a real feeling of safety. She felt that. So did I. It's extremely compelling and not very common. I would not ever want to be in your path if you went on full alert."

He laid dead eyes on her and growled. "I'll let ya know."

Ruby flinched. "That's awful," she said. "Don't quit your day job."

FORTY
Ruby in the Cockpit

CROCKETT HAD A TRAVEL CASE and a hanging bag by the basement door when Ruby came up the stairs. She was dressed in one of her new Jane Junior League meets Smokey the Bear outfits, and looking fine for it. The sun was just coming up.

"I'll drive," she said. "We'll grab some breakfast in Columbia."

"Why don't I drive, and we'll eat in Blue Springs."

"That's the very reason," Ruby said. "It'll take you forty-five minutes to get to Blue Springs. I'll have us all the way to Columbia in less than an hour and a half."

"Sweet Jesus."

"My stuff is already in the car," she said, moving through the house, checking on lights, stove knobs, locks and the like.

"You're gonna drive, aren't you?"

"Without a shadow of a doubt," Ruby said.

"What about my leg?"

"We can rebuild it. We have the technology."

"Shit."

"Grab your cane and lock the door behind you," Ruby said, heading off down the stairs with his bags.

By the time Crockett was settled in the car they were on I-70, Ruby had her radar detector dialed in, and they were streaking across Missouri like a low level A-6. The Corvette loved it. As Blue Springs flashed by, he could no longer contain himself.

"Hey, Uhura, we at warp speed yet?"

Ruby grinned. "Almost," she said. "I'll let it out in another mile or two."

"Let it out?"

"Yeah."

"How the hell fast are we going now?"

136

"Little under a hundred," she said, squirting past something green and blurry.

"A little under a hundred!"

"Yeah." Something red disappeared in their wake. "Little over now. 'Bout one-ten."

"Oh, hell."

"Take it easy, you wimp. This car is built to do this and so am I. Don't be such a pussy."

"LaCost, if you kill me while engaging in this macho dance of death, I will never forgive you."

"It's all under control," she said, and he could feel the car accelerate a bit. "Besides, I wouldn't wanna do any damage to the duck. How is the duck, anyway?"

"Trying desperately to return to the egg."

She laughed. Crockett peeked at the digital speedometer.

It said 126.

Columbia appeared in view long before it should have.

"Cracker Barrel," Crockett said.

Ruby dove for the exit. By the time she'd made the five or six turns necessary to get a space in the parking lot, he felt like he'd been on a Tilt-A-Whirl. Ruby peered at him.

"You okay?"

"Do I look okay?"

"You're a little pale."

"I'm a little green."

"I thought you just got airsick."

"Motion sickness is what they call it, Ruby."

"Oh, Crockett, I'm sorry. I got a little carried away. I kinda like this car. Let's go eat."

She breezed into the Cracker Barrel as if she owned the place. He lurched along behind her like Renfield on a bad day. Thank God, they were seated quickly. Their waitress arrived.

"Hi, Folks! Coffee?"

"With cream," smiled Ruby.

"Compazine with a side of Demerol," Crockett said.

"Beg pardon?"

"Just water."

"Okay. Be right back!"

"So, what's good here?" Ruby said, her face buried in the menu.

"You'll have to decide for yourself. I can't talk about food right now."

"I really did a number on you, didn't I?"

"Pretty much," Crockett said.

Ruby struggled to keep from grinning and maintained a concerned expression.

137

"Have you always had this problem," she asked, "or is it a symptom of your advancing age?"

"LaCost, you are a cruel insensitive slut, and I despise you totally."

Ruby smiled. "Feeling a bit better, are we?" she said.

"Bite me."

"Ooh. Dessert?"

Crockett couldn't help it. He laughed.

"That's my big boy," Ruby said. The waitress returned.

Ruby ordered the Extra Greedy, Big Man's, Eat More Than You Can Possibly Stand, Stomach Stuffer Special breakfast. Crockett, battling mightily with his digestive system, had one poached egg and dry wheat toast. She finished before he did.

Ruby put down her napkin and beamed at him.

"Ready to go?" she said.

"I want some Dramamine."

"We passed a drugstore on the way in, didn't we?"

"How do I know? My eyes were closed."

They had. Ruby stopped. Crockett took two. She drove back to I-70 very carefully.

Dramamine is an effective downer. Crockett reclined his seat a bit and leaned back. He dozed for what felt like twenty minutes until Ruby rubbed his shoulder.

"'Bout ten miles out of Champaign on I-57, Sweetie. Time to come back."

"Whah?"

"Time to wake up."

"Wheh?"

"Almost to Champaign."

"Already?!"

"You've been sleeping for hours! You even slept through a gas and potty stop."

"I did?"

"Yes, you did. Champaign's coming up. Where am I going?"

"I-74 East I guess. Look for motel. Stop. Gotta whiz."

"Okay. Cold coffee in the paper cup. Take a hit and try to focus. Damn, can you snore!"

"Part of my charm."

"Check that sign," Ruby said.

"Slow down, I'm not a speed reader."

"Marriott Courtyard on I-74."

"Suits me," Crockett yawned, looking around. "God, I don't recognize anything. The whole damn place is different. I bet the cop shop has moved or something. I'll have to make some calls."

Ruby took the I-74 turnoff with considerable decorum at less than eighty miles per hour. They passed the exit for Prospect Avenue and the Marriott came up on the left side of the road. She grabbed the exit and drove like she had a will to live. Ten minutes later they were in their rooms and Crockett felt much better. He had just finished calling a rent-a-car company to have some transportation delivered when Ruby came in through the connecting door. She was wearing knee-high boots with two-inch heels over amazingly tight blue jeans, with a bulky cable-knit creamy white sweater and an open sheepskin vest.

"This country is flat," she said.

"Best farmland in the USA," Crockett said, slipping into a broad mid-western accent. "Summers is awful hot, winters is terrible cold. They say there ain't nothin' between here an' the North Pole 'cept one bob-wire fence, an' it's down."

"You get real country when you're this close to your roots, huh?"

"You can take the boy outa the country, but—"

"Yeah, yeah, yeah. Let's eat."

"LaCost, how come you don't weigh four hundred pounds?"

"Because if I did, I couldn't wear these," she said, turning around and shaking her butt.

"I see."

"It's my metabolism," she said, advancing on him. "My metabolism is very fast, Crockett," she continued, laying an arm on each of his shoulders. "Lots of warm-blooded animals have fast metabolisms. Did you know that Crockett? Did ya?"

She leaned into him a bit, and her voice dropped into a purr.

"Fuzzy little bunnies for instance, and cute little minks, and quick little foxes. They all have fast metabolisms, Crockett, just like me."

She leaned in a bit more from the pelvis, her eyes wide and innocent.

"All those furry little animals and I have something else in common too, Crockett. Did ya know that?"

Crockett couldn't answer without clearing his throat. He kept quiet.

"All of us, the warm bunnies, the sleek minks, the pretty foxes, and me, Crockett, we all have something we really love to do." She kissed him gently on the chin. "We really love to *eat*. Hurry up! I need food."

"I don't think I can walk right now."

"That your cane, Crockett? Or are ya just glad to see me?"

"Ruby!"

She chuckled all the way to the car.

FORTY-ONE
Playing

THAT EVENING Crockett took a hot soak in a pretty nice size tub for a motel, walked out into the room with a towel wrapped around his waist, and encountered Ruby sprawled on his bed, watching HBO. She whistled.

"Don't do it if you don't mean it," he said.

"For a decrepit old man, you could be worse."

"Don't you have a room of your own?"

Ruby bounced up off the bed and posed. "So, whatcha think?"

Ruby was wearing a long purple t-shirt, heavy white socks turned down to the ankles, and a ponytail wrapped in one of those white scrunchy things

Crockett peered at her critically, wishing he was wearing more than a towel. "Quite youthful," he said.

"That's it?"

"Ah—"

"I don't wanna put any pressure on you, Crockett. God knows you old guys can't handle pressure, but I dressed in this high school slumber party thing especially to see if I could embarrass you, and that's all I get?"

"Oh."

"Okay," Ruby said. "If this outfit doesn't tickle your fancy, what does? What do you like?"

"I beg your pardon?" he said, digging some sweats out of his suitcase while keeping his back to her.

"Sophisticated socialite, expensive call-girl, sleazy stripper, naughty nurse. What blows your skirt up, Crockett?"

"Gimme a minute," he said, and slipped into the bathroom.

"Me too," Ruby said.

When Crockett came back into the room she was gone, but returned shortly wearing black heels, dark hose, an above-the-knee leather

140

skirt, a long-sleeved dark blue blouse, and lipstick. Her hair was down. She sat at the table and put on a pair of glasses with thin black frames.

"And who would this be?" Crockett asked.

Ruby slowly crossed her legs. "The sensuous secretary, I should think," she said.

"Very nice," he said.

"Men are so strange about sex. We are led to believe that women are the ones who are coy, who must be manipulated and romanced, sought after and seduced, but on the whole, that's bullshit. It's really men who require seduction and fantasy to perform."

Crockett thought about that for a moment.

"You know, you're probably right."

"Ya think?"

"I really do, Ruby. I never looked at it that way before."

"For most men, Crockett. I make a generality. Generalities are fine until they are applied to specifics. You, for instance."

"Me?"

"Yep. The schoolgirl fantasy you encountered in this very room. You were turned on?"

"Sure."

"Thank you," Ruby said. "Now think about this. Was it the schoolgirl that turned you on?"

He considered carefully.

"No. It was you, playing the schoolgirl."

"And the secretary you see before you," she said, sitting very straight and proper. "How 'bout her?"

Ruby's pen slipped from her grasp.

"Oh, excuse me," she said. "My pen seems to have fallen to the carpet. Would you please?"

Crockett leaned down to retrieve the pen from where it had fallen beside her feet, and Ruby slowly crossed her legs.

"You writing a book, LaCost?" he said.

"Private research. The secretary?"

"You playing the secretary."

"I see."

"No. That's not quite right. Just you playing. Trying to get a peek at the duck, or harassing me, or putting your feet in my tub, or bumping me with your butt, or a thousand other things you do or have done. The play."

"You enjoy it when I play?"

"You bet. Do you?"

"I love to play."

"That's it then," Crockett said. "I would not enjoy your play nearly as much, if at all, if you did not enjoy it also."

"I am an exhibitionist, I suppose."

"But a selective one. You do not leave your curtains open, or wear trench coats to schoolyards."

"I do, however, wear provocative clothing."

"But that is not what we are talking about, is it?"

"No. That is a tool, a means to an end," she said.

"So why me? Because you're safe with me? You have control?"

She thought a moment. "That's probably part of it, subconsciously at least."

"What's the rest of it?"

"The fact that I love you," she said. "Plus, you seem to enjoy it, even when it embarrasses you."

Crockett laughed. "I love you too, LaCost, and I do enjoy it. If what you said about men's needs is true, then women don't need that type of stimulation as much as men do?"

"Speaking in generalities, no, they don't."

"So you enjoy my responses and I enjoy responding."

"Another question," Ruby said. "Do I go too far? Or, perhaps, not far enough?"

He smiled. "There's safety there for me too, Ruby."

"Ah. Performance concerns?"

"Sure. Also fear of rejection."

"That's fair. I sometimes wish I could be more accommodating."

"I sometimes am glad you are not."

Ruby smiled, bouncing her leg up and down to distract him.

"So, how would you, a man, define this twisted relationship the two of us battered souls share?"

"Other than control and power for the female and torture and retribution for the male?"

"Other than those."

"We are lovers, Sweetheart," Crockett said, "in all of the really important ways."

Tears leapt to her eyes. She removed her glasses and crossed to the bed to put her arms around him. Her nylons whispered and he smelled White Shoulders.

"Aw, Crockett. That may be the best thing anybody has ever said to me in my life."

Crockett flopped on his back, reached out, and patted her bottom.

"Not to change the subject, LaCost, but that sure is a great butt ya got there."

She shifted her position a bit, up onto one hip.

"Always more where that came from, Big Boy."

"Aw, shit," he said, and flopped over on his stomach.

"You can't win, Crockett. But don't let the fact that you'll never beat me dissuade you from trying. I do so love it when you try."

Face down on the bed he muttered at her.

"Kiss my ass."

She pulled down his sweats, did exactly that, and snapped them back up.

"LaCost!!"

Ruby giggled, enjoying herself.

"Gotcha," she said.

FORTY-TWO
Old Friends

THE NEXT MORNING Crockett called the Champaign Police Department and got the address on East University Avenue for the building containing the office of the Chief of Police. He cleaned up and got dressed in his best new suit, a charcoal-gray double breasted with a tiny cranberry stripe, a white shirt with French cuffs, a dark cranberry silk tie, and black dress loafers.

Ruby walked into the room without knocking as Crockett was adjusting his tie in front of the mirror. He saw her and posed a la Sears catalogue.

"Damn, Crockett," she said, "if you'd looked like that last night, even I might have handed over my honor."

"You don't have any honor."

"The cane really sets the whole thing off. You look almost good enough to eat, so to speak, but aren't you a little overdressed to take me to Pauline's Pancake Pavillion, or wherever it is we're going for breakfast?"

Crockett shook his head. "Daniel Beckett, special investigator for the Department of Justice, and/or The Illinois Bureau of Investigation, has an appointment with the Chief of Police in about thirty minutes. Hopefully I'll get to see the County Sheriff today, too."

"Do you mean that I am to be abandoned to my own devices?"

"Would any of those devices be battery powered?"

"Only three of them," Ruby said. "Proof that a man can be replaced by the Energizer Bunny."

Crockett climbed into the black Chevy Impala he'd rented and headed for downtown. He only got lost once and made it to the Chief's office five minutes early. The receptionist smiled.

"Good morning, may I help you?"

"I made an appointment yesterday afternoon to see the Chief this morning. Daniel Beckett?"

"Yes, Mr. Beckett. You're with the Department of Justice?"

"That's correct. By the way, who is the Chief? I don't know his name."

"Daniel Harter."

Crockett chuckled. "When you let Dan know I'm here, tell him I'm very angry and upset with him, okay? I absolutely promise that you won't get into any trouble."

"You know him?"

"I was his T.O. when he was a rookie."

"You were the Chief's training officer?"

"Yup."

She smiled, picking up the phone and pushing a button.

"Chief, your nine o'clock is here, the guy from Justice ... yessir ... I don't know sir, but he's really pissed about something ... he was talking on a cell phone when he came in. Said something about reaming you out ... yessir, right away, my pleasure!"

"Good job," Crockett said.

She grinned and her eyes crinkled. "That's the door right over there," she said. "He's ready for you."

Harter was sitting behind a massive oak desk, his back to the door, looking out the window. He seemed poised in his chair, obviously not prepared to take any shit from some Justice Department weenie. When Crockett slammed the door, the Chief neither flinched, nor turned around. He did, however, growl.

"When you come in my office, Bub, you shut the door, you don't slam it. That way, maybe I'll let you stay a while."

Crockett growled back. "When I come in your office, Asshole, you turn around and address me properly. That way, maybe I won't throw you out your own fucking window."

Harter bolted to an upright position quickly enough to propel his chair violently into the desk, and whirled around like he's heard a rattlesnake.

Crockett laughed. "Jesus Christ, Rookie, slow down. A man your age shouldn't move that fast. It's bad for the blood pressure."

Harter froze and peered across his desk. "Crockett?"

"The way you treat visitors, it's a damn good thing it is. That badge goin' to your head, or you always this grouchy nowadays?"

"Jesus Christ! Crockett!"

Their hug was long and loud and full of all sorts of stereotypical male-bonding. After they stopped pounding on each other and trading insults, they sat down. Harter picked up his phone.

"Patty," he said, "get in here!"

Still smiling, Patty was through the door in less than ten seconds.

"I don't blame you for this," Harter said. "He always could talk anybody into anything. Just don't ever relax around him. He's not a nice person."

"This old reprobate gives you any shit, Patty," Crockett said, "you just let me know. I'll personally hand you a list of a few of his rookie fuck-ups. That kind of privileged information will absolutely guarantee your immediate promotion out of this hell-hole and into a much better position."

"How can I reach you?" Patty said.

"If Crockett asks for the keys to my car, wants to rip off the wall paper, shoot the school board, or sell the furniture," Harter said, "it's on my unqualified authority. He and I have been through it together and I'd go through it with him again. In a heartbeat. You understand?"

"Yessir," she said.

"Here's the situation," Crockett said. "You did not hear him call me Crockett. As a matter of fact, I wasn't ever here. We've never talked, you've never met me. Okay?"

"Yessir. Okay."

Harter glanced at Crockett, then turned to Patty. "What's my schedule for today?"

"Mayor at ten, city manager for lunch, Judge Tillman at two, department of human resources at three, city council dinner and meeting tonight."

"Jesus."

"Yessir, Jesus."

"How 'bout tomorrow?"

"Morning is full, lunch with councilman Ryan, two o'clock with some women's group."

"Blow off Ryan and the women. Something very important has come up."

"Yessir. Consider it done," she said, and left.

Harter squinted at Crockett. "What's all this crap about the Justice Department?"

Crockett placed both his ID's on his desk, along with his new driver's license and credit cards. "Or the IBI," he said. "Your choice."

"Any of this stuff legit?"

"Run any checks you like, Chief. Every piece will prove out. Justice and the IBI will tell you I'm real, but not what I'm doing. The driver's license is valid, the credit card is solid gold. The only thing that isn't legit is me, but I got some power behind me that is real scary. I'm after a guy that needs to get got, and I'm gonna get him. Legally if I can, but illegally if I have to. The object here is not law, but justice. One way or the other, justice will be served."

"What do you need from me?"

"Maybe nothing but an introduction to the Champaign County Sheriff. The last one I knew was Everette Hedrick. Maybe a lot more than that."

"Whatever it is, you got it, Crockett."

"Thanks. You're pressed for time. I'll give you the whole story on this at lunch tomorrow. Wear plainclothes. We don't need publicity."

"We don't need to eat in town either," Harter said. "Meet me at the Hen House on I-74 at the Mahomet exit around noon. And do us both a favor. Stay the fuck outa trouble at least until lunch."

"You know me," Crockett said.

Crockett drove around a bit, thinking about how great it was to see Harter again and how good it was to have a friend in the area, then headed for a grocery store. He picked up a pound of fresh steamed shrimp, a wedge of brie, a couple of bottles of a nice Australian Shiraz, and arrived back at the Marriott Courtyard a little after noon. Ruby's car was in the lot. He knocked on her door.

"Who is it?" she asked.

"Titus Canby, and his wonderful whiffle bat," Crockett replied, repeating a line he had rehearsed for two miles.

"Can you come back in a couple of hours, Titus? The Flying Wallendas are here right now and I don't wanna throw off their timing."

"Two hours?" he whined.

"Yeah. And it's BYOB."

"But I have booze!

"Batteries, Titus. Batteries."

FORTY-THREE
Time Warp

CROCKETT CHANGED CLOTHES and they went out for lunch at one of those cookie cutter joints. He drove the rented Impala. Ruby bitched.

"Jesus, what a hippo! I should have driven the Corvette. You could have taken nine Dramamine and missed the whole thing."

"Thought we'd take a jaunt around the old home town," Crockett said. "I haven't been here in a very long time."

"I'm right here if you need me."

"If I need you?"

She patted him on the leg. "When you need me. You really haven't been back here since you moved to Kaycee?"

"Never. Walked away from it. Well, limped away from it," Crockett said.

"You had a lot of it with you when you first came to me."

Crockett turned the corner onto State Street.

"You see that row of town houses? Used to be duplexes. Karen and I had our first place there. Gone now."

Most of it was. They spent about three hours driving around the city. Almost every place that Crockett was attached to didn't exist anymore. Where he grew up, where his first girlfriend lived, his apartment before he and Karen got married, a couple of the clubs they used to go to, all gone. Everything all seemed smaller and more seedy.

"How ya doin, Crockett?"

"Any chance of getting a little pity?"

"Nope."

"Pretty good. I keep waiting to feel bad or something, but it's just not happening." They stopped at a red light and Crockett looked at her. "Am I repressing a bunch a shit?"

"I don't think so. You body language doesn't say you are. I'm not getting many signs of internalized stress. Anything you'd like to say out loud that you're whispering internally?"

"I don't think so."

Ruby studied him as they passed his old high school and went on to cruise down Church Street to First, then onto Green, heading for the campus to see if the Steak n' Shake or Abe's Red Hots was still around.

Ruby sighed and shook her head. "We see this type of thing in my profession from time to time, Crockett. It's not common, but it does manifest itself in some people."

"Shit. What?"

"Sanity."

"Huh?"

"You've moved on, Big Guy. You have reached the point where the demons of your past are placed in proper perspective with your present and aligned with your future. You have acquired an internal balance and an equalized perspective. Are you cured? No. Nobody is ever cured. There is no destination for this trip we take. But you, David Allen Crockett, with the exception of still some guilt over Paul's death, are proceeding on your journey with very little negative baggage from what has gone before. You, of course, owe it all to me."

"As I look around," Crockett said, "none of this seems real."

"It isn't any more real than a dream."

"That corner over there, Fourth and University? The police Chief, Dan Harter, and I took twenty-one rounds of automatic weapon's fire through our squad car there one night. It really doesn't make any difference to me now."

"I pronounce you recovered from the effects of those days," Ruby said.

"Well, if that's true, why do I keep you around?"

"Overwhelming respect for my supreme ability as a therapist."

"Sure."

"Overwhelming curiosity about my life as a female homosexual."

"No doubt."

"Plus, you love me. And, in your heart or hearts, you desire access to my charms."

"Every man should have a goal."

"Congratulations, Crockett."

"Thanks, but I don't feel like I really did anything. It's like I was struggling to climb a mountain, and then I looked around and the mountain wasn't there anymore. I didn't reach the top or anything, it just went away."

"That's the way it's supposed to feel when it goes really well," Ruby said. "You didn't kill it, you didn't beat it, you just released it. The popular myth is that to achieve we must fight and struggle. We must declare war on something. That's all ego-based bullshit. It's much easier on us to just let it go than it is to strangle it to death. You done good."

"Thanks, Ruby."

"Before we bring up all the twisted neurosis that you haven't dealt with yet, it's celebration time. Find a Baskin-Robbins, or someplace like that. We'll have some ice cream, then go back to the Marriott. You'll take a soak, I'll take a shower, we'll drink Shiraz, eat Brie, suck shrimp, and I will tantalize you with my naughty wardrobe."

"Sounds perfect."

Ruby smiled. "Perfect it ain't, Crockett," she said, and patted him on the knee, "but it will damn sure do 'til perfect comes along."

FORTY-FOUR
Something Wicked

CROCKETT DIDN'T WAKE UP until nearly nine the next morning. Ruby had been in rare form the night before and it was nearly two before she toddled off to her room. He lay awake until nearly three. When he came out of the bathroom, slightly hung over and moving low and slow, she was sitting at his table, looking lovely and composed in a deep red sweater and her gray skirt, complete with charcoal tights and her black boots. Her hair was down and her make-up was perfect. She smiled at him.

"Hi, Sailor. New in town?"

Crockett clutched at his towel. "Anybody ever teach you how to knock?" he said.

"Sure, but I find that I get to see a lot more interesting things if I don't."

"You are amazing."

"That's true, but what makes you say so this time?"

"You look like you just stepped out of a picture frame. I look like shit, I feel like shit, and there you stand, rested, refreshed, and so pretty it almost breaks my heart. Do you ever look like hell?"

Ruby glared at him. "You make a compliment sound like a accusation, you grouchy old bastard," she said. "The answer to your so elegantly phrased question is no. Even with the stomach flu and screaming diarrhea, complicated by ringworm, a head cold, and a boil on the end of my nose, I teeter on the brink of perfection. I also never lose my white hat in a bar fight."

"I was afraid of that," Crockett said.

As he moved behind her to get some clothes, he patted her butt.

"Ooh," Ruby said. "Fondling my bottom and the day has barely begun. Something wicked this way comes."

"Why don't you fondle your way to the lobby," Crockett said, "and bring back some of that bad coffee and a couple of those dry pastries while I get dressed?"

"Okay," she said, passing behind him and grabbing his butt. "That, for future reference, was a grope."

She giggled as she went out the door. Crockett hurried to get dressed.

He was fully clothed by the time she got back.

"Aw," Ruby said, "you put it all away!"

"Eat your heart out."

She kissed him on the cheek and put a small tray on the table. The coffee was in real cups, not Styrofoam containers, and the pastries looked recent.

"China?" he asked.

"Only the best for us, Crockett. I ran into the chef. The coffee is from his private urn and the cinnamon rolls are from his oven. First class all the way."

"You just ran into him and he volunteered to bypass all the normal procedures and do all this just for you."

"Well, I may have offered him some encouragement. He is a man and therefore putty in my hands, so to speak."

"You coerced a poor, defenseless chef!"

"Jealous?"

Crockett took a sip of the coffee. "Delighted, actually."

"Do you think I'm terrible, Crockett?"

"I think you are admirably honest. A rare quality that often makes life more difficult. To capitalize on it when you can is not only not terrible, it is richly deserved. Especially when it benefits me. Good coffee. Thanks."

"A quality we share, Crockett. You could have done the same thing if it were a female chef."

"So could you."

She laughed. "There's that."

They munched in silence for a time, then Ruby looked at him.

"So, what's the agenda for today?"

"We'll leave for lunch pretty soon."

"How long does it take to get there?"

"About ten minutes out I-74 from Champaign to Mahomet. The restaurant is right off the highway. I wanna be there at least an hour early. We'll take both cars. You'll wait until I'm inside for about five minutes, then come in and sit as far away from me as you can, where you can watch the whole room."

"Ooh! Spy stuff."

"Sorta. I wanna know who comes in before the scheduled meeting and I want you there to look for anybody looking at me or Harter."

"Will I meet this guy?"

"If everything seems okay after a while, I'll call you over. You'll maintain your cover completely."

"Bond," she said. "James Bond. I'm with Universal Export."

"Eat your roll and do the boogie," Crockett said. "I'll be about five minutes behind you. Park where you can view as much of the lot as possible. After I arrive, watch for any cars that follow me in. If somebody looks suspicious, get the license number before you come inside. You know the drill in the dining area."

"I-74 west to Mahomet."

"About ten miles, exit south, the Hen House is right there. Go, James."

Ruby stood up, put on a short trench coat, and headed for her room. Stopping in the door, she smiled.

"You know, you're the only one for me, Moneypenny."

Crockett laughed. "In this room," he said.

With a furtive glance from side to side, she shut the door. In a few seconds, Crockett heard her outside door slam.

It had begun.

FORTY-FIVE
Rosebud at the Henhouse

CROCKETT WAS ABOUT HALFWAY to the Mahomet exit when his phone rang.

"Yeah?"

"The horn blows at midnight," Ruby said.

"Jeremiah was a bullfrog," he replied.

"Wrong," she said. "The password is swordfish. I saw it in a Marx Brothers movie. I'm in the parking lot."

"LaCost, the way you drive, you've probably already had something to eat."

"The bacon is fat, the eggs are greasy, but the gravy ain't bad."

"Go away," Crockett said.

"Rosebud signing off," she replied.

When Crockett pulled into the parking lot, he spotted her Corvette near the back. Not many cars. He parked in the front row, got out, and walked inside. Several people glanced his way when he entered. The place was about half full. He grabbed an empty table near the rear, away from the counter. A waitress hurried over. Forty, skinny, bottle-red hair, chewing gum. If she had worn a nametag, it would have said Flo.

"Canna gitcha, Hon?"

"Just a cuppa mud. S'posed to meet a fella. Gotta while to wait."

"Ain't seen ya before. Trucker?"

"Naw. On the way to Bloomington. Just gotta meet a guy. Okay to smoke?"

"Betcha. Mud comin' up." She sashayed away.

Crockett looked around the room. Maybe thirty men and ten women. Nobody seemed to be paying any attention to him. He lit a Sherman and Flo showed up with a coffee pot and a clear glass ashtray. No water.

"There ya go, Sweetie. Gitcha anything else?"

"Naw, thanks. This'll be just fine. I may be here for a while though. You won't forget about me, willya?"

"Honey, five rum an' Cokes wouldn't git me to forget about you," she said, and headed back to the counter. At that moment, Ruby came in the front door.

The noise level in the room dropped by half and many heads turned. Slowly, and with complete indifference to anybody in the place, she removed her trench coat and hung it by the door. The noise level dropped again, and everybody in the room knew she was there.

Deliberately, Ruby strolled through the dining area, down the counter, and took a sideways seat on a stool near the end, on the opposite side of the room from Crockett. She let her gaze flick over the patrons, leaned an elbow on the counter, casually crossed her legs, and smiled to herself. The place gave a collective sigh and gradually the noise came back up. She owned the room and everybody in the joint knew it. Crockett smiled, betting she pissed Flo off.

Dan Harter arrived a little before noon as the place was beginning to fill up. Crockett stood up to get his attention. Harter saw him, walked over, shook hands, sat down, and grinned.

"What the hell are you into, Crockett?"

"I'm after a very bad man. He abuses children in the worst possible ways, he killed his wife about thirty years ago, he murdered his daughter, or had it done, late last summer. He is prominent, he is wealthy, he is respected, and he is going to be dealt with."

"Sweet Jesus."

He gave Dan a brief rundown on the whole story. As Crockett talked with him, now and then Harter's gaze wandered to Ruby. She ignored him.

"So what do you wanna know about the Champaign County Sheriff?" Dan asked.

"He okay?"

"Straight arrow. Tough. Marine vet. We get along okay. His name is Mike Shipley. He's been County Sheriff eight or ten years."

"I wanna talk to him about the Hyatt County Sheriff."

"You figure this Morrison owns him?"

"Probably, or a piece of him."

"I wouldn't doubt it. I don't really know him, met him a couple a times. Lester F. Dawkins is his name. He's been Hyatt County High Sheriff for twenty years or so. Every time there's an election somebody runs against him, but it doesn't seem to make any difference. Hyatt County is a whole different world."

"I used to have an uncle that raised hogs out that way. It was country as hell back then."

"Probably worse now," Dan said. "I think the population is stagnant, maybe even dropping. You watch your butt, Buddy." His eyes flicked back to Ruby. Crockett grinned at him.

"Well, damn!" Harter said. "I'm not too old to look. I don't think I'd ever be to old to look at that. That is one handsome woman."

"You want a closer peek?" Crockett said, and stood up.

"What the hell are you doing?"

"Maybe she'll join us," he said, walking away.

"Jesus. Crockett!"

He collected Ruby and they walked to the table. Dan was squirming like a butterfly on a pin.

"Randi," Crockett said, "may I present my old friend Dan Harter, chief of the Champaign City Police Department. Dan, this is Miss Randi DeMoss. Randi is my partner in this venture."

Dan blushed and stood up. "My pleasure, Miss DeMoss," he said.

Ruby laid a long slow smile on him and Crockett could feel Harter's knees get weak.

"I've been watching you for a long time," she purred, extending a hand. "I'm so glad Crockett finally ended the suspense. I was hoping we'd get to meet."

Harter took her hand, and Crockett watched his ears get red. He winked at Ruby, and she chuckled.

"Please take your seat, Dan," she said. "Just think of me as one of the guys."

"Not very damn likely," Harter said.

"I accept the compliment," Ruby said, "and thank you." She sat down.

"Just to let you know who you're dealing with, as I assume Crockett has not done, I am a clinical psychologist employed to assist Crockett in his investigation and empowered by the same agencies that he is."

"Miss DeMoss—"

"Please, Dan, call me Randi. I don't want to be uncomfortable around you."

"Okay, Randi. From what I have been told, the two of you are doing something that needs to be done. Crockett and I have been through some very tough stuff together. Although he will not admit it, I credit him with saving my life on at least two occasions. I will do anything within my power to help him and, of course, you."

"He told me even before we came here, that we could count on you. Thank you, Dan."

Harter tore his eyes away from Ruby and turned to Crockett.

"What can I do?" he said.

"A call from you to set up an appointment with Sheriff Shipley and a commercial to establish me as a good guy from the Justice Department. You've known me for years. I only work on very serious stuff. It

156

would be a feather in his cap to help. I'm a top cop, super trooper, all that stuff. Just don't tell him what it's about. I'll do that."

"You got it. What else?"

"Hopefully nothing, but there may be. When I eventually go see this Hyatt County Sheriff, if he is dirty, he's not gonna like me one little bit. When I do that, I'm gonna use Champaign as my base of operations. Something may come up. I want a phone number where I can reach you anytime, day or night. I may have to ask for a favor in a hurry, without the time to go through channels."

"You got that, too. Next?"

"I don't have any idea. Probably not a damn thing, maybe a bunch. I won't know until I know. We'll be in town until I talk with Shipley, then we'll pull out. When we come back I'll let you know we're in the area. I wish I could be more definite than that, but I can't. We're winging it. That's why I want to get as much background on the Sheriff and Morrison as I can. I'm probably going to have to pressure one or both of them to make a move and see what flushes out."

"If what you have told me is accurate," Harter said, "this could be some dangerous shit. You watch your ass, both of you. You packin'?"

"Nope."

"That's stupid. You're licensed, you're legal. Carry a gun, goddamn it!"

"Rather not."

"Christ, Crockett! Randi, how 'bout you?"

"Not me."

"Idiots. A couple of idiots! If you change your minds, I'll get you anything you want or need, you got that?"

They nodded. Harter pulled out two business cards, and wrote on the back of each.

"Here's my hotline number. I keep a special cell phone with me at all times. It's even within reach when I shower. You call this number and, if I'm not dead, I'll be on the other end within eight rings. You need me, you got me."

Crockett thanked him and gave him both their cell phone numbers.

"I'll call you by five today and let you know when Sheriff Shipley is expecting you. Keep me posted, Crockett. It's great to see you. When this is all over, we'll get drunk and you can tell me the whole story. Same goes for you, Randi," Harter said, and stood up. "Maybe I could even talk you out of your real name."

Ruby laid a sultry smile on him. "Dan," she said, "there is probably very little you couldn't talk me out of."

"Right," Harter grunted, and walked out of the restaurant. Ruby looked at Crockett and yawned.

"LaCost," he said, "you are incredible. You could probably get damn near anything, from damn near any man on the globe!"

"I don't want anything from any man but you, Crockett. And I already have that."

"Yeah, you do," he said. "So, what do you think of Harter?"

"He's got a lot of respect for you. Some deep sorrow there, too."

"He was first on the scene after I got shot. He had a real tough time with it."

"Still does," she said.

"Yeah."

"He'll do anything we want, get anything we need. We can count on him."

"We can trust him to try to do what he says he'll do, no doubt about that, Ruby, but it's *us*, and only us, that we can count on. If the shit gets deep, Darlin', we will be the ones in it."

"Aw, Crockett," she said, "don't beat around the bush. You can be totally frank with me."

FORTY-SIX

Dolphins

CROCKETT TRIED TO FOLLOW RUBY back to the motel, but she left him in the dust. As he pulled into the parking lot, the phone rang. It was Dan Harter.

"Tomorrow morning, seven-thirty, my office, you and Sheriff Shipley."

"That was quick."

"Just got off the phone with him. He suggested you two meet somewhere other than his office."

"What else did you tell him?"

"That you were a federal agent, that you were a good guy, we were old friends, and that this was a very special situation. Stuff like that."

"You tell him my name?"

"Nope. I didn't give him a name at all. I wasn't sure how you wanted to handle that."

"I'm not either. Can I trust him?"

"Yeah. I think so."

"What makes you say that?"

"He hates assholes."

Crockett laughed. "How's he feel about you?"

Harter chuckled. "Can't stand me," he said.

"You gonna be there in the morning?"

"I'll be around long enough to introduce you guys and put you in a room."

"The room clean?"

"I'll make sure. I got a couple of pretty sneaky dicks around."

"Ain't they all. Sounds good. Thanks Dan, I mean it."

"And I meant what I said. Anything, anytime. Now, five years from now, whatever. I'm just glad to see you."

"Well, you'll get another peek at me in the morning. I'll be there at seven-thirty."

"Oh! How do I introduce you?"

159

"Agent Beckett will do just fine."

"Don't wanna use your real name, huh?"

"Better not. The bad guy probably knows it."

"Randi's real name Randi?"

"Nope."

"Bet that's about the only thing that ain't real."

"If you only knew," Crockett said.

"Don't wanna know," Harter said. "Fantasies are a lot safer. Woman like that could roll over in her sleep and cripple ya for life. Just lookin' at her'll fuck up my blood pressure for two days. She gonna be there tomorrow?"

"I don't think so."

"Probably safer."

"For who?"

"See ya in the morning, Crockett."

When Crockett walked into his motel room, the connecting door was open. Ruby yelled from the other side.

"I'll be right over. What took you so long?"

"On the phone with Harter. I meet the sheriff early tomorrow," Crockett said. He was hanging up his jacket when Ruby spoke again.

"Me too?"

"No. You've done enough damage to local law enforcement as it is," he said.

Crockett flopped on the bed and slipped an extra pillow behind his head. Ruby walked in wearing an oversized dress shirt over her tights. She was barefoot.

"Are you saying that I had a negative effect on Chief Harter?"

"I don't know if negative is the right word. Effect certainly is."

"He was peeking at my legs the whole time you were talking to him."

"And at your chest the whole time you sat with us."

"Yes," Ruby breathed, batting her eyes. "I know."

"So you enjoy it when men look at you?"

"I dress for it, so I have no right to bitch about it," Ruby said. "Women that do, piss me off. Cleavage to the navel, a skirt to the ass, spray painted jeans, or a nipple-factory sweater, and 'Oh! He looked at me! Men are such pigs!' Please. Then there's the whole other thing. 'I'm a liberated woman, I have the right to dress any way I want! These male chauvinist assholes just take advantage of me by leering when I claim my freedom to dress as I please!' That makes as much sense as a stripper telling the audience not to peek!"

"Let's see," Crockett said, "where did I leave that soap box?"

Ruby laughed. "To get off the pulpit and answer your question—"

"And that question was?"

"Do I enjoy it when men look at me."

160

"Ah. Yes."

"Let's say that, if I'm asking for it, I appreciate it when men look at me."

"Power trip?"

"Sure," she said. "Except with you."

"Me?"

"Yeah," Ruby said.

She smiled, sat down on the bed next to him, and stretched. "I like it when you look at me."

"Aw jeeze."

"Whaddaya mean, 'aw jeeze?'"

"You know damn good and well what I mean, you shit," Crockett said. "You'd rather tease me than eat!"

"As opposed to the reverse of that statement," Ruby said, bopping her foot up and down.

"Jesus, Ruby!" Crockett laughed, as it dawned on him what she meant. He struggled on, trying to change the subject. "Is that my shirt?"

"The very one you wore yesterday."

"You've got on my dirty shirt?"

"Sure. It smells like you. I like the way you smell."

"Oh-oh."

"Oh-oh? Whadaya mean oh-oh?" she said, her eyes getting wide and innocent. "Scent is very important. I read somewhere that scent has dolphins in it that attract people. Don't you think I smell good, Crockett?"

"Oh, Christ. Here we go."

"Here," Ruby said, leaning over him. "I'll get closer so you can smell my dolphins and see if they attract you. It's like an experiment or something! I think science is so exciting don't you? It's where we got Velcro!"

"Ruby, goddammit—"

"Okay, okay," she said, bounding up off the bed, and bouncing on her toes. "I'm hungry. Why don't you order us a pizza, we'll eat, and then maybe we can experiment with my dolphins some more."

Crockett got up to look for the phone book. There was no other refuge.

FORTY-SEVEN
Off the Record

CROCKETT WAS UP EARLY the next morning fully dressed in sport coat, slacks, tie and such by seven AM. Ruby came wobbling in wearing her short white silk robe and, as far as he could tell, nothing else. She yawned and scratched her head. Even rumpled, she looked terrific. Her voice had a throaty rasp.

"Mornin', Crockey."

"Crockey?"

"Umm-hmm," Ruby grunted, and snuggled her face into his neck, hugging him. "Doan gimme shit. I still sleepin'," she muttered, leaning against his chest.

"Crockey?"

"Yeah, Crockey. You big an' warm an' fuzzy an' right now you feel like a Crockey," she grumped, her speech slurred by his collar. "Jus' stan' there an' hold me, willya?"

"Coffee and bad rolls on the table," Crockett said, doing as he was told. "I'd hoped for better, but I didn't get a shot at the chef."

"Likes girls." Ruby mumbled, squirming into him. "When ya leavin'?"

"Two minutes."

"No."

"Yes."

"No. Stay an' snuggle me."

"Can't."

"Won't.

"Can't."

"Okay," Ruby muttered, pulling away and adjusting her robe. "I hereby withhold sex."

"Ruby, you have been withholding sex from me for years."

"Come back to bed with me and cuddle."

"I have to go meet the Sheriff."

"Okay. I forgive you."

162

"Does this mean you'll stop withholding sex?"

"You nuts? I'm a dyke! Get outa here or you'll be late."

Crockett slipped on his trench coat and stepped out into the cool morning air.

Since Crockett knew where he was going and traffic was light, he arrived ahead of schedule. Dan Harter pulled in just after Crockett shut off the engine, headed for the building, and motioned him to follow. They went up a back set of stairs and entered directly into Dan's office through a side door.

"My bolt-hole," he said. His badge winked gold and silver on a custom-tailored uniform. "Coffee?"

"Sure."

Dan poured Crockett a hot cup from a pot on a timer and took one for himself. They heard noise from the outer office.

"That'd be Patty," Dan said. "I asked her to come in a little early. She'll let Shipley in when he arrives." His phone buzzed. "Yeah? Okay. Thanks for coming in." Harter looked at Crockett. "He's here already," he said, "be right in."

Crockett leaned his cane against the desk and took off his coat. The door opened, and Sheriff Shipley entered the office.

Shipley was about five feet ten, forty-five years old, around two hundred pounds, and not fat. His hair was high and tight, his uniform well pressed, his shoes shined, and his posture perfect. A Smith and Wesson model 686 with custom grips nestled in a high-rise holster on his left hip. He crossed to Dan and held out his hand.

"Mornin', Chief," he said.

His voice was thin and a little reedy, with a Midwest twang.

"Hello, Sheriff," Dan said. "Thanks for coming by. This is agent Beckett. Beckett, Sheriff Mike Shipley."

They shook hands. Shipley exerted just enough pressure to convince Crockett he was taking it easy. Jack Webb would have loved this guy.

"I've got a meeting," Dan said. "Why don't the two of you just use my office. I won't need it for an hour or so. Patty will see to it that you have privacy."

"Thanks, Dan," Crockett said. "If I don't see ya again this trip, I'll let you know when I'm back in town."

"Watch your ass, Buddy. Say goodbye to Randi for me."

"She'll be sorry she missed you."

Dan smiled. "I bet," he said, and left by the main door.

Crockett looked at Shipley. "Coffee?"

"Thanks," Shipley said and moved to a chair by a small table. Crockett poured him a cup and sat down. Shipley's gaze flickered back and forth between Crockett's cane and his limp.

"That your cane?" he asked, glancing toward the desk.

"Yep."

"You're Justice Department?"

"That's right," Crockett said, showing him some ID.

"What can the Champaign County Sheriff's Department do for the Department of Justice?"

"This isn't about agencies, Sheriff," Crockett said. "It's about people. I need information, off the record if you like."

"About what?"

"Lester F. Dawkins."

A smile teased the corner of Shipley's mouth. "Why?" he asked.

"I figure he's probably in the bag to a man named Martin Morrison."

"Morrison. I know the name. Head doctor or somethin' like that. Got a clinic in a big old place out in Hyatt County?"

"That's the guy."

"He the one you after?"

"He's the one."

Shipley thought for a moment. "What for?"

"Two murders, child abuse, other stuff."

"This personal?"

"I believe he is responsible for the death of a woman I loved and her mother. There is probably a lot more."

"Got proof?"

"No."

"Can you get it?"

"Maybe."

"Make any difference?"

"Not one damn bit."

Shipley grinned. "You gonna be breakin' laws in my county?"

Crockett shook his head. "I refuse to answer that on the grounds that you don't really want to know," he said.

"Can't help ya do that."

"I can do that by myself. I just need to learn all I can about Dawkins."

"Keith Mackey. Ran against Dawkins in the last election. Was a deputy for seven or eight years. Said Dawkins was a hairball. I expect he'd be willing to talk to ya."

"Keith Mackey," Crockett repeated, reaching for a pen.

"Ex-Jarhead, like me. Works in the lumberyard over in Hixon, the Hyatt County seat. Had to give up his job as deputy when he ran against Dawkins a couple of years ago. Not real bright, but smart enough to think Dawkins stinks."

"What do you think?"

"Tell ya what I don't think. I don't think you're Justice. I don't think you got that limp in a skateboard accident. I don't think your name is Beckett. I don't think I want to know what this is all about."

"Now tell me what you do think."

"I think Dawkins is as dirty as a dairy barn floor. Hyatt County don't pay their cops shit. Deputies have to use their own cars, buy their own weapons, uniforms and gear, even the red lights for their vehicles. Dawkins has been top dog for years. Runs that county like it's his own little kingdom. He's a disgrace to anybody behind a badge and his deputies are no better. If something is goin' on at that clinic or with Morrison, you can bet your last bullet if Dawkins ain't in on it, he damn sure knows about it."

Shipley took a sip of coffee.

"I think Keith Mackey will go out of his way to give you any information he has. I think you'll have a hard time proving anything, and I don't think that makes any difference to you. I think if you can do anything to cause Dawkins trouble, you're doing the world a service. That sonofabitch ain't worth a dead hog on a hot day."

"You know Mackey?"

"Not much."

"If I ask him to call you about me, what are you gonna tell him."

"I saw your credentials, I talked with you, I think you got good reason to do what you're doing, and I believe that if what you are doing works out, he'll will win the next election."

"Thanks, Sheriff. I couldn't ask for more."

"Lemme ask you a question. How come you ain't wearing a gun?"

"My strength is that of ten, because my heart is pure."

Shipley laughed. "Pure heart won't stop a bullet. Dawkins is a coward with some power. That makes him a dangerous man."

"So am I."

"I don't doubt that one bit. You got the eyes." He stood up. "That all?"

"That's all. Thanks for the help. I reserve the right to give you a call, if that's okay."

"Sure," Shipley said, handing Crockett his card. "Just don't tell me anything you're doing. I might have to stop you. Neither one of us would like that."

"Not a word," Crockett said.

They shook hands.

On his way out, Crockett stopped by the desk.

"Patty," he said, "if you ever get tired of that old fart you work for, find me. You can restore my youth and I'll renew your faith in men."

She beamed a lovely smile at him that grew into a grin. "If I get five hundred offers today," she said, "that'll still be the very best one." She dropped her voice to a whisper. "'Bye, Crockett. Be careful."

He blew her a kiss, and headed out the door.

165

FORTY-EIGHT

Breakdown

ON THE WAY BACK TO THE MOTEL it began to dawn on Crockett how changed his life was. Less than six months ago he was comfortably alone, relatively isolated from the world. Nudge and he were pulled back up into their cave, safe, secure, sedentary. Nobody made any demands except the occasional recording studio or agent. His time was his own, he was not responsible to anybody on the planet except himself. Then Ruby called asking if he had a gun. That simple inquiry dragged Crockett out of his hidey-hole and pushed him into the sun and the rain, the calm and the storm. He met Rachael and fell in like, and then in love, for the first time in twenty-five years. A few weeks later she was dead. Jesus.

He schlepped into the motel room in a funk. Ruby, dressed in country club frontier, was packing his stuff.

She smiled and wiped an errant lock of hair off her forehead.

"Hey, Sweetie," she said. "Let's go get some breakfast and head for home. Crockett? What's wrong?"

"Aw, Christ, Ruby. What the hell do I think I'm doing?"

She stopped packing and steered him to a chair at the table. "Sit," she said, taking a seat beside him. "Talk."

"About what?"

"About anything."

"The weather?"

"Great. Weather is good. Talk about the weather."

"Kinda gray out there today. Chilly, too. I don't know what I'm doing, La Cost."

"Whadaya mean?"

"I mean, I don't know what I'm doing! I've got a county sheriff and a police chief jumping through hoops, I got some mega-wealthy old woman from Chicago hanging her hopes on me, I got some Texi-can ex-spook of some kind opening doors I didn't even know existed, I've left my home and my work, I've spent thousands of dollars of

166

somebody else's money, I got over a hundred grand of that money stashed away for a rainy day, I got people expecting me to come up with a way to lay low some dirty bastard I've never even met, and ahead of me, as I slide down this shit-covered slope, I'm pushing you, the best person I have ever known!"

Crockett pulled his tie loose so violently, he popped the top button of his shirt.

"To top all that off, Rachael is dead. She's as dead as Julius Caesar. She will always, always be fucking dead! God damn this, Ruby. God damn this! This fucking sucks! I don't know what I am doing here! I can't handle this, Ruby. I can't handle it! I'm not equipped. I don't have the knowledge, I don't have the training, I don't have the expertise, I don't have the heart. And whether I do it or not, whether I succeed or not, whether I even try or not, Rachael will still be dead!"

Crockett's nose was stopped up and tears were streaming down his face. Ruby took his hands and led him to the bed where she undressed him and put him between the sheets. Weak as a kitten, he lay on his side and could not stop trembling. In a few minutes Ruby slipped into bed behind him and curled up against his back and legs. She wrapped her arms around him and kissed the back of his neck. That tender gesture, the warmth of her breath and the kindness of a simple kiss, pushed him over the edge. While Ruby spooned him and held him in her arms, Crockett sobbed like a child.

He groaned his way out of the bedroom around dusk to use the john and Mother Ruby was still there. She fed him four aspirins with a glass of chocolate milk and put him back to bed, sitting on the floor beside him as he slipped in and out of self-pity, blotting his tears with toilet paper. He woke up again a little after dawn when Ruby carried in an insulated carafe of hot coffee and a box of donuts. She smiled at him from her position beside the table.

"How are you?"

"Groggy," Crockett rasped. "My whole head hurts. Gotta whiz."

"Go whiz. Then I'll feed ya lots of complex carbos. Get your blood sugar up."

Only after he swung his feet to the floor and stood, did Crockett realize he was nude.

Ruby smiled. "Something is already up," she said. "Bring your own donut rack, or are you just glad I'm here?"

He lurched for the bathroom.

Ruby chuckled. "Aw, Crockett," she said, "I wanted to play ring toss."

He was standing under the shower, his forehead pressed into the wall, letting the hot water beat on his low back, when Ruby's dulcet tones wafted over the curtain.

167

"If you'll get your moldy ass out here and munch a donut or two, you'll get some goddammed energy! C'mon, Crockett! There's underwear, wind pants, and a sweatshirt on the sink. Shake a leg, or whatever else you might prefer."

When Crockett dragged himself out of the bathroom, Ruby, looking extremely L.L.Beanian, was sitting at the table. Across from her were two glazed donuts and a cup of coffee with cream.

She grunted at him. "Food. Eat much. Grow strong."

Crockett slumped into a chair. "Jesus," he said. "What the hell happened?"

"No talk now. Eat. Talk soon."

He took a bite of donut that he didn't want. It was wonderful. "Damn, that's good."

"You've had one glass of chocolate milk in twenty-four hours, Crockett. Load up on carbs and sugar. When we get out of here, we'll hit some protein to back it up."

"What was that?" he asked, between bites and slurps.

"A breakdown. It was overdue. I'd been expecting it for some time, but good old male bullshit kept pushing it away. Sometimes you people really piss me off."

"You people?"

"Males. You testosterone-ridden, beetle-browed, knuckle-dragging pansies, that are so afraid of being seen as even momentarily weak, you'll make yourselves sick with grief and doubt and worry rather than own up to the simple fact that you are just as sorry, just as scared, just as pathetically human as the rest of the species."

"Oh, us."

"Eat."

"Holler, but don't hit."

"You have been running on the ragged edge since we got back from Ivy's. You have not grieved sufficiently for Rachael's death, you have not gotten enough rest, you have not compartmentalized our mission, you have not talked enough, and you have not released stress. Yesterday that all came to a head. Thud."

"Did I do anything right?"

"Yes."

"What?"

Ruby grinned. "You hung around with me."

"Yeah, well, I've been thinking about that," Crockett said.

"What about it?"

"It's pretty strange."

"Certainly atypical," Ruby said. "You want a divorce?"

"I've just been thinking how fortunate I am. Thanks, Ruby. Not for just yesterday and last night, but for every day and every night and all these years."

"Crockett, you know that I don't do very damn much that I don't want to do."

"I know."

"Just remember that, any time you start getting overloaded with gratitude. I am where I am and with whom I am because I choose to be."

"I just wanted you to understand that I take very little of this thing of ours for granted."

"Part of any good relationship is being able to take certain things for granted and then celebrating the fact that you can take those things for granted. Your ears getting red on cue, for instance."

Crockett grinned around his last bite of donut. "I like living with you," he said. "I'm gonna miss that when all this is over."

"Me too, Raoul. It has crossed my mind that our living together is a pretty good arrangement."

"Mine, too."

"Unfortunately, any women that either of us were to become involved with might not totally appreciate the subtle nuances of our twisted relationship."

Crockett leered at her. "Unless you brought one or two home that batted from both sides of the plate."

"I might be a preevert, but that's a little much."

Crockett laughed. "It wouldn't work."

"No, it wouldn't," Ruby said. "Kinda nice, huh?"

"Yeah. Okay, since we're being honest here," he said, "lemme ask you a question. Were you ever jealous of Rachael?"

Her big brown eyes carressed Crockett like a flannel sheet.

"Jealous? No. Envious? Yes."

"Really?"

"Now that both Frank and Ernest are here, you bet. Envious that you and she could relate in ways that you and I cannot. Then I realized that you and I related and relate in ways that you and she could not. The envy went away and I was very happy for both of you."

"I see."

"Understand that I'm not just talking about fucking, Dolt."

"Did you just call me a fucking dolt?" Crockett asked.

Ruby ignored him. "I'm talking about a certain intimacy that comes between people who not only love each other, but are, or have been, lovers. There is something there that cannot be achieved in any other way."

"Ruby, Ruby, Ruby," he said, shaking his head. "I don't know, but I think a good man could straighten you out."

"Really?"

"Yep."

"And who, pray tell, could this marvelous individual possibly be, I wonder? Someone we both know?"

"Well," Crockett said, "just for the sake of argument, and speaking hypothetically, me."

"Zat right?"

"Yeah. Crockett to the rescue."

"What if I don't need to be rescued?"

"We all need to be rescued," Crockett said.

Ruby rose and came around the table, wiggled her way onto his lap, and gently pulled his earlobe with her teeth. Goosebumps ran up the back of his neck.

"Crockett," Ruby whispered, "what most of you people believe to be so invaluable to women, can easily be replaced by a medium size cucumber. Why the hell do you think it takes me so long to fix a salad?"

Crockett's ears got hot.

"Aw, shit!"

Ruby gave him a wet kiss on the cheek and giggled.

"Another Crockett moment," she said.

FORTY-NINE

Otters

THE RIDE HOME was uneventful, at least for Crockett. As Ruby predicted, he ate a huge breakfast and slept through most of the trip. After they got home and put everything away, she started fussing around in the kitchen. Crockett called Clete.

"Hey! How ya doin?"

"Fine, Cletus. Ruby's keeping me on the straight and narrow."

"What a burden for you," he chuckled.

"You have no idea. Need a favor or two."

"Shoot."

"Information on a couple of guys. Number one, Lester F. Dawkins. He is currently the county sheriff of Hyatt County, Illinois. Everything you can get from personal finances and expenditures, to campaign contributions, to IRS information, to what he likes for breakfast, immediate family, military record if any. I'm looking for dirt. I wanna know enough about this man to scare him to death."

"Gotcha. Who's next?"

"Keith Mackey. Ex-Dawkins deputy, ex-military, ran against the High Sheriff in the last county election. Only kind of location I have on him is that he works in a lumberyard in the county seat, Hixon, Illinois. Him I wanna impress with my wealth of knowledge and power. I want him to know that I'm ready to cause Dawkins trouble."

"Got it. I'll get after this tonight. You guys on the web?"

"Ruby! We on the web?"

"No! Soon."

"Not yet, she says, but soon."

"When you are, get me your E-Mail address. Meantime I'll send this stuff to ya Fed-Ex or something like that. Take three or four days. Anything else?"

"No," Crockett said. "That's about it. You want a report on what we're doing or anything?"

"Don't need it. Whatever you think is best is fine with us. Just yell if there is anything, and I mean anything, we can do on this end. As if it would be enough, give Ruby my best."

"Consider it done, Clete. Thanks."

Crockett wandered into the kitchen. Ruby was finishing putting sandwiches together.

"Smoked turkey, avocado, sprouts, baby Swiss, mayo, and dill pickles," she said.

"Dill pickles?"

"Yeah."

"They start out as cucumbers don't they?"

"They certainly do and I'm very fond of 'em. Don't give me any shit, Crockett. How's Cletus?"

"He asked me to give you his best."

"I don't think ol' Clete's best would be good enough."

Crockett laughed. "He said the same thing."

Ruby chuckled. "Might be more there than meets the eye. So, now what?"

She moved the sandwiches to the table and poured some water over ice.

"Now, nothing. We wait. We wait to hear from Morrison about your visit to him, we wait to hear back on my two guys from Clete. Things are out of our hands for a while."

"You okay with that?"

"Nothing I can do about it, one way or the other."

"Yes, there is," Ruby said. "You can chafe and worry and be impatient, or you can relax and enjoy the pleasure of my company. You may not have much control over our current circumstance but you have definite control over how to manage your reaction to it. Now would be a great time for you to lighten up and take it easy for a while."

"Okay," Crockett said. "Let's relax here for a day or two, then go to Omaha and visit the zoo."

"Isn't it a little cold for the zoo?"

"I will escort you through a salt water reef where sharks swim above our heads, I will walk you through three different tropical rain forests and, if we are very lucky, the otters will be so glad to see us they'll go nuts."

"In Omaha?"

"In Omaha."

Ruby sat across from him. "Crockett," she said, "never before has anyone ever offered to spirit me off to such exotic locales. You have a deal."

"If you have a desire to immerse your body in water while surrounded by a gaggle of screaming children, as I play miniature golf

172

and wave lovingly at you over the pinball machines and video games, we can even stay at the Hollidome on I-80."

"As wonderful as that sounds, on top of everything else it might be a bit much. I don't want sensory overload."

"Well," Crockett said, "as much as I hate to miss seeing you frolic with the children, I suppose there is somewhere else we could stay. We'll kick back tonight, then tomorrow afternoon head for Omaha. Okay?"

"Okay."

"We'll take the truck," he said. "I'll drive."

"I knew there'd be at least one string attached."

FIFTY
Cowboys and Indians

THE TRIP TO THE ZOO was a blast. Ruby behaved like a ten-year-old. She and Crockett wore themselves out enjoying the jungle and aquarium, stomping through the outside cold and acting like a couple of idiots. Crockett was right. The otters were so glad for company, they behaved as badly as the humans did just for the joy of it. Ruby bought an immense stuffed toy gorilla that she named Ego. He rode between them all the way back. It created quite a stir on the highway.

They returned home late Friday afternoon as a Fed-Ex van pulled up in front of the place with an envelope for Crockett. He left it on the kitchen counter while they unloaded, then carried it into the living room and lit the gas log.

Ruby took a break from bustling around the kitchen. "What's in the envelope?" she said.

"It's the info on Sheriff Dawkins and his ex-deputy."

Her cell phone rang upstairs. "Damn," she muttered, and headed up to answer it.

Crockett was still reading the stuff from Clete when she came back down. Ruby appeared a little pale and was chewing on her lower lip.

"Everything alright?" he said.

Ruby's voice was a monotone. "I just got off the phone with Martin Morrison," she said.

"You okay?"

"I think," she said. "That call was from Randi's office in Lincoln. He'd called there in response to the letter I sent. My cell phone is issued from Lincoln so while I had the nerve, I called him back. We have an appointment for one in the afternoon a week from this Monday. He's going to fax directions to his clinic to Randi's office. I'll get us on the Web tomorrow or the next day so the girl can E-mail the stuff to me. Jesus."

"Sorta scary, huh?"

174

"Up until now this has all been kind of a game."

"It's no game."

"No, it isn't," Ruby said. "I mean, I knew that. I knew it wasn't. I know it isn't. I know how serious all this is, but I guess it just didn't register until I heard his voice."

She crossed to sit on the couch beside Crockett, changed her mind, and went into the kitchen. Wine glasses clinked.

"You must be serious about this, Ruby," Crockett said, "but you cannot take it too seriously."

She put two glasses and a bottle of Merlot on the coffee table and flopped down next to him.

"What the hell is that supposed to mean?" she asked, her hand trembling a bit as she poured the wine. Crockett paused as he accepted a glass.

"It means cowboys and Indians," he said.

"Huh?"

"Look. When I was a cop, we had to do stuff all of the time that sane people would just not do. Sane people don't go in a dark warehouse to find a possibly armed burglar. Sane people don't knock on the front door of a house where the neighbors have reported a family fight with shots fired. Sane people don't drive a vehicle with a target on each front door through an area where they are likely to take fire."

"But you did all that."

"Yeah, and much worse, many times."

"How?"

"By knowing it damn sure is not a game and then treating it like one. On the way to a call with a life-threatening potential, we would usually be cracking jokes. We would treat the situation seriously, but not take the situation seriously. Take it all seriously, and in a very short time you'll be a Moon Pie."

"A Moon Pie?" Ruby said.

"Or a banana split, or a cherry parfait, or a hot fudge sundae, you get the drift."

"Would you still love me if I were a Moon Pie?"

"Absolutely not. But it would make it easier to get at your tender filling."

"And tender it is. It would seem to me that I must come to terms, on a mental level, with all that is occurring, while attempting to maintain a certain amount of detachment from the situation, the personal danger to me, the fear of what might happen to you, and related emotional encumbrance that can be manifest in a situation such as this."

"That's what I said. Cowboys and Indians."

"Exactly. And you'll help."

"And I'll help."

"Christ, Crockett. I have an appointment with the sonofabitch!"

"Randi DeMoss has an appointment with the sonofabitch," Crockett said.

"Right. Now who the hell is Randi DeMoss?"

"She is the woman who wrote him the letter. She is the woman who talked with him on the phone this evening. She can simply be you, LaCost! He doesn't know you, he's never talked with you, he's never heard from you. You don't have to fool him into believing you are someone you are not. The only possible thing he might know about you is your appearance, and you've changed that. You are another doctor coming to him with a problem. That's all. We've got a long week to work all this out. Relax."

Ruby changed the subject. "Anything good from Cletus?" she said.

"Sheriff Dawkins can be had. He will not run for election again."

"Really?"

"Yep. And that's how I get his ex-deputy on my side. He's got a family, makes less that twenty-two thousand a year, and is hungry. If I can guarantee him Dawkins is out of the picture and hand him a few grand for his election campaign, we got him. We get him, we're that much closer to getting Morrison."

Ruby cocked an eyebrow and lowered her voice. "Oh, Crockett!" she said, "could it possibly be that you are devious?"

"Anything's possible."

"I find this very exciting," she said. "I never even suspected. My goodness!"

"If you're gonna run with the big dogs, ya better know how to bark, Baby."

Ruby laughed and killed her glass of wine.

"So, order in, you cook while I slip into something to tease and tantalize, or go out? Make up my mind, Crockett. The only unacceptable option is for me to prepare a repast."

"Sweet and sour chicken, fried rice, crab Rangoon, egg rolls, and egg drop soup."

"Great! You order and set everything up. I'll bounce in the shower and slip into something more comfortable."

"Oh-oh."

"Do I detect a note of trepidation in your voice? What about access to my tender filling?"

"Every time you slip into something to get comfortable, it winds up affecting my comfort level too, you know."

"Yes, I know. Filmy and sheer, short and sexy, or slinky and sleazy?" She batted her eyes and gave him a toothy grin.

"For Christ's sake, Ruby. Whatever makes you most comfortable."

"Oh, goodie!" Ruby bounced off his lap and headed for the stairs.

Crockett was arranging the food on the coffee table when Ruby came down. She was wearing a dark blue terrycloth coverall, white socks, and had a towel wrapped around her head.

"Comfortable?" he asked.

"Yes," she said, "but never predictable."

FIFTY-ONE
Promises

DURING THE NEXT FEW DAYS Crockett watched Ruby gradually become accustomed to the fact that she was a secret agent. Her fear at facing Rachael's father declined to apprehension, then to nervousness, acceptance, confidence, and even eagerness. It crashed back into fear on the drive to Illinois, after they crossed the Mississippi.

"Crockett, I'm afraid."

"So am I. Slow the hell down."

"That's not what I mean."

"That is what I mean. You are forbidden to talk to me while this thing is in afterburner."

Ruby slowed to less than ninety.

"Better?"

"You may speak."

"You know that I am not the type of person to be riddled with doubt," Ruby said.

"Yes, I do."

"You also know that I sustain a fairly high degree of self-confidence."

"Indeed."

"I also believe that you are aware of the fact that when I have committed to a course of action, I strive to see it through."

"You are one of the great strivers," Crockett said.

"I'm serious," Ruby said, shooting him a disgruntled sideways glance.

"So am I. What's on your mind, Ruby?"

"For the past four or five days I have dealt with the fact that Monday I am going to meet, and attempt to deceive, a killer. And not just a killer, but one who is accomplished at dealing with the intricacies of the human mind, at ferreting out the truth, at seeing through the ruse. I have examined the situation. I have examined myself. I have come to terms with my fear and I know that I can do this."

178

"But?"

"I'm still scared."

"Okay."

A rest area sign whizzed by. Ruby backed off the gas and coasted up the ramp to a parking space in the dog walking area. A cocker spaniel dragging a fat lady in stretch pants that had no choice, lurched in circles and shivered in the wind.

Crockett grinned. "Just a slight change in dietary habits and life-style, LaCost," he said, "and in two years or less, that could be you."

"Naw," she said, swiveling in her seat to better face him. "I don't like cockers."

"I'd heard something to that effect about you people."

"You weasel. You are not going to let me obsess about this are you?"

"Nope. Fear isn't important unless it were to make you irrational. Irrational ain't a factor with you, Ruby. Most people don't understand fear, even though they spend a great deal of time being afraid. They're afraid of their boss, afraid of their past, afraid of their future, afraid of their spouse, the neighbor's dog, their age, God, their body, their desires, their parents. Thousands of everyday fears that nag and punish us relentlessly from cradle to grave."

Crockett cracked his window and lit a Sherman.

"Most people never have to do what cops or soldiers or firefighters have to do, to deliberately go into harm's way time and time again. To sit and tremble with adrenalin shakes after it's all over trying not to vomit on your shoes. To go do a deed that ninety-nine percent of the population would have the good sense to run from, simply because you promised you would."

"That's it, isn't it?" Ruby said.

"Yep."

She smiled. "I promised I would."

"Exactly," Crockett said. "And a promise—"

"Is a promise. Christ, Crockett, it really is that simple."

"For people like us, yeah. We're warriors, Sweetheart. We're the ones who do the things that most people won't, or can't. Ivy knows it, Cletus knows it, now you know it."

"I'm a warrior."

"Sure. It has nothing to do with training, it has nothing to do with weapons, it has nothing to do with occupation, it has nothing to do with cultural or social issues, parents, heritage, or anything similar. We warriors, Ruby, like the joy of battle and we make promises to get what we like."

"You're right."

"Whether we crawl around inside somebody's head, or down some alley, the risk is there, the fear is there, the battle is there. And whether the opponent is a masochistic feces-fondler or Goliath on the plain, the true enemy is always us."

"Crockett! You wax!"

Crockett flushed. "I guess I do," he said. "That's okay. The best warriors are philosophers, too."

"Well, I am going to battle my way to the restroom," Ruby said. "You may accompany me to the door if you like."

They walked against the north wind. The sky felt like snow.

In and out of the bathroom, Crockett was trying to decide on the least offensive choice from the candy machine when Ruby's arms came around him from behind. Her warm breath tickled his left ear.

"You are one helluva man, Crockett," she whispered. "It is not uncommon for you to restore my faith in people from time to time, but today you have restored my faith in *me*. Thank you."

"You are very welcome," he said, resting his palms on the outside of her hips. She leaned her pelvis into his butt.

"I just wanted you to know that you are appreciated," Ruby murmured, lightly kissing the back of his neck. Crockett shivered.

"Ooh," she said. "The warrior trembles. Of what else, I wonder, am I capable?"

"I can tell you one thing," Crockett said.

"And what would that be?"

"You can damn sure make a duck stand at attention."

"Crockett!" Ruby blurted, and began to laugh, releasing him as she giggled.

Crockett turned to face her. "Damn!" he said. "That was almost a LaCost moment!"

Ruby pointed her finger at him. "Don't let it, so to speak, go to your head," she said. "It took two of you. You didn't do it alone."

FIFTY-TWO
Meeting Marlene

THEY CHECKED INTO THE MARRIOTT COURTYARD about five-thirty and went out for some dinner. On the way back Ruby stopped at a K-Mart and Crockett purchased some first aid supplies, safety pins, a canvass all-weather hat, and a roll of duct-tape. Ruby wisecracked a couple of times, calling it duck-tape, and eventually asked what it was for.

"Disguise," he said.

"As what, The Mummy?"

"You'll see."

When they drove back to the Marriott, Crockett had Ruby continue on down the frontage road a bit. Sure enough, only a short distance away, was some sort of two-story, low budget motel. Semi-sleazy exterior, badly lighted parking area, no restaurant. Perfect. When they got back to their rooms Crockett dug out the magic number and called Dan Harter. He answered on the third ring.

"Chief Harter."

"Bullshit."

"Hey, Asshole! How the hell are ya?"

"Great, Dan. Need a favor. Nothing serious."

"Shoot."

"I need a two or three block ride in a marked squad car."

"When?"

"'Bout an hour."

"Where are ya?"

Crockett told him.

"I'll grab a blue and white and be there."

"Just come on up and knock."

Ruby was looking at him with raised eyebrows.

"Grab your warpaint, Tonto," Crockett said.

"Huh?"

"Get out your make-up. I need a couple of shiners and some bruises."

For the next hour, Ruby diligently disfigured him. She seemed to enjoy it. Just before Harter arrived, she slipped into her short white robe. She seemed to enjoy that, too. When she answered the door, Dan certainly did.

"Randi," he said. "I was hoping to see more of you."

"And now you are," she smiled. "I'm running a bit late." She excused herself, and went into her room. Dan watched her go, then turned to Crockett.

"Jesus Christ! What happened to you?"

Crockett grinned. "I pissed Randi off. Be careful."

He had two black eyes, a bandage over a broken nose, and a badly bruised chin.

"That all make-up?"

"Yep."

Harter laughed. "Well, ya look like hell," He said. "Nobody'll know ya, and they sure won't like to look at you very much. Good idea."

Crockett put on a shirt and handed Dan the roll of duct-tape.

"Here," he said, "help me be the one-armed man."

Harter was taping Crockett's left wrist to his left bicep when Ruby came back in wearing jeans and a sweatshirt.

"What can I do?" she said.

"Grab those safety pins and pin up the left arm of my trench coat," Crockett said. "Then pull the filters off about four of my cigarettes."

Soon he was ready. A badly abused, one-armed man with cigarette-filter swelling under his lower lip and a newly broken nose.

"The desk clerk will remember you," Ruby said, helping him on with one glove, and peering critically at his hat.

"Exactly," Crockett said, "I'll be in touch shortly."

When Harter pulled up in front of the little motel office, a young woman clerking at the counter stared at the police car through the window. Dan shook his head.

"This never happened," he said.

"That's right," Crockett said, opening the squad car door. "Never did. Thanks, partner."

"Anything else, just call." Harter said, and drove away.

Crockett hefted his suitcase in his one remaining hand and limped inside. The girl at the counter was staring at him.

"Good evening, my dear," he slurred in his best British accent. "Pray, do not be alarmed. I have been the victim of two swine who beat me and made off with my wallet, passport, and identification. The constable was kind enough to bring me here from the hospital."

The hostess was in her late teens, slightly chubby, with stiff blond hair and freckles. Sympathy shone from her black-rimmed, wide blue eyes. She seemed so taken with Crockett's plight that she actually stopped chewing her gum for a moment.

"You okay, Mister?"

"Well no, actually, I am not. But I shall be, young woman, I shall be. I require a room for a few days. I am here to lecture at the University and then back to Manchester at the middle of next week. I shall need something away from noise and the street, top floor, do not disturb and all that. Do you have such an accommodation available?"

"Yeah. I mean, yessir."

"Jolly good. And the compensation for the hostelry would be—"

"Huh?"

"The charge for the room, my dear."

"Oh. Thirty-five dollars a night."

"Very well. I shall engage the room for eight nights. As I am sure you require identification and I do not have any, and because you have been so cooperative thus far, I will pay you four-hundred of your dollars in rental and ask you to retain the overpayment balance for yourself."

She looked at him for a moment as the wheels ticked over, then began to rapidly chew her gum.

"Sure!"

"Wonderful," he said, fishing a roll of hundred dollar bills from his coat pocket and passing it to her. "Please take the four you require. I wish not to be annoyed. I wish my room not to be entered unless I request it. If it is entered, I shall know. If it remains inviolate during my stay, before I leave, I will pay you an additional one hundred dollars. What say you?"

Her chew rate increased noticeably.

"You bet!"

"Excellent! Now, give me my keys, I shall go to the room and see you again in eight days with your additional compensation."

"You need anything, Mister, anything at all, day or night, even just some, you know, company or somethin' like that, my name's Marlene. I'm here almost all the time. I sleep in the back of the office. Just dial five, and I can come right up. Yours is room 232, on the corner at the back of the second floor. Have a nice stay and don't forget to call me if you get lonesome or something."

Crockett took the extended key, picked up the bag, and walked outside and up the stairs. His taped arm was on fire.

The room was as tacky as he assumed it would be. When he got the tape ripped off and some circulation back, he phoned Ruby.

"Randi DeMoss."

"It's me."

"Hi, Spy. You get in from the cold?"

"Yep."

"You still look like shit?"

"Yes, but Marlene didn't seem to mind."

"Marlene?"

"Just a friend I made on my recent travels."

"Am I going to have to scratch someone's eyes out?"

"Jealous?"

"Of course."

"I didn't get jealous when you flaunted your body at Dan tonight."

"You didn't?"

"No."

"You didn't?"

"No."

"You didn't?"

"So come get me, willya?"

"I don't know," Ruby said. "Maybe Marlene could bring you back."

"No good. It'd blow my cover."

"Blow might be the operative term here. What's this minx look like?"

"A young Garbo, only more sultry."

"Not your type."

Crockett chuckled. "Yours either," he said. "She is rather attractive, if you're into gum and lots of dark eye-liner."

"I see."

"And, she was kind enough to offer me the pleasure of her company, just a short phone call away."

"Before you corrupt this poor innocent child, perhaps I should spirit you away from such fleshy temptations."

"Come to the rear by the back stairs and honk. I'll be down. Avoid the office area."

"Wouldn't want Marlene to think you were unfaithful."

"Of course not," Crockett said.

While waiting, he put out some tell-tales to see if anybody would come into the room during his absence. He even did the old Sean Connery/James Bond trick with a hair across the drawer front. It felt very spyish. Crockett was about to phone Ruby again when he heard her horn. He grabbed the suitcase and headed down the stairs. The trunk lid popped open and he dropped the luggage inside. As he opened the car door, he was hit by a wave of heat. There sat Ruby in her green teddy, hose and heels, with her white silk robe untied and open. It stopped him dead in the door.

"You know what I bet you're not doing, Crockett?" she said.

"What?"

"I bet you're not thinking about Marlene."

FIFTY-THREE

Meeting Mackey

SATURDAY Ruby worked on her story for her meeting with Morrison. About ten in the morning, Crockett phoned Keith Mackey at home. No answer. He tried the lumberyard.

"Hixon Lumber."

"Keith Mackey, please."

"Out in the yard."

"That's fine. I'll wait for you to call him in."

"Pretty busy."

"I'm not. I'll just hold on."

"Gotta number he can call?"

"No."

"Look, he's got work to do."

"You his boss?"

"Yeah."

"I'm gonna buy thirty-thousand board feet of yellow pine and five-hundred squares of shingles today. I may order it from you guys, I may order it from somebody else. Mackey was real nice when I was in a couple of weeks ago. I'd like to talk with him. I have time to wait. Why don't you take your head out of your ass and see if you can find him. If I hang up, I won't call back. While you're looking for Mackey, add up how much money you may have just lost."

"I'll call him in right away."

"Very kind of you. Take your time."

Mackey came to the phone in less than a minute.

"Keith Mackey."

"Mr. Mackey, if your boss is nearby, look happy. I just led him down the primrose path a ways. He seems like an asshole, so I punished him a little."

"Yessir," Mackey chuckled. "He said this was about a bunch of lumber and shingles. What can I do for ya?" Baritone voice with the flat Midwestern, slightly nasal twang. Definitely a farm boy.

185

"My name is Daniel Beckett," Crockett said. "I'm a special investigator with the Department of Justice. You and I need to talk."

"You want that many board feet, I'd be glad to talk with ya."

"If you like, please check with the Champaign County Sheriff, Mike Shipley. He knows me. What time you get off work?"

"Noon on Saturdays, Mr. Beckett."

"Can you be in Champaign by one?"

"No problem. For a shot at your business, I can probably leave now. Lemme check with my boss."

A hand went over the receiver, and Crockett heard mumbling. Mackey came back on the line.

"Where do I find ya, Mr. Beckett?"

Crockett gave him the location and room number.

"Drive straight to the rear and come up the back stairs. Avoid the office."

"Yessir," Mackey said. "Be there in about an hour."

Crockett hung up and noticed Ruby standing in the connecting doorway. She was wearing a bright yellow warm-up outfit in lightweight satin and white running shoes. She pirouetted slowly to give him a good look.

"Whatcha think, Crockett? Too tight across my lovely bottom? Too snug over my heaving bosoms?"

"Yes on both counts. It's nearly perfect." She threw out her lazy smile and advanced on his chair, straddling Crockett's legs and sitting on his lap, an arm on each of his shoulders.

"I called the rental place for you. They have a Monte Carlo on the way over. They'll leave the keys at the front desk."

"A Monte Carlo?"

"Live a little, you old fart. Got a 'pointment?"

"Mackey, in about an hour, over at Marlene's place."

"Marlene, Marlene," Ruby sneered. "What's she got that I haven't got?"

"Absolutely nothing."

"What can she possibly do for you that I can't?"

"Absolutely nothing, but can't isn't the issue. Won't is the issue."

"I walked into that, didn't I?" Ruby said.

"Yeah, but I'm sure that half a loaf with you is infinitely more rewarding than would be a full loaf with Marlene."

"That's sweet," Ruby said, and kissed him lightly on the lips. "More rewarding perhaps, but maybe not as satisfying."

"You're pretty satisfying, Sweetie."

"Why Crockett, what are you saying?"

"Too much, probably."

"Ooh. It's a shame you have to leave or I'd worm this out of you. Am I your fantasy fem, Davey?"

"Get off my lap, you slut, and set me free. Marlene awaits."

186

"We will continue this later, Big Boy. I refuse to lose you to the wicked Marlene."

Ruby giggled and scooted away as Crockett swatted at her butt and missed. The room phone rang.

"For God's sake, Crockett, straighten up and answer the phone. Your car is here. I'll just stay all by myself and wait for you to come back."

Ruby grinned and shut the connecting door.

Crockett had been at Marlene's place for about twenty minutes, watching a talk show on a TV that advertised adult movies at reasonable rates, when a knock came. He opened the door.

"Keith Mackey?"

"That's me. You Mr. Beckett?"

"Call me Dan," Crockett said. "C'mon in."

Mackey was an inch or so taller than Crockett, raw-boned and thin, wind-whipped and creased. In his mid-thirties, he carried the crows-feet of a sixty-year-old around constantly moving gray eyes in a long face. He had large hands with heavy knuckles and a quiet handshake. He was angles and joints and he slumped into a chair like a pile of sticks. Crockett laid his credentials on the table. Mackey ignored them.

"What's this all about?"

"Ultimately, it's about Martin Morrison."

"Martin Morrison, Morrison," Mackey mused. "Fella that's got that hospital for crazy kids out in the southwest part a the county?"

"That's the one."

"The Sheriff used some a Morrison's money to beat me when I run against him in the last election."

"Morrison dirty?"

"Probably," Mackey nodded. "You must think he is or you wouldn't be here."

"That's right. I know he is. I just can't prove it. That's why I need your help."

"Shit. I can't do ya no good. I can't spit in that county without old Lester F. knowin' about it."

"When is the next election?"

"Little over a year."

"Want it?"

"Want what?"

"Do you want to be elected Sheriff next time?"

"Well, hell yes!"

"What if Dawkins was out of the picture and you had ten grand or so in your election fund?"

"You can do that?"

"What if I can?"

187

Mackey grinned. "Mister," he said. "As a general rule, I don't kiss strange men, but you better be ready to pucker up!"

"Save the kiss for your wife. Dawkins will not run again."

"How the hell can you make somethin' like that happen?"

"You graduated from Mahomet-Seymour High School with a C average, where you played football okay and basketball pretty well. You enlisted in the Marine Corps when you were eighteen, wound up being in recon in Desert Storm, came back home, went to work at the Lumberyard. You have two brothers and one sister. She died in an auto accident in the spring of 1995. Your parents are both living, although your mother has chronic liver problems and your dad's had heart surgery."

Crockett shifted in his seat as Mackey gaped at him.

"You have two daughters, Ruth and Sara. Their mother is your high school sweetheart that you married when you came out of the military. You are a year late on your federal income tax, as of last week your bank balance was less than four-hundred dollars, you have slightly over eleven hundred dollars in savings, and you make less than twenty-two grand a year at the lumberyard. Two years ago your marriage got in trouble because of a short fling you had with the woman who used to be your wife's best friend, and when you were fifteen and a juvenile, you were busted for blowing up mailboxes with cherry bombs. That's what I recall off the top of my head. I have a lot more than that on Sheriff Dawkins. He will not run again."

"Damn."

"You in?"

"All the way."

"Good. Go home, kiss your wife and hand her this five-hundred dollars," Crockett said, counting out some bills. "Consider this a bonus. I won't call you at work again. When I take care of the Dawkins mess, I'll be in touch. Then we'll get to work."

"Is what we're gonna be doin' against the law?"

"Some of it. Make a difference?"

"Nope. Just curious."

They shook hands and Mackey started out the door, then stopped. "Thanks a lot."

"You'll earn it, Mackey," Crockett replied. "Every dime."

FIFTY-FOUR

Country Roads

AFTER LUNCH Ruby and Crockett took a ride in the country. He drove, she fidgeted.

They went west on I-74 to the Mansfield exit, then south out into the country following the map Morrison had sent Randi DeMoss. In about thirty minutes they were winding down an oiled country road under leaden skies, looking for landmarks. At length, turning at a metal grain bin, they moved into a series of twists and turns bordered tightly by trees and ragged hedge. The road became a series of short hills and the customary weedy barbed-wire fencing gave way to white boards and stately pines on the left side of the car. Through the trees they could catch glimpses of a vast lawn, dotted with huge blue spruces and the occasional immense, winter-barren oak. Almost a quarter of a mile back from the road on a low hill, sheltered nearly completely from view, they saw flickers of a large, white, three-story mansion. The fence broke for a wrought-iron gate framed in field-stone columns. On the right column was a bronze plaque that read 'Morrison.'

"Jesus," said Ruby.

In about another three hundred yards the road made a hard left and the fencing and pine trees continued on that side of the car. The right side opened up onto a gravel pit, the land falling nearly vertically away only a few feet from the fence. A hundred feet or so farther on, a gravel road turned off to the right, heading down a steep slope into the pit, which was at least a half-mile across. Rusting heavy equipment dotted its floor, sixty to eighty feet below the level of the road.

Ruby grimaced. "Wouldn't wanna miss that turn," she said. "No signs or anything."

"Welcome to the country," Crockett said. "Everybody that drives these roads lives here. They know the gravel pit is there. Who needs signs?"

189

They'd missed the Morrison mansion while looking at the huge hole. Crockett turned around at the next wide spot and retraced their route, attempting to see the side of the house through the thick trees. Not much luck.

"Big place," Ruby said. "What was it Ivy said? Over sixty acres of lawn?"

"Something like that. Nine bedrooms and twelve or thirteen bathrooms."

"Nothing like Ivy's place, but pretty nice for gravel pit country," Ruby said. "I'll get a better look Monday, I guess."

"How you doing with that?"

"A lot better. In for a penny—"

"You need to get as good a look as possible," Crockett said. "Con him into a tour of the grounds and the home if you can."

"Shouldn't be too hard. Ivy's big rich. This Bozo is little rich. Little rich usually likes to show off. I can be a very receptive audience."

"You'll do fine."

"Actually, I think I'm kinda looking forward to it," Ruby said. "I sometimes enjoy the playing of roles."

"No!"

"Yes."

"I had no idea. Would that be the sleazy stripper, the man-hungry meter maid, the copulating cowgirl, or someone else?"

"Copulating cowgirl?"

"Aw, man."

"Copulating cowgirl?"

Crockett flushed. "Gimme a break, willya?" he said. "It was the best I could do at the time."

"Christ, Crockett," Ruby laughed.

"I shoulda stopped with the meter maid."

"You shoulda stopped with the stripper. I don't have a meter maid outfit."

"You have a stripper outfit?"

"I expect I could assemble something suitable," Ruby said. "Would you like that Crockett?"

"Whatever it takes to help you relax in the face of your upcoming ordeal is fine with me," Crockett said. "After all you have done for me, the least I can do is assist you in any way I can."

"Ha! How'd it go with Mackey?"

"Changing the subject?" he asked.

"Only for the moment," Ruby said.

"Mackey is in the boat. It remains to be seen how well he can paddle, but it looks good so far."

Mansfield was coming up. Rather than taking I-74, Crockett turned on route 150 and took the two-lane into Mahomet, then went south on 47 to route 10 and followed it into Champaign.

190

"Where we going?" Ruby said.

"The old way, the two-lane way."

"Some of Crockett's old stomping grounds?"

"Just making sure everything still goes where it used to. Always pays to know the lay of the land."

"Or routes of escape?"

"Or routes of escape."

"This could get very serious?"

"Yeah, it could," Crockett said. "An instructor in one of the FBI training courses I went through said that if somebody wanted to get me, he had a ninety percent chance of succeeding. The best I could do was to make my ten percent as fat as I possibly could. He also claimed a properly motivated and fat ten percent was pretty equal odds to a self-assured and complacent ninety percent. I am not self-assured or complacent. Monday you meet the bad guy. Tuesday I go after the Sheriff of a whole county. Wednesday I want us in one piece and together. I am fattening our ten percent."

"There is a real change that comes over you at times like these," Ruby said.

"Oh, yeah?"

"Your eyes shift. They seem to gaze instead of look and never stop moving. Your body becomes more still. Although it does not relax, it appears to relax. The line of your jaw shifts, your movements are slower and more deliberate. It's like your awareness of where your physical self is expands or something. Your concentration becomes more acute. I'll bet your pulse rate even drops a little. Somebody who didn't know you would think you had just become complacent."

"Jesus. What are you, an analyst?"

"I know this. If we were enemies in a room together and I watched this mini-mutation occur, I'd want out of that room."

"You would, huh?"

"Real fucking quick, Crockett."

"Just think how fearsome I'd be if I really was a badass."

"I like your ass just fine the way it is. I expect that it is bad enough."

"Why, Ruby!" he said, "don't you just say the sweetest things?"

She chuckled. "So, now what?"

"Now we go back to the rooms, freshen up, go out to dinner, and check the paper. I noticed that the University Of Illinois Jazz Band is playing someplace in town tonight. We will find out where that is and we will go. You'll love it. Tomorrow we will sleep late if we like, catch a movie, go shopping, hang out, whatever. We will make every effort to have a good time and relax. Our business will still arrive on schedule."

"Can I get all gussied up?"

"You betcha. Randi is gone for the weekend, and Ruby's back in town."

Ruby shifted in her seat.

"Oh, Crockett," she purred. "And you thought Monday and Tuesday could be dangerous."

FIFTY-FIVE
Randi Undercover

MONDAY WAS A BITCH. They went out for a late breakfast, but Ruby wasn't hungry. She stirred her food around a lot trying to look busy while Crockett played along with excessively witty banter as he forced down bacon and a waffle. Back in their rooms, she dressed in a gray conservative wool suit, a pale pink blouse buttoned to the throat, and only a little makeup. She hung a small black leather purse over her shoulder and carried a slim black briefcase. She kept slipping in and out of character as she waited for the rental company to deliver a dark green Taurus. The car arrived almost exactly at noon. Ruby put on her trench coat and rested her chin on Crockett's shoulder.

"I love you, you know that?" she said.

"Sure. Never doubted it."

"Suppose Morrison can monitor cell phones?"

"Probably not. Want me to call?"

"If you don't hear from me by three, yeah," Ruby said.

"I'll take care of it. I'll even route the call through Lincoln, just in case."

"See," Ruby said, "I told you that you were devious."

"Get on the road, Champ. You'll do fine."

She kissed him very gently on the lips. "See ya soon, Crockett."

"Betcher ass, Cutie."

And she was gone.

Crockett was so uptight, it only took eleven hours or so to get close to three o'clock. About one o'clock he lost his breakfast. He never felt sick, just so tense that digestion was not an option. He paced, he sat, he turned on the TV, he turned off the TV, he hummed, he shut the hell up. He resisted the urge to get in the Chevy and drive to within range of the mansion. He worried, he fretted, he fidgeted, he spent the longest afternoon of his life. About a quarter to three, he phoned Randi's office in Nebraska.

"Doctor LaCost's office. This is Rose." Woman's voice, mid-fifties, high plains accent.

"My name is Crockett. Does that mean anything to you?"

"What is your middle initial, Mr. Crockett?"

"A."

"Your upline sponsor's name?"

"Cletus."

"Your dog?"

"My dog uses kitty litter and his name is Nudge."

Small chuckle. "Very good, Crockett. What can I do for you?"

"I'm going to hang up in just a moment. When I do, forward all Randi's office calls to her cell phone. Okay?"

"Fine."

"After twenty minutes, stop forwarding the calls, okay?"

"Very well, Crockett," Rose said. "Always good to hear from you. Have a pleasant afternoon."

He waited five minutes longer and called Ruby's cell phone.

"Doctor DeMoss."

"Randi, it's Carl at the office."

"Yes, Carl. Is there a difficulty?"

"I'm awfully sorry to bother you, but the young Dickson girl attempted to commit suicide early this morning. Her father just called. He's at the hospital with her mother. Tiffany is stable and in no danger, but I promised to get word to you as soon as possible."

"That's fine, Carl. You did absolutely the right thing. Contact them and give them my number. No, not this one. Did I give you the number at the Hotel?"

"Yes, I have it."

"Give them that number, it's to my room. I'm at the Morrison clinic at this time. Tell them to call between six and eight this evening. Reassure them, as best you can, and advise them I'll be waiting for their call. Express my sorrow and let them know that they are in my thoughts."

"Fine. Again, Randi, sorry to disturb you."

"It was totally appropriate," Ruby said. "Thanks for calling."

She hung up and Crockett was holding a dead phone.

Oh, man.

Crockett washed his face, drank some ice water, then whanged around the room like a demented ping pong ball for about a day and a half. He was thinking about changing his sweat-soaked shirt when his phone rang. He glanced at the clock. A little after five.

"If this isn't you, I'm gonna want to know why," he said.

Ruby was almost singing. "Relax Crockett," she said. "Just little ol' me, free as a bird and on the way back."

"Are you okay?" Crockett said.

"I am now. I have never been more glad to hear your voice."

194

"How was it?"

"Enlightening. Martin Morrison is a very suave, very attractive, very charming older man. He's also as phony as a forty-year-old hooker in a prom dress. This guy makes Hannibal Lecter look like Peter Pan."

"Did he bite?"

"He can't wait for my return call. He only gets twenty-five hundred bucks a week per patient. Not bad, huh?"

"Jesus."

"Yeah, times five or six kids. Nice little piece of, ah, nice little piece of—"

"Whazzamatter?"

"God, Crockett, I'm starting to shake."

"Where are you?"

"Coming up on Mansfield and I-70."

"Stop at a gas station or somewhere and eat a candy bar. Follow that with some milk. You're running on empty. You been on an adrenalin rush and now it's crash time."

"I'm okay."

"Listen to me, dammit! You are not okay. You cannot judge your condition. I don't care how you think you feel. Stop."

"I can be back in twenty minutes, Crockett."

"Ruby, you don't have twenty minutes. Stop the fucking car, get a candy bar and a pint of milk, eat and wait for a half hour. Then drive on in. Please, listen to me. Please."

Anger rippled through Ruby's voice. "Okay, okay," she said. "Jesus. If it'll get you to shut the hell up and get off my back, I'll stop. Goodbye!"

He waited about fifteen minutes and phoned her.

"Crockett?"

"Hi. How ya doin'."

"I'm sorry."

"No prob."

"Yes, it is. I should have listened to you. I got the car stopped and the bottom fell out. I barely made it inside! I don't think I ever felt like that before."

"Comin' back to yourself now?"

"Yeah. I still feel a little fuzzy, but I'm better."

"Good. Give it another ten minutes or so, then if you feel okay, drive on in. We'll go out, find us a big steak, lotsa potatoes, and a decadent desert. After the dinner, you can ply me with a little wine, give me all the grisly details, and I will rub your lovely bottom."

"Suits. I'm getting really hungry, and I've had so much smoke blown up my skirt this afternoon, my bottom could use a rub. Thanks, Crockett. Sorry I was such a bitch."

"Bitch is one of your best features."

"Aw. Smooth talker."

FIFTY-SIX
Managing Morrisons

THEY ARRIVED back at the motel around eight, stuffed and relaxed. Ruby went to her room to change, Crockett kicked off his shoes, leaned his cane against the wall, and opened a bottle of wine. He put it and two plastic glasses fresh out of their plastic bags on the plastic tabletop and dropped into a chair. About five minutes later Ruby sauntered in wearing her short white robe and nothing else that he could notice. She carried two cigars. She stopped in front of him, turned around, and waggled her butt. He patted it.

"That was not a rub," she said. "That was a pat."

"I don't wanna get you too excited."

"Bullshit you don't. You don't wanna get you too excited."

"You may be right."

"I'm always right, Crockett. I'm surprised you have not admitted that to yourself before now."

She smiled at him and took the other chair.

"You pour, I'll light."

They traded cigars and wine and settled back. Even expensive motel chairs are not comfortable.

"This sucks," Ruby said. "We need a couch."

"No couch."

"Move to the bed, Big Boy. I'll go grab my pillows."

A few minutes later they were settled on the bed. Crockett was propped up on the headboard while Ruby sat cross-legged, not quite facing him, a cigar clamped in her teeth, a wineglass in her hand. He couldn't help smiling.

"What?"

"You are a class act, Lady."

Ruby grinned and blew smoke at him.

"You noticed," she said, and guzzled most of her wine, then belched. "Ain't I somethin'?"

196

"You'll do 'til the roads dry up. Feeling okay?"

"Thanks to that huge dinner, not to mention your greatly resented advice while I was driving back, I'm back to normal, or at least myself again. Fill my glass, you wonderful man. It appears to be empty."

"Tell me about Morrison," he said, passing her the wine.

"Over sixty, six-two, full head of silver hair, professional tan, fresh manicure, trim, fit, quite attractive in a senatorial kind of way. Could easily have been a successful lawyer, evangelist, politician, real estate developer, CEO, like that. Inspires confidence, speaks well, displays convincing enthusiasm, dresses beautifully. He played me like a banjo, or at least thought he did. An impression I cultivated, I might add."

"I'm sure you did," Crockett said. "You are expert in cultivating impressions."

"He is expecting my call within two weeks concerning my patient. He knows he can help her. His rules and regulations state that the parents cannot see their child except at his discretion as long as the child is under his care. He told me he rarely lets the parents visit during the first three months. Average stay is six months."

"What's he do?"

"His own version of behavior modification. He accepts children from six to nine years old with extreme behavioral problems, violent tendencies, resistance to discipline, excessive temper outbursts, like that. Nothing that is physical in origin. He takes the child for a week and then decides if his treatment is indicated. If not, the parent or parents come get their kid, no charge. If the child is accepted, no visitation for three months, no un-monitored visitation ever. Twenty-five hundred bucks a week. His acceptance rate for kids is about fifty-five percent. He claims a success rate of about sixty percent."

"Is that good?"

"It ain't bad. I met two of the children currently in residence. A little Stepfordish, but that's not unexpected. I don't know anything about how constant that success rate is as they grow into their teens. I expect it's pretty fair. It was still working on Rachael to an extent."

"What?"

"Remember the fish hooks?"

"Oh, yeah."

"That's why she spaced out when you asked her about them. She was still under suggestion control from him, even though she had not been around the man for twenty years."

"Jesus," Crockett said, his throat closing up a bit.

"Jesus has nothing to do with this guy. His sister either. Boy is she a piece of work! Marian is definitely the power behind the throne."

"No shit?"

"Close to seventy, much like him. Tall, silver, thin, polished. Chip a tooth on that bitch anywhere you tried to bite. Unlike her brother, she does not go out of her way to charm. She, I believe, is management. He is labor. She claims to be a psychiatric nurse, and she may be, but she is damn sure not his psychiatric nurse. She ain't anybody's anything. That old broad rules the roost. Count on it. She also appears to be completely asexual, although I would not be surprised if she and her darling brother were not extremely close in years past. It would have been another method she could have used to bind him to her. She has hitched her wagon to his star, then rebuilt the star to her specifications."

"Good grief."

"My thoughts exactly," Ruby said. "If there is abuse going on among his patients, I'm sure it is relatively low-key. The two kids I saw had no physical evidence of it. Nor could it be very severe. Parents may not visit, but they can remove their children at any time. Something is going on in that place, Crockett. I know it. I can feel it. I don't believe in evil as such, but I do believe in evil deeds. There is some stuff in progress in that house that leaves nasty in the dust. I think the whole set-up may be just a righteous front for something else entirely. He's not a right guy, Crockett. The sister will make the hair on the back of your neck stand up."

"Why don't the parents notice that kind of thing?"

"Parents come to him exhausted from trying to deal with a terrible problem, hopeful that he can offer relief. Or, they are excited to get their child back and begin a whole new relationship. At that point they believe him to be a miracle worker. They are not emotionally in a place to notice anything other than their own sorrow or joy. Plus, Marian has only limited contact. She was not with us for more than ten minutes."

"But you picked up on all this."

"Sure. I was not emotionally distressed or looking for help. I'm trained and experienced, and, in certain situations, I get feelings. I got feelings, Crockett. Great big hairy-assed feelings."

"I trust your feelings, Ruby."

She drained her glass. "I got a feeling I need more wine, and I got a feeling we need to stop talking about this for a while, okay?"

"Sure," he said, refilling her glass.

She took a sip, and settled in against his right side. "Wanna hear about some of my other feelings, Crockey?"

"Crockey? Again with Crockey?"

"Uh. I feel like I wanna snuggle. C'mon, Crockey, snuggle me."

Crockett put his arm around her and Ruby burrowed into him like a puppy. When he woke up at about three AM, his arm and shoulder were numb, his back ached, and his leg had gone totally south. Ruby was smiling in her sleep. He didn't wake her.

FIFTY-SEVEN
Leaning on Lester

AT AROUND FOUR-THIRTY Ruby woke up and helped him get untied.

"Jesus Christ, Crockett, why didn't you get me up?"

"You were sleeping."

"You were suffering, you idiot! You're not a knight in shining armor, you know. You have the right to be comfortable, too!"

"Did you sleep well?"

"Yes, I slept well. I slept great, if you must know."

"Then my job here is through, m'am."

"You cheeseball."

"Look, Ruby, I've got to go intimidate a sheriff today. I would have been restless all night anyway. You were beat to shit and really needed some rest. You got it. I'll just slip into the tub for a while and I'll be as good as new."

"Yeah, yeah, yeah. Thanks, Crockett."

"You don't have to thank me. While you were unconscious, I fondled your private parts and peeked inside your robe. Now I've got fantasy fuel for another month at least."

"So it wasn't a noble gesture?"

"Not for a second."

"That's a relief. I couldn't stand you if you got all noble."

"Me either. Love your mole."

Ruby was chuckling as she walked back to her room.

An hour and a half in the tub put Crockett most of the way back together. They had breakfast at a Bob Evans, Ruby said she'd wait in the room until he got back, and by ten o'clock Crockett was on the outskirts of Hixon, the Hyatt County seat. Finding the center of town was not difficult, there wasn't much town. As with so many places, the courthouse was in the mid-town square, an old stone building of three and a half floors and a half basement. It was built to resemble a small castle and failed miserably. What had once been slightly regal had become outdated and grubby.

Over half the businesses on the square were closed, most of the open ones faced the front entrance to the courthouse from across the narrow street. There was a small restaurant, a hardware store, a drugstore, the post office, an insurance agency and down the street next to a boarded up building, a barber shop squatted beside the cracked sidewalk. The entire place seemed to be crumbling, going back to the earth, robbed of promise by time and Wal-Mart.

He parked diagonally in front of the building, walked up the flaking steps, and went inside. The Sheriff's Department was on the left. The small lobby smelled of furniture oil and disinfectant. A faint odor of urine wafted up from the jail downstairs.

A bored looking deputy glanced up from behind the counter. He studied Crockett for a moment, finished cleaning a fingernail with his Swiss Army knife, slowly rose to his feet and walked to the reception desk. A toothpick wobbled in the corner of his mouth and his cowboy boots clunked on the hardwood floor.

"Yeah?"

"Sheriff Dawkins, please." Over the deputy's shoulder Crockett could see a glass door and a uniformed older man sitting alone at a desk.

"Who wants him?"

"I do."

"Gotta 'pointment?"

"Nope."

The deputy leaned back and looked Crockett up and down. "You ain't from around here, are ya?"

"No. I traveled to this scenic bastion of law enforcement just to talk with your boss."

The toothpick froze and the deputy squinted. "What's yer name, boy?"

"Beckett. What's yours?"

"What the hell you wanna know my name for?"

"So I can remember whose attitude was so badly in need of adjustment."

"Huh?"

Crockett laid his Justice Department ID on the counter. "I'm a fed, Sweetcakes. Get the sheriff and put your dick away before I break it off."

"You really Justice?"

"Call 'em and find out."

"We ain't never had nobody from Justice in here since I been on the job," the deputy said, slightly excited. "Lemme git the sheriff."

"Thanks, Deputy. I appreciate it."

He went into the office and shut the door. He and the older man spoke for a moment, then the deputy returned to the counter.

"You can go in, Mr. Beckman."

"Beckett."

"Yessir."

Crockett walked into the office. The sheriff stood up.

Two or three inches shorter than Crockett, most of that because of the lack of neck, Lester Dawkins rose from behind his desk and extended his hand. They shook. The man's hand felt like a piece of wood. Dawkins looked at Crockett steadily out of cold blue eyes from a heavily jowled face under a high forehead. What was left of his hair was sandy-gray in a crew cut, and a dirty t-shirt showed through the open collar of his uniform. He was thick through the waist but not fat, with short arms and large shoulders, and he didn't seem impressed by Crockett at all. Bullshit.

"Dawkins," the sheriff said.

"Daniel Beckett," Crockett replied. "Department of Justice."

Dawkins eyed Crockett's cane. "I didn't think them federal boys let no cripples work for 'em."

Crockett smiled. "I'm the exception," he said. "I'm sort of a special investigator. As I told your deputy outside, the one who is probably on the phone right now to let somebody else know that I'm here, feel free to call my headquarters in Washington and ask about me. They'll verify I'm who I claim to be." He sat down across from Dawkins' desk. "Please, take a seat, Sheriff. I won't need much time."

Dawkins remained standing. "What's the Justice Department want from me?"

"It's not what they want," Crockett said. "It's what I want."

The Sheriff snorted. "Well, just what the hell do you want?"

"I want a new sheriff in this county."

"A what?"

Crockett smiled. "A new sheriff," he said. "New blood. Somebody who's not as crooked as you are, Dawkins. I'm here to convince you not to run again and announce that fact in the next week or so."

Red spread up Dawkins' neck and into his face as his jaw clenched. "I been sheriff here near twenty years! Quit, my ass!"

"No, no, no. Don't misunderstand me, Lester. You don't have to quit. Nobody wants to embarrass you. All you have to do is announce you are not going to run again and bow out of the next election. You can go ahead and rip the county off, and lie, and cheat, and steal just like you've been doing for another year yet, but that year is all you get, Sheriff. After that, you're out."

"What the fuck do you mean out, you sack a shit? Out? I ain't outa nothing, you cocksucker!"

Crockett adjusted his grip on the cane. "Now, Lester," he said, "there's no need to raise your voice. You can still get through all of this gracefully. You keep yelling and everybody is gonna know that I'm pushing you around. That won't look good for the High Sheriff, will it?"

"I'll kick your fuckin' ass all over this fuckin' room!" Dawkins yelled, and came striding around the end of his desk. Crockett pushed the tip of his cane into the man's stomach.

The sheriff grabbed it like Crockett knew he would and pulled. Crockett thumbed the release and Dawkins was left holding the cane's shaft, looking down at twenty-one inches of Damascus steel stiletto, the point of which was touching his low belly, just above his crotch.

"Stand real still, Lester," Crockett said, "and you may live through this."

Crockett removed Dawkins' old Colt Python from its holster, keeping it low so the deputy out front wouldn't see it.

"Now, just lay the shaft of my cane on the floor and go sit behind your desk. Keep your hands on top where I can see them and keep your crooked mouth shut so you can hear. You get itchy and I will shoot your Hyatt County ass with your own gun. Count on it."

Lester F. walked back around his desk, sat down, put his hands on the blotter, and calmly looked at Crockett. He had guts, no doubt about that.

"You ain't from Justice," Dawkins said.

Crockett smiled. "I *am* justice, Lester. Justice that you've been missing for years. Your time is up. Here's the way it's gonna be. I know about the bank accounts in Champaign, Decatur, Bloomington, and Springfield. I know about the other two accounts in your wife's name. I know about the cabin in Michigan and the safety deposit box in Saginaw. I know about your brother in Memphis and the little side-line the two of you have going there. I know about your arrangement with Carter who owns the liquor distributorship, I know about the lab out by the forest preserve, and I know about your lady friend in Farmer City. I know your net worth is over a million dollars that we've traced, and probably that much more we've missed."

Crockett tapped the tip of the stiletto on the worn floor.

"I know about you, Dawkins, even about the kid who disappeared here in ninety-two and your six-cell flashlight that went into the river with him. I know a lot of shit and the only thing that keeps it from covering you up is me. You don't want to go to jail, Lester. They won't like you in jail. You do as you're told, you keep it all and retire. You screw with me, you white-trash piece of shit, and I'll hang you so high the crows won't be able to reach your body! What do you say, Lester? Walk away or twist in the wind?"

Dawkins was white and shaking, looking at his desktop. "Walk away," he mumbled.

"Sorry, Lester. What did you say? Speak up."

"I said walk away, you sumbitch," he growled.

"Good choice, Lester! You win the grand prize. I'll be watching the papers for the big announcement, plus, I'll keep an eye on you so you don't get frisky down the road a ways and decide to back out on the deal. You really need to understand the danger that you're in. Your life depends on what you do in the next few days. Do what you've been told and you never see me again. You don't want to see me again, Lester. Look at the bright side. You got a whole year left to steal from the folks that voted you in."

Dawkins glared as Crockett unloaded the magnum and put the shells in his pocket. Crockett laid the gun under a chair, reassembled his cane, and stood to leave.

"Don't get up, Lester. I know the way out. Just remember our agreement. Nice doing business with you."

Crockett said goodbye to the deputy and went out to his car. About three miles out of town, he noticed a beige pick-up behind him. He saw it again outside of Mansfield. He turned onto old Route 150 and saw it again. It seemed that Lester didn't think he was serious. He phoned Ruby.

FIFTY-EIGHT
Crockett in Motion

"CROCKETT! Are you alright?"

"So far. Don't talk, just listen. Save your comments until I'm done. Put on slacks and running shoes. Grab the key to Marlene's place off my nightstand. Get the roll of duct tape from the closet shelf and a pair of socks out of my suitcase. Take the rental car and hustle over to Wal-Mart. Buy a bottle of ammonia, some decongestant nasal spray, some Saran wrap, a small cassette recorder, and get to Marlene's as fast as you can. You with me?"

"Yes."

"Good. Go into the room, pull the cases off the pillows, put the socks, the ammonia, the recorder, and the duct tape on the nightstand. Lay the pillowcases on the foot of the bed. Don't lock the door, pull the drapes closed and shut off all the lights. Oh, and put your gloves on before you get to the store. Leave them on for the duration. The room is clean. I don't want your fingerprints in there. I'm taking the long way home and I'm about forty-five minutes out. We have company, two of them I believe. They will be armed, they will be serious. We will deal with them. Questions?"

"No."

"Then go. I love ya."

"On the way. I love you."

"Ruby, wait!"

"Yeah?"

"If you're wearing perfume, wash it off and sample some after-shave while you are at the Mart."

"Gotcha."

"Call me as soon as you're in the room."

"Right."

"Go get 'em, Tonto."

"Ugh."

Crockett dawdled on the drive as much as he could. Finally his phone rang. Ruby's voice was tight with emotion.

"I'm here," she said. "Everything's ready."

"Good. For sure, two guys are tailing me. I'm a few blocks away, in traffic. Stand inside the door so when I open it, you'll be blocked from view."

"Okay. It's unlocked."

"Tear off ten or twelve strips of duct tape about two feet long and stick one end of them to the table. More if you have time. I'll be there in a couple of minutes." He hung up and slipped on his gloves.

When Crockett got out of the car, the boys in the truck hung back and watched. He took his time so they'd be sure to see which way he went, then climbed the stairs to the room. Ruby was waiting behind the door when he went in.

"Listen close," he said. "They'll be here real soon. They're not good at this, so they'll hurry. Stand behind the door. When the knock comes, I'll open it so it is perpendicular to the wall. As soon as I open it that far, you put all you got behind it and slam it as hard as you can. Then, as quickly as possible, open it again. I'll be going through it in a hurry. Understand?"

"Yep."

"I don't want these guys to see you. Fade back as soon as you open the door. Watch from the bathroom or something. Don't come in unless I get in trouble. If that happens, bust ass and get away. Call Dan and get back to the motel. Got it?"

"Got it," Ruby said, her voice rigid and thin. Shadows flickered on the drapes.

"Here we go, Champeen," Crockett whispered.

There was a knock on the metal door.

"Yeah! Who is it?"

"It's the day manager, sir. Important message for you."

Crockett put his left hand on the knob and held the cane in his right. "Just a minute," he said, and immediately pulled open the door.

He caught a flash of a shape with a gun, and Ruby slammed the door like the Jolly Green Giant. When she whipped it open, Crockett went through it, holding his heavy cane by the tip end, like a baseball bat.

The one the door had hit was down against the wrought iron railing, his idiot partner bending over him in a crouch with his back to the room. Swinging the cane like a golf club, Crockett blasted him squarely on the tailbone. The man shrieked and went headfirst into the railing beside his buddy. Crockett hit him again, this time in the kidney, and his squalling stopped as his body went into spasm.

Grabbing him by the jacket, Crockett pulled him into the room and threw him into a chair. He stuffed a sock into the bad guy's mouth and secured it with duct tape. The man began to come around, confused and in considerable pain. Crockett used the heel of his hand for a short strike to his temple. The guy sagged and became quiet. Crockett pulled his unconscious friend inside and taped his forearms, wrists, and ankles to a chair. Then he did the same for number two, and dropped a pillowcase over his head.

Number two, the man who had been hit by the door, had a badly damaged forehead, broken jaw, and possibly a broken nose. Crockett shot some nasal spray up his nostrils so he could breathe, gagged him, and used the other pillowcase. He then retrieved a Smith and Wesson .38 and a Glock nine from the walkway outside the room and sat down on the bed to rest. Ruby walked quietly out of the bathroom, kissed him gently on the cheek and stared at the two hooded figures, her eyes wide.

After he caught his breath, Crockett checked the men's pockets for ID. Nothing. Number two groaned and shifted in his seat. Crockett held the open bottle of ammonia under the front edge of the pillowcase. The man began to snort and thrash around.

"How's your ass, Motherfucker?" Crockett said, and rapped him on the tailbone with his knuckles through the open back of the chair.

The man squeaked around the gag and threw his head back and forth.

"I think it's busted, Motherfucker. What do you think?"

Using the head of his cane, he gave the broken tailbone a strong tap. A muffled shriek came through the case.

"Yeah, busted. Your kidney's fucked too. Even if you get to a hospital pretty quick, you're gonna be pissin' blood for at least a week. It's bleeding in there right now. You're not in good shape, Motherfucker. You need help. Wonder where you're gonna get it?"

The hooded head rocked from side to side, and Motherfucker tried to shout around the sock stuffed in his mouth. Crockett casually backhanded him across the face through the pillowcase.

"Shut up, Motherfucker. You'll talk when I want you to talk." The man tried to stamp his feet and started to sob.

Ruby looked at Crockett, her face awash in shock. He winked at her. She gaped at him for an instant, then her eyes crinkled and she looked away.

Crockett turned his attention to the second man. "Let's check on your partner, huh? I think he's still alive."

Crockett held the ammonia under the second pillowcase. It took a little while, but the head finally jerked away from the fumes. Soon, little cries and snorts wafted through the room. Crockett motioned Ruby back to the bathroom and pulled the pillowcase off his next subject. The man was badly injured and having difficulty breathing. Crockett reached for the nasal spray and tried to use it, but his victim attempted to pull away. Crockett grabbed his shirtfront.

"You can hold still, Asshole, and breathe, or I can let you suffocate. You choose." Asshole froze. A few seconds after the spray hit his nostrils, he started to breathe.

"Asshole," Crockett said, "you are a mess. You got a broken jaw, a broken nose, maybe even a fractured skull. How ya feel?" The man glared through his tears.

"Aw, now don't look so pissed, Asshole. I've already done you a favor. If that sock wasn't in your mouth and your jaw could move, you'd probably pass right out. What do ya think?" Crockett tapped him gently on the chin and a scream ripped through the gag. "God, I bet that hurts. Your buddy, old Motherfucker over there, has a busted tailbone and a bleeding kidney. Which one of ya is in the worst shape ya think?"

Asshole's face was beginning to swell and change color. Crockett turned his attention to his first captive and removed the man's pillowcase.

"Hey, Motherfucker," he said. "Take a look at Asshole over there. How long do you think it will be before he can't breathe through his nose and suffocates? Suffocation would be a terrible way to go, doncha think? If I take that gag out of your mouth, suppose you could tell me who sent you guys?" The man grunted and shook his head. "No?" Crockett picked up the Saran Wrap Ruby had purchased and reeled out a couple of feet. "Let's see if I can change your mind."

He wrapped the plastic film around Motherfucker's head a few times, opened the door, and left.

Outside on the landing, Crockett counted to thirty before went back in. Motherfucker's face was red and he was struggling against the plastic. When he stopped thrashing, Crockett pulled it off, picked up the recorder, and held the ammonia under the man's nose. He jerked and gasped, drawing in massive amounts of air through his nostrils.

Crockett held the recorder below the man's line of sight and turned it on.

"Whatcha think now, Motherfucker?" he said. "Funny thing about torture. If there's enough time, it works. Always. I can keep doin' this 'til I decide it's time for you to die. And then, I still got Asshole to play with. Ready to be the first one on your block to have a little conversation?" Motherfucker nodded weakly. "Great. Now don't yell when I take the gag out, or you'll be in worse shape than Asshole, okay?" He nodded again. Crockett removed the gag.

"Who sent you?" he asked.

"The sheriff," Motherfucker gasped.

"What sheriff?"

"Dawkins," the man rasped, his voice a little stronger.

"Who?"

"Dawkins, goddammit. Lester Dawkins."

"Hyatt County Sheriff, Lester F. Dawkins sent you two guys to kill me?"

"Yeah, but only if we had to. We was supposed to scare you off if we could."

"Didn't work, did it?"

"Naw."

"What's your name?"

"Alan Dale Rooter."

"And your partner?"

"Ronnie Herbst." Crockett shut off the recorder.

He gagged Motherfucker again, taped the two men together back to back, gave Asshole another big shot of nasal spray, replaced the pillowcases, gathered up the supplies, grabbed Ruby and left. They abandoned his rental car and went back to the Marriott in hers. Crockett phoned Dan on the way.

"Harter."

"Crockett."

"Trouble."

"Afraid so. Got a mess for ya. Two young stalwarts tried to kill me. They're alive, but need some help. No ID, but I persuaded one of them to tell me their names. I left their guns with 'em in the room. Can you hold 'em for a couple of days? They'll both probably be in the hospital for at least that long."

"I'll take care of it."

"Thanks, Dan. Better hurry, one of 'em isn't breathing too well."

Crockett gave him the location and room number and rang off. Ruby and he went inside. Crockett put the recorder in his pocket, gave her a kiss, and requested Ruby's car keys.

"Where the hell are you going?" she said, handing him the keys.

"Back to see the sheriff."

Ruby watched him open the door.

"Aw, shit," she said. "What are you going to do?"

"Something large," Crockett said.

FIFTY-NINE
Dealing with Dawkins

DURING THE DRIVE, Crockett mused on how Ruby had taken the confrontation with Asshole and Motherfucker. Even though she seemed a little horrified, she'd hung in there, doing what he needed her to do. He hoped it wouldn't crawl too deeply under her emotional skin. Hell, he hoped the same thing about himself.

Nearing his destination, Crockett allowed his anger to bubble toward the surface. One of the things he appreciated about being a Taurus was that when anger finally did arrive, it was not difficult to sustain for a while. He needed it to do what he had to do.

He reached the outskirts of Hixon a little after two. The sky had turned very dark and was spitting tiny flakes of snow. Far from Currier and Ives, everything was gray and heavy, dense and oppressive. The courthouse crouched, hunching its shoulders against the leaden overcast.

When Crockett passed the barbershop, the lights inside made it brighter than the dim afternoon street. He glanced in. The sheriff was sitting in the barber chair. He drove around the block. Only two cars were outside the courthouse and no other traffic was moving. He was alone on the street. He passed the barbershop again as Sheriff Dawkins was getting out of the chair. Crockett parked in front of the abandoned store next door and quickly stepped into the space between the buildings.

What he thought was an alley was actually an old loading dock. The street entrance had been boarded up years before and half the rotten wall that ran parallel to the sidewalk was still standing. Garbage and refuse were scattered about the dark interior. Unless Sheriff Dawkins crossed the street in front of the barbershop, he would pass by the loading dock. Crockett leaned his cane against the brick wall and waited.

In just a few moments, Dawkins strolled by on the way back to his office. As he passed the narrow entrance, Crockett stepped out behind

209

him, grabbed Dawkins' collar in his left hand, the sheriff's pistol in his right, and pulled the man violently back behind the wall.

Lester's Colt came out of his holster and Crockett used it to club him low on the back of his skull. As Dawkins dropped to his knees, Crockett stepped in front of the hurt and bewildered man and kicked him squarely in the crotch. Dawkins went over backwards in the kneeling position and shrieked as one of his knees popped. He gasped and collapsed on his side in the filth. Crockett rolled him on his stomach, secured the man's wrists with his own handcuffs, pulled him over to the greasy brick wall, and sat him up. He opened his mouth to shout and Crockett kneed him in the chin. Dawkins head bounced off the wall, his eyes glazed, and he slumped.

While the sheriff was foggy, Crockett retrieved the pistol, emptied it, and removed Dawkins' sap from a front pocket. It was a nice one, spring loaded, packed with about eight ounces of lead shot at the business end, capable of breaking a forearm or fracturing a skull. He slipped it in his hip pocket, grabbed Dawkin's upper lip, and dug his thumbnail viciously into the cleft just below the man's nose. When Dawkins started to come around, Crockett pushed about three inches of the Colt's barrel in his mouth, keeping the cylinder low enough that the sheriff couldn't see that it was empty. Dawkins' eyes snapped open.

"Lester, my man! How you doin'? Surprised to see me? Got something for you to hear."

Crockett took out the recorder and played the portion of the tape where Dawkins' stooge identified him. The sheriff lost all the color he'd gained since regaining consciousness. Crockett put the recorder back in his pocket and retrieved the sap.

"Jesus, Lester," he said. "I bet that front target sight really hurts digging into the roof of your mouth like that."

He bounced the gun up and down a little. Tears came into the bound man's eyes. Crockett looked closely at his face.

"Look at that," he said. "You're bleeding a little bit. Uh-oh, looks like I may have chipped a tooth, too. This is the second time today I've taken your gun away from you. You gotta be really embarrassed, huh? You're not very fuckin' smart, are you? You didn't believe me when I told ya how things had to be, and now you're sitting on your ass in the dirt, cuffed with your own hardware, suckin' on your own gun. Damn, Lester, I bet you feel really stupid, doncha?"

Dawkins stared at Crockett, his eyes full of hatred.

"Now see, you're getting' all pissed off," Crockett said. "I don't want you pissed, Lester. I want you humble. I want you to understand that you are not dealing with some poor bastard that's been afraid of your little dictatorship for fifteen years. I want you to know that I am not some lost runaway kid you can beat to death and drop in the river. I want you to realize that your narrow ass is mine, you pea-brained country fuck!"

Crockett thumbed back the Colt's hammer and Lesters' eyes grew wide.

"Here's the deal, Dawkins. You don't have to pull out of the election anymore. Now you have to leave. I tried it the easy way, and you sent a couple of guys to kill me. In three days, Lester. In three days you will be gone, out of the area, absent. Resign your position and leave. I don't care where you go, but you can't stay here. Do I have your attention, Lester?"

Dawkins never moved, just glared. Crockett hit him across the collarbone with the sap.

"Lester, do I have your attention?" A whimper came from around the gun barrel. "Good, and thanks for not shouting. You yell and this thing might go off, being cocked and all. So, that's the deal. Seventy-two hours and you are gone. You're gonna need some help, though. I think you have a dislocated kneecap, and I'm pretty sure you have a broken collarbone. What the hell, though, you're still alive, huh? That's pretty good, everything considered, wouldn't you say?" Dawkins nodded.

Crockett leaned over so the two men were eye to eye.

"Now you listen to me, Dawkins. You are gone from the county in three days, or you are a dead man in four. You will not get another chance to do this right. You do exactly as I say and you get to live. Fuck up, even just a little bit, and I'll kill you. Don't resign, I'll kill you. Stay an extra day, I'll kill you. Think you're tougher than me, I'll kill you. You have one chance to live and a dozen chances to die. It's up to you. I don't give a rat's ass. I'd just as soon pop a cap on you as eat a steak. Understand?"

Dawkins nodded.

"Leaving town?"

Dawkins nodded.

"Seventy-two hours?"

Dawkins nodded.

"Well, that's real fine, Lester," Crockett said. "You get to keep all your money and start a new life. Good choice. I'm gonna take this gun out of your mouth now. If I were you, I wouldn't yell or anything, okay?"

Another nod. Crockett removed the pistol and stood up.

"Been fun, Sheriff. I'd really like to be here when you flop out of this hole in the wall, but I gotta go. You oughta get that knee and shoulder looked at, maybe see a dentist too. You don't look so good. I'll be back in a few days. To be honest, I'd love to see you again. Just once more. You take care."

Crockett dropped the gun, picked up his cane, walked out of the loading dock, got in Ruby's rental, and headed back to town. He didn't make it five miles before he had to stop and get over the shakes.

SIXTY
Orange Freeze

CROCKETT WAITED until after he stopped shaking before he phoned Ruby. He didn't want her to hear his voice tremble.

"Crockett?"

"Praise the Lord and pass the ammunition."

"Jesus! I've been worried sick."

"Not to worry, my dear child, all is well."

"Get back here, so I can kick your ass!"

"Oh good. More violence."

"Where are you?"

"About ten miles out. I'll be there pretty quick. Let's go eat. I'm starved."

She hung up. Uh-oh.

Crockett walked through the motel room door to find Ruby standing with her hands on her hips.

"Just who the fuck do you think you are?" she snarled. " I watch you damn near kill two guys you've never even seen before, then you blithely take off in search of your next victim! No goodbye, no kiss my butt, nothing. Meantime, I'm left standing around like Hogan's goat, waiting for the other shoe to drop!"

"Oh, shit."

"Oh shit is right, you mindless refugee from a five handed, crossways, Lithuanian cluster fuck! You think I don't care what happens to you? You think I don't give a shit if you live or die?"

"I think you might have lost touch with your professional detachment in this particular case, Doctor," Crockett said.

"Oh! That's what you think, huh? How 'bout I personally detach your ass, you sonofabitch, and cram it down your self-centered throat! Jesus H. Christ! You ever display such a total disregard for my feelings again, and I swear to God I'll, oh, hell. Jesus. Crockett, are you okay?"

"I was better before I came in here."

213

"Hold me, you insensitive clod," she said, moving into his arms.

"It's what I live for," he said.

Ruby cried for a long time.

They went to a Steak n' Shake. Crockett had a triple steakburger with extra Thousand Island dressing and a double order of fries. Ruby had Boston Baked Beans and a salad. After Crockett wolfed down his food, Ruby looked at him over his orange freeze.

"You are one nasty sonofabitch," she said.

"Thank you."

"When I agreed with Ivy that you could be very ruthless, I had no idea that you could be as brutal as you were today."

"Nobody died."

"No, especially not you."

Crockett smiled. "Speaking of brutal," he said, "you damn near killed that old boy with the door over at Marlene's place."

"I did, didn't I?"

"Betcher ass. Fun, huh?"

Ruby thought for a moment, removed the straw from her Coke, stuck it into his orange freeze, and took a sip.

"Yeah, it was. God! Crockett, that's awful!"

"No, it isn't."

"Yes, it is! I caused that man a terrible injury!"

"So what? He wasn't some innocent walking down the street that you attacked with a claw hammer! He and his pal would have killed you just for laughs. Not to mention what they probably would have done to you before they killed you."

"Not to mention what they would have done to you," Ruby said, and Crockett watched as she took another long drink of his orange freeze.

"You want one of those of your own?" he said.

"Naw."

"Well, I do," Crockett said, and signaled the waitress.

"Law of the jungle, huh?" Ruby said.

"No. The jungle isn't like that. The vast majority of the brutality that happens there, happens from necessity, not greed or avarice. That's pretty much our bailiwick."

"Yeah," Ruby said, "it is. But God, Crockett. I hate to admit it but I actually liked it. I really did. Christ! I was even grinning when you had those two taped into the chairs. I can't believe it!"

The waitress arrived with Crockett's new orange freeze, and Ruby, oblivious to almost everything, pulled it over in front of her and stuck in a straw.

"Another orange freeze, please," Crockett said. The girl grinned and hustled away.

"Another thing," Ruby continued. "When you had those two tied up and were, ah, dealing with them—"

"I was abusing them, Ruby. It was deliberate and planned. I did it on purpose."

"I wanted to come out there and punch 'em or something. I really did."

"Sure."

"Sure?"

"Sure. They frightened you. They came there for no other reason than to hurt or kill me, and you, if they had known you were there. Why shouldn't you want revenge?"

"Is my veneer so thin?"

"You're the psychologist, for chrissakes. You tell me."

"Your motive was more, of course, than just revenge."

"Right."

"If revenge had been your only consideration you would have just killed them."

"Right again."

"You needed to scare them to secure information. So you did that with the most expeditious protocol you had at your disposal."

Crockett's orange freeze arrived, and he swept it to him as rapidly as possible. Ruby smiled.

"Did you enjoy it?"

"The expeditious protocol?" he asked.

"Yeah."

"I enjoyed the fact that those two idiots who were so confident I was gonna be a cakewalk wound up helpless and hurt, yeah. But I didn't particularly enjoy hurting them."

"So Ivy was right on that score, too."

"Huh?"

"She said you were a non-violent man, capable of extreme violence."

"I kinda like that."

"You are exactly like that," Ruby said, twisting his words. "So, how's the sheriff?"

"Ah. Lester is going away. He leaves to search for safer pastures within the next three days. At least I believe he will."

"What did you do to him?"

Crockett slipped into his best Brando.

"I made him an offer he couldn't refuse," he said.

Ruby snorted. "Is he hurt?"

"His body will be fine. His pride, however, will bleed for some time."

"So, now what, Vito?"

"Now we go back to the motel after a stop by a liquor store. We drink wine, you flaunt your body for my tired old libido, we talk until the wee hours, and we help each other through the emotional repercussions of what has transpired today. There will be repercussions."

"No doubt about that."

"Then tomorrow, or the next day, we go back to Kaycee and wait for the events we have set in motion to play out a bit, before we resume our business. Now is the time to see what develops."

"Ooh," Ruby said. "You gonna finish that orange freeze?"

SIXTY-ONE
Dawkins Departed

TWO DAYS LATER, from the Quality Hill townhouse, Crockett called Keith Mackey.

"Beckett?"

"Yep."

"Man, what did you do?" Mackey asked, excitement surging in his voice. "All hell has broke loose around here!"

"What's goin' on?"

"Lester F. is gone, Son! Yesterday he called Herb Yount, the head of the county commission, said he was quittin' his job, said he was leavin' to go live in Michigan or someplace like that. This morning, a big ol' truck showed up at his house and guys are throwin' furniture and shit in it like a flood is comin'. Lester is limpin' around with his arm in a sling, yellin' at everybody, throws his wife in the car, and heads out! Jesus, Beckett, what'd you do to that sonofabitch?"

"Who's sheriff?"

"Lester's dumbass head deputy for right now. One of the county commissioners was in the lumberyard today. Told me they was gonna have to have a special election, or somethin' like that, to get a new sheriff to fill out the term until the regular election came around. Said he didn't know what was goin' on either, 'cept Lester had a bad knee, a swole up mouth, and a broke arm or somethin' and was just leavin'! He give 'em a letter that said he quit. I drove by his place when I got off work. Looks like a cyclone hit it and empty as hell."

"Well, whadaya know."

"Beckett," Keith said, "what the hell did you do?"

"So what's the high sheriff job pay?"

"Forty-one thousand."

"Damn near twice what you make now, huh?"

Mackey nearly shouted with excitement. "And a car!" he said.

"Not bad. Gonna run?"

217

"Aw, I don't know. I'm pretty busy at the lumberyard."

Crockett chuckled. "Let's not ruin our relationship with lies," he said.

"Goddammit, what the fuck did you do to Lester?"

"We had a chat."

"Let's not ruin our relationship with lies," Mackey crowed.

"Let's just say I persuaded him that it was in his best interest to retire. How's your campaign fund?"

"What campaign fund?"

"Watch the mail. I sent you a big old dictionary yesterday. Fascinating reading. Leaf through the pages carefully. There are a hundred certificates in there with Ben Franklin's picture on them. That oughta kickstart the old campaign for you."

"Goddamn! What are you, my fairy godmother?"

"Watch the fairy talk, Redneck."

"Beckett, I owe you. Bigtime."

"We'll talk about that after you're sheriff. Just keep Morrison and his clinic in the back of your mind. This goes well, and the new Hyatt County Sheriff will clear up a couple of murders that nobody even knows are murders. That should keep you in office for awhile."

"Thanks, Dan."

"I'll be in touch, Mackey. Keep the faith."

Ruby, wearing yellow tights and a short, brown angora sweater, came padding in from the kitchen, barefoot. She was munching on a tortilla wrapped around a bunch of veggies and had ranch dressing on her chin. She sat beside him on the couch and leaned in, holding the sloppy wrap with both hands.

"I got stuff on my chin?" she asked.

"Yep."

"Bet it looks kinda erotic, huh?"

"Jesus, Ruby!"

"God, I love catching you off guard," she said.

Crockett's ears were warm. "You sure seem to," he said.

"How's Mackey?"

"Damn," Crockett said, trying to recover. "You change gears faster than a roadracer."

"Part of my charm. How's Mackey?"

"Amazed. Getting ready for a special election. Grateful. I told him the money was on the way. Now we just lay back until he's sheriff. Then he and I start working on Morrison."

"Lay back. I like the sound of that."

"You gotta keep the dressing off your chin, Ruby. It screws with your libido. Why don't you pick on somebody your own gender?"

"Why don't you?"

"Why don't I what?"

"Pick on somebody my own gender?"

"No likely candidates at this time."

"For chrissakes, Crockett, they're everywhere. Don't you heteros just go hang around a bar until somebody jumps your bones?"

"Not this hetero."

"Not your style, is it, Sweetie?"

He grinned. "I have no style."

"Oh yes you do. Maybe we need to find you a victim."

"A victim? Someone of whom I could take advantage?"

"Bingo!" Ruby said. "I could consult my little black and fix you up!"

"C'mon, Ruby."

She looked at him thoughtfully. "You know, that's not necessarily a bad idea," she said.

"Yes, it is."

"Maybe not, Crockett," she said.

"Jesus."

"What? You think I don't know any available straight women?"

"Ruby—"

"I can think of two or three right off the top of my head."

"Put a hat on, for chrissakes."

"Think about it, Crockett. I know a lot of women. Some of them are even attracted to waterfowl. You could use a little female companionship. You have money. You aren't driving that piece of shit truck anymore. You've got a new wardrobe. You're damn near presentable!"

"LaCost, I am not interested in a relationship right now!"

"Who said anything about a relationship? Go out, have a good time, get laid."

Crockett laughed.

"Make sex a two person sport for a change!"

"Christ, Ruby, gimme a break!"

"You got something against having some fun?"

"Alright. How 'bout you?"

"We're not talking about me."

"Maybe we should, you horny old broad. When's the last time you got your bell rung?"

"This morning, if you must know. I just happened to be alone at the time. I'm not interested in a relationship either," she said.

Crockett cracked up. When he settled down, Ruby smiled at him.

"So, it's just us, huh, Big Boy?"

"Seems like it," he said.

"Well, that ain't too bad."

"Ruby, dear Ruby," Crockett said, looking into her big brown eyes. "I got you, I got half a bottle of Vaseline Intensive Care, and I got a brand new box of Kleenex. I am a satisfied man."

She actually blushed. Crockett's first LaCost moment.

219

SIXTY-TWO
Home for the Holidays

THE HOLIDAYS ARRIVED. A couple of days before Christmas, Ruby flew to Dallas to spend some time with friends. Crockett declined her invitation to go along. Before she left, he gave her a pendant with a crystal heart suspended in a delicate gold wire cage. She gave him a wonderful old pocket watch.

Watching him lift it from the case, Ruby smiled. "It's an antique," she said. "But so are you. See you on the fifth or sixth of January. You will be sorely missed, Crockett. Know that."

"I do, Sweetie," he said, "as will you. Have fun." She gave him a long hug, licked the tip of his nose, and headed for her cab. Crockett went to the video store.

An hour later, he staggered back in the house with a half dozen movies and two bags of groceries. Alone! God! He'd spent years alone. He liked being alone. He missed being alone. Crockett put on a huge pot of chili, boiled up a dozen eggs to devil, and made up a big bowl of tuna salad, working the rest of the day on stockpiling food. He finished the preparations about in time for dinner, but had cooked too much to be really hungry, so he settled for a glass of V-8 and a couple of pieces of toast with peanut butter.

That evening he took a long soak with William Goldman, smoked three Shermans, put on his ratty old robe and schlepped back downstairs into the kitchen. He shut off the burner under the chili so it could cool, fixed a small grilled cheese and tuna sandwich, grabbed a Coke and a bag of chips, slipped a disc into the DVD player, settled back in his recliner, turned the volume up loud, and waited for History Of The World, Part 1 to hit the screen. Munchies and Mel. What could possibly be better? Evidently something. Even Mel Brooks couldn't hold his attention. Before Crockett finally gave up and went to bed, he tried Remember The Titans, A League Of Their Own, As

Good As It Gets, The Man Who Would Be King, even the director's cut of Abyss. Nothing worked.

He put the chili in the fridge and crashed for the night. Lying there in the dark, the horrible truth came thundering down on him. He missed Ruby. He missed her bitching, her laugh, her smell, her wise mouth, her eyes, her teasing, her heart, her humanity, her presence. Jesus. He had to get a grip.

By the time New Year's Eve rolled around, Crockett was pretty much settled in, basically numb, once again used to being alone. He went out to eat in the late afternoon before the drunks took over the street, neither happy nor sad about the holiday. It was snowing when he arrived back at the townhouse. He parked on the street and shook snowflakes off his shoulders as he came through the door, stamping his feet in the entryway.

"Happy New Year, Crockett."

Ruby stood in the living room, a lopsided smile on her face.

"I missed you" she said.

"Welcome home, LaCost. Good to see ya."

It took them five minutes to stop hugging, blubbering, laughing, and giggling. They were sitting at the table, Ruby pounding down some nicely aged chili. Crockett watched her eat. Ruby waved her spoon at him.

"Crockett," she said, "I was halfway to Dallas when I realized I wanted to be here with you. I am happier in your company than I am when I am not in your company. How sick is that?"

"You tell me, Doc."

"Pretty damn twisted, that's how sick it is."

"I like you better than Mel Brooks," Crockett said.

Ruby looked at him for a moment, her eyes shining.

"Does that justify me returning here five days early?"

"Oh, yeah," Crockett said. "It justifies you not leaving at all."

"Very well. Consider the compliment accepted."

"Ruby, what the hell is going on here?" Crockett said, relieved he'd mustered up the courage to broach the subject.

"God," she said. "I have asked myself that a thousand times in the last few days. I'd like to say we are unusually bound together because of the mission we are on, or that we are emotionally connected because of Rachael's death, and both of those are true, but they do not account for this mess. I fear that we are in love, Crockett. I have known for some time that we love each other. I can deal with that. I'm just not exactly sure what to do with the prospect that I may be in love with you."

"Shit," Crockett muttered. "Don't get me wrong, Ruby. The prospect of you being in love with me makes my toes tingle. I just don't know if I can handle being in love, not just with you, but with anybody."

"Rachael?" Ruby asked, one eyebrow rising.

"Rachael."

"Okay," she said. "It's easy to see how you feel that way, and please understand that this mess is just as screwed up for me as it is for you. I am not trying to talk you into anything. That is not the purpose of what I am going to say. Got it?"

"Got it," Crockett said.

"Little happy hubby loves his wife, his daughter, his infant son, his sister, his father, his brother, and his niece, Matilda. Different types of love, right?"

"Right."

"Wrong," Ruby said. "There are no different types of love. There are only different applications of love. In all honesty, I suspect that we have been a bit in love with each other for years but avoided that can of worms and decided to just love each other, primarily because we are both sexually attracted to women."

"That could do it," Crockett said.

Ruby laughed. "Has so far," she said. "This is a very strange situation, Crockett. It is possible to be in love and not be lovers. If we were both gay, it would balance quite nicely. See, it's simple. You just have to start being queer."

"Ain't likely. Why don't you just stop?"

"Ain't likely," Ruby said. "I do know that I have never missed anyone in my life as much as I missed you."

"Likewise," Crockett said.

"Not even Rachael?"

Crockett stared at his hands for a moment, then raised his gaze to her face.

"No, Ruby," he whispered. "Not even Rachael."

"Jesus. This isn't remotely fair to you, Crockett."

"Not fair to you either, Sweetheart."

"Yeah," Ruby said, "but I'm the deviate here, not you. You have a complete right to expect certain things from a loving female companion, you know."

"We've been over this before, LaCost. I don't expect one damn thing more from you than you are prepared to give."

Ruby took his hand. "Christ, Crockett," she said, "where the hell do you hide your wings?"

"They're at the cleaners. I keep getting them dirty."

"I am who I am, David."

Crockett smiled. "Been good enough up 'til now," he said. "So what the hell do we do about all this?"

"We live together."

"We are living together," Crockett said.

"See? It's working already. We spend time, we enjoy, we see if this continues on an emotional level, or just burns out. There is no right or wrong here, there just is what there is. I think we relax and let whatever is going to evolve, evolve."

"What about when all this detective shit is over?"

"Answer me this, Crockett. Are you happier with me than without me?"

"Oh, yeah. A lot."

"Then, as weird as this whole thing is, we continue to live together. Maybe a duplex or something equally twisted, I don't know. I'm flying blind here, Crockett."

"I know one thing, Champ," he said.

"What's that?"

"I'm just awfully glad you came home."

Ruby glanced around the townhouse as if she'd never seen it before.

"I really did, didn't I?" She said, tears in the bottom of her eyes. "Home. Wow. I came home."

SIXTY-THREE

Recon

ON ONE PARTICULARLY GLOOM AND SNOW-RIDDEN AFTERNOON in mid-January, Crockett pulled a heavily laden cookie sheet from the oven and placed it on top of a cutting board, admiring the toll house goodness that graced its slick surface. Hot chocolate, slightly seasoned with cinnamon and just a touch of Bailey's, simmered on the stove, and a fire flickered cheerfully from the gas log as he carried some cooled cookies into the living room and put them on the coffee table. Returning to pour the hot chocolate, he yelled for Ruby, busy on the computer in the den.

"Succulence is at hand. Meet me on the couch."

Ruby yelled back. "This better be good. I've had other offers today," she said.

He carried in the steaming mugs just as Ruby entered from the hall.

"Ooh, Crockett," Ruby said. "When you decide to ply a girl, you do not fool around. You know how cookies and hot chocolate make me feel. Let's dunk!" She took her cup and flopped cross-legged on the couch, pushing up the sleeves of her sweatshirt.

"Nobody I'd rather dunk with than you," Crockett said.

Ruby's voice trembled when she spoke. "You've dunked with others?" she said.

"As painful as it is to admit, you are not my first dunk," Crockett said. "You certainly are, however, my best dunk."

"I suppose, considering your age, it is a bit unreasonable for me to expect you to have kept your cookies dry all these years."

"That's true, but they have not been wet for some time. I have been saving myself."

Ruby reached for the tray. "Then allow me," she said, dipping a cookie in the hot chocolate, and holding it out to Crockett. The soaked half broke off and fell on his foot.

"A failed dunk," he said.

Ruby patted his hand. "Don't you worry about it, Honey," she said. "It happens to every man now and then. You're probably just nervous because it's been so long for you. We'll try again after while. I'm very good at this kind of thing. Before I worked with the Keebler Elves, they wouldn't even come out of their tree. Now, nobody's safe."

Crockett fought to keep from spitting crumbs all over the table.

"Sorta puts a new meaning on the term 'short fuck', doncha think?" Ruby said.

"Damn, LaCost!" Crockett choked. "Lemme swallow, willya? Whacha been doin' on the computer?"

"Making you a rough lay-out of Morrison's place. The relative locations of the house, the barn, the garage and stuff. If I show it to you, Crockett, willya help me get my cookies?"

"Anytime."

"Really?"

An hour or so later they sat at the kitchen table, looking over her sketch of the Morrison grounds. Ruby pointed.

"The house is three sides of a square. The entire top floor is given over to the kids' rooms in the east wing, ten of them I think, treatment areas in the north connecting center structure, and a kitchen-dining area and play space in the west wing."

"Big place."

"Nothing like Ivy's, but very large. The second floor has Hansel and Gretel's clinic offices, a staff office, and a pharmacy below the kids' rooms. There is a reception area and records space, plus private visitation rooms and such in the center. The second level of the west wing is private bedrooms and sitting areas for the family. Below that on the ground floor is the kitchen and pantry, dining room, library and stuff. Ground floor center is the front entryway, sweeping staircases, and a parlor. The east side is a huge living room and a great room-home theatre section."

"Jesus."

"And then, there is the basement," Ruby said. "Under the west side is the playroom. Crockett, the playroom is about forty feet square with nine-foot ceilings, a huge mahogany bar, full-mirrored walls above the wainscoting, and get this. The grand piano, the doors, the furniture, and the entire ceiling are all upholstered in buttoned and tucked white leather."

"Home sweet home. What's under the center and east sections?"

"Morrison said it was just storage."

"That's a lotta storage."

"Twice the space of this entire townhouse. Maybe more."

"All underground."

"Yep."

"Okay. What else?"

Ruby pointed to the sketch. "Off the east wing, right here," she said, "is what was once a two-story carriage house, I guess. At one time it was converted to a six or eight car garage. It is now a three-car garage with living spaces for an older married couple who are the houseman and the cook, and a small apartment for the grounds man. It also has a sleeping area for two night staff members of the clinic. The cleaning crew comes in from the outside, as does the cook for the kids."

"You got a lot of information from this guy."

Ruby batted her eyelashes. "I was very charming," she said.

"I bet you were."

""Back here, to the north of the house about sixty or seventy yards is a stable. It has a small indoor riding arena and ten or twelve large box stalls. Morrison keeps a couple of ponies there for the kids. Behind it is a board-fenced paddock for riding outside, and to the west is a spring-fed pond of about an acre, with willow trees all down the far side. It's quite lovely, Crockett. It has ducks. I was reminded of you."

He ignored her grin. "What about security?"

"Not much," Ruby said. "There is a TV camera over the front door and various outside lights, some of them motion activated. The board fence we saw goes all the way around the grounds of the house, about a hundred acres. It is six feet high and backed continuously with well-maintained chain link, except for the iron gate. The gate is electrically controlled from the house through an intercom built into the left stone column. The fence is not designed to keep people out as much as it is there to keep the dogs in."

"Dogs?"

Ruby shivered and crossed her arms. "God, yes," she said. "Big, nasty bastards."

"You saw 'em."

"I was ten feet from them. Morrison keeps them in a steel cage attached to the outside of the stable. There is a big, insulated doghouse built against the wall to give them shelter and a door to the inside of the stable that slides up the wall on tracks when you pull a rope. The box stall inside the stable that's connected to the dog's pen has been lined with chain link fencing up to about twelve feet."

"What kind of dogs?"

"I don't know. Big, ugly, rangy animals. Short haired, sort of flat faces, dark brownish-gray color. Kind of look like pit-bulls on steroids."

"Canary Island."

"Who?"

"Canary Island dogs," Crockett said. "Supposed to be real bad-asses. At least that's what they sound like."

"That's something else."

"What?"

"Sound. They didn't make any. Well, that's not true. They kinda whined, but they didn't bark. They tried, but no noise came out."

"Whadaya mean, they tried?"

"They went through the motions of barking, but they didn't bark."

"Shit. He had their vocal chords severed."

"What!"

"Yep," Crockett replied, shaking his head. "Keeps 'em quiet. That way, whatever they're after doesn't know they're coming until it's too late."

"Ick!"

"That pretty much sums it up, Sweetie. They ain't guard dogs. They're attack dogs."

"What's the difference?" Ruby asked.

"Guard dog training is very discipline based. It's why a police dog, for instance, can bite and even restrain a bad guy with his teeth, but will also play with the family's five-year-old. Attack dogs are way different. Have you ever seen a film of the dogs at a military base or someplace, where the handler has the animal on a very short leash, patrolling the perimeter."

"Yes."

"Did you ever notice that the guy, unlike everybody else, carries a pistol and not a rifle?"

"No, but why?"

"The pistol is to use on the dog. Attack dogs enjoy their work."

"Shit."

"And it has little or nothing to do with the breed. It's all in what the trainers do to them. Like pit-bulls. People caused their terrible reputations, the dogs were the victims. How many of these maniacs does Morrison have?"

"Two. Thor and Loki."

"That's cute."

"He said that in warm weather, the dogs run loose on the grounds at night."

"Jesus!" Crockett said. "If one of the kids got outside, they'd tear him to pieces!"

"He said that the children were well monitored."

"They better be. Anything else?"

"Nope. That's all I have except for feelings."

"Gotta trust those."

"I have to contact him soon," Ruby said. "It's been a month or more since I was there. He expected to hear from me a couple of weeks ago about the patient I had for him."

"Call him in the next day or two. Stall him. Tell him the parents haven't made up their minds."

"No problem. That's a common scenario."

"Tomorrow I'll phone Mackey and see what's going on in the law enforcement biz. Then we'll consider what we're gonna do next. I wanna know what's in the rest of that basement."

"You may need to know, Crockett, but I'm not sure either of us wants to know."

"I'm scared you're right. Woof! I've had too many cookies, too much hot chocolate, and way to much Morrison for one day. Think I'll gimp upstairs and take a nice hot soak."

Ruby puffed her hair and preened. "All by yourself?"

"I was thinking of asking Dan Jenkins to join me," Crockett said.

"What's Dan Jenkins got that I haven't got?"

"Billy Clyde, Old 88, and Barbara Jane."

"Well, can I at least look in on you from time to time?"

"Of course."

"And can I look in *at* you from time to time?"

"Of course."

Ruby grinned. "Ah," she said. "Tiny pleasures."

SIXTY-FOUR
Getting Equipped

THE NEXT EVENING Crockett called Mackey.

"Beckett! Where you been, Son? I thought you dropped offa the earth."

"Still hangin' on. How's by you?"

"February first, I am the Hyatt County Sheriff!"

"The hell ya are!"

"Actually, I'm sorta the Sheriff now. Officially only a deputy, but I'm more or less in charge. Come next month, the salary kicks in. I get the car, which I'm drivin' anyway, and all kinds of benefits, even a big old life insurance policy! The wife's real happy about all that shit."

"I'll bet she is," Crockett said.

"They had that special election right after the first a the year, an' I run all by myself! Cost me a thirty-five dollar filing fee. I still got all that campaign money you sent."

"That's yours, Keith. Do what you want with it."

"No shit?"

"No shit, no taxes, no records. All yours."

"I damn sure ain't earned it. Maybe that's why you called, huh?"

"You sly devil, you saw right through me."

Mackey laughed. "Hell yes," he said. "I'm damn near the sheriff!"

"What I need you to do has to remain totally unofficial. If we can get enough together, then we'll make it official, but right now it's all on the QT, okay?"

"Okay."

"I need all the local information on Morrison and his clinic you can get. How many people work there, what they do, and when they come and go. If he has any unusual traffic in and out of the clinic, how often he travels away from the place, anything you can think of. As much intelligence as possible. If you know anybody who works there, what they think of him and his set up, stuff like that."

"Gotcha. But I can't do this officially, right?"

229

"Right. You have to be sneaky. If this comes to an open investigation and arrests, your department and I will handle it. The Justice Department will stay out of the picture. All the credit goes to you and your guys. The problem is, I don't even know what I'm looking for. The ultimate end in all this is to obtain enough information to prosecute Morrison for the murder of his wife about thirty years ago and the murder of his daughter last fall."

"No shit?"

"This is a very bad man, Keith. God only knows what's going on out at that clinic, but it's a hell of a lot more than meets the eye. We need reasons to legally get in there and look around, even if we have to get in there illegally and look around first."

"Why don't Justice just send in a bunch a guys?"

"Can't. We have to appear to be working totally inside the law, or nothing we got would be admissible in court. That's why we sometimes send people like me, to find people like you, to do all the set-up work. The glory of the bust doesn't mean shit to my department. This is a tiny little local case to them. They just want to make sure this guy is dealt with. We get enough information, then we create logical sources for that information, secure the warrants, I come along, and you and your guys serve 'em. Hyatt County gets credit for the bust, the Department of Justice picks up the tab and prosecutes. Everybody wins. Justice gets the asshole in a sack, your office is full of heroes."

"I'll start lookin' around," Mackey said. "There's an ol' boy that's got a farm back behind his place that was a friend of my daddy's. I'll talk to him some. Plus I know the guy that's leased that land across the road to be dug out for gravel. Could be I can get on his place and watch the clinic. I'll get to diggin', Beckett. Something goin' on, we'll find it."

"Good man. If this works out, there'll be a bonus in it for you and maybe some federal money for your department. I'll be back in touch in two or three weeks, Sheriff."

"That's me?"

"That's you, Mackey."

Across the table, Ruby munched a slice of apple and looked at Crockett.

"You're telling him an awful lot, but you are not letting him know very much, are you?"

"Nope," Crockett said, lighting a Sherman.

"Don't trust him?"

"No reason not to."

"Don't trust him?"

"Not when it could be my nuts hanging from somebody's rear view mirror."

Ruby snorted. "Graphic image," she said.

"We'll see how he does. I'm not suspicious, just cautious."

"Pizza's on the way. Should I change for dinner?"

"To what end?" Crockett said.

"To cultivate one appetite as we satisfy another?"

"Please do."

"You talked me into it," she said, getting to her feet and moving to lean a hip against his shoulder. "The pizza will be here in about thirty minutes. I'm off for a quick shower, then I will show you my new heels, my new red silk robe, and my new lacy white teddy. You'll love the neckline, or lack thereof."

"Go away, LaCost."

Ruby kissed him on the ear and headed toward the stairs.

The next morning Ruby went grocery shopping. Crockett dropped in a load of laundry and called Cletus.

"How you doing, Texican."

"My God, the voice of the Crockett is heard in the land. I thought maybe the junk yard dogs got you, Old Man."

"They been nippin' at my heels sure enough, but I don't fight fair."

"No need to. How much trouble you gettin' in?"

Crockett related to him recent events of interest concerning the upset of Sheriff Lester F. Dawkins.

"Christ on a crutch, Crockett! You leave anybody standing?"

"It got a little tense."

Clete laughed. "Goddamn, I guess!" Clete said. "Remind me not to piss you off. Where do ya go from here?"

"I need to get into the clinic, look for records, check out the basement. Ruby's got some bad feelings that the whole thing is a cover for something more sinister. We know this guy's proclivities. She claims they're not being satisfied with what she saw. I'm inclined to trust Ruby's feelings."

"I would be too."

"Any way we can get a phone tap on this fucker?"

"Naw, don't think so," Cletus said. "That takes warrants and such. I could get ya a cell phone scanner, but they're not very reliable. Damn shame we didn't get Ruby some insects to scatter around while she was inside."

"Yeah, I know. It never occurred to me to bug the place. We could try to get her back in, but I hate to chance it."

"No, no, no. Too big of a risk. She got in and out clean once. We sure don't need to push her luck any farther than that. Getting her hurt is unacceptable."

"What about me?"

"People like us," Clete said, "are expendable."

"So," Crockett said, "I need some stuff."

"Stuff I got, or can get."

231

"I need three good night vision devices, not the kinda things you buy at sport shops, but top of the line light collection optics with magnification capabilities and infra-red assist."

"I can get ya the same shit the SEALs use."

"Perfect. I also need a good, long distance, listening device. Parabolic or something better."

"No problem. What else?"

"I need a way to put a couple of very large, very mean, very well-trained dogs down fast, and for a while."

"Shotgun."

Crockett smiled. "No," he said, "not a shotgun."

"Simple solutions are almost always the best."

"Gotta be quiet."

"Night?"

"Probably."

"Flashgun could attract too much attention. I'll get ya something to put in some meat that'll knock 'em out for a few hours."

"I don't wanna kill them."

"Right. Take a few minutes to work, but it'll work well. They'll be okay. What kinda dogs we talkin' about?"

"The way Ruby described 'em, Canary Island I think."

"Shit."

"You got that right."

"Shotgun'd be best," Clete said, "but I don't want to offend your tender sensibilities."

"Thank you. Send two of the vision units and the doggie downers to me. The rest goes to Keith Mackey at the Hyatt County Sheriff's Department. Stick a sheet of paper inside that says 'From Beckett', or something like that. Okay?"

"With my compliments. I'll give Ivy an update, carefully edited of course. This'll take me a few days. I'll send it FedEx from Chicago. Watch for it in about a week."

Crockett heard the basement door slam. "Thanks, Clete," he said. "Ruby just came in. Wanna say hello?"

"Just send her my love from afar. Watch your ass, Crockett. Watch her ass too. That's the best part of the whole job. So long."

Ruby set two bags on the counter and raised an eyebrow at Crockett. "Cletus?"

"Cletus."

Ruby hung up her jacket and headed for the coffee pot. "How is ol' Clete?" she said.

"He told me to watch your ass."

Ruby turned around and stuck out her bottom. "Now that is some good advice," she said. "But, right now, my ass needs a rub. It's cold out there."

"What are friends for?"

SIXTY-FIVE
Treat and Treatment

IT'S TRUE that waiting is the hardest part. For the next three or four weeks, Ruby and Crockett killed time. Not to say that Ruby wasn't a fine partner for waiting and time killing, but Kansas City is not the most entertaining of places in winter. As a rule, winter never really arrives in Kaycee. Once or twice there will be a significant snowfall, then significant slush and ice with alternate filth and freezing for a few days. The expositions are too crowded, indoor soccer and the occasional season or two of second-rate hockey too boring.

They saw a lot of movies, snuggled by the fire, played grab-ass, and really got to know each other. Out of sheer boredom, they even journeyed to Springfield, Missouri for a few days. They did not take a ride-through trip at Fantastic Caverns, and they avoided Branson like it had herpes. At Crockett's request, the duo did make it to the world headquarters of Bass Pro Shops and wandered about that vast emporium for a few hours. Ruby liked some of the clothes and tagged along through the rest of it, a sympathetic smile of tolerance on her face. Being an outdoorsy type, at least compared to Ruby, as they stood in front of an immense aquarium watching bass stare balefully back at them, Crockett was foolishly hopeful enough to suggest they go camping together in the cool of the coming spring.

"Crockett, I love you. But you must understand this. I wouldn't spend the night in a tent with you, or anyone else for that matter, if the cities were on fire. Anyplace I can't walk in heels, I do not go."

"Lotsa fresh air."

"Gives me gas."

"Chirping birdies."

"They shit on things."

"Lovely campfires"

"Smoke gets in my eyes."

"Gorgeous sunrises."

"Bedtime."

"Mother nature."

"No toilets."

"Forest primeval."

"No showers."

"LaCost, you are a stick in the mud."

"That's another thing," Ruby said. "Too many sticks, too much mud. Roughing it is when room service is late. As much as I adore you, Tarzan of the Flakes, you shall never induce me to accompany you into the wilds. The great outdoors is something to be passed through on the way inside."

Ruby turned from the aquarium and leaned against the railing, resting her elbows on the polished brass.

"If it is your sincere desire to return to nature with a female companion," she said, "I can offer you a plethora of hairy-fisted, knuckle-draggers for your inspection. I will assist you in making the least potentially painful selection and cheerfully wave goodbye as the two of you depart on your expedition. I will unselfishly do these things because you are the love of my life, and I want you to be happy. But if you expect me to slip into a muskrat loin cloth and swing through the trees, you can, and I say this with all possible kindness and sympathy for your unfortunate condition, kiss my lovely ass."

Crockett looked at her. "How 'bout we go home, I start a fire, you slip into a silk loincloth, swing through the living room, and I kiss your lovely ass?"

"Ooh! Ungawa."

An elderly lady who had been standing nearby, walked past them.

"You go girl," she said.

In the last week of February, Ruby and Crockett trekked back to Champaign. Avoiding the area of the Marriott and Marlene's place, they took a couple of rooms at the Clarion Hotel on south Neil Street. After settling in, Crockett took a cab south toward Savoy. He stopped at a Best Western and, claiming his luggage was misplaced at the airport, rented another room for a few days, paying cash. On the way back, the cabbie swung through a Chinese joint so Crockett could pick up some sweet n' sour chicken, egg rolls, and shrimp-fried rice. Feeling the need to see a happy cab driver, Crockett got him an order of crab Rangoon.

Ruby, in a long black satin robe and impossible black heels, was waiting in Crockett's room when he returned. Her hair was damp, her grin, lopsided.

"Well now," she said, "isn't that nice. Something to munch on."

"Always thinking of you," Crockett said, putting the sacks on the table.

"And you brought food, too," Ruby said, wrapping her arms around his neck.

"Damn, Ruby. I got things to do tonight."

"Isn't this nice," she said, leaning back and looking slightly down at him.

"This," Crockett said, patting her on the bottom, "is excessively nice. The food is getting cold."

Ruby released him. "Crockett," she said, "you are amazing."

"That's me," he said, opening the bags and putting out containers.

"I'm being serious here. Any other man I have ever known would either be pawing me like some sort of troglodyte, or bouncing my butt out on the street. You, you amazing male, just keep hanging in there, in spite of the way I treat you. You have to be very frustrated."

"Oh, sure," he said, sitting down to eat and pushing out a chair for her. Ruby sat.

"Why do you put up with me?" she said.

Crockett thought for a moment before he answered. "One: I love you," he said. "Two: while most men, and even you a lot of the time, would look at the way you treat me as being really shitty, I don't. I think you are just doing the best you can in a situation that is frustrating for both of us. Three: Hope springs eternal that some day you will eschew your misguided ways and become my wanton sex slave." He bumped his eyebrows. "Three's the big one."

She grinned. "It's always about you, isn't it, Crockett?"

"So far."

"Okay," Ruby said, "then tell me this. How 'bout if I said that tonight was the night?"

"I'd black out."

"All that blood rushing away from your brain, no doubt."

"The truth is, I'd probably turn you down."

"Revenge?"

"No. I'd be afraid you were in a moment of compassion for my plight, or something like that. Making love with you would, I hope, be a joyous event. A pity fuck could ruin us. I will not have us ruined, Ruby. We are too good to be allowed to go bad."

Tears leapt to her eyes. "Jesus, Crockett," Ruby said. "You are a piece of work."

"Eggroll?" Crockett replied.

SIXTY-SIX
Snuggling

AFTER DINNER, Crockett took a soak to ease the effects of the long drive. Ruby spent most of that time popping in and out of his bathroom. She washed his back, hung around to talk and generally made a nuisance of herself. She claimed it was to keep an eye on the duck, but Crockett sensed a deeper motive. He suspected she wanted to make a nuisance of herself. After the bath, declining her very kind offer to assist in his drying off, he phoned Keith.

"Sheriff Mackey, please."

"Beckett! Good to hear from ya."

"Keith?"

"Yeah."

"God, I didn't recognize your voice. It has so much more authority in it now that you're sheriff."

"Hey, bite me," Mackey said.

"How ya doin?"

"Great. Makin' progress. We gotta talk."

"Tomorrow morning, ten o'clock, the Best Western north of Savoy, room 120."

"You're here?"

"Yup. Come in your own car, in plain clothes. Will the boss let you off in the morning? Oh! Wait a minute. You're the boss, huh?"

Crockett could hear his grin. "I'll be there, Beckett. See ya tomorrow."

Ruby walked in wearing one of his dirty shirts over red panties, and sat on the side of the bed. "Seeing Mackey in the morning?"

"Yeah. Ten, at the other motel."

"Why not here?"

"To the best of my knowledge, nobody knows about you. I want to keep it that way. If I manage to fuck this whole thing up, I don't want any repercussions coming back on you. You are the woman who was never there."

"So you still don't trust him."

"I trust you, Sweetheart."

"Just me?"

"I don't distrust Keith. I'm just not sure yet. If, all of a sudden, you were introduced into the equation, too many other things would become suspect. Who I really am, what I'm really doing, stuff like that. Mackey has a pretty firm picture of who he believes me to be. I don't want to screw with that. Plus, when all this is over, Beckett can just fade away, never to be seen again. No ties, no complications."

"Gotcha."

"Yes, you do," Crockett said.

"For better or worse?"

"I dunno. So far, it's all been better. What is this thing you have for wearing my filthy clothes?"

"I don't have a thing for wearing your filthy clothes! I do, however like to put on your slightly soiled shirts. They feel like you. I like the way you feel. They smell like you. I like the way you smell. It's a girl thing, Crockett."

"If I had a letter jacket, I'd let you wear it to the pep rally."

"Why don't you come over here and sit with me, and I'll see if I can rally some of your pep, Big Boy."

"Now, don't start, Ruby. It's late and I'm tired. Tonight I just wanna go to bed. Nothing personal. I need to get some rest."

Ruby crossed her legs and began to bounce her foot. "Are you sure? This is a very nice offer."

"I realize how nice the offer is. Now behave yourself, get out of here, and let me go to bed."

Crockett turned in. He read for a while, then put up the book, rolled on his right side, shut off the light, and settled in. He was almost asleep when he heard the connecting door open. Ruby lifted the covers behind him and slid in against his back. She wrapped one arm around his chest and kissed the back of his neck.

"Just wanna sleep with you, Crockett," she whispered.

He reached back and patted her leg. "Always welcome, Sweetheart."

Ruby snuggled deeply against him. "I know that," she sighed.

In two minutes she was snoring. It took Crockett quite a while longer.

SIXTY-SEVEN
Pillow Talk

THE NEXT MORNING was unusual. Crockett woke to find Ruby in his bed, lying on her side, looking at him. It gave him a bit of a start. He flinched.

"Thanks a lot," she said.

"No, no, no, it's not personal," Crockett rasped. "I'm just not used to being watched when I wake up."

"Good morning," she smiled, laying her hand on his chest.

"Good morning," he stretched, enjoying the warmth of her palm over his heart.

"Sleep well?"

Crockett grinned. "Very well," he said, "considering there was an orangutan in bed with me. How 'bout you?"

"You hog covers."

"Sleep well?"

"You snore."

"Sleep well?"

"Yes, I did," Ruby said, collapsing back on the bed and looking at the ceiling. He could see a slight flush on her face. He rose to an elbow and looked down at her.

"Good," he said, and kissed her on the cheek.

"Now don't get any big ideas, Buster. This doesn't mean we're gonna go shopping for baby clothes and a vine covered cottage."

"Not me, Ruby," he said, and kissed her cheek again.

"This was ... I don't know what this was. Shit."

He kissed her on the cheek for the third time. Slowly. She squirmed, and hunched up her shoulder.

"Crockett—"

"Call me Davey," he said.

"Aw, Jesus. Crockett, don't read anything into this."

"Why would I read anything into this? You just groped me all night long."

"You jerk! You and I both know we didn't do anything, I needed a warm bod to snuggle against. This is not an indicator of future behavior or any significant change in the relationship that you and I maintain. Got that?"

"Absolutely," Crockett said, and kissed her cheek again. Very slowly.

"You just needed a teddy bear and I was handy, right?"

"Exactly. We are not going to be writing love letters and picking out china patterns. And stop kissing my face."

"Okay," he said, and kissed her ear.

"Crockett!"

Crockett chuckled. "Call me Crockey," he said, "or some of those other wonderful things you called me last night."

Ruby laughed. "Christ, Crockett," she said, "knock it off!"

"Any minute now," he replied, and kissed her ear again.

"Now listen, goddammit!" Ruby growled, her voice muffled by the bedspread she'd pulled over her head. "None of this means shit."

"I know that, Ruby. The fact that you came sneaking into my bed last night, doesn't mean a thing."

"Right."

"Or that, instead of fleeing back to the sanctity of your own lesbian hideaway next door, you have chosen to still be lying abed with me, a dreaded man."

The bedspread lowered to just below her eyes.

"You are such an asshole."

"Having fun?" he said.

"Yes."

"Want me to rub your bottom?"

"Yes."

"Gonna let me?"

"No."

"Then get thee from my bed, miserable harlot."

"I can't."

"Why not?"

"I'm naked."

"Who are you, and what have you done with the dyke?"

Ruby blushed to the hairline. "Goddammit, Crockett," she snapped, "lemme have the sheet."

Crockett laughed and grabbed onto the covers.

"No chance," he said. "You made your bed. Lie in it."

"Very well," Ruby said.

Gathering her dignity, she threw back the bedspread, rose to her feet, and sauntered to the open connecting door. When she reached it, she turned around and looked at him.

"Will we have time for breakfast before you leave? I'm hungry."

239

Crockett grinned and looked her up and down. "Sure, Ruby," he said. "We'll leave in about thirty minutes, if that's alright with you."

"That will be fine," she said, and went through the door.

Ruby lied. She was not naked. She was wearing socks.

White ones.

Breakfast was weird. Ruby was congenial, friendly, nice, and not really there. Unless actively engaged in conversation, she drifted away on her thoughts. Gradually Crockett just left her alone. Between bites of his eggs, he glanced at her. She was looking at him thoughtfully. When his eyes found her, she flushed a bit and turned away. Almost immediately she looked back at him and held his gaze.

"What?" he asked.

"You."

"Well, that clears it up."

"Trust me, it ain't clear."

"I'm agog," Crockett said. "This is something I didn't think I would ever see. Ruby LaCost, confused."

"Confused isn't a strong enough word. I'm teetering on the brink of freaked-out here."

Crockett leaned forward and took her hands in his.

"Look," he said, "you need to understand some things. I love you, LaCost. Nothing is gonna alter that. We Crocketts are known for our loyalty. I am not attempting to change our relationship, alter your lifestyle, or get in your knickers."

"Sometimes I wish you would."

"Get in your knickers?"

"No, you twit. Alter my lifestyle."

"Not my job."

"I know that, Crockett, and more importantly, so do you."

"Thank you."

Ruby smiled. "You're welcome," she said.

"I love you," Crockett said. "Love is a damn site more important than anything else."

"I love you too, David."

"Be a fool not to."

"Don't I know it."

SIXTY-EIGHT
Pieces in Place

AN HOUR LATER, Keith Mackey came through the door of the Best Western.

"Beckett," he grinned, shaking Crockett's hand, "how ya doin'?"

"Fine, Keith. How's the sheriffin' business?"

"Got three new deputies, two new staff members. Some of the folks that'd been there for a spell got real nervous when Lester F. left, an' quit. Kinda glad to get shed of 'em. The county even voted me some more money for equipment and such, and everbody got a eight per cent raise. Guess a bunch a people is glad Lester took off. I know I am. Thanks again."

"Glad to help. What do you know about this whole Morrison business?"

"I watch the place two or three evenin's a week. Them night glasses you sent are great! That listnin' post ain't worth much. I'm peekin' in from over a quarter of a mile away. Can't hear nothin' special. I did find out a ol' boy I went to high school with is a part-time grounds keeper there, an' I talked to him some. He claims that Morrison an' his sister don't leave the place much, an' never on no regular schedule. He does know the combination at the gate box an' when the dogs are out, though."

"Well, that's something."

"He says he ain't seen much around the place that's very suspicious, except for Morrison's sister. Claims everybody calls her 'Darth' behind her back, an' she gives him the creeps. He says that ever three or four months things get kinda hectic around there for a few days, then ten or fifteen cars and trucks show up for a day or two, then things settle back down. I told him I might wanna get in there and look around. He said he'd lemme know if Morrison and his sister was gone and would help out, if he could. I trust him. He's a pretty good fella."

"That sounds promising."

241

"I was watching the place when they got food deliveries. A truck shows up ever Monday from a wholesale grocer here in Champaign, down on Market Street. Thought maybe you'd wanna talk to them."

"Sure do. Anything else?"

"How long ya gonna be in town?"

"Long as necessary."

"Good. Why don't you call me ever day or two. Meantime I'll keep in touch with my friend and watch the place. If anything comes up, we can be ready. Gimme a yell at home or the office. I gotta go now, though. Gotta noon meetin' with the County Commission at a place down in White Heath." He stood up. "Keep after me, Beckett. Somethin'll break."

Crockett checked the yellow pages for the address and, twenty minutes later, pulled up in front of Metro Wholesale Grocers. The lobby was small and seedy. So was the receptionist.

"Can I help ya?" she said.

Crockett laid his ID on the counter. "Please," he said.

"The Illinois Bu-bureau of Investigation. Yessir. Whacha need?"

"Your boss, or whoever heads the company."

"That'd be Mister Norman. He's probably out on the warehouse floor. I'll page him."

"Thanks."

Four or five minutes later a short, heavyset man of about fifty hustled into the lobby clutching a clipboard. He wore a white shirt with the sleeves rolled up his forearms, an open collar around a loose tie, and a concerned expression below dark brown messy hair with no gray. He spotted Crockett and came over.

"Art Norman," he said. "What can I do for you?"

"Mr. Norman, My name is Daniel Beckett. I'm with the Illinois Bureau of Investigation. Could we talk for a few moments in private?"

"You bet," Norman said. "You boys don't handle parking ticket prosecution, do you?"

"No," Crockett smiled.

"Well, that's fine. At least I won't have to call my wife's attorney. Janelle will show you to my office and get you something to drink. I'll get this last truck outa here and see you in about ten minutes, if that's okay with you."

"Just fine, Mr. Norman."

"Shit. Call me Art."

Crockett pulled back into the Clarion in time to see Ruby doing the same thing. She got out of her car carrying a grocery bag, saw him, and smiled.

"Perfect timing, Crockett. Who could expect less from two such as we?"

242

"Who indeed?"

He trailed her down the hall, unlocked his door and followed her inside.

"Whacha got?" he said.

Ruby began unloading her bag. "Emotional comfort food," she said. "I need it. So do you. French vanilla ice cream, real vanilla, real cream, real French, with chocolate fudge topping, real chocolate, real fudge, and whipped cream, real cream, real whipped. Plus, my personal favorite, Maraschino cherries. I can put a knot in one of these stems in twenty seconds, with my tongue tied behind my back. Interested?"

"Who do I have to kill?"

"And disposable plastic bowls and spoons," Ruby said, pulling the last items from the bag. "The fudge is hot. I nuked it before I left the store. Take off your coat and whatever else trips your trigger and dish up the ice cream. I'm going next door and divest myself of garments. Perhaps when I return, we'll see how creative we can be with whipped topping."

She kissed him on the cheek and went away.

Crockett started spooning French vanilla into the bowls. He was opening the jar of cherries when Ruby came back, wearing dark blue calf-length tights, a big, floppy cable-knit sweater and dark blue socks. She took the jar as soon as he got the top off and plucked out a cherry. He retrieved the jar and placed one on top of each of the piles of whipped cream. Ruby put her arms around Crockett's neck and kissed him on the lips, slipping a cherry into his mouth with her tongue. There was a knot in the stem. She leaned back and looked at him, mischief shining in her eyes.

"Ooh. You got my cherry, Crockett. Was it good for you?"

"If I buy the angora," he said, "will you wear my class ring?"

"To every game for the rest of the season," Ruby said.

SIXTY-NINE
Big Business

DEBAUCHERY IS FAR TOO MILD A WORD for what occurred in that room over the next thirty minutes. A quart of ice cream, most of an eight ounce bottle of chocolate fudge, and all but about three squirts of a can of Reddi Whip disappeared. Ruby ate more than Crockett did, and he went way overboard. She called it a pity pig-out and maybe it was, but there didn't seem to be a lot of pity in the air. Ruby licked the last of her fudge from her spoon some moments after Crockett finished.

She hiccoughed and peered at Crockett in a nearsighted manner.

"Oh, God," she said. "Crockett, it is a real shame you no longer possess that cheesy mustache of yesteryear. This can of whipped cream is not quite empty."

"Sorry."

"Perhaps there is somewhere else I could squirt it?"

"Perhaps not."

Ruby twirled the can. "Let's see," she said.

"Where is the woman who seemed so riddled with regret and perforated with uncertainty this very morning?"

"She has changed her mind," Ruby said. "She was not a healthy person, and she was up to no good. She was looking a gift horse in the mouth, she was assuming some sort of failure had occurred, and she was scared to death she had made a terrible mistake."

"And just what drew her to these revelations?" Crockett said.

"You did. Never, not once, have you put any pressure on me."

"Not true," he leered.

"Okay. You've never put any emotional pressure on me."

"True."

"Whereas I have put intense pressure of all types on you."

"Also true."

"Plus, you made a very nice statement. You said nothing matters as much as love, or words to that effect."

244

"Sure."

"So," Ruby said, "I am going to really try to not get all uptight about what may or may not be happening here. I am going to sincerely attempt to allow whatever is happening to happen, and not concern myself with what may be happening. Get it?"

"Clear as mud."

"Good. I knew you'd understand. Now, back to the Reddi Whip."

Ruby picked up the can and eyed him speculatively.

"Crème Duck?" she said.

Later that evening they were propped up on Crockett's bed, watching some sort of special effects ridden, lust encrusted, muscle-bound epic featuring bodies in the streets and blood on the moon, wishing they had eaten less ice cream. Ruby shifted a little lower against his arm.

"So, how'd it go with Mackey today?" she asked. She even sounded bloated.

"Pretty fair, I think. He knows some guy that works there he thinks can maybe get us in, and I talked to the man that supplies the clinic with groceries. Interesting."

"Interesting?"

"Yeah. It seems that the clinic has about the same food in the same amounts delivered week after week for about ten or eleven weeks in a row. Then, for two or three weeks, the amount of kid's food, lunchmeat, milk, eggs, bread, canned pastas, puddings, peanut butter and jelly, things like that, skyrockets to two or three times the normal amount. During the last few days of that two or three weeks, the call for steaks, lobster, shrimp and luxury foods goes up a thousand percent or more. Then the whole thing falls off radically and gets back to normal. In another ten or eleven weeks, the process starts all over again."

"That is interesting."

"Also, Mackey's friend that works there says every three or four months, things get a little hectic around the old homestead for a couple of weeks, then several cars and trucks arrive for a day or two. After they leave, everything relaxes again. This is confirmed by a farmer who lives behind the clinic."

"What the hell is going on?"

"The food is the real indicator. If you look at it alone, it seems that about four times a year the population of children at the clinic booms. Then, shortly thereafter, a group of adults must be fed and fed well. Then the excess adults and excess children all go away until the next time."

"That's weird. What are they doing?"

Crockett shook his head. "No way to know for sure," he said. "Could be any number of reasons for the evidence. There is certainly not enough grounds for any kind of formal action. But, if I had to make a wild guess, knowing Morrison's proclivities and such, I'd say he's a slaver."

"A slaver?"

"Yeah. Selling kids. He buys a group, fattens 'em up, so to speak, vets 'em out, then contacts clients and has a sale."

Ruby sat up straight. "He's selling children?!"

"Could be."

"Jesus Christ, Crockett! That's awful!"

"Yep."

"What for? I mean, what's he selling them for?"

"Who knows? Child pornography, torture, adoption, medical experimentation, organ harvesting, prostitution, snuff films. There's a hell of a list and damn near everything on it is terrible. Big money though. Millions a year."

"God! Can that be true?"

"It's just one possible explanation. No proof, just supposition. I am damn sure gonna find out, though. We stay here until Mackey comes up with a way to get us inside. If I can get information that'll pass muster, we give it to Clete. He gets it into the right hands and Morrison and Darth go downtown."

"Jesus!"

"Thousands of kids, not just young people and runaways, but kids, little kids, vanish in this country every year. And that's just this country. The problem is huge in central and south America. Children are stolen, parents sell their kids to brokers, phony adoption services are all over the place. Women are paid just to get pregnant, have babies, and give 'em up to the dealers for re-sale."

"Big business."

"Huge business. Bigger every year."

Ruby had almost screwed herself into his side. Crockett shifted his posture and she relented.

"Sorry. Guess I was trying to crawl away from it all."

"We're going after this guy, Sweetheart. If he can be had, we'll get him. Mackey has some good connections. With luck, we may be able to close this thing down in a few days."

"I hope so, Crockett. Then what?"

"Then we live happily ever after."

"Really?"

"Really."

Ruby slid down on the bed and rested her head on Crockett's chest.

"I wish it were that simple," she said.

Crockett twisted a strand of her hair around his finger. "That's the problem with simple," he said. "We tend to complicate it a lot."

Ruby chuckled. "Crockett," she said, pushing her ear against him. "I can hear your heartbeat."

"LaCost," he said, rubbing the back of her neck, "you *are* my heartbeat."

SEVENTY

Attack

FOR SIX DAYS they knocked around Champaign-Urbana. Ruby and Crockett toured some of his old stompin' grounds, what little was left, and just generally relaxed and played with each other. Every day he called Keith at the sheriff's department, and every day Mackey had nothing to report. On the seventh morning, a Friday, things changed.

"Dan. Glad you called." Keith's voice betrayed a little excitement. "Morrison's got a speech to give in town tonight at some kinda dinner. His sister always goes with him to these things. They'll be gone from the place 'til midnight or better. I can't get us inside the house, but I thought you might wanna take a look around outside."

"Sure."

"Great. We can go in on foot from the back of the place, get up to within fifty yards or so of the stable, and look the set-up over. Week after next, Morrison and his sister are goin' outa town for a couple days. Hopefully we can get inside then. After tonight we'll have a lot better idea what we'll need to be doin' when they leave."

"Sounds good to me, Keith."

"You been to his place?"

"Drove by it once."

"'Member the sharp turn at the gravel pit?"

"Yep."

"Just a little ways after the turn is a road off to the east."

"I know where it is."

"Right after ya go through the gate, there's a flat spot to your left. I'll be waitin' there at nine in my old truck. We'll drive to the backside of Morrison's land and walk in. Suit you?"

"Suits me."

"It's still cold enough the dogs shouldn't be loose. Long as we stay outside the board fence, we'll be okay even if they are."

"Fine," Crockett said. "See ya at nine."

247

"I'll bring a thermos a coffee. Probably be cold as a mother-in-law's kiss tonight."

"Well, you dress warm, Honey."

Mackey chuckled. "I will, Mom," he said.

Ruby had come in during the last half of the conversation, wearing her satin warm-ups. She straddled Crockett's lap and sat down, draping an arm over each of his shoulders, and leaned forward to kiss the tip of his nose.

"LaCost," Crockett warned.

"Going out tonight?"

"Yeah."

"Mackey?"

"Mackey," Crockett said, squirming a bit.

"Woof," Ruby growled. "More."

"Goddamn it, Ruby, get up. You're killin' me, here."

She did, turned around, and sat down again, leaning back against his chest and stomach. Crockett reached his arms around her waist. She put her hands on his.

"Going to Morrison's?" Ruby said.

"We're gonna take a look around the grounds. We'll try to get inside in a couple of weeks. We finish this bit of business tonight, and it's back to Kaycee for a while."

"Speaking of unfinished business," she said, moving his hands down to the tops of her thighs, "don't we have some of that?"

"We have a shitload of that."

"Ever notice how good my bod feels through thin satin, Crockett?" she said, sliding his hands down to the inside of her thighs.

A tiny warning bell jangled in the back of Crockett's brain. This was not the usual LaCost fun n' games.

"Ruby, quit it! C'mon, get off."

"Okay, Crockey," she said, leaning forward and wiggling her butt. "The question is, can I get off and get up, too?"

"Dammit, Ruby."

"Plus, if I don't get up, you might get off."

"Shit."

Ruby got to her feet. "I can't help it," she said. "I'm horny."

Crockett patted her on the bottom. "You are also gay," he said.

"Yeah. It's amazing how I can be this gay, and not happy about it."

"I'm not too happy about it either, you know."

"I know, Crockett. Can I go with you tonight?"

"No, no, no. Too many questions, too much hassle. Besides, we're just going to look around. We won't be inside the board fencing. I need to look at the place before we try to actually get in the house."

"Okay. I'll just stay here, all by myself, and decide what I should be wearing for you upon your return. Any preferences? Bi-sexual business woman? Virgin baby-sitter? Nasty nurse? C'mon, Crockett, help me out. What do we do fornication like this?"

"How 'bout a nasty, bi-sexual, virgin nurse?" Crockett said, not really appreciating the by-play.

"Too complicated. I might have an identity crisis."

"Some people would say you already have an identity crisis."

"Yeah, but they're all Republicans."

"I'm a Republican."

"Nope. You're a Crockett. That means you're way too smart to believe the Democrat's bullshit and way too aware to buy into the Republican rhetoric. You are enlightened enough not to have anything against those of us who are gay as a group, but, specifically speaking, the fact that I am gay pisses you off."

"Bingo!" he said.

She grinned and put her arms around his neck.

"A Democrat would celebrate the fact that I wouldn't screw him. That's phony. A Republican would be pissed that I wouldn't fuck him because I'm a dyke and be convinced that if he could get in my knickers he could change me. Ignorant, but honest. You, Dear Man, are pissed because you actually understand my feelings and sympathize with my plight. Aware and caring."

"That would be me."

"Yes, it is. Would you want me to put aside my feelings and fall into bed with you for a pity fuck?"

He grabbed her bottom with both hands and stared thoughtfully into the distance.

Ruby giggled. "Crockett, what are you doing?"

"I'm thinking," he said. "I'm thinking."

SEVENTY-ONE
Abuse

RUBY MADE CROCKETT'S LIFE mostly miserable through the rest of the day. Her play was not significantly different than from other times and situations, but she was. There was an edge to her behavior, almost a bitterness. She used her gender nearly as a weapon. Crockett didn't like it. It was a little scary.

She pursued him through lunch, teased him all afternoon, taunted him through dinner, and put Crockett in such a state of sexual battering he felt he needed professional help. Back at the hotel, he told her so.

"What kind of professional help? A hooker?"

Crockett snorted. "No," he said, "not a hooker."

"Need the old pipes cleaned, Crockett? How 'bout a plumber? I told you before that I knew several women with a fondness for waterfowl. I even offered to put you in easily accessible proximity to these fair maids, but no, you would have none of it."

Ruby grinned. Her smile was brittle. "You had your chance and my assistance," she said. "You chose the moral high ground. Now you are suffering. Whose fault is that?"

"What's going on, Ruby?"

"It's a LaCost accost."

"You got that right."

"I choose not to be horny alone," Ruby said, challenge in her tone.

"Bullshit."

She looked at him for a moment, then sagged. The nearly frantic light in her eyes softened.

"It is, isn't it?" she said.

"Yes, it is."

"Christ, Crockett, I don't know. Some sort of perverse need to keep the carrot just out of reach, for some reason."

"Testing me?"

"Maybe."

"Okay. If, for whatever reason, you feel I need to be tested, I'll play along."

"Well, it's no fun testing you if you know you're being tested. Jesus, Crockett, don't you know the rules?"

"Sorry to take all the joy out of it."

"This is terrible! I have no reason, much less any goddamn right, to test anybody, least of all you! I apologize."

Crockett got pissed.

"That is not a sincere apology, goddammit, and you fucking well know it! I don't want your apology anyway, Ruby. I want you to understand that the only way you are going to get me out of your life is to tell me to go away. It's just that simple. What has been going on with you today has not been fun and games. It has not been your usual level of teasing. It has not had the honesty of a green silk teddy and ear nibbling. It has not been playing in a see-through shower. It has been empty of joy, LaCost, and you are the most joyful person I know."

Crockett could see anger darkening Ruby's eyes. He plunged ahead anyway.

"It has been a sexual assault tempered with emotional cruelty," he said. "It is beneath you, it is beneath us, and I don't like it! I have put up with it because you are obviously troubled by something and I love you, but understand me. I do not, in any way, deserve this type of treatment. If you want some kind of punishment fuck, go find a hairy-legged bull-dagger and get it over with. I will be here when you get back and I will help you get through the aftermath. If you choose not to do that, I am still here for you. If you do not want me here, tell me to leave and I will show you my heels, but stop the rest of this crap right now! I'll put it as plainly as I can, in an effort to communicate as efficiently as possible. Get off my back."

"You through?" Ruby snarled.

"Pretty much."

"Who the hell do you think you are?"

Crockett looked at her for a moment before he answered.

"I'm the guy that's registered in this room," he said quietly, feeling tears behind his temper. "Through that door is your room. I think it would be best if you went to it before one or both of us gets emotionally out of hand. I've taken all the shit I can today and I've gotta work tonight. Go away, Ruby. I'll see you tomorrow."

Ruby glared at him. "Fine!" she said, and stomped out.

He lay back on the bed and felt like shit.

At about ten 'til eight Crockett roused himself and got up. He changed into jeans and a pullover sweater, a pair of short Thinsulate-lined hiking boots, and got out his goose down car coat. He checked the pockets for gloves and an ear-band, slipped his phone out of the charger and into a pocket, grabbed his wallet and phony ID, and was picking up his cane when he heard a knock on the door from Ruby's room. It was the first time she had ever bothered to knock.

"Come in, Ruby."

She was dressed in dark blue sweats. Her face was puffy, her eyes red, her hair messy, and she had some difficulty looking directly at him. She schlepped in like the world was on her shoulders.

"Ah, Crockett?"

"Yeah?"

"I'm really stupid. I have behaved very badly today, and I am so sorry. I swear I don't know what's going on inside my head. I must be nuts."

"As a doctor," he said, "you would know that."

"You have every reason to be angry with me," she said.

"I am not angry with you, Sweetheart. I'm just concerned about you."

"Of course you are," Ruby said, and a tiny smile flickered across her lips. "I'm really embarrassed and I'm really confused. I have a favor to ask."

"Name it."

She held out a piece of paper the way you'd hold a scrap of meat out to a tiger.

"I want you to put this in your wallet, okay?"

It was a comment card for the hotel. On the printed side she'd lettered instructions to see the reverse side. The back contained Dan Harter's name and number and Randy DeMoss' name and number, designated as those to call in the event of an emergency. Crockett put it in his shirt pocket.

"Wallets get stolen," he said.

"Aw, Crockett," Ruby said, "I am such a shit. Hold me." She came into his arms and they stood, swaying a little, until he pulled away.

"I gotta go, Ruby. Mackey's gonna be waiting. We're on a fairly tight time line."

"You come back, goddammit. You come right back here to me."

"Count on it. I'll see ya before morning."

Ruby kissed him. Hard.

"Be careful, Crockett," she whispered.

"As a rat in a cat factory," he said, and went out the door.

SEVENTY-TWO
Lights out

THE NIGHT FELT EDGY. The sky was totally clear and, while the lights of the city did not disclose many stars, the three-quarter moon was crisp and well defined. Crockett's breath hung in the air, and he walked through it again and again on the way to the Chevy. The vinyl seat creaked when he got inside, as stiff and reluctant with the cold as his leg. Pulling out of the parking lot, Crockett tried to push Ruby and her behavior from his mind. She was not the situation that needed to most concern him at the moment. He was on the way to do something he didn't like to do. Sneak around.

Crockett could have been an armed robber. There is a directness in confronting someone and removing something from his possession by force or the threat of force. Robbery is a despicable act, but it is face to face, exposed, an open encounter. What Keith and he were going to do was much more like burglary. To skulk and prowl was not Crockett's nature and the prospect of it made him jumpy. He turned his thoughts to Martin and Marian Morrison and what they had done to Rachael. He needed anger to remain focused. It wasn't hard.

Driving through the country at night, the Chevy's tires crunching the gravel, the occasional gleam of roadside eyes gleaming in headlights, took Crockett back to the days of underage beer drinking, fogged car windows, frustrating bra snaps, and semi-permanent erections. He actually caught himself grinning a couple of times as rural Hyatt County slid by; remembering what it was like to be ignorant and immortal and seventeen. When he turned into the gravel pit road, shut off the headlights, and crept along the crusty path, he could almost feel Cheryl Blanzy next to him on the front seat, eager and tentative in the darkness. Parking lights flashed to his left and, behind some scraggly saplings, he could see the shape of a truck. Keith was waiting. Crockett sent Cheryl home.

"Hey," Mackey whispered. "Get in."

Crockett walked around to the passenger side of the old pick-up, slid onto the seat, and eased the door closed. The motor was idling and the cab was warm. As his eyes adjusted to the darkness, Crockett could see quite clearly. Keith handed him a cup of very hot, very strong, very black coffee.

"Thanks."

"Sure. Here's the deal. Morrison and his sister left about six o'clock to go to some dinner in Urbana. He's one of the speakers. Shouldn't be home 'til midnight or later. The day staff is all gone by now, the kids most likely in bed. The help that lives there will be off work except for the night nurse. She stays upstairs in a room next to where the young'uns are. Even with this goddammed moon, we oughta be able to get in and out without bein' seen. The dogs are penned up next to the stable. Man, them dogs are somethin'! Big old sonsabitches, nasty lookin', but in all the time I been watchin' this place, I ain't heard a peep outa either of 'em. The damn things don't bark!"

"Really."

"Not a sound. So, we don't havta worry about them. There's a pond just inside the rear fence. It's fed by a pretty good spring. The overflow runs away from the house out the backside of the property. It's made a cut through the field. We can go in that way, if ya like. Pretty rough. The rest of the backside is in clover stubble and stuff like that. We march up through that, we'll leave tracks like a super highway. I'd just as soon they didn't know we'd been here."

"Sounds fine to me."

"Okay," Keith said, slipping the truck into gear. "We'll leave your car stashed right where it is. Watch your coffee."

The pick-up jerked on the gravel, hot coffee sloshed onto Crockett's hand and they were off, driving dark to the rear of the Morrison estate.

It took them nearly an hour to walk from the back of the property to behind the fenced grounds. The streambed wound its way all over the place and Crockett's back and leg were on fire by the time they reached the fence. His cane was useless in the terrain; the night-vision goggles worthless in the bright moonlight. Both remained in the truck. Crockett leaned against the board fence and waited for his hip to settle down.

"Big place," Mackey whispered, wrapped tight and nervous. "The fence gets closest to the house on the other side of the stable over there, and the house has no rear windows in that area. When you're ready, we'll slide over that way and take a look."

"Sorry 'bout slowing you down."

"Don't worry about it. We got plenty of time."

Crockett rubbed his leg and looked around. Even coming out of winter, the place was neat as a pin. Well-maintained gravel paths connected the house, the stable, the arena, the pond, and the rear of the garage to one another. Nothing was out of place, nothing untidy. A fox barked in the distance and he watched a raccoon ramble across the backyard in that head-down shambling gait they have. When Crockett again knew where his foot was and could use his leg with some certainty, he told Keith they could move on.

Mackey took the lead and they slipped along the fence to the east side of the stable. The fence turned south and moved to within about thirty yards of the northeast corner of the house. They stopped by a gate in the shadow of an immense spruce and looked around from a different angle. From his left, Keith pointed across in front of Crockett.

"Jesus Christ," Mackey said. "Will you look at that?"

Crockett turned to see what Keith was pointing at, and the lights, as they say, went out.

SEVENTY-THREE
Belly of the Beast

A SLAP PULLED HIM BACK. Crockett's head throbbed with his heartbeat, the worst of it from just below and behind his right ear. He tried to move and couldn't, jerked his neck and hissed with the pain of it. He stopped struggling and awareness seeped slowly through the fog. He was still wearing his coat and was fastened securely in a wheelchair by wide padded-leather restraints at his wrists, biceps, waist and ankles. Carefully lifting his head, he gazed at a tall silver-haired man. He was smiling, standing directly in front of the wheelchair, wearing a quilted maroon smoking jacket and an ascot. The room swam slowly into focus.

"Mr. Beckett," he beamed down at Crockett. "So good of you to join us. I have heard so much about you. I am Martin Morrison. We have a mutual acquaintance, Sheriff Keith Mackey." His voice held a trace of an English accent.

Mackey was casually sitting on the edge of a desk about ten feet behind Morrison, grinning at their captive. The room was large and low, obviously underground. Opposite Crockett, against the back wall, was what appeared to be a closet. The door was partially open to reveal a portion of the interior. A small elevator. File cabinets and a couple of computers were at opposite sides of the room and two or three armchairs were scattered about. Sitting in one of them was an elderly woman. She was obviously Morrison's sister. Dressed conservatively in a dark blue pant-suit and plain white blouse, she was not smiling.

"Good evening, Marian," Crockett said, and slowly swung his head back to look at Morrison.

"Considerable pain I should think, Mr. Beckett," Morrison said. "I could give you an injection for relief, and gladly would, if it would not interfere with my plans for later. Terribly sorry."

Crockett slipped into a broad Brit accent.

256

"Think nothing of it, Old Thing," he said. "Terribly good of you to show such concern for my condition, however. I'll muddle through somehow. Lovely ascot. Pick it up on the Row?"

Morrison reddened, Mackey snorted, the sister shifted in her chair.

"Don't make the mistake of taking me lightly, Beckett!" snarled Morrison, suddenly without accent. "I am not a man to be trifled with!"

"Sure you are, you fuck," Crockett said. "If it wasn't for your sister, you'd be working in some public health facility someplace, getting your jollies over the internet. She's the brains and balls of all of this. She scares me. You just bring a bad taste to my mouth."

Morrison stepped forward, his face red and contorted. "You will leave my sister out of this!" he shouted, and raised his hand to strike a blow.

"Don't!"

Marian's voice was dry and flat. It stopped Morrison dead in his tracks.

"Not part of the exercise, Martin," she said. "Later, we'll find some entertainment for you."

From command, her voice had gone to cajole. He wilted.

"Very well," Morrison said, and collected himself. "I would assume you have some questions, Mr. Beckett."

Crockett looked at him.

"Come, come, Mr. Beckett. Nothing to say?"

Crockett swung his aching head and tried to focus on Mackey.

"You're a dead man, Keith."

"Mr. Beckett," Morrison said, "you are hardly in a position to make threats." Mackey smirked.

"Oh, I'm not threatening anybody," Crockett said. "I'd love to see Keith alive and in prison. A cop who protected a killer and abuser of small children, slammed away in the Graybar Hotel, would get exactly what he deserved over and over again. I'd enjoy knowing Mackey would be around for all that. He'll be much better off dead. You'll be doing him a real favor, Morrison."

"Fuck you, Beckett," Mackey said. "Some federal fuck comin' in here, gonna throw his weight around. You don't know shit, you ain't shit. All the time you thought you was playin' me, I was playin' you. You ain't so fuckin' smart now, are ya?"

"You don't get it, do you, Sheriff? Sometime tonight you are going to kill me. Unless I miss my guess, your department will even investigate my death just to be sure the investigation gets controlled. You think old Martin here can let you live after all that is over? You think he really intends to pay you as much as he has promised to pay you? He's a businessman, Keith. You'll be unfinished business. One phone call and, in a few days, you are just a memory. You stupid shit. I actually feel sorry for you. You're so goddammed dumb, you even think

257

I'm lying to you. At least you'll be out of the gene pool. You're just paddling around in the shallow end anyway."

"I'm gonna enjoy killing you, Beckett!"

"You better, you dumbass shitkicker. It's gonna cost you big."

"Keith," Marian said, "go get his car."

"Yes, M'am," Mackey replied and headed for the elevator. After he was out of the room, she turned to Crockett.

"You have a great deal of this figured out, don't you Mr. Beckett?"

"Some of it. You are the power behind the throne, I know that. The clinic is a front for other things, probably selling kids. Your brother is a chronic abuser of children. He murdered his wife."

"She didn't understand my needs," Morrison said. "Marian does. She's very good to me and I owe everything to her. She makes it possible for me to have my lovely toys to play with."

"I'm sure she does. How many kids a year do you sell?"

"Sixty to seventy-five. Fifty to sixty thousand dollars apiece. How much do you make a year, Beckett?"

"Mexico?"

"And Central America. I have suppliers as far south as Brazil and clients all over the country that buy from me or pay for the exhibitions."

"The exhibitions?" Crockett said.

Morrison glanced at his sister. She nodded.

"My clients are individuals of unusual tastes; tastes that the average person would find very difficult to satisfy. My function is to feed these uncommon appetites. Whenever I get a shipment, I save several head back. That way, I have something to play with until the next shipment, and I also have some disposable stock."

"Disposable stock?" Crockett said.

"Exhibitions. One of the favorites is to place one or two of the five and six-year-old children in a special stall in the stable, then release Thor and Loki upon them. The live performance can net close to a hundred thousand dollars. The films and tapes will more than double it. Very lucrative."

"Five and six year olds?"

Morrison's voice assumed the tone of a lecturer.

"That's about the right age," he said. "It's close to the upper level of what my clients appreciate, but if one uses children much younger than that, they give up or are too easily overwhelmed by the dogs. Plus, the child must be of sufficient age to have good self-awareness and a well-developed fight or flight reflex. In three and four year olds, the reptile brain is often too easily overwhelmed by naked fear. Entertainment value is lost. I find children that young are better utilized for superficial torture, burning, pricking and the like."

"Fish hooks and pellet pistols."

"Exactly!" Morrison said. "Mr. Beckett. You surprise me!"

"What about your daughter?"

"My daughter is deceased."

"By your hand, I assume."

"She was on the edge of becoming a threat."

"Nice work. Everybody thought it was a suicide."

Morrison smiled and settled into a chair.

"Quite simple, actually," he said. "She was my original subject for behavioral modification. It's the same type of protocol I use on the children upstairs. To keep within layman's terms, the use of certain chemicals such as Scopolamine, Clozapine, even something as mundane as Valium in bolus, when combined with hypnosis, can be used to format the mind so that a key word or phrase will render the subject completely malleable."

"Manchurian Candidate kinda thing, huh?"

Morrison laughed. "Hardly," he said. "I know my daughter was frightened of me, just as I know she had actually engaged an analyst. I could not allow some of her buried memories to surface. When I found out that she had acquired an ex-policeman to teach her how to use a weapon, I knew I had to act. I went to Kansas City, phoned her apartment, told her the key word, and she happily admitted me to her home."

Crockett's heart ached. "Key word?"

"Yes. Tundra, in her case. Not a word commonly used in conversation. She was conditioned to react to that word and my voice. After we got upstairs, at my request she filled her tub, wrote a note, disrobed, settled into the water and allowed me to open her veins. She was smiling when I left. Suicide. What else could it be?"

The elevator door opened, and Keith Mackey walked into the room.

"Car's out front," he said.

"Very good, Keith. Mr. Beckett, would you care for a drink?"

"No, thank you."

"I believe you would, Mr. Beckett," Morrison said. "In fact, I must insist."

While Mackey held Crockett's head and nose, Morrison managed to pour about a pint of whiskey down his throat. Keith grinned.

"All you gotta do, Beckett, is sit here awhile and get drunk. See ya later." The three of them left.

Crockett knew he was screwed. He had no help, he couldn't escape, and in fifteen minutes he'd be drunk as a skunk. Slim consolation was that Morrison would not get away with it. Ruby knew too much; Dan Harter would be told the truth. The clinic would fall. So would Crockett. He couldn't really get upset about anything except leaving Ruby alone. The more he thought about it all, the less he could think about it all. Soon Keith came back, and wheeled him to the elevator.

"You're gonna have a accident, Agent Beckett, sir," he said. "You're gonna miss the curve down by the gravel pit and go over the edge. It's about eighty feet to the bottom. Nobody'll find ya until tomorrow morning when the pit workers come in. Damn shame you was drinkin' so much or you might have made the corner. My department'll work its ass off, but it's just a plain old accident. One dead-drunk, dead drunk. Them head injuries'll take a fella out."

The door opened onto the mansion entryway. Morrison and his sister waited beside Crockett's car. The scene spun in front of him as Keith wheeled the chair to the open passenger side door.

"Anything to say, Boy?" he asked.

Crockett spat on him.

"Go ahead," Morrison said. "To the forehead, I should think."

Mackey grinned and reached for a hip pocket. He withdrew an immense, spring- loaded lead sap and drew back his arm.

"Say goodbye, Beckett," he said, and his arm flashed forward.

Crockett's world stopped.

SEVENTY-FOUR

Return

IT WAS DARK. Crockett was warm and comfortable, drifting aimlessly, completely at ease and at rest. The light came out of nowhere.

"Stop it," he said.

It went away. It came back.

"Get the light outa my eyes!"

It stayed.

"Goddammit! You deaf? Get the light outa my eyes!"

It left. As if from a distance, Crockett heard a voice.

"Jesus! Quick, get Kelso in here. I think he just tried to say something!"

"Shut up and let me sleep, willya?"

The light came back. He slapped at it.

"Hurry up, for chrissakes! He's twitching now and making noise!"

"What the hell is the matter with you? Get outa here and leave me alone! I wanna sleep!"

"David? David! Can you hear me?"

"Shit. Yeah, I hear you."

"Can you hear me? David? C'mon, David. Can you hear me?"

"I hear you, I hear you. What the fuck do you want?"

"David, it's time to wake up! Wake up now. It's time for you to wake up!"

"Wake up, my ass! Get outa here and lemme sleep."

"Open your eyes, David. C'mon, open your eyes. It's time to come back. Come on back David. David!"

"You better have a damn good reason for bothering me, asshole!"

"Wake up! David, wake up! It's time to wake up! David, Wake up! David! David! David!"

"For God's sake," Crockett said, "Call me Crockett!"

He opened his eyes.

Everything was muddled and hazy. Light streamed in through a window and Crockett squinted from the glare. Silhouettes moved be-

261

tween him and the light, but he was unable to focus or follow the movement. One of them leaned over the bed where he lay and laughed.

"Okay, Crockett. You got a deal," said a rich male voice. "I'm going to put a straw in your mouth. Try to sip a little bit of water. It'll make it a lot easier to talk."

Crockett sipped, but couldn't tell if he got any liquid or not.

"Try to stay calm, Crockett. Everything is all right. I know your vision is blurred, I know you can't feel your body. I know you are confused. None of that matters. You are in good hands and you are going to be okay. You'll go back to sleep in a minute. Just focus on the fact that you are among friends who are helping you. You are safe and you are going to be well."

Safe? Well? Why wouldn't he be safe and well?

"Before you go back to sleep, there is someone here to see you for a moment." Another shadow moved between Crockett and the light, and came very close to his face.

"Aw, Crockett. You came back. I told 'em you would. Good to see ya, you old fart. I love you."

Ruby. Reality returned with a rush and his eyes filled with tears.

The darkness crept back in.

SEVENTY-FIVE
Reunion

THE LIGHT RETURNED. Crockett opened his eyes. Ruby was looking down at him. She smiled. He tried to say hello, but nothing worked.

"Here," she said, holding a glass with a straw to his lips. "Take a sip. Slowly."

He did and felt water trickle down his throat. He sipped again, watching Ruby slip in and out of focus. Another woman moved to the other side of the bed and peered at him.

"Hi," she said. "I'm Darlene, your night nurse. You're stuck with me for another couple of hours yet. How ya doin'? Can you speak?"

"Yes," Crockett croaked.

She smiled. "More or less. Ruby will get you some ice shavings. That'll fix you up."

"Drink."

"No. I don't want anything to speak of going in your stomach," Darlene said, wiping his face with a damp cloth. "You are a sick puppy, David. You're gonna be fine, but we are going to do all of this the right way. Doctor Kelso will be in to see you after while. You're stable, your vitals are good, you are actually picking up some color. Ah, here's Ruby with your ice. Let me slip some of this in your mouth."

Crockett felt cold slide between his lips. It was wonderful. He closed his eyes for a moment.

"That's a good boy," Darlene said. "Slow and easy, David. Everything slow and easy."

"Call me Crockett," he whispered.

"Fine, Crockett," she said. "That's nicer than a lotta stuff I've called you since we first met. I'm gonna go get things ready to change your IV bags. If you are still awake when I come back, it's time for your bubble bath. If not, I'll just hose you off in your sleep. See ya."

263

"More ice?" asked Ruby. He tried to nod, but couldn't move his head. "One blink is yes," she said, "two is no." He blinked once and got more ice. It helped.

"Can't move," Crockett murmured. "Para—?"

"No, you are not paralyzed, just very weak."

"Where?"

"Ivy's house."

Ruby put a little more ice on his tongue. He let it melt for a moment.

"Not hospital?"

"No," she smiled. "Ivy wouldn't allow it. She wanted you to have the best. She brought the hospital to you."

He tried to grin. It almost worked.

"How I?"

"You are going to be fine. That's the truth. In some ways, you will be better than you have been in years. Your recuperation will take time, but you will recover completely. You know I wouldn't lie to you."

"Know."

"Good. Take my word for anything you need to know. If I don't have the answer, I'll get it for you. You will receive no song and dance here, Crockett, I promise you."

"Okay. Ice?" She gave him some more. "How long here?"

"Well, brace yourself, Sweetie. Next week will be three months."

"Wha?"

"It's the second week in June."

Crockett felt the bed tilt and a low roar filled his ears. He closed his eyes. When he opened them, Darlene was there.

"Sorry, Crockett. I sent Ruby away. I'll let her come back in now that you are stable again. We're boosting your adrenals a bit. That shouldn't happen any more. Don't get scared. You're doing very well. By the way, I'm really a doctor. You have three full-time orderlies who are really nurses, two full-time nurses who are really doctors, and one head physician who is really God. At least he thinks so. His name is Alfonse Kelso. I'm married to the bastard and he still gave me the night duty. Said he wanted a Kelso with you all the time."

She patted his forehead with a light cloth.

"We live here, Crockett. On this floor, in this wing. Believe me, nothing is going to be allowed to happen to you. Ivy would kill us. If she were too busy, Clete would do it for her. If not him, Ruby. You're getting better treatment than the President and, from what I hear, you deserve it. You seeing better now?"

"Yes."

"Great. Now you can tell how cute I am. Love me while you can, Crockett, 'cause in a few days, you may not like any of us very much. But, you will get better. I'll go tell Ruby that you're alive. My hubby

264

ought to be in soon." she smiled and winked at Crockett. "He's a real sonofabitch, but he's the best goddammed doctor on the planet."

She bounced out. Ruby was back in a flash.

"You okay?"

"Okay. June?"

"Yeah. Sorry to sneak up on you like that. You've been in a coma."

"Jesus."

"Let me tell you some stuff," Ruby said, perching on the edge of the bed and gently stroking the side of his face. "You just listen for awhile. Your cheesy mustache is back, and so is that little wispy thing on your manly chin. I've kept them trimmed. You've never been more lovely. You also weigh about one-fifty. You've lost nearly seventy pounds. Not exactly the weight loss program I'd recommend, but effective nonetheless. The piercings on your ear have been opened up. Now that you are awake, I can probably put your earrings back in for you. Your hair is actually shorter than when you last saw it. Your head had to be shaved in places, so I told them to shave the whole thing."

Ruby used a tissue to wipe some saliva from the corner of Crockett's mouth.

"Martin Morrison is shut down. His sister had a stroke a few days after you were there. She nearly died and just recently has gone home, confined to a motorized wheelchair. The clinic is closed, the patients gone, no staff remains but a cook and a houseman. The Morrisons believe you are dead. Oh! Keith Mackey has disappeared. Vanished. Nobody has seen him in two months or more. Even Cletus can't find him."

"Dead. Morrison hire him kill me, then kill him."

"That bastard! I'm glad he's dead. After what you did to help that sonofabitch, and he did this to you?"

"Yes."

"Asshole! I hope the shit-eater rots in hell!"

"Miss LaCost, something for your blood pressure perhaps?"

The voice was baritone, congenial, and belonged to a stumpy, slightly overweight, forty-year-old man with great teeth and almost no hair.

"Yeah," Ruby said. "Single malt scotch, if you have it."

"Buying you a drink could possibly cause me certain difficulties with my wife."

"Not if I can come along," Darlene said, walking in with a new IV bag. "If these people are bothering you, Crockett, I'll throw them out."

"Maybe later," he whispered.

"Crockett," said the man, "I am Alfonse Kelso. I am responsible for assembling the collection of misfits, magicians and meddlers that has brought you back from the brink and will push you on to new heights. In spite of all that, and the propaganda you will doubtless receive

265

from the tempting and twisted lips of my spouse, Darlene, you may call me Al. How ya doin?"

"Pretty okay."

"Good! We need to talk. Ruby, if for no other reason than I do so enjoy watching you walk away, please leave."

"See ya later, Crockett," she said.

"First things first," Kelso went on, as Darlene clanked around the head of the bed, adjusting hardware. "All through this mess, Ruby has never left your side except to eat and sleep, and she has done precious little of either of those. She has read at least twenty-five paperback books to you, she has shaved you, she has bathed you, and, during the entire period of the coma, she always maintained that you would come back when you were ready, that you were just taking a break. It would appear that she was right. She is an amazing woman, Crockett. Truly amazing. Did I leave anything out, Darlene?"

Darlene looked down at her patient. "She loves you, Crockett, and she has a deep and steady faith in you and confidence in the fact that you love her. It has made the rest of us feel like emotional infants. And I can see now that her feelings are not misplaced. Not one person in a hundred thousand would have made it through what you have been through. Nobody here thought you would ever wake up, except Ruby. She was certain you would."

"Love her," Crockett said, feeling a tear trickle past his temple and toward his ear.

Al smiled down at him. "Make a note, nurse Kelso," he said. "The patient's tear ducts seem to be functional." Darlene wiped Crockett's eyes and patted his cheek.

"Now then, Crockett," Kelso said, "Darlene is adding a bit to your intravenous cocktail that will cause you to sleep for a time. As that takes effect, I will give you some information about your injuries, if you like."

"Keep simple."

"Certainly. Starting at the top. A mild fracture near the base of your skull at the right rear and the resulting displacement of the atlas-axis. A second and severe fracture to the forehead above your left eye. That one was responsible for the coma and required extensive surgery. A portion of the bone was removed and replaced with a composite plate that will not set off metal detectors. It is a Teflon-graphite substance with many unique properties and a composition that I am not familiar with. It is not my specialty. I deal in trauma and coma, not carpentry."

Kelso gently touched Crockett's face.

"The orbital area, brow ridge, socket and such of your right eye were also shattered. The eye was repaired and will function normally with time, although you will doubtless need a contact lens. The bone structure around the eye and cheekbone was also shattered. They have

266

been replaced with a substance similar in many ways to what was used for the skull. This rebuilding has changed your facial structure a bit. According to Ruby, the results are quite satisfactory. Your left shoulder was badly broken, along with your collarbone and three ribs, one of which pierced your lung. The lung is fine, the shoulder has been rebuilt with man-made products, including a new socket and the attending skeletal structure. You doing okay? My machines tell me your blood pressure and heart rate are fluctuating a bit."

"Okay. Jus' freak."

"That's understandable," Kelso said. "Thirsty?"

"Ice?"

"Certainly."

Darlene slipped some slivers between Crockett's lips.

Crockett began to feel nice and warm, and relaxed a bit. Kelso leaned against the bed.

"Now, to continue, while you are still awake," he said. "Your left hip sustained some minor damage, your left thigh was badly broken. When the team repaired the break, they also did some extensive work on your hip, replaced the socket, tuned up your sacrum a bit, balanced your pelvis, cleaned away some calcification and spurs, and repaired some damage and adhesions from that old bullet wound. We had some very good people with some cutting edge techniques and new products with which to work. I would suspect that a great many of the problems you have had in the past with your back, hip, and upper leg are over."

"Thas nice," Crockett said through the fog that was beginning to surround him.

"So, any pain anywhere? Any complaints?"

As best he could, Crockett thought for a moment. "Jus' one," he said.

"And that would be?"

"My foot itches."

"Which one?"

"Lef'."

"No, it doesn't."

"Yes, it do."

"No, Crockett, it really doesn't."

"It doesn'?"

"No."

"Why na'?" Crockett asked, just barely hanging on.

Kelso smiled. "Simple," he said. "You see, your foot is, well, it's not there anymore, actually."

"Oh," Crockett said, and went to sleep.

SEVENTY-SIX

Spike

CROCKETT OPENED HIS EYES and there was Ruby. She leaned in and kissed him on the cheek.

"More," he said.

She kissed him on the other cheek.

"More," he said.

"Take it easy, Studley."

"Take off clothes," Crockett rasped. "Want hospital visit fantasy." He tried to bump his eyebrows. She chuckled.

"Jesus Christ, Crockett. Back from the brink of eternity, and all you can think about is committing carnalities. Can't you give me a break?"

"No."

"Seems like totally appropriate behavior to me," Doctor Al said, striding into the room and moving to stand by the bed. "How ya feelin', Hotshot?"

"Hungry."

"Dammit, Crockett! You just ate three months ago. You gotta give the Kelso diet time to work. We'll have you down to eleven pounds in no time. Spike! Our boy is hungry."

A wiry little redhead appeared on the opposite side of the bed and looked down at Crockett.

"Hey," she said. "Welcome back. Glad you decided to join us."

She had lime green eyes, frizzy orange hair, thousands of freckles, great cheekbones, and that translucent skin common to the Irish and Scots. Eight inches shorter than Ruby, she weighed about a hundred pounds.

"Spike?" Crockett said.

"My name is Katheryne Margaret Maureen O'Neal."

"Nice to meetcha, Spike."

"Well," Kelso said, "while the two of you get acquainted, I am going to escort the lovely Miss LaCost to the sunroom where we will

268

have dinner and discuss your overall condition with Ivy. My bride will be by to attend to your every whim later, as will Ruby, I should think. In many ways, Crockett, you are to be envied."

Ruby kissed him on the forehead. "Take it easy, Champ. I'll be back after while."

"See ya, Ruby."

Spike and he were alone. She patted him on the arm.

"I'm your new day gal, Crockett. That's right isn't it? You prefer to be called Crockett, I'm told."

"Yep. You a doctor?"

"More or less. I have degrees in nutrition, pharmacology, and physical therapy."

"Jesus. What do you do in spare time?"

"Work out," she said. "My job is to get you in shape. Right now your digestive system is shut down. You haven't eaten anything in months. Your body has done nothing more strenuous than heal and breathe. This evening we'll get you started on some pre-digested liquid protein. You'll love it. It tastes just like bat shit."

Spike's eyes flickered over the various monitors.

"Over the next several days, we'll get you worked back up to soft foods and get ya poopin' like a good boy. We'll also get you lifting weights, like your arms and legs and head. It ain't gonna be easy, and it ain't gonna be fun, but it is gonna be real rewarding. You are gonna get well if I have anything to say about it, Crockett, and I have everything to say about it."

"You don't scare me," he said.

Spike laughed. "Sure I do," she said. "I scare everybody."

"If you physical therapist, how come not from Sweden, six feet tall, name Inga?"

"'Cause you couldn't get that lucky," Spike said.

"My luck just fine," Crockett said.

Then he remembered. The room receded and his vision reddened at the periphery.

"Just breathe, Crockett," Spike said. "Nice and slow, deep into the lungs."

She slipped a mask over his nose and gave him some straight oxygen. Gradually things leveled out and the numbness left his hands. He opened his eyes.

"Better?" Spike asked.

Unable to speak, Crockett blinked slowly.

"Good. Got a little shocky there, Big Guy. I'll rig you up a nasal line," she said, fussing around with some tubing, "so you can get rid of the mask and talk."

In a few moments she had him set up and wiped sweat off his face with a tissue. "How's that?"

"Okay."

"Something blew your dress up, Crockett. What scared ya?"

He swallowed, his tongue thick and unruly. Spike slipped some ice into his mouth. He let it melt a bit before he spoke.

"No foot," Crockett said. Spike looked puzzled for a moment.

"Oh, yeah. That. Your foot is gone. Your lower leg too, from about six or eight inches below the left knee. Don't worry about it. By the time we're done with you, you'll be the one-legged man who wins the ass-kickin' contest."

"Right."

"I'm serious. I don't know what you like to do, but you'll be able to play softball, bowl, run, rock climb, kick small dogs, whatever."

"With wooden leg."

"No, not with a wooden leg. With the leg we'll give ya."

"Bionic man, huh?"

"Nope, not bionic either. No moving parts at all actually. It's spring steel strap. Nothing to wear out, nothing to replace, absolutely simple and very reliable. Works really well. A little practice, and nobody will ever know if it's live or Memorex. As a matter of fact, we can even make it height adjustable. How 'bout it? Stand on one foot and be seven feet tall. Of course, you'll only be able to walk in a circle."

Crockett couldn't help it. He grinned.

"That's better," Spike said, removing the tubing and letting her hand rest on his shoulder. "Somebody will be by in a couple of weeks to do a gel cast of your stump, which has healed very nicely I might add, to create the correct size socket for your leg."

She checked his monitors again, and smiled down at him.

"Honest, Crockett. I know this whole thing is real scary, but it's the truth. You'll walk on it the day it's fitted to you. Just a few weeks later you'll be running on your new foot. It's amazing. I could show you case history after case history of the stuff people do with these things, from high-schoolers to grandmas. The leg will not be a problem. It will be the easiest thing we have to do. Okay?"

"Yeah. Okay."

"Good. Now, you need to nap for a while. I'll wake you up before I go so you can drink some bat shit. We gotta get those intestines humming along. Tomorrow the work begins. Love me while you can, Sweetie Pie, cause very soon, you're gonna think I'm the bitch-queen of the universe. And you'll be right. Go to sleep, Crockett," she patted him on the chest. "It's nice to be workin' with ya."

She closed the drapes and left. Crockett lay in the gloom and tried to sleep, but couldn't get comfortable. His left foot itched.

Shit.

SEVENTY-SEVEN
Availability

THE NEXT FEW WEEKS were awful. Crockett's digestive system, much to his embarrassment and the disgust of everyone around him, rumbled back to life. Spike fed him all types of noxious substances, battered his body with her thumbs and elbows, pushed him constantly to exercise and stretch, and got him into a wheelchair. Manual, of course. Kelso and his crew departed and left him in Spike's hands.

Ruby was ever there. If Crockett woke up in the middle of the night, he'd almost always see her sitting beside his bed. They'd talk, she'd let him get freaked out, then love him through it. She was available when he needed her although she was never intrusive or in the way. She seemed a little sad, but did not indicate she wanted to talk about it, so Crockett left it alone.

About a month after his awakening, after finishing a few hot laps up and down the hall on crutches, Crockett was on the floor mat trying to do tummy crunches with Spike holding down his thighs. The two of them had spent nearly eight hours a day with one another for almost four weeks.

"Take a break," Spike said.

Crockett flopped back and lay there sweating. She scooted on her butt up beside his head and sat with her arms around her knees.

"So, Crockett, what's with you and Ruby?"

"Whadaya mean, what's with me and Ruby?"

"C'mon. You know what I mean. You two lovers, or what?"

"Sorta."

"No. Can't be sorta lovers any more than somebody can be sorta pregnant."

"We love each other."

"I can see that. I can also see she's gay, huh?"

"Yes, she is."

"And you aren't."

271

Crockett grinned. "I'm not?" he said.

Spike smiled. "I was workin' on your upper adductors this morning, Crockett," she said. "Gay you ain't. I know what to look for."

"How are my upper adductors?"

"Coming along. Your whole body is responding very well. You weigh about one-eighty-two, muscle tone is improving, reflexes are much better. Your leg will be here tomorrow. You available?"

"What?"

"Are you, David Allen Crockett, available?"

"You mean like, available, available?"

"Yeah."

"Jesus, Spike, I don't know what to say." He rolled up onto an elbow so he could see her. "I mean, you're my therapist."

"That doesn't stop you from looking, Crockett. You look a lot," she said. A grin overtook her face. "Sweet Jesus. He blushes!"

"Shit," Crockett said. Spike chuckled at him.

"Your ears are red and you didn't answer my question," she said. "You available?"

"Spike, don't you think I'm a little old for you?"

"How old are you?"

"I turned fifty-two while I was in the coma."

"I got a daughter in graduate school."

"What?"

"Yep. Scary, huh? We Irish age well when we're not in Ireland. Plus, I work very hard to look like this."

"Damn! How old are you?"

"Showroom new and probably fifteen years older than you think I am."

"Wow."

"Look. I think you're a right guy. I like you. I enjoy being around you. I'm free at the moment, not looking for anything in particular, and I just thought that when all this settles down a little, maybe we could have dinner, be social and, if all goes well, screw each other's brains out. I could use it, and God knows you could."

Crockett laughed. "Spike," he said, "I like your style."

Spike bounced to her feet. "You ain't seen my style," she said. "Think it over. I don't make this kind of offer every day."

She held her hands out to him and pulled Crockett to his foot, then slid under his left arm for support, a bit more closely than usual, as he hopped to the bed and sat.

"Bath time, Crockett. We gotta get you cleaned up and dressed. You're going out tonight."

"I am?"

"Yep. Dinner with the lady of the house. Ruby got you some new clothes that should fit. Need some help with your bath?"

"Who's asking?"

"Your therapist, Smartass."

"Thanks, Spike. I can handle it."

"So can I, Crockett. Dump the dyke for a night sometime and find out. I'm just two doors down. If you're concerned about me being your therapist, I'll take an over night leave of absence. It ain't part of your therapy, but it could be very therapeutic."

At around six, Ruby showed up with a sport shirt, slacks, and a shoe.

"I hope you brought the right one," Crockett said.

Ruby smiled. "That's exactly the one I brought," she said, and kissed him. He got dressed and she pinned the left trouser leg up out of the way. "C'mon, Big Boy. I'll take you for a ride."

"Nope. Thanks for the offer, but I think I'll walk."

"Long hike on crutches."

"Yeah, but I need the exercise."

"I thought Spike gave you a lot of exercise."

"She does."

Ruby grinned. "Whadaya think of old Spike?"

"I been givin' old Spike some thought," Crockett said.

"Have you come to any conclusions regarding Ms. O'Neal?"

"She reminds me of you."

"Does she."

"There is one major difference in how you and she relate to me, however. She seems to be more serious about my physical self in her approach to our relationship, whereas you are more serious about my emotional self in your approach to our relationship."

"Hell yes, Crockett. She is your body's therapist. I am your mind's therapist."

"There's also another major difference. Spike took a run at me today."

"Zat right?"

"Shit. You knew, didn't you?"

"Not that she took a run at you today," Ruby said, "but I was pretty sure she was going to."

"How the hell did you know that?"

"She asked me if it was okay."

"What!"

"Yeah, three or four days ago."

"Jesus! And you didn't say anything?"

"And destroy the moment?" Ruby said. "Not me."

"What did you tell her?"

"She asked me if I was gay and I told her yes. She asked me if I loved you and I told her yes. She asked me if I would be offended if she were to make herself available to you. I said no."

"Just no, huh?"

273

"Actually, I believe I said something like I thought it was a terrific idea and that it was fine with me. I may have even told her it was a kick-ass idea, that you are a wonderful man, and that you have enough swollen libido stored up to affect the Richter scale."

"Oh, Jesus!"

Ruby looked at him for a moment.

"What did you say?"

"I sorta left it hanging."

"Crockett, you do whatever you think you need to do, but if you are avoiding contact with that lovely, bright, gorgeous little hardbody because of some sort of loyalty to me, let me remind you of something. We are not going steady! We have made no vows! We may love each other, but we are not lovers."

"I know that."

"I love you more than I have loved anybody in my life, but if Spike had made me the same offer she made you, she would definitely not have had to ask twice. You cannot be unfaithful to me, Crockett, because you cannot be faithful to me. Ours is not that type of commitment!"

"I know, Ruby. I just don't feel real stable right now."

"You don't think that Spike might offer you some stability? Your life has been turned upside down. Wouldn't it be nice to grab a bit of normal, not to mention a bit of Spike?"

"I don't know. Maybe."

"Ah. Okay, Crockett. I'm gonna say something to you now that is very important. I want you to listen closely. You may react to it however you feel is necessary. You cannot offend or embarrass me."

She took his head in her hands and put her face just a few inches from his.

"Spike knows that you only have one leg, David. She doesn't care. Neither do I."

About ten minutes later she dried his face and iced his eyes.

"Crockett, I don't give a shit if you and Spike do a nasty on the lawn or not, but I do give a shit about you. Not only do she and I have some things in common, so does Spike and chicken soup. A little chicken soup couldn't hurt."

"I guess not," he said, and they began their walk.

They were almost to the dining room when Ruby stopped and turned to him.

"Oh, Crockett," she said. "I keep forgetting to ask you. How's the duck feel about Spike?"

"Jesus, Ruby," he said, and started to laugh.

"God, you're easy," she grinned, and patted his butt. "Welcome back."

SEVENTY-EIGHT

Backstory

BY THE TIME Ruby and Crockett made it to the dining room he was about worn out and they were both giggling like school kids. In the space of a few minutes' walk all had been washed away and was new again. Crockett felt wonderful and LaCost was positively glowing. Ivy was waiting and rose to her feet to greet them as Clete grinned in the background.

"It is well to hear laughter in these old halls, Children," Ivy said, giving Ruby a brief hug. Then she turned to Crockett.

"Crockett," she said, her eyes shining. "Dear, brave Crockett."

She approached him and laid her hand on his face.

"Oh, you do look well. Your ordeal has been so terrible, and yet you shine so. I do believe that you are the first angel I have ever seen on crutches."

Crockett's ears got hot and he grinned at her.

"Ivy, if you see an angel here, it is only your reflection in my eyes. You look lovely. I can't thank you enough for all you have done for me."

"Nonsense," she said, patting his cheek. "I have total monopoly on all gratitude in this house. It is in my charge, I shall dispense it. I apologize for not coming to see you, but I wanted our first meeting during your recovery to be on your terms rather than my own. Cletus has been out of the country on my behalf since a day or two before you awakened. He has returned to us only this morning. I thought it the perfect time for reunion."

She stepped back to allow Clete access. He took Crockett's offered hand.

"Son, I thought we'd lost ya. Damn, you are one tough sumbitch!"

"Praise indeed from you, Texican. Good to see ya."

"You too, Crockett. You look good. You really do. C'mon, git off them crutches and set. We'll jaw awhile. You can tell us what happened if Ruby don't mind hearin' it again."

"I've never heard it the first time," Ruby said. "Crockett and I haven't talked about that night from his side or ours."

"Well then, we got some story tellin' to do. You feel like it, Crockett, go ahead on with your end. Then we'll fill in the blanks for you."

He told them every bit of it, right down to how badly Mackey had suckered him. He left nothing out.

"Damn," said Clete. "They wanted you dead before they ran your car over the edge of that pit. You took two massive blows to the front of your head. Mackey probably figured he'd killed ya."

"Over the pit?"

"Yeah. They ran you over the edge of that gravel pit out across from Morrison's, where the road has that sharp bend. Near as the cops could figure it, you fell nearly ninety feet to the bottom. The driver's door came open, or was left open I expect. The force of the strike to the ground knocked you out of the car; then it rolled or bounced over on the left side of your body. That's how you got your shoulder, ribs, and leg all busted up. Like to scared a couple of kids in the gravel pit to death."

"What kids?"

"The young couple that was attending the submarine races down in the gravel pit. Your car didn't miss theirs by more than thirty feet. Damn near fell right on top of 'em."

"Jesus!"

"I guess so. They were from Mahomet. Arrow ambulance serves Mahomet and they had a cell phone. They figured out that you were still alive and called the medics right away. Smelled gas, got scared the car was gonna catch fire, and pulled you away from it. The bottom of your leg was tangled up with the door. They pulled you loose anyway and drug you away from danger. Maybe that's how your leg got so screwed up, who knows? When the girl checked your heart, she found a slip of paper in your shirt pocket with Dan Harter's name and phone number on it and called him. Over to you, Ruby."

"Dan called Arrow Ambulance and told them to take you to Carle Hospital emergency trauma. Then he called me, found out where I was, and sent a squad car to pick me up. I called Clete on the way to the hospital. I got there about ten minutes before the ambulance arrived, and the joint was swarming with cops. Champaign and Urbana police had every intersection cleared on the route to the hospital and squad cars running interference. I heard an EMT tell a cop that you died three times on the way in. He said that if those kids had not covered you with their coats, you would have been dead at the scene."

"The rumors of my death have been greatly exaggerated."

Clete grinned. "After Ruby called me, I got busy and called Ivy's doctor. He pulled a bunch of strings and four hours later his team was on the way to Champaign-Urbana in an air ambulance."

"Funding major wings on teaching hospitals allows one to throw one's weight around," Ivy said.

"After I called Ivy's doctor, I called the Governor. Thirty minutes after you arrived at the hospital, the area you were in was locked down by agents of the IBI. Six hours after you arrived, me and Ivy's team of medicos swept in and took over. Twenty-four hours after you arrived, you and three doctors, including the two Kelsos, were on another ambulance helo coming here. The second floor of the cold wing had been opened, staffed, and outfitted for trauma care and staff accommodations. In two more days it was set for surgery and recuperative care."

"My God. You people moved heaven and earth!"

"While you were incapacitated," Ivy said, "each of the two young people who aided you at the scene received a fifty thousand dollar scholarship to the colleges of their choice, the Champaign City Police Department's Protective and Benevolent Association received a one hundred thousand dollar donation to its scholarship fund for continuing education, and Carle Hospital got a new, mobile emergency services unit."

"Ivy," Crockett said, "you are quite a gal."

"I have lots of it and I hear I can't take it with me," she said.

The soup arrived.

As they lingered over desert, Ivy spoke.

"Martin Morrison is finished," she said. "The severe incapacitation of his sister, who was the center and driving force of his life, has left him broken in his way as much as she is in hers. The clinic is closed, the staff is gone, the estate is in shambles. He is a recluse. He can no longer harm anyone and suffers in his own hell. His sister cannot walk or care for herself and is confined to a wheelchair. Justice, as I knew it would be, has been served. While I have given only money toward this end, you, Crockett, have sacrificed nearly everything. You died for it, and through the grace of God, were returned to us. You have given of your heart and your spirit and of your body. None of these things did you do from greed or avarice but from the highest of all motives, love. It makes me happy to know that men such as you still walk the earth. It makes me proud to know you. It makes me humble to sit at this table in your company. Sir, I salute you."

"Thank you, Ivy."

"Through all of this, Ruby," Ivy said, "you have been oak. You too have suffered so much. You have had possibly the most difficult job of all. Waiting. Showing incredible strength through these long months, you have kept your confidence in this man, you have held onto your connection with this man, and you never wavered. No matter how bleak it all looked, you remained steadfast in your belief that all would be well. What an incredible person you are. And you did it all for that most pure of motives, love. What a joy it is to have you in my home.

277

What riches have come into my life from knowing you. Madam, I salute you."

"Thank you, Ivy."

"All that is why I have taken certain liberties that neither of you shall deny me. Before you leave this place, after Crockett is completely recovered, each of you will accept a check from me for two hundred-fifty thousand dollars. From this day forward, during the first two weeks of every new year, you will each receive a payment of at least one hundred thousand dollars for the rest of your lives, from a fund I have set aside for that purpose. The vehicles provided for you are now yours, free and clear, as are any and all furnishings or household goods you purchased while acting on my behalf."

Ivy sipped her coffee and continued.

"The credit cards and such that you have shall remain at your service until after the first two weeks of the coming year. I expect you to use them, Darlings. Have a wonderful time. You can afford it. It is not my desire to make either of you wealthy. You are not the type of people who would wear such a mantel well. It is my desire that you be independent, and independent you shall be. I look at the two of you and I see three lives. The life that each of you must have for yourselves and the life that you must have together. It is a very strange circumstance. I suspect that, at times, it will not be easy, just as I am sure that it has been difficult in the past."

She smiled at them and her eyes shined.

"I know things, Children. I know things. One of the things I know is that the two of you are absolutely destined for each other. It is up to you to find the way for that to happen. I sometimes think that poor Rachael's true purpose was to make sure the two of you really discovered one another and the power you create together."

Beneath the table, Crockett took Ruby's hand.

"Well, that, as they say, is that. I have said what I have to say. I will brook no protests, I will accept no gratitude. I have done what I have done to please myself, I have succeeded, and I thank you. The proper paperwork has already been attended to by Cletus. Enjoy your dessert. I am going to bed. Day after tomorrow is Sunday. I shall expect your company at my Sunday morning fun club for a flagon or two of Mother Marshal's Magic Elixir. Good night, Children. I love you all."

She stood and left the room.

Clete stretched and yawned. "Well, boys and girls," he said, "I guess you can send my saddle home, too. I got a case a jet lag that is tearin' me up. Even though it's not even nine yet, this ol' boy is goin' to the house. The two of you have a great night. I'll drift around and see ya tomorrow. Night, ya'll."

They were left alone.

"Well, shucks, Podnuh," Ruby said.

"Believe ah'll light me a shuck, an' git on ta bed," Crockett drawled. "Ah'm plumb tuckered out."

"Want me ta walk to the bunkhouse with ya, Jeb?"

"Right neighborly of ya there, Earlene," he said, and collected his crutches.

They walked in silence for a moment, until Ruby spoke.

"I think you should give this Spike situation some serious thought," she said.

"Nip it," Crockett said.

When their walk took them past Spike's room, Ruby knocked on her door and ran off, leaving him standing alone in the dark hallway. There was nobody home.

Crockett was relieved.

Sort of.

SEVENTY-NINE

Crockett Rebuilt

CROCKETT SLEPT LATE the next morning and was only semi-awake awake when Spike came zipping in. She had a slight sheen on her face, her hair was damp, and she was dressed quite fetchingly in speedo-style tights to mid-thigh, a very short t-shirt, tenni-runners and white socks. Her hair was in a ponytail, her eyes were shining, she had on a bit of make-up, and her navel was very French.

"You conscious?" Spike said.

"Not quite. Late night last night."

"Out drinking?"

Crockett yawned. "Eleven bars in five blocks," he said. "Where you been?"

"I did four miles this morning," Spike said. "Bailed out of the shower to come work you over and you, you slug, are barely conscious."

"Great belly-button," Crockett said. "Why don't you see if the kitchen can get me a sweet roll and some coffee, while I go to the john. Get something for yourself too, whatever you step-arobaddicted, nautalusted inquisitors have for breakfast."

"Pretty heavy talk for a man with the body fat of a small walrus."

"You should have seen me before the coma," he said, standing up on his crutches about a foot from her. "Eskimos used to follow me around and smack their lips."

Spike giggled, but didn't step back.

"That's okay, Crockett. For a man your age, you could be a lot worse. Now that you have me to fight off the Eskimos, you'll be fine."

"Now that I have you, huh?" he said, leaning toward her a little. "Do I have you, Spike?"

She looked up at him with those lime-green eyes and slowly traced her finger up and down his sternum.

"You do have me, Crockett, and someday, if I have anything to say about it, you will have me. And I will have you."

She pushed him back an inch or two with her finger, then let him lean forward.

"My, my, my," Crockett said. "Spike, you are beginning to have a serious effect on me."

"And I'm just using this one finger," she said, pushing him back again. "Go to the john, clean up, and I'll get us breakfast. You need help with your shower?"

"Nope," he said, turning away. "I can do it all by myself."

Spike chuckled. "That's a real shame," she said. "A man like you shouldn't have to do anything all by himself."

Three hours later they had finished breakfast and Crockett had worked out with exercises and a Nautilus machine until he saw God and only partially satisfied his therapist. Lying face down on a table with Spike's elbow so far into the back of his left thigh that he was beginning to see God again, he squeaked in protest.

"Breathe," she said, as if he could. "Breathe right through where it hurts. See it in your mind. Breathe through my elbow."

He tried and, as dumb as it sounded, it worked. The pain fell off almost immediately.

"Good boy," Spike said, lifting her weight off his leg. "Don't things go better when we listen to those brighter than ourselves?"

"While you're back there, you heartless bitch, why don't you kiss my ass?"

"You're just looking for an excuse to roll over," Spike said, moving her elbow up a couple of inches and starting again.

"Jesus," Crockett grunted.

"Breathe," she said.

"Miss O'Neal?" came a voice from the doorway.

"Leo! Good to see you," Spike said, releasing Crockett from his agony and pulling up his sweatpants.

He struggled to a sitting position to see a smallish man of about sixty standing in the doorway. He had thin gray hair, thick glasses, was dressed in a dark blue suit, and carried a sizeable black suitcase. His wingtips were black and white.

Spike reached out her arm toward him and he advanced into the room. "Leo Vitali, this is David Crockett. Crockett, Leo Vitali. Leo has your leg."

"Thank God," Crockett said, extending a hand. "I've been looking for the darned thing for months. Where'd you find it?"

"Ah," Leo said, taking Crockett's hand, "humor. Levity has its place, I suppose. It would seem you are in good spirits, Mr. Crockett."

"I am, Leo. Your arrival has caused Spike here to stop torturing me. Ever since that house fell on her sister, she's been in a terrible mood."

"Of course. A reference to the Wizard of Oz. Jocularity is sometimes quite therapeutic I'm told." Leo set his case down. "I have your appliance here, Mr. Crockett."

Crockett resisted the urge to ask for a toaster.

"Call me Crockett," he said.

"Oh, no. I could hardly do that. If you would be kind enough to pull up your left trouser leg, we'll get on with the fitting."

Spike was grinning from ear to ear. A half hour later Crockett was standing on his own two feet. One original equipment, the other aftermarket.

"So, Mr. Crockett, if you need anything at all, just phone and I'll come right out," Leo said. "The stump will alter in shape slightly as you move about and put weight on it. We will re-fit as necessary until your leg is fully settled in. A certain amount of discomfort is normal, but not pain. Your stump is quite lovely, the fit is as good as we can make it and we are the best. You should expect things to go smoothly. The length is correct, the foot is correct, the shoe is correct. You seem to be ready to move on. Good. The more you do, the more you will be able to do. I have known Miss O'Neal for some years. You could have no better assistance than she can render. I will call on you again in two weeks and we will examine the fit and assess your progress. Good luck, Mr. Crockett. I believe you will do quite well."

"Thank you very much, Leo," Crockett said, as the small man picked up his case and headed for the door. "You are very understanding."

"Of course I am," Leo said, and pulled up his left pant leg. Strap steel. "Mid-calf amputation eighteen years ago, Mr. Crockett. The right one is just like it. Goodbye."

Crockett could hear him chuckling as he walked down the hallway.

For the next hour or so he limped up and down the hall, first with crutches, then with a hospital-type cane, then holding onto Spike's shoulder. It was amazing. Crockett's back didn't hurt, his hip didn't hurt, and his leg didn't burn. The stump ached and pinched a little, but only a little. Spike said that was normal and it would either go away or slight adjustments in the boot would fix it. He sat on the bed grinning a lot and panting a little, and crossed his leg, something he hadn't been able to do for quite a while.

Spike beamed at him. "You are doing great, Crockett," she said. "I mean it. Really well."

"It's kinda like walking on a stilt or something. I can't feel my foot, but I can sorta feel the floor. When can we go outside?"

"Slow down, Hotshot. You are gonna cover a lot of miles in the halls before we go out into the world of bumps and humps. You'll get there, and you'll get there more quickly than most, but you will not get there today."

"Okay," he said. "I am at your mercy. Whatever you say goes."

"Happy?"

"You bet I am," he said, carefully standing up and bracing himself on the elevated mattress. "A celebration of some sort is in order."

"Would this celebration be for just you, or could anyone participate?"

"I haven't decided yet."

"Speaking as your caregiver and being aware of your weakened condition, I would urge you to keep a healthcare professional close at hand," Spike said, slowly advancing on his position.

"Close at hand, huh?"

"The closer the better. It's a safety issue."

"Really?"

"Oh, yeah," she said, a wicked little smile on her lips.

Crockett settled back into a seated position. "Well, if it's for my safety," he said, "come here and gimme a kiss."

"Who's asking?" Spike said.

"Crockett. The incredible, two-legged man."

"I don't know," she said, easing between his knees. "As Crockett, my patient, you are a lazy, unmotivated slob, undeserving of my affection. But—"

"Tight little butt?"

"You have no idea."

"Not yet, anyway."

"But, as Crockett the incredible two-legged man, you are the closest thing to a hero I've seen in a long time. It's not everyday a girl gets to kiss a hero."

Spike took his face in her hands and bored in. The room actually tilted. Crockett was just rounding one of Jupiter's moons when she backed off.

"Jesus," Spike said, looking a little startled.

"Holy shit," Crockett grunted. He could hear his pulse in his head.

Spike peered owlishly about the room. "Honest to Christ," she said, "my knees are weak. My fucking knees are weak!" She flopped down on the bed beside where he sat. "I got a daughter in graduate school. One kiss does not make my knees weak!"

"I feel like I'm high," Crockett said picking absentmindedly at the sheet.

"I haven't been this buzzed since college," Spike said.

She fell to her back and rubbed small circles near the base of Crockett's spine. He shivered.

"Crockett, this is deeply weird."

"Deeply," he said.

Spike sat up and turned to face him.

"I mean it!"

"So do I," Crockett said. "I feel like I been de-boned."

"Well, not totally."

Crockett laughed. "No, not totally," he said.

"We are veterans, Crockett. We are not a couple of sixteen-year-olds in the back seat at the drive-in, goddammit!"

"Katheryne Margaret Maureen O'Neal, it was never like that when I was sixteen. Little birdies were chirping. Lady, you scare the shit outa me."

"Likewise. This ain't good. It was wonderful, but it is not good."

They sat in silence for a few moments before Spike took a very deep breath and exhaled noisily.

"How ya doin?" Crockett said.

She got up. "I'm fine I think. No, I am. I really am." She looked at him as if he was some sort of specimen.

"Me too," Crockett said, and meant it.

"This didn't happen," Spike said.

"It didn't?"

"Nope. Crockett, there is no way that I can continue to treat you and work with you and be next to you all the time, with this kind of whatever the hell that was, hanging over my head. Christ! I went from zero to sixty in less than two seconds!"

"Me either. I ain't up to it."

"You were a minute ago," she said.

"You know what I mean."

"This won't work. I cannot spend as much time with you as I need to, if everytime I touch you I start to pant!"

"So, now what?" Crockett said.

"Now we continue as we were. As long as your treatment is ongoing and we both stay here under the same roof, we do not put ourselves in an awkward position."

"You've been putting me in awkward positions since two days after I met you."

"Jesus, Crockett! Gimme a break, willya?"

"I can do that," he said.

"But when we pick this back up, consider yourself warned. No matter how completely you are recovered, by the time I get through with you, you are gonna need a physical therapist."

"Know one that specializes in prostate massage?"

"Yeah," Spike said. "Me. C'mon, get up and walk around, test your balance and stuff."

"If you are going to so coldly rebuff me," Crockett said, "I am going for a hike."

"Great idea," Spike said. "Take the crutches. I'll be back later to beat you up some more."

She kissed him the cheek and fairly skipped out the door.

Crockett gathered up his crutches and, using them as little as possible, headed off down the hall and across to the other wing, in search of Ruby. It took him almost ten minutes to reach her room, the same whorehouse she'd stayed in on their first visit. He leaned the crutches against the hallway wall and knocked. The door swung open and there she was.

Ruby was wearing a light blue cotton sundress with a short skirt, tall sandals, and impeccable make-up. Her gorgeous eyes lit up, her magnificent mouth grinned, and that deep contralto chuckle swept over him like warm water.

"I was just comin' to see you, Crockett."

"My God. You are lovely, Ruby. Just lovely."

"So are you, David," she said, tears springing to her eyes. "Just lovely."

She moved into him, kissing his face a dozen times in half a dozen seconds, then burrowed into his neck and began to sob. He held her, standing there in the open doorway on a phony leg, trying not to fall backward into the hall, he held her. She cried for a while.

Finally Crockett moved Ruby to the bed and sat beside her, his arm around her shoulders. He handed her a box of tissues. She blew her nose, laughed, and blew it again.

"Shit, Crockett. I'm behaving like a girl."

"Looks good on ya."

"I was so scared for so long and I tried so hard to be brave. You died three times, and you went away and I couldn't reach you and you had, like, eleven surgeries and they rebuilt your poor face and you lost your leg, and you didn't come back and you didn't come back and I talked to you and read to you and sat with you and loved you, and I couldn't reach you, Crockett! I couldn't reach you!"

She blew her nose again.

"And then I open that goddammed door and you're standing there on two goddammed feet with that goddammed goofy grin on your goddammed face! And I'm so goddammed mad at you, you sonofabitch! If you ever do anything like that to me again, I'll neuter you! And I treated you so badly the night you went to Morrison's. I was just a shit to you, Crockett, and I'm so sorry. I was mean and hateful and you went off and got killed."

Ruby looked at him intently for a moment, then reached out and touched his face. "You're going back, aren't you?"

"Yeah."

"Why?"

"Unfinished business."

"Morrison and his sister are finished, Crockett."

"No. They're just outa business."

"This some sort of macho, male, masculine shit?"

"Something like that."

"I can't talk you out of it, can I?"

"Not if you ever want me all the way back. I left too much in Morrison's basement, Ruby."

Ruby shredded the tissue for a while, then looked at him.

"When?"

"I dunno. Three or four weeks maybe."

"Shucks little darlin', there's things a man just has ta do, right?" Ruby said.

"Yeah, that's pretty much it."

Ruby slumped, staring at the floor for a few moments, then sat up and squared her shoulders.

"So, three or four weeks."

"Whenever I feel like I'm ready and Spike agrees."

"How is old Spike?" Ruby said, grateful to shift the subject.

"None of your business, you nosey dyke."

Her eyes sparkled. "Ooh, secretive. Perhaps that is an indicator of progress on the Spike front, so to speak."

"Spike and I have agreed that this is not the time or the place to advance our relationship."

"Oh yeah?"

"Now what the hell does that mean, LaCost?"

"It's a professional term. You, as a layperson, wouldn't understand it."

"I see."

"Hey, Crockett, as I allow my eyes to travel down your lean trim body, I notice two feet at the end of it. Is that a good sign?"

"A very good sign. Ready to go dancing?"

"What, the horizontal mambo?"

"Don't knock it, if you haven't tried it."

"I have tried it."

"But not with me."

"What makes you think you'd be any different than the hundreds of others," Ruby said.

"I love you."

"That could make a difference."

"And you love me."

Ruby smiled. "So could that," she said.

EIGHTY
Out of Character

FOR THE NEXT MONTH AND A HALF, Crockett worked. At two weeks he was walking outside for at least two hours a day, inside for another two hours. At four weeks, an hour of his inside hiking was up and down stairs. He had also started to jog morning and evening. At six weeks, he did two miles a day, could run a hundred yards in less than sixteen seconds, could trot up and down the stairs, and did isolation exercises and weight training for an hour and a half a day. He spent part of each morning and afternoon with Spike, evenings with Ruby, and slept alone. After one weekly Sunday Morning Fun Club, he cornered Clete.

"What's up?"

"I need a vehicle," Crockett said.

"Okay."

"Untraceable, four-wheel drive, fictitious plates. I'll return it."

"How soon?"

"Week."

"You got it. Goin' back?"

"Yep."

"I figured."

"Got it to do."

"I spose you don't wanna gun."

"Don't like 'em."

"Suit yourself. I'll get ya something' to drive and pack you a nice lunch," Cletus said. "Leave your heart here. Use your head there."

"Good advice, Clete."

"Only if ya take it."

Crockett went at it extra hard that week. Thursday afternoon, Spike walked in as he worked on the Nautilus. She was dressed in street clothes.

287

Spike grinned. "Dear me," she said. "My heart gets all a-flutter watching a big strong man sweat."

"Especially if he's looking down at you, I bet."

"Actually, I like looking down at him a lot, too."

"Dominance?"

"More freedom of movement."

"Shit, Spike. Let's not go there. We get into some monkey-fuck talk here and things could get outa hand."

"Relax. It's okay. As of this moment, you are officially released from my tender care."

"What?"

"Yep. Stick a fork in old Crockett. To be truthful, I could have been outa here a week or two ago, I just didn't wanna leave ya. You are done, Son. I'm gonna take my pile of money and go home."

"Well damn, Spike. I don't want you to go."

"You ain't seen the last of me, Crockett. You've got an appointment with Leo in another three weeks for an adjustment and a new gel-cast. Leo's office is in Downer's Grove, about thirty minutes from my empty and lonesome apartment. I'm gonna be free that whole week, with nothing to do but lie around the house. Did I mention my apartment is empty and lonesome?"

"Yes, you did."

"I expect you to spend three or four days there. That oughta be enough time for us to damn near kill each other. Sound like fun?"

"Sounds like a near-death experience. I wouldn't miss it for the world."

Spike placed her palms on his chest. "Great," she said. "See ya then. You know what they say, abstinence makes the heart grow fonder."

She leaned in and kissed each side of his neck. The hair on the back of Crockett's arms stood up.

"Grrrrr," Spike growled, and backed up.

"I'll be there. How do I find you?"

"My address and phone number are in the nightstand. I have your number. Got it from Clete. He could barely stop grinning. Three weeks, Crockett. Just follow the directions and look for the light in the window. See ya."

She headed for the hall.

"Count on it, Spike."

She paused in the doorway. "Oh, Crockett, what do you drink?"

"Anything but single malt scotch or Shiraz," he said.

Sunday Morning Fun Club was rather subdued. Word had spread that Crockett was going back to Morrison's and that Ruby and he would soon be leaving. Afterwards, Cletus led him outside. Next to the garage was a two or three year old Jeep with a soft top. The plate was from Wyoming.

"How's that?" Clete asked.

"Perfect."

"Gotcha a automatic transmission. Didn't know how you'd do with a clutch."

"This is great."

Clete opened the passenger side door. "I know ya don't use a cane much anymore, Crockett, but I figured you might need one since your old one was never recovered. Got a friend that's a pretty good craftsman. He made this one for ya."

From out of the Jeep he took Crockett's new cane. It was round, tapered from top to tip in some sort of very hard wood that was so dark green as to be nearly black. The butt was a viper's head in silver alloy with blue star sapphires for the eyes. Behind the head, the body coiled around the shaft all the way to the tip, which ended in a rattlesnake's rattle where the cane touched the ground.

"Jesus, Clete! This is beautiful!"

"Not another one like it on the planet," he said. "It ain't lightweight, but I didn't think you'd mind."

"Not one damn bit. Thank you."

"Nope. Thank you. If you and Ruby hadn't done what you did, Ivy'd be dead by now. As it is, she's better than I've seen her in years. When you settled this whole thing, you gave her a new lease on life, Crockett. I owe ya. Anything I can ever do for you is done. Got it?"

"Got it."

"The ID's and such are yours. Keep 'em. Never know when ya might need 'em. Goin south tomorrow?"

"Early."

"See ya when ya get back. Get it done, Son."

"Absolutely."

Crockett worked out for most all of the rest of the day, trying to quiet his mind with activity and sweat. He showered before dinner and walked over to eat with Ruby. As he expected, she was distant and a bit withdrawn. He gave her space. She never mentioned the Morrisons. They made small talk and about eight o'clock he kissed her goodnight and went to his room. He got undressed, put his crutches in easy reach, took off his leg, and settled in with a book. At nearly ten, he said goodnight to Elmore Leonard and reached for the light. There was a small knock on the door.

"Crockett? You awake?"

"Sure, Ruby. Come in."

She sat on the edge of the bed. "Crockett, are we okay?"

"Aw, Sweetheart. We're fine. There's just a lot of stress right now."

"I just don't wanna shut you out or get stupid like I did last time."

"Ruby, this time and last time are totally different."

"Just so you know that I love you and I believe in you and I want you to come back," she said, adjusting the belt on her long black robe. "I can't do without you, Crockett. Ivy knows what she's talking about. She is an amazing woman."

"So are you."

"Amazingly screwed up."

"Who ain't?"

Ruby smiled. "Nobody in this room," she said.

"Or any other one."

"You have really done well, Crockett. You have worked so hard to come back from the mess you were in. It makes me proud."

Crockett smiled. "A hundred and ninety-six pounds of sparkling personality," he said. "Couldn't have done it without you."

"You couldn't have done it without Spike."

"Spike helped."

"Not as much as she wanted to."

"Maybe not."

"You and Spike really didn't, ah—"

"No, we didn't ah."

"Just checking."

"Ruby, I meant what I said about not being able to make it without you. I didn't come back just to go through all this pain and rehab, you know. I came back because you are here and because you didn't give up. Where you are, I need to be. Ivy's very smart."

Her eyes filled with tears. "I gotta go, Crockett," she said.

"I know, Sweetie. I'll see you late tomorrow and call you when I head back. In a couple of days we'll go home."

"Home."

"Yeah. Home. Goodnight, Ruby."

She kissed him on the cheek. "Sleep well, Crockett."

He shut off the lamp and lay awake in the light of the full moon as it splashed around the room. About a half-hour later, as Crockett was dozing off, his door opened. Ruby stepped into the pool of pale light beside the bed. She was wearing her short white robe.

"A vision," he said.

"Oh good. You're still awake."

"Barely."

"Sorry to disturb you Crockett, but I forgot to ask you something very important last time I was here."

He shifted up on an elbow. "And that would be?"

"Well, it's kind of delicate."

"Ruby, you can ask me anything. You know that. What's wrong?"

"Aw, Jesus. It's sorta embarrassing. Okay. Here goes. Crockett, it's been on my mind a lot the past few days. I really need to know."

"What?"

"How's the duck?"

Crockett laughed. "The duck? The duck is fine, Ruby."

She dropped her robe to the puddle of moonlight on the floor and lifted his sheet.

"I'll be the judge of that," she said. "Move over."

EIGHTY-ONE

Cry Havoc

CROCKETT WOKE UP ABOUT FIVE, alone, a little disoriented and wondering if Ruby had even been there. In the center of the passenger-side pillow was a perfect lipstick kiss. He smiled, put on his leg, and got ready for the trip.

The Jeep was noisy, windy, and had no radio, so the drive left him considerable time for contemplation. Crockett rolled over in his mind everything that had led him to being an hour south of Chicago on I-57. From Ruby's phone call asking if he had a gun, to Rachael's death, to the lunch with Ivy, to his near death, to Spike, to Ruby's amorous and out of character visit the night before. Jesus, what a trip.

He was less than an hour out of Champaign when he realized it had been almost a year since Rachael had been killed. The impact of that realization was stunning. He pulled into a rest area and sat for nearly an hour, unable to drive, unable to cry, unable to do anything but stare at the cars that pulled through, the little dramas that rolled by.

It was just short of noon when he hit Champaign. He stopped at a hardware store and picked up a heavy-duty pry bar and some wire cutters, then, surprised that he was hungry, went to a Cracker Barrel for lunch. After gassing up at a Quick Trip, he headed out I-74 to the Mansfield exit, then south into Hyatt County. Twenty minutes later, he drove past the Morrison Mansion. The place had really gone downhill.

Crockett circled to the rear of the property and found the cut Mackey and he had walked up a lifetime ago. It was dry and dusty with horseweeds growing to six or eight feet high on either bank. He got out of the Jeep and snipped the five strand barbed wire fence, pulled the wire back to allow passage, then eased the Jeep through and began the slow grind up the rocky trail to the rear of the house. About fifty yards from the board fence, he found a spot wide enough to accommodate the Jeep's short wheelbase and turned around. Taking the pry bar, he left the vehicle and pushed his way through the weeds, heading for the rear of the mansion as fast as he could go.

Within sixty seconds, he was leaning against the wall beside the back door to the foyer, panting. During the run, he confirmed that there were no windows facing the rear of the house from the staff quarters above the garage. As he paused to catch his breath, the dogs watched him from their pen against the stable, thirty yards away.

The storm door was open and the pry made short work of the entry door. Crockett left the bar outside and slipped into the house, cane in hand. He heard the elevator rattle and waited beside it, just out of sight. The door opened and Morrison stepped out, his back to Crockett. He was wearing a wrinkled bathrobe, lightweight slacks and slippers over bare feet. His hair was disheveled and thinner than Crockett remembered and he seemed to be shorter.

"Surprise," Crockett said.

Morrison whirled, and shock fastened onto his face.

"Y-You!" he stammered.

Crockett jabbed him in the throat with the butt of the cane.

Morrison went to the floor immediately, clutching at his neck and retching. Crockett grabbed him by the hair, stood him up, and shoved him into the elevator. He fell against the rear wall, his eyes wide with fright, rubbing his throat and coughing. Crockett stepped in and closed the door.

He slammed the heel of his hand into Morrison's forehead and the rear of the man's skull thudded into the elevator wall. He gave a low wail and slid to the floor. He wasn't hurt, just scared.

"Listen to me," Crockett growled. "One shout from you, one yell, one noise, and I will use this cane to beat you to death. Understand?"

"Y-yes," Morrison gasped.

"There is a slight chance you might survive today. It depends on you. Understand?"

"Yes."

"How many servants in the house?"

"Only two."

"Man and wife?"

"Yes."

"Is there a phone in your basement office so you can contact them?"

"Yes."

Crockett pushed the down button. In a few seconds the door opened onto Morrison's office. The frail man huddled where he was and stared at Crockett.

"But, you're dead!" he groaned.

"Not any more," Crockett said, and threw him across the floor.

Morrison rolled to about five feet in front of his sister. Marian sat, slouching to her left, in a motorized wheel chair, halfway into the room. She had lost a great deal of weight. Her skin had a gray pallor, the left side of her mouth turned cruelly downward. She emitted a grunt of surprise and gaped at Crockett with a startled look in her eyes. It only took a few seconds to shift to hate. He smiled at her.

"Hi, Darth. How ya been?"

An umbrella stood just inside the doorway. Crockett grabbed it and shoved it through the spokes of the wheels on her chair. She tried the hand control a few times, but the wheelchair could not roll. She glared at him and mouthed some gibberish, as her brother struggled to rise from the floor. Crockett hooked his ankle with the cane's handle. Morrison sprawled again and began to weep.

"Get your shit together, you sonofabitch," Crockett growled, "or I'll kill you where you lay. Get in touch with the staff. Send them to their room. Use whatever is necessary to get that job done. You say one thing out of line, you pass out one hint that anything is wrong, and I'll let you watch while I kill that twisted bitch in the wheelchair. Clear?"

Genuine fear registered on Morrison's face. "Yes. Whatever you want, Beckett. Just don't harm my sister."

"Up to you."

Morrison got to his feet, wobbled over to a desk, sat heavily in the chair and took the phone in hand.

"Irene," he said. "You and Charles remove yourselves from the main house please. I desire extreme privacy. Take the afternoon off but remain in your area. Do not go outside or enter the main house. Do you understand? Good. Thank you, Irene."

He dropped the phone into the cradle and looked at Crockett.

"Satisfied?"

"Good for you, Martin. Keep it up and you have a chance."

"What do you want?" he asked. "What more could you possibly want? You've taken all there was."

Crockett could hear the chair whir and thump as Morrison's sister fought with the locked wheels.

"Go disconnect the power on that wheelchair," Crockett said. "It makes me nervous. You don't want me nervous."

Morrison crossed to his sister, pulled a lead from the rear of the chair, returned to his desk, and sat.

"You bastard," he choked, rubbing his throat, "you've taken all I have. My practice is gone, my lovely children are gone, my toys are gone, my income is gone, and my sister is gone!"

Tears began to stream down his distorted face.

"Look what you've done to me," he cried. "Look what you've done! Look at her. The most understanding, wonderful woman who has ever walked this earth, broken and condemned to that hideous machine. Unable to talk or move on her own. Look what you have done to her! My precious sister!

"Not like my wife," Morrison seethed. "Marian understood my needs. She always gave me my toys. My wonderful little children to play with."

His face became wistful, almost serene.

"Don't you see how much they mean to me? Don't you understand how I need them?"

Crockett shook his head. "I understand that the only person on earth who has less right than you to beg for understanding is the ghoul in that wheelchair. She knows it's wrong. You, you contemptible bastard, have no idea what an abomination you really are!"

Morrison's sister uttered a croak and Crockett turned to look at her. A drawer scraped, and he whirled back. Morrison had a small, chrome-plated revolver in his hand.

"Don't move, Beckett," he spat. "Don't you dare move."

Crockett raised his cane and shot him.

The .22 magnum hollow point hit Morrison high on the left shoulder, breaking his clavicle. The pistol bounced on the carpet and Morrison fell backward with a screech. Crockett picked the revolver up, dropped it in his pocket, and looked down at the bleeding man. The wound was not serious, but the broken collarbone was causing him a lot of pain. Blood seeped slowly through the bathrobe. Crockett went into the restroom, grabbed a towel and tossed it to him.

"Pack this around the wound and get your ass into a chair. Pull another stunt like that and your sister pays for it."

Morrison whimpered and did as he was told. After some color came back into his face, Crockett pulled a chair up in front of him and sat down.

"So, how ya feel, Martin?" The man stared at Crockett with hollow eyes. "Not so good, huh? Well, you're not hurt very bad. You'll probably be okay if you cooperate. Here's what I want. The names, addresses, and related information on everybody who bought children from you, who attended your little sporting events, who bought and sold your home movies, and who sold children to you. All of it. Everything. Simple."

Morrison screwed up his tiny courage.

"No," he said.

"Martin, maybe I'm not making myself clear. You are going to give me the information I want. You are, Martin. You really are."

"I won't."

Crockett grinned at him. "Sure you will," he said, and stood up.

"Wh-what are you going to do to me?"

Crockett emptied a small garbage can on the floor.

"To you, Martin? I give you my word, that as long as you do what I ask you to do, I will not kill you. I will not torture you, I will not harm you in any way. You will not suffer at my hands, if you cooperate fully. I will not even turn you over to the police. If you fail to cooperate, well that's not in your best interest. Where are the records, Martin?"

"You'll never find them. They're hidden."

"I don't have to find them. You are going to tell me where they are."

"What makes you think so?" Morrison said, a ten-year-old, getting cocky.

Crockett lifted the plastic bag liner out of the wastebasket, walked to the man's sister, and slipped it over her head. One eye bulged, and she sucked part of the bag into her mouth, rolling her head from side to side, fighting for breath.

"Noooooooooo!" Morrison screamed, and Crockett got in his face.

"Yes! Yes, Martin. We'll stand right here and watch her die, just like you watched your daughter die, you fuck. Just like you watched all those babies die, you soulless piece of shit!"

"I'll tell! I'll tell! Get it off her, Beckett! Get it off!"

Crockett poked a hole in the plastic and the elderly woman struggled to wheeze through it.

"Where, Martin?"

"In that file," Morrison said, pointing to a large gray cabinet against the wall. "The back wall of the top drawer is false. Open it all the way and push the lock mechanism. It will release. Now, take that bag off her head!"

Marian was breathing okay, but Crockett pulled the bag off anyway and checked the file cabinet. Sure enough, the back of the drawer fell forward and revealed about a half-inch of hidden space. In it were two computer disks. He checked the rest of the drawers. Two more contained disks, for a total of seven in all. At Crockett's encouragement, Morrison pulled up some information on a couple of them at his computer. Suppliers, wholesalers, customers, a wealth of information that Cletus would be able to get to the right people. Morrison was finished and so was his network and pipeline, from Washington State to Caracas.

"Gosh, Martin, this is wonderful. See what can be accomplished when we work together?"

"Get out," he pouted. "You said you'd leave us alone. Now leave us alone!"

"I'll be gone before you know it, but I don't want you calling anybody until I get away, so we have just one more little thing to do."

"What?"

"I'm going to lock you and your sister in the stable. The help will discover you later and I won't have to worry about you when I leave."

"But I won't call anyone," Morrison said, attempting to regain a bit of his dignity. "You have my word."

"Get in the elevator, or the sack goes back on her head."

With Martin leading the way, Crockett muscled the heavy electric wheelchair and Morrison's sister into the elevator, outside, down the gravel path and into the stable. Morrison peered at him through the dusty gloom, as Crockett opened the caged stall and motioned him inside.

"I won't go in there," Morrison said.

"Why not?"

"Because that's the stall we, where we—"

"Where you put the children, right Martin?"

"Yes," he said, holding the bloody towel to his shoulder.

Crockett pulled the chair backwards through the door, leaving it in the middle of the stall.

"You promised you wouldn't hurt us," Morrison whined.

"And I won't, Martin. I will not hurt you. This is the only stall that locks. I don't want you to get out."

Crockett could hear the dogs scratching at the bottom of the connecting door to their pen. The rope that lifted it was tied to a stanchion on the outside of the stall.

"Get in," he said.

"No!" Morrison shouted, backing up.

Crockett grabbed him by his good shoulder and pushed him into the enclosure. He was struggling to his feet as Crockett locked the door. The dogs were throwing themselves against the sliding door in the outside wall, their snuffling made more frightening by their inability to bark. Marian began to moan and cry.

"I said I wouldn't hurt you, Martin, and I won't," Crockett said, grasping the rope.

"Beckett," Morrison pleaded. "No! No, Beckett, please. Beckett, no! Beckett! Beckett!"

Looking through the welded wire above the wooden sides of the box stall, Crockett took a strain on the rope and smiled.

"Call me Crockett," he said, and loosed the hounds.

297

EIGHTY-TWO
King of the Wild Frontier

ABOUT HALFWAY BACK TO THE SUPERHIGHWAY, as Crockett was attempting to rescue his cell phone from where it had fallen on the floorboard of the Jeep, his thoughts turned to the night before and his visit from Ruby. Not for a moment did he believe that anyone's life direction had been changed, but he did have his triumph. If memory in the midst of passion served him correctly, he recalled that at one point during their encounter Ruby had referred to him as Davey Crockett, King of the Wild Frontier. Crockett smiled at the thought of bringing that up during casual conversation.

After all, he'd hate to waste a LaCost moment.

Coming Soon
another CROCKETT novel

GENERATION GAP

A woman cruelly murdered over fifty years ago needs help to save her granddaughter's life. Crockett and Ruby embark on an investigation into a forgotten crime from a forgotten time, as they struggle to keep history from repeating itself.

Also by David Lewis:

BLOODTRAIL

Tired of his life and weary of his sins, Joseph Casey places his fate in the hands of medical researchers. A NOSFERATI in the power of mere humans, he asks for one thing in return: help to find his fourteen-year-old daughter, a young woman he has not seen in over one hundred and fifty years.

"This book held my attention. It is the first lengthy fiction piece I've finished in more than 20 years. BLOODTRAIL by David Lewis is a story of love, lust, science, and intrigue set in the Midwest haunts of Chicago, Kansas City, and Colorado. Lewis can weave a tale like nobody else. Check it out if you dare challenge the darkness. You won't regret it."

Brian Kubicki of the *Platte County Landmark*

"Looking for something scary that sucks…as in a book about thirsty vampires? Orrick, Mo. author David Lewis may have just the ticket via his book BLOODTRAIL. Plus it's peppered with Missouri references as opposed to the standard somewhere in Transylvania shtick. I really like the new spin he [Lewis] puts on an old story."

Angela Colvin reviewing for Hearne Christopher, Jr. in the *Kansas City Star*

Also by David Lewis:

ONCE UPON AGAIN

Transplanted to Kansas City from the East Coast by an inattentive husband, Lucin Montgomery begins a journey of self-awareness that leads her from visions of ancient Japan to the appreciation of her own sensual essence, as she learns that femininity is without limit, and love has a life of its own.

"As a reader, I feel the tremendous impact David Lewis has had on me. Since D.H. Lawrence, I hadn't experienced a writer describing so well a woman's conflicts, lack, ennui, and perhaps the discovery of her own body. The epigraphs transported me to another world. This is a page-turner. One of those books you feel sorry when its over."

AP

"Couldn't put it down. Started in the morning, finished in the late afternoon. Neglected my laundry."

SD

www.ingramcontent.com/pod-product-compliance
Lightning Source LLC
Chambersburg PA
CBHW031110030726
47496CB00002BA/473